TOUCH THE SKY

TOUCH THE SKY

Christa A. Jarvis

Dedicated to Daniel Lee Shatswell.

"Strengthen what remains."
Your faith will always be an inspiration.

Prologue

The house is empty except for our brown Labrador retriever, Rooster. The thought causes a small ache in my chest.

Solitude. Not by choice but through calamity.

In the kitchen, I wait for a cup of coffee to brew, my eyes staring at the dark skies through the small window above the kitchen sink. The first storm of the cool spring season each year is a subtle reminder that creeps over our small town in the same way dark shadows steal away light at the end of each day. I fill my coffee mug and retrieve Rooster's favorite bone from the pantry where I keep it hidden, meant only for special occasions. Rooster and I walk together to the screened-in porch off the back of the house. A soft thump sounds through the quiet house as I toss Rooster's bone to the floor. I sink into the cushioned chair, positioned to overlook the distant river.

Here I sit, waiting, watching.

Energy builds inside my chest, fueled by anticipation, as the storm grows louder. The feral streaks of white electricity rip through the dark sky, mirrored on the river's glassy surface. The thunder echoes through my hollow chest.

Hollow.

Empty.

Rooster's ears perk up, and he moves to sit by my side, studying the sky. A minor tremble shakes his body, and he lets out a soft whimper, not out of fear but excitement. If I would allow him, Rooster would be outside, face-to-face with the storm, his ferocious bark a challenge to the wind.

I feel the tension in the air and know the peaceful night sky is about to erupt in a war within itself. I picture the few others who are also awake, scattered throughout town as they sit on their porches or lie in bed, plagued with anticipation of the first storm.

The scarlet mark of the date to come.

A date none of us will forget.

1

Black

It was a humid summer day in August, 1995. Laughter filled the old, rusty Buick as the car made its way down a highway flanked with farmhouses and endless fields. Old classics played over the radio, and a thirteen-year-old girl with wavy, brunette hair that reached past her shoulders, smiled, her hand out the window, palm open in rivalry with the wind. The wind whipped her unruly curls around her face, and her silver eyes were full of life as she sang along to the Temptations.

Her father took his eyes from the road long enough to smile at her. "Such a beautiful voice," he said.

The girl shook her head in disagreement. "No. But it is a beautiful day!"

With a chuckle, her father shot her a sly grin. "Now, aren't you glad I talked you into getting off the couch to enjoy your last day of summer before school starts?"

The girl rolled her eyes. "Yes. I'll admit it. You were right." She leaned over to check the gauges behind the steering wheel. "How much more do we have?"

The girl and her father had felt adventurous when they left their small apartment in St. Louis. It was his idea to pack the car with their swimming suits, a few snacks, and fishing gear before driving westbound on the highway until they had to pull over or run out of gas. They would spend the day in whichever town they ended up in. The Buick's departure from St. Louis had been close to three hours ago, and the girl was anxious.

Her father smiled and turned on his blinker. "Looks like this is it. We're on empty."

The girl strained to read the exit sign. "'Belle'?" she asked. "They named their town after a fairy-tale princess?"

Her dad chuckled. "Belle means 'beautiful' in French."

"Beautiful," the girl now whispered to herself.

Her face an inch from the taxi's backseat window, Gray's warm breath left a light fog against the glass. The memory, now eleven years old, was a vivid movie playing in her mind as they passed the highway exit sign, which displayed the city's name in large, white letters. The sun began to set, and Gray slipped on a pair of sunglasses to shield her eyes as the taxi turned off the highway.

Moments later, the taxi pulled into a parking spot in front of a small floral shop in the heart of the small town.

"Here we are." The older, female cab driver glanced through the rear-view mirror. "I can start unloading your boxes if you'd like."

"Thank you." Gray's voice was quiet. She checked her notes to make sure she was at the right place and sucked in a deep breath before she pushed her door open to step into a new world.

A chime above the shop door rang as Gray entered the building. A woman who seemed to be in her early forties with long, soft, blonde hair looked up from behind the counter. Her face had a gentle glow, and she smiled as Gray approached the counter.

"Hello." The woman had a soft tone to her voice. "You must be Gray. I wasn't expecting you until tomorrow."

Gray wondered if her black lace dress and gray leggings had been the obvious indicator that she was not from around here. The walls of the shop were adorned with religious artwork and farmhouse décor. Gray instantly felt out of place and second-guessed her decision to move to Belle.

"Yes, I am." Gray pulled at the lace on her dress as she walked up to the counter. "And you must be Mrs. Henning."

"Please, call me Vera." The woman reached under the counter to retrieve a clipboard and paper. "'Mrs. Henning makes me feel so old."

Vera set the clipboard on the counter along with a pen. "I'm about to close the shop. If you would like, I could help you unpack and show you the town. Dinner would be my treat."

Gray focused on the paper. "No, thank you."

Vera hesitated for a moment. "That's all right, maybe next time." She motioned to a corner of the shop. "There is a table and chairs over in that corner if you don't mind looking over the lease and signing it. I just need your driver's license to make a copy for my records. I received the check in the mail for the first month's rent and your deposit, so you are all set as soon as the lease is signed. If you have any questions or concerns about the lease—"

Gray signed the paper and pushed the clipboard back across the counter along with her driver's license. "You won't have any problems with me."

With a curious gaze, Vera pursed her lips together. "All right." She picked up the license and walked into the back office to make a copy. Her kind smile was back in place when she returned.

"Thank you." Gray slipped the license into her small, empty wallet.

"Oh, wait." Vera slid the clipboard back over to Gray. "You wrote the wrong date. Today is March 29, 2006. This says March 27."

Gray scratched out the twenty-seventh and wrote the twenty-ninth.

"I'm sorry," Vera said as she walked out from behind the counter. "I've had a very busy few weeks between weddings and the high school's formal dance. The apartment has been listed for over a year and a half now without interest, and I had given up hope that it would be rented in the near future. When you emailed me, I expected to be able to get up there and give it a thorough cleaning, but like I said, I've just been so busy. This is the first break I have had, and I set aside the evening to clean, expecting you to be here tomorrow. I can tidy up while you unpack if you don't mind the company."

"Don't be sorry." Gray clasped her hands together. She wanted to retreat to the apartment alone. "I don't mind cleaning it myself."

"Oh, no. I couldn't possibly—"

"No, really," Gray insisted. "I can manage."

Vera dropped her hands as guilt flooded her once-cheery face. "If you insist."

Gray offered a weak smile. "I insist."

"Do you need any help moving your things in?" Vera peered around Gray at the taxi driver, who had unloaded the last small box onto the pavement of the walkway in front of the building.

Gray ducked her head, and her hair fell into her face to hide her cheeks as they warmed with embarrassment. She turned to leave. "No, thank you. I travel light."

"Well, all right." Concern veiled Vera's sweet voice. "Have a good night then, Gray, and welcome to Belle. I look forward to seeing you around."

Gray wished Vera a good night and stepped out into the cool, spring weather. The rented space was one of two small apartments above the shop. The building had caught Gray's eye when she had searched online for a place to rent in Belle. Not unlike the adjacent buildings along the few blocks that made up the heart of the small town, the floral shop had been built in the 1800s and had originally been a physician's office. The stonework and architecture were beautiful, and a similar apartment in St. Louis would have cost her twice her limited income.

In the center of the building was a door off the sidewalk, which opened to a stairway leading up above the floral shop to the apartments. Gray picked the first small box up off the sidewalk just as Vera shut off the lights inside of the shop and flipped the "*Open*" sign to "*Closed*." Vera offered Gray a small wave good-bye through the window before she turned and disappeared into the dark. The garden lanterns that hung in the large viewing windows gave a dim, fairy-like light to the plants inside.

The door which led to the apartments creaked as Gray heaved it open. She made a mental note of her black mailbox mounted on the wall just inside the narrow entryway before heading up the stairwell. At the top, the apartment to the right was marked with a jade-green, artsy, wooden "1," while the apartment on the left was marked with a similar, yet orange, "2."

Through the window above apartment number one, Gray saw lights inside, and she heard the sound of a TV. She set her box down and lifted the brightly colored welcome mat in front of apartment two to find the set of keys Vera told her were hidden there. Belle was a trusting town.

After Gray shoved the key into the lock, she pushed the heavy, solid wood door open and stepped into a dark apartment. The soft thud of the box against the wood floors echoed through the empty apartment and she took a moment to look the room over. The original wooden floorboards in the living room were dusty along with the off-white, out-dated curtains. To her right, the kitchen seemed to be in similar order. With a sigh, Gray turned and walked back into the hallway.

Seven small boxes and a lone suitcase were carried into the apartment in multiple, stealthy trips without disturbing her neighbor. Gray shut the apartment door behind her and locked both the door handle and the deadbolt out of habit. The solitude of the apartment suffocated her, and she sank to the floor, her back against the door. Her head in her hands, she stared into the dark living room and let a single tear slide down her cheek.

A few minutes ticked by before she pulled herself together and stood. There were two windows in the living room opposite the front door, and she pushed the curtains back to be greeted by the brick wall of the building next door, only two feet away. A previous tenant had done a breathtaking job of painting a sunset scene over the brick. Dust filled the air as Gray let the curtain drop.

The apartment had two bedrooms. Gray ignored the smaller bedroom to the left of the living room, and her shoes echoed against the hardwood floors as she walked into the second bedroom on the right side of the apartment. On the far wall, two windows overlooked the road in front of the building. Gray peered out over the empty street below. On the opposite side of the road was a guardrail followed by a gradual brick decline, which led to the rushing Gasconade River below. Streetlights lined the cobblestone street and cast an orange glow over the choppy water of the river. A couple walked along the shoreline, hands linked together as they looked out over the waves.

Inside, Gray turned her attention to the black, cast-iron bed frame with a full-size mattress, still in its original plastic. She ran her finger along the frame and a layer of dust stuck to her fingertip. Vera had mentioned to her during their previous correspondence that the apartment included a new mattress and bed frame. She said she considered the mattress to be her housewarming gift to her new tenants. Gray rubbed her thumb and forefinger together to brush away the dust and wondered how many new tenants Vera had been through. She assumed it hadn't been many. People didn't come and go in a small town such as Belle.

Gray thought about her future in Belle. Vera seemed friendly enough, but she had not come to make friends.

She was here to find her father.

The silence of the room closed in around her and Gray forced the thought of her father from her mind. She unpacked a large down comforter from her things. The French-style blinds were left open which allowed the lights from the street to illuminate her ceiling.

In the quiet of her apartment, she slipped under the covers and heard the rush of the river outside her window. With her eyes closed, she let herself be swept away and the years eroded from her mind. Once again, Gray was a thirteen-year-old girl, her eyes mesmerized as she looked out over the river's choppy surface.

2

Black

As Gray and her father, Jack, pulled off the highway, anticipation strained Gray's young face. The outer road off the highway led deeper into the trees for another few miles before it broke out into a small, southern town. They bumped along over red brick cobblestone, and small mom-and-pop shops stood on either side of the road with American flags hung next to their doors. Jack drove over a small bridge overlooking the Gasconade River, which divided the town. On the other side of the arched bridge, the Buick met a long line of traffic as they waited to turn into the local park.

"Looks like there's a carnival in town." Jack strained, his neck arched as he tried to see past the cars in front of him. "So, how 'bout it?"

"Yeah, Dad! Let's go!" Gray saw the Ferris wheel peeking out from above the park's tall oak trees.

A man in a bright orange vest directed them to a parking spot. Moments later, Gray and her father walked away from a booth, carnival tickets in hand.

"So, what first?" He stuffed their tickets into the zipped pockets of his swim trunks as they walked. They both wore their swimsuits under their casual clothes. The purple one-piece suit irritated Gray's shoulders, and she pulled at the straps under her white T-shirt as they walked.

"That one!" Gray pointed to a ride with small, enclosed seats.

Jack watched as the passengers were seated and the ride began, twisting and turning, flipping upside down and spinning in every direction. He winced.

"If that's what you want to ride."

"Yeah," Gray squealed as she grabbed his hand and dragged him to the long line.

When they reached the front of the line, her father gave the ride attendant their tickets and followed Gray to a cart. The safety bars were lowered, and Jack gripped them with white knuckles. The metal screeched as they lurched forward and he whispered a prayer under his breath. Gray laughed and threw her hands up in the air as the ride hit full momentum.

As they headed out the exit gate, Gray turned to look at her pale father. "What were you saying while the ride was going? I couldn't make out what you were trying to tell me."

"I wasn't talking to you, honey," Jack said, as he wiped the sweat from his palms onto his T-shirt. "I was getting right with my Maker."

Across the park there was a horse show, and near the parking lot, a large stage had been set up where a live band was now playing their cover of "Fire and Rain" by James Taylor. Between the horse show and stage, a series of small red-and-white striped booths had been set up, and they offered anything from handcrafted jewelry to kettle corn. A few of the booths had been reserved for games, and they approached one.

"So, what do I have to do to win?" he asked as he assessed the booth.

"You have to throw these baseballs to break those clay plates." The old man behind the counter pointed toward the terra-cotta plates as he spoke. "The smaller the plate you hit, the more points you win. If you get 100 points, you win the large teddy bear or the goldfish."

Jack furrowed his brow as he studied the distance to the plates versus their size and then calculated his chances of winning. "How many chances do I get?"

"You get four baseballs."

After a moment of hesitation, her father provided the necessary tickets, and the man set the basket of baseballs in front of him on the counter. A few people stopped to watch him play. He pulled his right arm back, zeroed in on the smallest plate, and then swung his arm forward to release the ball, which missed as it hit the back of the tent with a loud thud.

"Three more," the man said from where he stood in the corner of the tent.

Jack's second throw was a solid hit, and the ball sent pieces of the small plate in every direction. The onlookers clapped in support. He made his third pitch, which was another hit.

"If you hit one more small plate, you win the prize," the carnival man said.

"Come on, Dad!" Gray bounced on her feet.

With the last baseball in his hand, her father rolled it over in his fingers a few times before he drew his arm back. He took a deep breath, zeroed in on the last smallest plate, and then made the pitch.

Gray burst out into cheer and threw her arms around Jack as the plate shattered.

"Very good, sir," the man behind the counter said. "Which bear would you like?"

"The light-brown one!" Gray pointed to a bear toward the middle of the group. When the man handed it to her, Gray snuggled the bear.

"Thank you, Dad." She hugged the bear. Its fur smelled like popcorn and funnel cake.

"You're welcome, sweetie." Jack smiled proudly as they left the booth, which now had a small line formed behind the counter.

Gray walked with her arm looped through her father's sturdy arm until they reached their car. The bear was left in the back seat, and they returned to explore more rides. When evening rolled around, they had played bumper boats and arcade games, had ridden the Ferris wheel, and Gray had somehow convinced Jack to try three other rides, which had left her father's palms in a perpetual state of perspiration. Jack asked a few locals about the best place to eat in town, and they headed back to their car.

Twenty minutes down a winding back road, Gray sat forward in her seat, her silver eyes in search of the small, unmarked gravel road they had been told led to a small café off the river. When they reached the road, the car jolted up and down as they rode over the deep potholes and dodged tree branches. The gravel ended at a large clearing and a paved parking lot full of cars. A large, wooden, hand-painted sign, which read "Marie's Café," hung over the wraparound porch of the Victorian-style home.

Jack parked the car, and they walked together up the weathered, wooden stairs of the porch. Two elderly men sat in wicker chairs near the door and sipped on cups of coffee. The men nodded to them as her father opened the door for Gray. The smell of coffee and pastries lingered in the air. The Victorian house had been converted into a café. The main level of the home had been opened to accommodate a kitchen, a large bar, and several tables and chairs. The waitress seated Gray and Jack on the back deck, which overlooked a small, grassy yard followed by a white fence before a steep drop-off to the rushing river below.

They ate, tipped their waitress and headed back to their car to retrieve her father's fishing pole and lure. With his aviator sunglasses on his face, Jack turned to Gray, who gathered her towel and beach bag into her arms.

"The waitress told me about a river access space just down the property lines a bit. Shouldn't be too far of a walk. Ready?"

Gray gave a small nod. The warm, summer air carried the cool moisture from the river in the melancholy breeze. It danced over her skin as Gray walked behind Jack. He carried the fold-up lawn chairs from the trunk, and they made their way down a gravel path that led away from the café. Not far from the parking lot, Gray saw the path was marked with a small, rusty sign that read "Fishing and River Access." A small, wooden dock jutted out into the slow current where a few flannel clad men sat, fishing poles in hand.

Jack set his fishing pole down on the rough, weathered wood of the dock as he sat next to Gray, and then he brought the hook up to eye level. Gray followed his motions.

"Now, here's how you bait the hook." Her father slid his sunglasses to the top of his head to see more clearly. He picked a worm out of the container he had bought from a tackle shop in town. "You want to make sure the worm covers the entire hook, and there isn't much of the worm left hanging from the hook. If too much of the worm is left unhooked, the fish will miss the hook, stealing your worm and leaving you empty-handed."

Gray bit her lower lip as she mimicked her father's movements to bait her own hook. When she was finished, she held out the end of her line for her father to examine. "Is that right?"

"Good job, Gray."

Gray's first cast was tangled in a fallen tree at the edge of the riverbank, and Jack made his way down the bank to cut the line before he tied on a new hook. When he handed the pole back to his daughter, a small smile tugged at the corners of his lips. He stood to the side and studied her as she cast the line again, this time with a little more success.

"Much better." Jack patted Gray on the back before he sat back down.

Three worms later, Gray's line tightened as she felt a tug on the hook. When she noticed the bobber submerge before reappearing, Gray jumped to her feet and her lawn chair collapsed behind her. "Dad, I got one!"

"Good job, Gray!" Jack stood up to join his daughter. "Okay, now jerk the line back to set the hook. Good. Now reel it in."

The fish burst out of the water, thrashing in an attempt to free itself. Panicked, Gray dropped the pole, and the small sun perch fell to the deck with a thud where it continued to flop. Gray let out a small squeal and leapt away from the fish as if it were a venomous snake.

"Gray." Her father's eyebrows furrowed, and he took a step forward to lift the fish from the hot, dry wood of the deck. "You have to be more careful. He's not going to hurt you."

Her father took the fish in one hand and Gray mustered up enough courage to take a hesitant step forward. The spikes of the fish's fins were pressed down as he held it in his hands and removed the hook.

"*That's a good-size fish you got, sweetie.*" *He held the fish up a little higher in the air to examine it more closely. The fish began to flail about again, and Gray jumped back as a small scream escaped her lips.*

"*All right buddy,*" *Jack said to the fish as he bent over toward the river.* "*You're free.*" *He gave the fish a small toss, and it disappeared beneath the surface of the water.*

A quiet chuckle from one of the men behind them caught Gray's attention, and her face flushed red. She straightened herself out, set her lawn chair back in its place on the dock, and took a seat. A while later, after the men behind them had moved further down the beach, Gray scooted her lawn chair closer to Jack.

"*Dad.*"

He looked up at her.

"*I don't think I like fishing.*" *Gray motioned towards the water where he had released the sun perch.* "*The fish is just swimming along, minding his own business, looking for a meal, and then he gets caught and yanked out of the water. He didn't do anything wrong. Just doesn't seem fair.*"

Jack smiled. He leaned over and kissed her forehead. "*You've always been my tenderhearted girl. We don't have to fish.*" *He set his fishing pole down.* "*Looks like a pretty good swimming spot there just down the beach. Why don't we go check it out?*"

Gray nodded her head. They left their stuff on the dock and headed down the beach. The water was cool and calm, and they swam for an hour before hunting for neat looking rocks along the riverbank. Jack found one that was white with black stripes and Gray found a rock in the shape of a heart. She slipped it into her pants pocket after they had walked up onto the beach to retrieve their dry clothes. The sun had begun to set over the river when they made their way back to the dock. Gray lay on her towel, listening to the gentle hum of the river's peaceful current. Jack packed up their fishing gear and lawn chairs.

"*I'm going to carry this stuff to the car and grab a cup of coffee. We can hang out here for a bit longer.*" *He tucked the fishing poles under his arm.* "*Would you like anything from the café?*"

Gray shook her head. She was content. The dock swayed as he walked away. She watched the sun slowly sink behind the distant hills, the brilliant hues of the sunset giving way to the darkness of night. The stars had begun to appear when her father returned, a coffee cup in his hand. He lowered himself to sit next to her, and they looked out over the wide river.

The full moon reflected off the black, choppy surface of the water. Tree frogs chirped in the woods around them, joining a symphony of crickets. Occasionally, a bullfrog would give a bass vocal input to perfect nature's song. Gray turned onto her back to look up at the stars. Jack lay down next to her, his arms folded behind his head, and they both silently watched the sky.

"Wow," Gray whispered, transfixed by the glistening lights which floated carelessly above them.

Unlike the populated city where Gray had grown up, there was not enough skyglow in Belle to blot out the magnificent display of stars, which presented itself before them now. The Milky Way wound through the ebony sky like a ribbon of a million Christmas lights strung above them.

"We're never alone, baby girl." Jack closed his eyes and inhaled a deep breath of the cool, moist air. The scent from the cedar trees along the river carried through the breeze. "In moments like this, I can feel God. It's like we could just reach out and touch His face."

With her eyes closed next to her father, Gray focused in on the sounds around her: the crickets and frogs, the wind as it combed its graceful fingers through the branches of the trees, and the gentle sigh of the river as it moved beneath them. The cool night air kissed her cheeks as the breeze picked up and sent a small shiver down her spine. While her eyes were still closed, Gray reached both her hands out to the sky above her. Her fingertips longed to touch something real. She believed for a moment that God was there, reaching His hands down from Heaven, His fingertips disguised as the gentle caress of the breeze against her open palms.

3

Black

A soft knock on the front door woke Gray from her sleep. At some point, she had pulled the blanket over her head while she slept, and she now poked her head out from under the white down comforter as the sun illuminated her bedroom. Gray sat up and assumed by the sounds of the busy street outside of her window that it had to be early afternoon.

Another knock.

Gray stood and shook her head to chase the sleep from her dreary eyes. She made her way past the scattered boxes in her living room to the front door. She noticed a small tremor in her hands as she ran them through her wavy hair and sucked in a deep breath before she opened the large wooden door.

A woman with a bright smile and blonde curls stood on the other side of the door. She was shorter than Gray, though she looked to be the same age, and she had a curvy build accented by the brown sweater dress she wore. Gray ran her hands down the wrinkled dress that she hadn't changed out of from the day before.

"Good afternoon!" The woman's singsong voice matched her bouncing curls. "You must be Gray. I'm Emma, your neighbor. I just wanted to bring you this welcome gift and see how the unpacking was coming along."

Gray peered over her shoulder at her seven small moving boxes, scattered throughout the dimly lit living room. She stepped out into the hallway and pulled the door closed behind her. The gift bag Emma held out was decorated with a black, stick-figure house against a lime-green background and had the words "*Welcome Home*" in cursive above the roof.

Gray forced a smile as she accepted the gift. "Thank you. I don't have much more unpacking to do."

"Well, that was fast!" Emma exclaimed with a smile. "You just got in last week, right? I have been here for five years now, and I have thought about purchasing a house or finding a bigger apartment, but with all of the junk that I have accumulated over the years, I'm afraid of the work and the time it would take to pack it all up, haul it, and then I'd have to spend weeks just to unpack it all again. So, I'll just stay put. I like living in this apartment anyway. It's right in the heart of the town and Vera is one of the sweetest people you'll ever meet." She paused for a moment, but Gray didn't speak, so she continued, "I heard you moved here from St. Louis. I think you'll like it in Belle. It's one of those small, cozy towns where everyone knows everyone."

This time when Emma paused, Gray forced a weak smile.

Emma shifted from one foot to the other. "So, what brings you to town?"

The memories flashed through Gray's mind.

"My father," she replied.

Emma clapped her hands together. "Oh! You have family here in town? What's your father's name? I've lived here since I was born, and my parents also grew up in Belle, so I know most of the families in town."

A deep voice was resurrected from Gray's memory. The two words that had shattered her life rang in her ears with as much clarity as the moment they were first spoken to her ten years ago.

"*He's gone...*"

Gray shook her head to free herself of the memory. "He wasn't from around here. He passed away. Coming up on eleven years."

The vigor sank from Emma's face. "I'm sorry."

For a moment, Gray recalled the simple phrase that had been repeated by a countless number of people over the past ten years—a phrase that, while meant well, did nothing to take the edge off the emptiness she felt at the loss of her father. *"I'm sorry. . . I'm sorry . . . I'm so sorry . . . My condolences to you and your family . . ."* Coworkers, family friends, teachers at her school, even strangers whom she had never met until her father's funeral.

"It was a long time ago," Gray said, without any desire to keep up pretenses.

After a moment's hesitation, Emma took a step back toward the open door of her apartment. "I had better be getting back," she said as her warm smile returned. "I don't want to keep you; I just wanted to take a minute to say 'hi' and to welcome you. It was very nice to meet you, Gray. I hope that we can spend more time together, and if you need anything, just let me know."

A small pang of guilt stung Gray's conscience at the thought she may have offended this kind woman. "Thank you, Emma. And thank you for the gift."

"You're welcome." Emma stepped past the threshold before she turned back to face Gray with another big smile. "I hope to see you around."

"Thanks again," Gray offered and lifted the gift for emphasis.

Once she was able to retreat into the cold shadows of her empty apartment, Gray stood with her back to the closed door and stared at the drapes that hung lifelessly over the windows on the other side of the room. A torrent of emotions threatened to arise, and she let her mind wander aimlessly to the outdated drapes.

Gray thought about who had lived here when the drapes were hung. She thought about how long ago that might have been, and what that person might have been like. Was it a young woman, striking out on her own for the first time, filled with hope and promise? A man working overtime to make ends meet and living a quiet life of solitude? A married couple, perhaps; their first home together. Or maybe an elderly widow who downsized to apartment living after her children had all grown and moved away. She wondered what kind of lives had been lived in this apartment before her. She wondered if she should take the drapes down. The window opened to a brick wall and she didn't need the drapes for privacy. She thought about having to stare at a brick wall without the drapes. But then again, the dusty, limp drapes weren't much to look at either—

"Gray." A male voice cut through her thoughts and echoed in her mind. The deep voice beckoned her to relive a day that she had laid to rest. *"You have to calm down, Gray."*

"I'm calm," Gray spoke into the vacant apartment.

"Gray..."

She moved across the apartment and ripped the packing tape from one of her boxes. She retrieved the old, worn, brown teddy bear her father had won for her. The plush fur felt worn and tattered beneath her fingers. Though the popcorn and funnel cake scent of the carnival had long since faded, she held the bear to her face, closed her eyes and inhaled. Gray savored the memory of her father for a moment before she reached back into the box to retrieve a leather journal and a pen.

Once in the comfort of her bed, Gray sat the bear next to her and flipped the journal open as she searched for the next blank page.

"Gray... Gray... Gray..." The warped voice continued to ring in her head and threatened to bring the memory to the surface.

Her hand trembled as she held the pen to the paper. *Gray,* she wrote as the headline at the top of the page. *Have you ever wondered what a lifeless heart looks like? Drained of purpose. Drained of warmth. Drained of love. Long after a heart has stopped beating, long after it has been depleted, does it hold its shape? Is it cold to the touch? I've seen drawings of red broken hearts or hearts that are blue, but I'm not convinced. No. I know that cannot be an accurate depiction of a lifeless heart. Broken, it may be. But a lifeless heart is gray.*

The journal was snapped closed. She curled up under the covers and closed her eyes in a last-ditch effort to ward off the memories. But as she stared at the black of her closed eyelids, a distant light started as small as a pinhole in her peripheral vision and grew until every shadow in her mind had been chased away by the light. Gray was suddenly in another life—taken back to just three days after she and her father had visited Belle—and her small body was crumpled in a hospital bed with nothing more than scrapes and bruises.

A doctor in a white coat pushed the hospital door open and stepped inside the sterile room. Gray recognized his face. The doctor had worked alongside her father for years. His name was Paul, and she had grown up to know him like an uncle. She was always excited to see him when the holidays rolled around, but today as he entered the room, Gray's stomach sank. She watched as Paul made his way to the windows and opened the blinds to let the bright sunlight into the dull room. The sharp, metallic taste of blood was on her tongue as she licked her swollen, bruised lower lip and fidgeted with the white sheet that covered her. Paul turned from the window and knelt in front of her as he put his gentle hand over her quivering fingers.

"No," she whimpered. Gray pulled her hand away from his as she understood the news he had come to share. Paul met her eyes, and there was a darkness, which now masked his bright demeanor, that frightened Gray.

"No." Gray shook her head and fought back the tears. She wouldn't break down. Not here. Not after all she had been through the last twenty-four hours. She needed to be strong.

"Gray, I'm sorry." She turned away from his bloodshot eyes. This would be the first of many condolences to come.

All at once the air in the room became oppressive and the child within Gray fought for life. "No!" She screamed and pushed the covers away from her before she flung herself from the bed. "No! No!"

As she ran for the door, Paul jumped in front of her and wrapped his strong arms around her small body. "Gray, please," he said to her.

"No!" Blood pounded hot through Gray's veins as she fought against the man. "Let me go! It's not true! It's not true!"

"Gray, you have to calm down." Paul fought against her, his arms around her belly as her limbs flailed about violently. "The nurse will call security. You don't want them to medicate you."

"I don't care!" The heels of her feet pounded against the hard, laminate floor and her back arched as she fought to free herself from his grip. "I have to see him!"

Three male nurses entered the room, one carrying a syringe. Paul continued to hold Gray as he spoke in her ear. "Gray, please," he begged. "You have to calm down. He's gone, Gray. Your father has passed away, and there is nothing you can do to bring him back. You have to be strong, Gray. Your dad would want you to be strong."

"No," Gray moaned. Her soul withered, and her body fell limp as she heard the finality in Paul's voice. Gray's outstretched arms fell to her sides. There was nothing to reach for, nothing to fight for. He was gone. "No."

Tears poured down her cheeks as she fell to the floor, released from Paul's firm grip. Her face to the cold, white floor, Gray gripped her hair with her hands and wept as she rocked back and forth on her bruised knees. Minutes turned to hours without hope of an end to the tears.

Eventually, the nurses left the room. Time slipped by unnoticed as the sun set outside of the opened blinds and left the white room in shadows. Paul remained and sat in a chair next to Gray, his head bent in defeat and sorrow as he waited.

Long after the moon had risen, Gray grew silent and lay crumpled on the floor, her knees pulled up to her chest. After she had passed out from exhaustion, Paul lifted her weak body and placed her in the bed.

Throughout the night, her dreams echoed with Paul's voice. "He's gone, Gray . . . He's gone. He's gone, Gray. Your father has passed away.
"Gray . . . Gray . . ."

4

Black

"Gray?"

Emma's voice echoed through the empty apartment, muffled by the closed front door. A soft knock followed.

Gray pushed the covers away and wondered how long she had slept. The sky outside was filled with light, and her stomach ached with hunger. When she sat up, Gray's head spun, and as she lifted her hand to rub her temples, the empty bottle of whiskey resting on the floor beside her bed caught her eye. She didn't remember unpacking and drinking the bottle.

Another knock at the door.

"Gray, please . . ."

Gray stumbled through her apartment. She opened the door a crack to hide the fact she was still in the same black dress.

Worry strained Emma's face. "I'm sorry to be bothersome, but I haven't seen or heard anything from the apartment for the last four days—no light, no TV, not even the air kicking on and off . . ." Emma trailed off.

Had it been four days? How much of that time had she slept?

"I started to worry, so I just wanted to make sure that everything was okay." A frown fell limp across Emma's voluptuous lips. "You look pale."

Gray brought her hand to her face and noticed how clammy her flesh felt. She stood up taller and took a deep breath to steady her head.

"I'm fine."

"Are you sure?" Emma tried to meet Gray's eyes, but Gray looked away. "Why don't you come out with me tonight? I'll show you around a little."

Gray took a step back from the door, ready to find something to eat and return to bed. "No thanks."

Not willing to relent, Emma put her hand on the door. "Please, Gray. There is a carnival in town and —"

"A carnival?" Gray asked. "I thought the carnival wasn't until August."

Taken off guard by her sudden interest, Emma shook her head. "The town used to have the carnival in August, but they decided to move it up to the spring to avoid the heat. It's been this way for a few years now."

Images from the night at the carnival with her father faded in and out of her memory as she considered the offer to join Emma. A faint smile threatened to pull at Gray's thin lips at the memory of her father as he threw his head back in laughter while they rode the Ferris wheel. But just as quickly as the memory had appeared, a darker, more dreadful memory stole its place; the beautiful, sunny day at the carnival whirled into a nightmare, and the sound of her own scream echoed in her ears.

Gray turned away from Emma. "No thank you."

As Gray started to close the door, Emma stepped into the doorway and held her hand out to block the door. Startled, Gray stumbled back a step, which allowed Emma to view the empty, dark apartment in its entirety. Her eyes dashed from one end of the apartment to the other.

So lonely. So dark. So neglected.

"Gray," Emma whispered in a hushed tone as she stood frozen in the doorway.

Gray's arms fell to her sides in defeat. She could do nothing to explain herself to Emma, and she didn't bother to try.

Emma took Gray's hand and stepped closer as she spoke. "Gray, please." Emma held a look of desperation. "Please come with me to the carnival. You have got to get out of this apartment. It's not healthy."

Healthy? Gray thought to herself.

Gray had questioned both her mental and emotional health on a number of occasions over the past ten years. Soon after her father passed away, she had been referred to a therapist, but the sessions had done little to revive her.

But there was something in Emma's eyes—urgency, or maybe a spark of hope—that cut past Gray's reservations, and she exhaled as she nodded her head.

"I'll go," she spoke, "under one condition. After this, just leave me alone. I'm fine."

Emma glanced around her one last time and took a step back into the hallway. "I will be back in an hour. You can ride with me."

After a moment's pause, Emma turned and left Gray alone in her apartment with the door still open. Gray closed the door and trudged to the kitchen to find a pot and box of ramen noodle soup. As the water came to a boil on the small stove-top, Gray moped at the thought of having to shower. On first consideration, she wasn't going to bother cleaning herself up. But as she thought more about it, she didn't want to give Emma reason to be further concerned. She should *look* like she had her life in order.

So, shower it is, she thought.

Gray stripped down in the middle of the kitchen, a pile of wrinkled clothes left on the floor by the table. A moment later, the shower curtain screeched as it closed, and she turned on the faucet. Cold water poured over her shoulders, and goosebumps spread across her body. She bit back a gasp as her system adjusted to the sudden change of temperature.

Knots formed tight in her stomach as she finished her shower, but the longer she remained awake, the more thirst overshadowed the pains of hunger. The towels Gray owned were thin and worn, and she used one to cover her body and the other to wrap around her unruly hair.

The smell of her shampoo still lingered in the air as she left the bathroom. Gray fought the urge to return to bed as she entered her bedroom and dug through a suitcase of clothes, which lay in the corner behind the door. There was one closet in the apartment, which happened to be a coat closet in the living room, and Gray hadn't brought a dresser with her, so the suitcase did a fine job holding the clothes she had packed. She slipped into a pair of black cotton leggings and a loosely fitting, oversized T-shirt.

In the kitchen, Gray made her bowl of soup. As she waited for it to cool, she glanced around the small room that consisted of a handful of worn cabinets and a couple of outdated appliances. The olive-toned, one-door refrigerator looked old enough to be original to the apartment. With a sigh, Gray walked to the sink, filled her glass, and gulped down its contents. As she stood at the sink, empty glass in hand, Gray peered through the kitchen window to a large, covered back porch that overlooked an expansive garden. On the other side of the garden was a thin line of trees, which offered privacy from the buildings that lined the next block over.

The glass was set in the sink and Gray walked over to the table to eat her soup. She sat and awaited a knock at the door to rouse her from her sedated state. When no knock came, she stood and walked back into the bathroom. She pulled her hair into a loose ponytail and stared at herself in the mirror. Her eyes were droopy, her taught lips pulled into an uneven frown.

With a grunt, she gave in to herself and found her way back into bed where she settled beneath the covers.

Time escaped her, and Gray wasn't sure how long it had been before she awoke to the light tap on her front door. She cursed under her breath and steeled herself to leave the bed. Once in the living room, Gray pulled on a pair of slip-on black-and-white checkered Vans and opened the front door to greet the all-so-cheerful Emma. Gray offered a weak smile to Emma, who watched her.

"Are you excited?" Emma's words held triumphant hope as she spoke.

Gray forced a smile and pursed her lips together. She was determined to put on enough of a show to subdue Emma's concern. "Yeah."

Her response was enough to pacify Emma, who brimmed with delight and bounced down the stairs as she chattered about the carnival. Gray blocked out the mindless chatter; her head dipped low as she struggled to forget the memories that still dug their nails in the back of her mind and sent images throbbing through her brain.

Images from the night her father died.

The city park was a fifteen minute drive from the floral shop. The cool, spring breeze tickled the back of Gray's bare neck and sent goosebumps down her spine and across her pale cheeks as she crossed the parking lot. A large banner hung over the park's entrance that read, "*Welcome to the Belle City Fair.*" A small smile tugged at the corner of lips as she recognized the sign. She felt as though she was thirteen again, at the carnival with her father without a care in the world. Gray half-expected her father to walk up beside her, tickets in hand.

But the moment faded, and the realization she was alone in a town of strangers settled over her once more.

Emma noticed the pause and followed Gray's gaze to the sign. "Are you okay?"

Gray looked away and cleared her throat. She began to walk again. "Yeah."

The park surged with life as a kaleidoscope of colored T-shirts wove their way in and out of the candy-cane striped tents. There were booths set up across the baseball fields, rides on the soccer fields, and a large stage consumed a smaller parking lot near the restrooms.

"I know this band!" Emma shouted and grabbed Gray's hand and pulled her through the crowd to get closer to the stage. "They are members of our church."

Gray was sure Emma knew the vast majority of the people at the carnival and felt sick at the realization Emma would want to introduce her to every person who crossed their path.

A short distance away from the stage, Gray and Emma were crowded in by a mass of people singing along with the music. Emma shouted above the music, "This is as close as we can get! It's pretty packed up there!"

Gray didn't need to respond; Emma had already turned her attention back to the band that played a rock song, which Gray neither recognized nor cared to listen to. From what she could hear above the crowd, the band played well and would normally be the style of music Gray would enjoy, but right now her focus was on escape.

Emma caught a glimpse of a group of people gathered in lawn chairs just a short distance from the mob. She jumped up and waved until a thin, blonde girl from the group waved back. The group consisted of about a dozen men and women of various ages, and Gray bit her lower lip as she realized her fate. Gray hoped to ease her way out of the crowd unnoticed as she took a solitary step away from Emma. Unaware of Gray's discomfort, Emma took Gray by the arm and pulled her toward the group.

"Come on, I'll introduce you to a few people."

Gray stuttered as she fumbled for an excuse to get her hand free from Emma's grip. Her voice was drowned out by the crowd, which now cheered as the song concluded. Emma weaved through the crowd and bumped into a few people as they cut through. Gray was pulled to where the lawn chairs had been arranged to flank the stage. As Emma approached, a few people stood to greet her.

"Hey everyone, this is Gray! She just moved in next door."

Gray looked over her shoulder toward the exit, and her mind raced through plausible excuses, which might lead to her freedom.

A couple of people smiled and offered a friendly greeting before their attention was drawn back to the stage. Emma was engaged in conversation with another girl from the group, and Gray turned her focus to the band performing an upbeat song.

The group of guys on the stage had a rock edge to their music, and their unique sound reminded her of a band that had frequently played at a bar Gray and her friends used to visit regularly back in St. Louis. For a moment, Gray wondered if it had been the same band, but then dismissed the idea. Emma had said this was a church band.

To Gray, they didn't sound like a band that would play in a church.

Lost in thought, Gray didn't notice Emma had approached until she was once again latched onto her arm and guiding her toward the other side of the group.

"I want to introduce you to a few of my friends."

Gray's irritation grew, only matched by her urgency to leave. They came to a stop in front of two women who looked to be polar opposites of each other. One was blonde, short, and petite, with a model's face. Self-confidence radiated from the blonde woman's tanned skin. The other woman met Gray's eyes with a distant but friendly gaze. This woman was tall, pale, and thin with dreadlocks in her long, light-brown hair. She wore a cream-colored hemp skirt and a brown tank top without a trace of makeup on her clear, freckled skin.

"Tiffany, this is Gray." Emma nodded from the blonde woman to Gray, which forced Gray to return her attention to the woman's gaze.

"Gray just moved from St. Louis."

Neither of the women seemed fazed by the news. Gray was sure half of the town had heard of her arrival. She could hear the gossip in her mind about the strangely dressed loner locked in her apartment for days. Her cheeks flushed.

Oblivious to Gray's discomfort, Emma continued with introductions. "Tiffany owns Marie's Café. And this is her sister, Carla, who owns a clothing store called, 'A Flower's Petals.' She designs and hand makes all of the clothes herself."

"Hello." Carla had been the one to speak, while Tiffany offered a pinched smile.

In the background, the band concluded to a roar of applause before they exited the stage. The sudden quiet settled over the crowd as they waited for the next band to set up.

"So, you're from St. Louis?" Tiffany asked in a soft, southern accent. "I have been there a few times just to shop. Places here in Belle don't carry decent designer brands."

Tiffany eyed Gray's attire. Her plump lips pursed together as she looked Gray over.

"I'll pretend I didn't hear that," Carla mumbled from where she had settled into a quilted lawn chair, no doubt homemade.

"Shhh," Emma said as she turned to face the stage. A female singer stepped up to the microphone, her guitar strap looped around her thin shoulders as she began a slow country song. "It's Samantha Ray!"

"Do you like country music?" Carla asked Gray.

Tiffany had walked away to join a blonde-haired man with a matching tan who had exited the stage with the previous band.

"I haven't listened to country music for a very long time." Gray's mind clicked back through the years before it settled on a moment that seemed to be a lifetime ago. "I've never liked it that much, but my father loved country music."

Emma made a comment about the musician, but Gray's mind was in her father's office in St. Louis.

"Are you here to see your father, Gray?" the secretary asked from behind the sliding glass window. The window had information about the small doctor's office taped up across the glass along with other pages about co-pays. Gray always found that strange since her father ran a practice for low-income people without insurance and rarely asked for payment.

"I'm just waiting for him to get off work," Gray said with a smile. "He's driving me to my volleyball game."

The woman smiled back. "I'll let him know you are here when he is finished with his current patient."

"Thanks."

The phone rang and the woman turned away from Gray to answer the call. "You've reached the office of Dr. Wilcox... I'm sorry, he's with a patient right now..."

A song by Garth Brooks played over the small radio that sat on the counter near the window. Gray hummed along with the song as she flipped through the stack of magazines left on the coffee table in the center of the waiting room. Gray settled on Vogue *and sank into a chair near the office door. Only then did she notice the man who sat on the other side of the room...*

Gray shook her head to bring herself back to reality. The woman on stage sang, "Without you I'm so lonely, the pieces of my heart shattered on the floor . . ." Even as Gray tried to focus on the music, the man's dark-brown eyes haunted her thoughts as he stared up at her from where he sat hunched over in the small waiting room, eleven years in the past. Panic crept up Gray's neck and sent waves of heat across her chest. Her breath caught in her throat.

Emma was at her side again, her arm looped in Gray's. "Let me introduce you to a few guys from the band that was on stage."

With a sudden jerk, Gray freed herself from Emma's touch. The movement caught the attention of Tiffany and Carla as well as the blonde man, who now stood next to Tiffany. Four sets of eyes stared at her.

Gray cleared her throat.

"I, uh—" she pinched the bridge of her nose and closed her eyes as she rummaged through her brain for an excuse, but the man still sat haunting the dark corner of Gray's mind. Her lungs ached as the fear continued to rise. "I've got to go."

She hurried off, disappearing into the crowd. The faces around her were a blur, the smell of beer overwhelming as she forced her way through the ocean of bodies. Gray knocked into a man and spilled his beer all over herself and the woman who stood next to him, but she didn't stop. Her aim now was to get away. She had made a mistake to come to the carnival. She had chased her father's ghost and expected the carnival to bring him back to her. As she burst out of the other side of the crowd, Gray tripped over a thick, black electrical cord that ran to the stage and hit the ground with momentum.

A sharp pain ran up her right arm at the impact. Gray crumpled, pulled her arm close to her, and cradled it against her body. The pain forced the thoughts from her mind and rendered her motionless for a moment.

"Are you okay?"

A man with brown hair rushed to her side to help her up. "That was a pretty nasty fall."

"Yeah," Gray said, dazed from the impact. She sat up straight and scanned the outskirts for an exit sign.

The man offered his hand and helped her to her feet. He wore a white T-shirt with two black crows screen-printed across the chest along with a pair of faded jeans. His facial hair was short and scruffy, he had small wrinkles in the corners of his eyes, and his brown hair was shaggy and tossed. Gray was pondering whether or not his soft, blue eyes had flecks of green in them when she caught his look of concern.

A look she was all too familiar with receiving.

"Well, thank you for helping me up," Gray spoke as she took a step back.

"You're welcome," the stranger said. "To be honest, it's my fault that you fell. I had just uncovered this cord so that I could pack it up and put it in the back of the trailer when you came out of nowhere."

When Gray didn't respond, the man held out his hand to shake hers, but she left it to hang in the air. He let his hands drop to his sides as he rocked his heels and an awkward silence settled between them for a moment before he pushed forward.

"I'm Tony." The man gestured to a large van and trailer parked behind the stage. "My band just finished our set on stage." Tony bent over, pulled the thick, heavy cord up from the ground, and wound it into a large circle. "I was just packing up the last of our equipment."

Tony tossed the wound-up cord into a plastic tote and then brushed off his hands. "Get that out of the way before anyone else gets hurt. I'm really sorry about that." He took a step closer.

"I'm fine. Thanks."

Gray held her injured hand up in a slight wave as she turned to leave, yearning for the comfort of her dark, empty apartment. Tony stepped in front of her, took her arm in his hand, and held it up for her to see. The movement sent a wave of pain up her arm, and she cringed.

"It's bruised and swollen." Concern marked Tony's face. "We need to get you to the medical tent. You may have broken it. There's an ambulance on the other side of the park, and they can check it out and let you know if you should go to a hospital. I'll walk you there."

The bruise was already deep red in color, and the subdued panic rushed back within Gray. She stumbled backward as she pulled her arm from Tony's hand.

"No, no ambulance. I'm fine. I just . . ." Her voice trailed off, anxiety choking out the breath within her as she looked around for an easy get-away. When she turned, she absentmindedly collided with a passerby, which sent another wave of pain through her body, and she winced. Tony was at her side again.

"Please, let me take you to the medical tent. Just let them look at it."

She managed a small nod and they walked together to the tent next to where an ambulance was parked. When a paramedic approached them, Tony explained what had happened, and the man sat her in a metal folding chair. He examined her wrist after he took her blood pressure and information.

"It looks as though it's just badly sprained, but we won't know for sure unless you have an X-ray," the paramedic said. "We can take you to the hospital in the ambulance if you would like."

"No." Gray said abruptly, her uninjured hand clinging to the seat of her chair to ground her. "No hospitals. Please."

"But ma'am," the paramedic protested. "In my professional opinion, you need to go the emergency room for an X-ray. I can only assess—"

"No," Gray said. "Do what you can for me here, but I'm not going to a hospital."

Tremors shook her body as the memories stirred at the mention of a hospital. Like unruly river water beating against a worn, tattered dam, they threatened to destroy what was left of the composure she clung to.

The paramedic turned to retrieve gauze-wrap and an ice pack when Tony met her eyes. "Are you sure? I will cover the cost if that's what is holding you back. Like I said, it's my fault."

The paramedic handed Gray an ice pack wrapped with a paper towel. "The ice will keep the swelling down. You can purchase a sling and proper brace at your local drug store. Keep it wrapped and try not to use it for the next three to four weeks. That's all that we can do for you unless you go to a hospital and have an X-ray. If it's broken, the bone will heal itself without being appropriately positioned and—"

"Thank you." Gray stood.

Tony was at her side as she stepped into the fading sunset.

"It's not about the cost," she said to Tony and walked faster. "I swore never to step foot into another hospital again. I'll be fine, I just need to find the person I rode here with."

"Let me take you home." Tony kept pace beside her.

"No, thanks," Gray said, her voice raspy as the tremors settled. "I'm fine, really."

"I don't mind—"

Gray stopped and her eyes met Tony's with brick-wall determination. "I said I'm fine."

Gray caught sight of Emma, who was searching in every direction, no doubt for Gray. Tony stepped in front of her, which blocked her view of the exit and Emma.

"Please. It's the least I can do. It would make me feel better. Let me take you up the street to the drugstore to pick up the sling and brace, on me, and then I will take you home." Tony wore the same look of concern on his face as Emma did when she had come to Gray's door.

The options were for Gray to flag down Emma and ask her to leave early—no doubt further subjecting herself to the neighbor's already overbearing concern—or take Tony up on his offer.

"Fine," she said. "Where are you parked?"

"Just outside the south exit." He motioned to his left. "But you've got to at least tell me your name. My mom taught me never to give rides to strangers," he teased with a grin.

Gray cursed herself for coming to the carnival. "My name is Gray."

When they exited the park, the sky had grown darker, and Gray heard the sound of the carnival rides and laughter on the other side of the large chain link fence the city had put up for this event. Tony directed Gray down a quiet one-way street that led behind a couple of shops, which lined Main Street. The smell of funnel cakes lingered in the air, and Gray's stomach growled.

"Do you want to stop and get something to eat before I take you home?" Tony dug through his pockets for his keys as they walked.

"No, thank you. I just want to go home." Gray didn't look up as she trudged her way forward, her mind set on being curled up in her bed.

"No drugstore?"

Gray shook her head.

They approached a black Jeep Wrangler parked on the far end of the street, and Tony unlocked the passenger-side door for Gray before he walked around to the driver's side. Once they were both inside of the car, Tony backed out of the parking spot and drove down the dark street until they emerged onto Main Street and headed toward the other side of town. As they drove, the top to the Jeep open, Gray let the cool wind whirl around her and her thoughts wandered back to her friends in St. Louis.

On a Friday night like tonight, she would be out at Riffs, a local bar, with her boyfriend, Tyler, and childhood friend, Audrey Turner. The image grew in her mind, and it was as if she were next to them as they sat at their regular table in the back of the crowded, smoke-filled bar. Tyler would have a cigarette between his lips—Marlboro, his favorite—

as Audrey would eye the men clustered around them. A live band would play on the large stage on the other side of the bar, and Gray would sit there, distant and alone in the middle of all the chaos, her mind in another world as she threw back her usual—a Jack and Coke. By the end of the night, Gray would have had a few too many, and Tyler would help her out of the bar, a cigarette still between his lips. Audrey was usually just as drunk as she left with whatever man she had settled on for the night. Another Friday night like every other Friday night.

A long line of traffic exited from the carnival. Tony waited at a busy intersection to turn right. The officer who directed traffic waved the Jeep on and Tony accelerated as he pulled out into the busy street before turning onto a back road, which went the long way around the outskirts of town but avoided all the traffic from the park. The Jeep bounced across the potholes that littered the small, gravel road, and the night grew quiet as they distanced themselves from the crowd.

"Can you always see them this clearly?"

Gray's face was turned upward as she stared at the dusk sky.

Tony looked over at her. "What?"

"The stars," she said with her eyes still fixed on the sky.

"Yeah, you can see the Milky Way clear as crystal when you get closer to the outskirts of town. It's quite the show."

"The stars are beautiful." Gray's voice was just a breath into the cool, night air. "They remind me of my father."

Tony smiled. There was something warm and inviting about his eyes —they made Gray feel at home. The flecks of green in his irises stood out more clearly against the blue under the golden tinged moonlit hues of the dusk sky.

"What does your dad think of you moving all the way out here?"

Gray was quiet for a moment. "My father passed away about eleven years ago . . ." Her gaze returned to the flickering stars above them. "Three days after we visited Belle together on a summer trip."

Grief strained Gray's voice as she spoke those words. Tony didn't afflict her with obligatory condolences or prod any further. They drove in silence, and Gray slipped off into another world, her eyes locked onto the night sky as she tried to find the connecting piece among a scattered, intricate puzzle.

After parking in front of the floral shop, Tony got out of the Jeep first and walked around to open the door for Gray. He was careful to stay clear of her wounded arm as he helped her out of her seat. A solitary tear, which danced its way down Gray's defined cheekbone, glimmered in the streetlight. Tony shifted on his feet beside her and cleared his throat before he spoke.

"Gray." His voice was quiet and soft as he continued to hold her uninjured arm, though her feet were now safely planted on the cobble-stone street. "I have never experienced the death of someone I loved, and I can't pretend to imagine how deeply that hurt you. I think I understand why you are here, though, and I pray you find what you're looking for before you leave."

"Thanks." She didn't look up at him.

He released her arm. She stepped past Tony and left him to stand alone next to the empty passenger seat of his Jeep. As she walked to her apartment, reality weighed on her. She was a woman reaching out with all she had left in a vain attempt to change her past and bring the dead back to life. Gray had disappeared into the dark stairwell before she heard the Jeep pull away, and the desolate street fell silent.

5

White

Tony pulled into the parking lot of the local drug store. He shut off the engine and sat in silence for a moment. Images of Gray flashed through his mind; the sight of her in the seat next to him in the Jeep, her dark hair blowing in the wind as she stared up at the starlit sky with her silver eyes.

Her eyes.

Those moonlit irises had him captivated.

Tony shook his head and sighed before he stepped out of the Jeep. The drugstore was mostly vacant, and he made his way to the back aisle where the wraps and bandages were kept. Belle was a small town and word traveled amongst church pews, bar stools and salon chairs. He had heard about the mysterious woman who had moved into town, clad in black and keeping to herself. Townsfolk labeled her cold and uptight. But that wasn't the woman Tony had met tonight. The woman he had encountered was guarded yet vulnerable. There was something in those eyes that he recognized and identified with.

Perseverance.

His heart paused as he recalled those haunting eyes. How long had he been standing in the same place with the same wrist brace in his hand? His thoughts weren't on the wrist brace. He tucked it under his arm, grabbed a sling and headed to the cashier.

Not two months had passed since he had sat with his friend, Darren, and talked about how he was content with his life at the moment. Darren had been trying to set Tony up with a woman at church, but Tony wasn't interested. He lived alone on the outskirts of town, content with his vegetable garden and music.

A vegetable garden can't break your heart.

After checking out, Tony walked back to his car and drove home. He would give the brace and sling to Emma to pass along to Gray the next time he saw her. Tony had grown up with Emma. They had their first class together in kindergarten and stuck pretty close to each other through high school. Emma always had her own way of living life. Their freshman year of high school, she and Tony had a big falling out over some of the choices he had been making. He felt like she had been overstepping her bounds, and he severed their friendship. Years passed before they reconnected again, and now he cherished their friendship. He knew that she would welcome Gray, but he hoped that her tendency to smother wouldn't push Gray away.

The crickets chirped outside his bedroom window as Tony tossed and turned. How could a simple meeting with this woman vex him this way? Tony thought back on the commitment he had made last year. He had spent years making decisions that only brought him pain, and after a particularly deep cut, he had decided not to pursue love or companionship. But this didn't feel like an infatuation or mere musing. Whatever was afflicting him felt deeper than a mere attraction.

So, what do I do? He silently prayed.

Love her, he heard a voice say within. *Unconditionally.*

Love? Tony questioned his own sanity. He didn't even know her.

Agape was the word that came to mind.

Restless, Tony flipped on his bedside lamp and pulled out his Bible. He opened the concordance in the back of the book and ran his finger down the first page until he found *Agape*. In the margins of his Bible, Tony jotted down words that came to mind while he read about agape love.

Unconditional.

Transcending circumstance.

Self-sacrificing.

Unmerited.

Goodwill for *all* humanity.

Unreserved.

Tony sighed when he put the book away and turned out his light. Unreserved? He wasn't confident that he knew how to love like that anymore.

6

Black

Tears of fear burned down Gray's red cheeks as she clung to her overstuffed Raggedy Ann doll and buried her face in the plush to muffle her cries. Her loud sobs would only fuel her mother's anger.

The bedroom door across the hall slammed shut, and the loud rap music from her mother's room drowned out the voice of Gray's mom and the dark-haired man who came to visit when Gray's father was out of town. Hidden, crumpled under the Barbie bed her father had brought home for her after his last trip, Gray's eyes were fastened on her bedroom door, which was partially open. With her back pressed against the wall as she tried to put more distance between herself and the bedroom door, Gray feared that at any moment the door would fly open and her mother would burst into the room.

The image of her friend Sarah's Weeble toy formed in Gray's mind. Sarah would punch the Weeble, and Gray would watch as it popped back up into place, only to be knocked down again. The loud pop of Sarah's hand hitting the tough plastic echoed in Gray's memory. Gray squeezed her eyes shut and buried her face deeper into the plush doll. She covered her ears to block out the memories. The loud pop grew more thunderous in her mind, joined by her mother's shouts.

The memory of the Weeble faded, replaced by the image of Gray's mother as she stood over her, eyes red and bloodshot. She would scream an endless string of profanities as she raised her hand and repeatedly brought it down to land fierce blows against Gray's small body.

Pop.

Pop.

Pop.

The sound of flesh against flesh now rang in Gray's ears. She wished her father were here to hold her. Twice a month, Gray's dad would spend the weekend out of town as he and his partner, Paul, lobbied for support from local businessmen in an attempt to get their medical clinic off the ground. Gray's mom would hug him and wish him a safe trip. She watched out the front window for his car to disappear from view before she called the man with dark hair. He would arrive an hour later with little bags of white powder. Her mother and the man would spend the next two days locked in her mother's bedroom as they snorted cocaine, blared rap music, and occasionally came out to play Weeble-Wobble with Gray.

Gray didn't always bounce right back up.

Pop.

Pop.

Pop.

The noise grew in her mind and sent tremors through her little body until she screamed in an attempt to drown the noise out. Gray's brain told her to stop screaming, that her mother would hear her, but the memories rushed through her mind with an intensity that caused her stomach to burn. As much as she wanted them to close, her lips were forced wide open as the pain was vomited from the pit of her being.

A door slammed so hard that it sent a quiver through the small house. The screams choked off in her throat, and for a moment, Gray couldn't breathe. Her eyes snapped open, focused on her bedroom door as she waited for it to burst open. Angry, muffled voices carried through the house. With her face buried into her doll once again, Gray cried as she wished the Raggedy Ann doll was strong enough to protect her from the arms that would be here at any moment to reach under the bed and yank her out from her dark cave of protection.

The music from the bedroom cut off, and Gray held her breath as she listened for the footsteps. They fell heavily against the floor. The bedroom door across the hall slammed shut and Gray's bedroom door opened. As the footsteps came closer, she pushed harder against the wall behind her and hoped the wall would turn to Jell-O so she could slip right through to the freedom on the other side. A dark figure bent down and peered under the bed. Two large arms reached to grab her. Gray began to cry as the hands latched onto her thin arms and pulled her from her safe haven. With a wince, she waited for the first blow.

The hit never came.

When Gray opened her eyes, she was wrapped in a familiar embrace. With a tinge of hope, she inhaled and recognized the smell of aftershave.

"Daddy?" Her voice squeaked.

Her father's body quivered as he held her and tears streamed down his cheeks. He kissed Gray's forehead. "It's all right, baby girl. I'm here now. Daddy is home."

Relief overwhelmed Gray, and she clung to her father and sobbed. Time passed by as her father sat, broken, on her bedroom floor and held her as they cried together.

A small vibration shook the apartment as thunder echoed in the dark night sky and woke Gray from her nightmare. Beads of sweat ran down her forehead, and she sat up in her bed and wiped them away with the back of her trembling hand.

There was another flash of lightning followed by a sharp crack of thunder.

Gray forced the memory of her mother from her mind as she rose to her feet in the pitch-black apartment. She opted out of turning on the lights and decided to enjoy nature's brilliant show instead. In the kitchen, she stopped to pour herself a glass of Jack Daniels. With the glass in hand, Gray walked out of her apartment into to the rear hallway of the building and tiptoed past Emma's apartment door. The metal door handle that led to the back porch felt cold in her grip. She pulled the door open and let a rush of wind greet her. The wind pressed against her as she walked barefoot onto the rough, weathered wood.

Raindrops being carried in the wind hit her bare legs, and she tugged at the bottom of her oversized T-shirt to keep her boy shorts-style underwear hidden from any passerby that might happen to notice her. Goosebumps spread across her exposed, wet skin, but the weather was warm for the beginning of spring in Missouri. Gray sank to a seat with her back against the brick wall of the building. She watched as the trees arched and their branches danced. The heavy black lid of the dumpster behind her building was being lifted and dropped, and a loud *thump, thump, thump* echoed through the night air.

Gray bit back a shot of the whiskey and let the warm burn run down her throat.

After her parents' divorce, her mother had blackmailed her father and offered him full custody of Gray if she could keep the house. Gray felt sick to her stomach as she thought about her mother's willingness to trade her for a two-bedroom shoebox in the slums.

The cold glass knocked against her teeth as Gray threw back more whiskey.

The home she and her father had rented in St. Louis was a cute little craftsman-style home in a quaint neighborhood just a few blocks south of Forest Park. Her father ran a medical facility full time for low income people who couldn't afford or had been denied insurance. The two of them lived a modest life. The clinic survived off the funds and donations of larger corporations and wealthy philanthropists. A friend of her father owned the home and had rented it to them for next to nothing.

On nights like tonight, as the thunder cracked and the lightning flashed, Gray's mind wandered back to that house. A large porch fronted the home, and every time there was a storm, Gray would crawl out of bed, her worn old Raggedy Ann doll in tow, to find Jack out on the front porch swing as he watched the chaos unfold. He would pull her up next to him on the swing, and she would sit with him in silence as her heart pounded, until the storm passed. When the rain lightened and the thunder became a faint echo in the distance, her father would pick her up, carry her to bed, tuck her in, and plant a soft kiss on her forehead before he left the room.

Now as she sat alone, Gray looked out through the blinding rain at the town around her. She wondered how many people had been woken by the storm, and how many still remained in bed, in no way fazed by nature's phenomenon. The last bit of whiskey burned as she gulped it down. Gray sat still and allowed the wind and rain to swirl violently around her. She could faintly make out a tornado siren over the sound of the storm.

As Gray exhaled, she put her hand to her chest, over her heart.

The beat was slow and steady.

Gray leaned her head back against the brick and stared up at the roof of the back deck, rain on her face as she sat, unmoved. How many times had she sat outside and waited for a storm? Waited for her body to fill with adrenaline and for her heart to beat against her rib cage like it used to?

To feel.

The empty glass rested on the splintered wood as Gray stood up and walked to the edge of the deck, her hands on the railing, the wind at full force. The branch of a tree across the street snapped and fell with a loud crash to the pavement below. Street signs rattled fiercely. Lightning struck close enough for Gray to feel the warmth of the bolt on her face.

Then, as quickly as it started, the storm began to die down. The trees began to calm, and the street signs became still. The quiet dark of the night settled in over the sleepy town once again, and Gray was left to stand on the back porch, soaked in rainwater, as she watched the last of the drizzle fall from the sky, her heart still beating with an unsettling calmness.

Wet footprints followed behind her as she made her way back through the dark hallway to her apartment. She closed the door, stripped her soaked clothes off, and left them where they fell before she climbed into bed, naked, to fall fast asleep.

7

Black

When Gray woke to a soft knock at the door the next morning, the sunlight broke through her closed blinds. The down comforter was wrapped around her nude body as she stumbled to the door and pulled it open enough to see into the hallway.

"Surprise!" Emma stood in the hallway with a horde of women behind her, which included the blonde girl, whose mouth hung open at the glimpse of Gray's indecent attire.

Emma went on with her speech as if Gray's lack of apparel had gone unnoticed.

"I got a few of the girls together to come help you deep-clean this place. Vera and I felt bad about not getting it done for you before you moved in, and we felt even worse when we heard about your injury, so we thought we would come give you a hand."

Vera gave a shy wave from where she stood behind Emma.

Gray cursed Tony under her breath for sharing the news of her fall. She felt equally defeated and annoyed and let out a sigh as she opened her door the rest of the way. "Come in. I'll get dressed and join you in the kitchen in a moment."

Once in the privacy of her room, Gray threw the comforter to the bed and slipped into a black, cotton dress. She pulled her wavy hair back into a ponytail and headed to meet her unwanted guests in the kitchen.

As she entered the kitchen, her eyes scanned over their faces. Vera, Emma, the blonde girl, and her sister Katie, or Kim, or Crystal.

"You remember Tiffany and Carla from the carnival, right?" Emma nodded to the sisters.

Carla.

Carla held out a small cardboard box. "This is for you."

Inside the box was a wrist brace, still in its packaging, and a sling. Gray forced a smile. "Thanks."

"It's not from me." Carla shrugged and her dreadlocks fell over her shoulders with the movement.

"Okay, so I didn't tell you the full truth," Emma interrupted. "We will only help you if you agree to come to dinner with us after we are finished. Every month, the four of us get together and go to the café Tiffany owns just outside of town, and we would love for you to join us."

What could she do now? Say no and kick them all out? Gray spoke through gritted teeth. "Sure."

With a little bounce, Emma smiled and threw her hands into the air. "We're going to have so much fun! Let's get started."

Emma took charge. She assigned everyone to a chore. The half-empty bottle of whiskey still sat opened on the small counter, and Vera screwed the lid back on and tucked the bottle into the cabinet above the sink as Gray made her way to the bathroom.

The apartment took two hours to clean, top to bottom. Not a nook or cranny had been overlooked. Gray had managed to go most of the time without carrying on a steady conversation with any of the women, but now as she looked over the apartment, her breath caught in her throat and she couldn't help but smile.

And feel guilty.

These four women had given the last two hours of their time to scrub her home, unpack, iron and hang her clothes, and scrape the week-old Raman Noodles off her dishes.

"Thank you," she whispered as she looked over the house again.

Vera smiled and stepped forward to give Gray a tender hug. "We want to help you, Gray. Don't ever feel shy about asking."

The other three women nodded their heads in agreement.

Vera stood next to Gray and looked over the apartment. "We'll get you a clean coat of paint on the walls and ceiling here in the next month. You will be proud to call this home once we're through with it."

"Let's get this show on the road! It's party time." Tiffany smiled and walked toward the front door. "I have to go home, shower, and change, but I will meet you lovely ladies at Emma's house in an hour."

She paused at the door and faced Gray. "I'm happy you are coming tonight."

Taken off guard, Gray fumbled for a response as she felt the sharp blade of guilt sting her gut. "Thanks."

Tiffany offered a playful smile to the group before she turned to leave. Carla followed behind her a couple minutes later and gave Gray a hug on her way out the door. Vera and Emma left together while they talked about what they might order at dinner.

When the door closed behind them, Gray stood and stared at her clean, empty apartment for a moment. A mix of joy, guilt, and fear washed over her. Gray walked to the coat closet where her clothes now hung neatly and chose a casual, gray, linen tea-length dress, black lace leggings, and a pair of black, suede flats.

The clothes were set out on her bed, which was now made, and Gray slipped out of her now-dirty dress and then made her way to the small bathroom. Her own reflection peered back at her in the mirror above the sink, and she let her hair down so that the mass of loose curls encumbered her and tickled her exposed back. Her silver eyes scanned from her dark, wavy hair to her lips, which hid straight teeth, and then to her fair skin.

"Your mother wanted to name you Heather."

Her father sat at the table across from Gray and drank his morning cup of coffee. When she looked up at him, he smiled as he studied her face.

"But the first time I held you in my arms, you looked up at me with those beautiful, steel eyes. 'Gray,' I told your mother. 'Her name is Gray.'"

Throughout grade school, Gray had cursed her parents for giving her that name. She had never fit in, and her name made her an open target for crude jokes. In the fifth grade, she had run home from the school bus after one little boy had made a hurtful joke. Her father sat in the living room doing paperwork, when she burst through the front door in tears. After she spilled the entire story, her father held her as she cried until the tears stopped.

"Why are you crying, Gray?"

Gray was frustrated as she pushed herself up and stared her father in the eyes. *"Didn't you listen? Because that boy said—"*

"Why are you crying, Gray?" he asked again, his tone soft.

Gray stared at him, confused.

"Don't you know that God created you to be exactly who you are? He breathed His very breath of life into you. He knew you by name before you were even born. The same God who handpicked the stars and set them each into place. Not one of those stars is the same as another. And God cares about you even more than the brightest star in the heavens. There's nothing wrong with being different. We each carry our own light."

God.

Gray let a bitter puff of air slip from her lips as she thought back on the memory. If only her father had known what the next ten years had in store, he would have thought very differently about the God that he so obediently served.

If God was real, He deserved no such praise or admiration.

Gray slipped into the shower and let the steam rise around her and fill the small room. The hot water ran out before Gray finished her shower, lost in thought of an all-powerful deity lying in its bed of hypocrisy. After she toweled off, Gray ran a comb through her hair, added a dab of makeup, and then made her way to the bedroom where her clothes lay.

The simple fabric felt like silk under her fingers as Gray ran her hands across it, her mind in a trance. She slipped into the ensemble and sat on the bed. The dress was modestly cut, as was all her clothing, but still she felt naked. Exposed. Ashamed.

"God cares about you even more than the brightest star in the heavens . . ."

Her father's words echoed through the empty apartment. Frustrated, Gray stood as she pushed the thought away. Anger consumed her at the thought of God. She had no time for God.

She had no love for God.

With the front door open, she entered the dimly lit hallway and stepped toward Emma's door. She ran her hands through her untamed hair once again and wished she had pinned her long, asymmetrical bangs back. Before she could turn around and retreat into her apartment in search of a bobby pin, the door at the bottom of the stairs opened and Carla walked inside, followed by Tiffany.

Gray offered a small wave with her braced wrist as she waited for them to join her at the top of the stairs.

"Perfect timing," Tiffany said with a smile as she climbed the last stair and then reached past Gray to knock on Emma's door.

"No thanks to you." Carla huffed. "Tiffany would spend the rest of the evening in front of the mirror if I let her."

The stark differences between the sisters struck Gray again. Tonight, Tiffany had adorned herself in a fluorescent pink, sequined cocktail dress with a fluorescent orange clutch and matching orange heels. Her makeup was done flawlessly, and her platinum hair straightened, each piece in place. Carla wore a white wrap dress with a large yellow floral print, matching yellow bandana, and hemp wedge-style shoes.

"Hello!" Emma sounded surprised to see them as she opened her front door and ushered the women inside her apartment. "Come in. Make yourselves at home. I'm almost ready."

Emma left the three of them in her neat, modern living room. As Carla and Tiffany continued to bicker about time, Gray looked around at her neighbor's apartment. The space was practically identical to Gray's apartment, but there was only one bedroom. Emma's furniture was modern but cozy with a little pop of color. A bouquet of silk, pink flowers was perched on the side table by the couch, a bright green throw tossed across the armchair, and colorful paintings hung on the walls.

A soft tap came from the back door in the kitchen. The door opened a crack as Vera poked her head into the apartment. "Hello?"

"We're all in the living room," Tiffany shouted, as if the apartment were too large to see or hear the three women in the living room.

"You're right on time." Emma walked around the corner, dressed in a tea-length, purple, cocktail dress and matching heels. "I'm ready. Now that Vera's here, that's everyone, right? We're not waiting on anyone else?"

As Tiffany checked herself once more in the mirror and applied another layer of lip gloss, the women decided to take Vera's SUV, which was large enough to seat the five of them. Gray slid across the leather to sit beside Emma and Carla in the backseat and fidgeted with the hem of her dress.

Friendship had never come naturally to Gray. She watched Emma's face light up as she shared an inside joke with Tiffany, who bit back a sly grin. Vera's cool, green eyes darted back and forth between the road and the rearview mirror, her small crow's feet wrinkles more predominately on display in the corners of her eyes when she smiled. From where she sat in the passenger seat, Carla would turn around every now and again to chime into the conversation.

"That's not even close to the truth," Carla said now. "His hair came out obnoxiously purple after you dyed it. I can't believe he still called you after that."

Tiffany offered an innocent smile. "What can I say?"

Emma rolled her eyes. "You have Darren wrapped around your finger."

Darren. That must have been the blonde man with Tiffany at the carnival. Gray thought back about how he seemed to be absorbed in Tiffany's presence.

"You would think." Tiffany looked down at her tanned and manicured bare left hand. "Obviously not the right finger! It's been three years now and still no *ring* wrapped around my finger."

"It's only a matter of time." Vera's voice was always soft and confident.

"What about you, Gray?" Emma asked Gray.

"I'm sorry?" Gray's voice was quiet.

"Yeah, let's get the dirt on Gray." Tiffany winked.

"Any boyfriends back in St. Louis?"

Gray thought about her ex-boyfriend, Tyler. They had been together off and on for several years, and the relationship had ended painfully, which had fueled her need to get away from St. Louis.

"No, no boyfriend."

Silence settled over the SUV and the soft hum of music played over the radio, unnoticed before. Gray didn't look up to meet their eyes.

"We're here." Vera pulled the car into a large parking lot and came to stop in front of a Victorian-style home with a creaky wooden sign hanging over the wraparound porch. The sign read *Marie's Café.*

Like an electrical current, the memory of her father seized Gray. All four doors opened, and as she regained her composure, Gray slid out of her seat behind Tiffany.

Nothing had changed over the years. The wildflower garden that flanked the expansive porch was in bloom, but nothing else seemed to be different.

A hostess dressed in black slacks with a white, button-down shirt opened the door for them as they approached and welcomed them to Marie's Ladies' Night Out. The lights were dimmed, and candles lit each café table. The windows were open, and the cool, spring air filled the restaurant. A live, five-piece band played on a small stage in the corner of the café.

The evening passed and the sun began to set. Gray learned Marie was a widow whose husband had been killed in a car accident over twenty years ago. They had started building the Victorian home together, and after his death, the town rallied together. With the help of her neighbors, friends and family, the house was finished. To thank everyone for their support, Marie would cook them meals during the construction. One woman said her food was so good that she should open her own restaurant. Marie converted the main level of the home into a café which she owned and operated until three years ago, when Tiffany purchased it from her. Marie moved to Florida to retire but Tiffany kept the name of the café the same to honor Marie.

After they finished their meals, Emma suggested they each order the famous homemade iced tea and retreat to the back deck. The sun peeked over the wooded hills in the distance. The deck overlooked a small backyard area with a volleyball court, a couple of picnic benches, and the path that led to the river below. Three hills protruded on the other side of the river, which created a nestled atmosphere.

"So, what do you think?" Emma asked, as she sipped her tea.

"It's beautiful." Gray couldn't help but be taken aback by the scenery surrounding her.

Tiffany inhaled and took in the crisp, spring air. "It is, isn't it?" She smiled. "I got a job as a waitress with Marie here at the café while I was in high school because I needed a little extra money. A week into the job, I knew I would never leave."

The conversation flowed into talk of Tiffany and Darren's possible engagement, and Gray allowed herself to fade out of the discussion, lost in thoughts of the life she had left behind in St. Louis.

The ride home was quiet, and after they pulled into the alley behind the apartment building, the women each slipped out of the SUV one by one. Still lost in thought, Gray fumbled for the key to her apartment, and then turned to face the back porch. The light in her kitchen was on.

Gray stopped and considered the possibility that the light had been turned on at some point during the day and left on when she left to meet the women at Emma's apartment. Before she could decide if this was a realistic possibility, a figure walked past the window and cast a long shadow on the lawn beside her. Fear gripped her.

The realization that none of the other women had moved from where they stood behind her or spoken a word since their arrival dawned on Gray. When she turned to face them, Gray was greeted by the four women huddled together with grins plastered across their faces.

"What is this?" Gray motioned toward her apartment.

"You'll see." Vera's soft, kind voice made it difficult for Gray to stay irritated.

Emma waved Gray forward toward the stairs.

Gray sighed and climbed the stairs, followed closely by Emma, Vera, Tiffany, and then Carla. The back door had a tendency to stick, and as she pulled it open with a little force, she could hear the muffled sound of male voices on the other side of her apartment door, which was cracked open. Gray pushed the door open and peered into the interior of her apartment.

In the kitchen, white, sheer curtains hung over the blinds that covered each window, a three-tiered, hanging fruit basket was in the corner near the stove, the table was covered with a white cloth, and a bouquet of fresh flowers was placed in the center of the table near the window.

From where she stood in the hallway, Gray saw into the bathroom, which had new towels on a rack hung on the wall, a burlap and lace shower curtain, and a matching rug.

She walked inside the apartment and peered around the wall into the living room, which had a brown, suede couch and loveseat facing a wooden TV stand and TV. Sheer curtains had also been added to this room, along with a square ottoman and small bookshelf in the corner of the room.

Gray faced the four women who now stood in the kitchen behind her.

"Go on," Emma urged.

"There's more?"

A familiar face emerged from Gray's bedroom, an empty, black, trash bag in hand.

"You?" Gray's face showed confusion.

Tony offered her a crooked grin. "You."

After a beat of silence, Vera stepped in next to Gray. "Tony is my nephew, and I asked him and his friends to move this furniture in for us while we distracted you by taking you out. I knew if I offered the furniture to you, you would have declined."

Darren also emerged from the bedroom and walked past Tony, who still stood in the doorway, eyes on Gray. The front door opened, and a man with red hair carried a natural wood dresser into the apartment with help from a man with dark-brown hair. They were in an argument about which of them had come up with the best idea for hauling the dresser up the stairs. Two other men entered through the front door, and each carried two dresser drawers.

Gray was overwhelmed. She stepped back against the wall and let the men pass into her bedroom. Tony now stood off to her side to talk to Emma about timing and how the move had gone.

"I can't accept this," Gray heard herself whisper. Her eyes were wide as she looked up and down her apartment at each piece of furniture, the various rugs, and every small detail.

"Yes, you can," Vera stepped beside her and wrapped Gray in a gentle hug. "A few people from church donated the furniture. Think of it as your welcome gift, just a little late." She patted Gray on the shoulder and then walked toward the six men gathered in the living room.

"These are the guys who helped out," Vera said as she nodded toward the men. "They also lead worship at our church Sunday mornings. You are welcome to join us."

There was an awkward pause before Vera continued with her introductions, starting with Tiffany's boyfriend, Darren, who was already glued to Tiffany's side. Darren played rhythm guitar for their band. Next she nodded to a heavyset man with shaggy, red hair and full facial hair and introduced him as Frank, who played the drums. The bass player was the man who had helped Frank carry the dresser up the stairs, and his name was Vince. Opposite of Frank, Vince was thin and lanky with shoulder-length, brown hair. Then there was Peter, who donned leather sandals and had gravitated toward Carla. Vera introduced him as a keyboard and violin player. The last man to be introduced was a short, well-built man who stood off to the side of the group. Before Vera told her what Jim contributed to the group, Gray had assumed his role was technological based off of his black, square-framed glasses and Mario screen-printed T-shirt. Jim was the brains behind the operation, a point that his demeanor seemed to suggest he was proud of.

Gray thanked them all.

"One last surprise." Tony stepped out of the way, and Gray saw into her bedroom.

She stood with her hands pressed together and her fingertips to her lips. The bed was dressed in a suede duvet and matching pillow set, and a floor lamp with hanging paper lanterns was next to the bed. The room was tranquil and serene.

All of this for her? After the way she had treated everyone for the past month?

Guilt surged within and twisted her stomach. Gray fought back the emotions.

"It's perfect. Thank you."

Vera gave a warm smile before she announced she was leaving. Tiffany and Carla followed suit, and they said their goodbyes before they left through the front door, Tiffany hand-in-hand with Darren, and Pete alongside Carla.

Vince, Frank, and Tony grabbed armfuls of empty trash bags and bubble wrap and offered their farewells before they disappeared down the stairwell, leaving Emma in the room with Gray.

"I am so glad that you came tonight, Gray." Emma smiled before she walked out the front door to her own apartment. Gray was frozen in place as she stood in an apartment filled with the love of complete strangers.

There was a gentle knock on the partially open front door. Gray didn't speak as she opened the door the rest of the way for Tony, who stood in the hallway. He ran the palms of his hands down the front of his jeans as he looked over her shoulder into the living room.

"Vince can't find his cell phone," he said as she held the door open for him and he took a step inside.

With a deep breath, Gray pushed her emotions away and joined in the search. Together, they checked tabletops, on top of the refrigerator, and in the couch cushions, until Gray found it on one of the window-sills in the kitchen. As she handed the phone to Tony, his last words to her echoed through her mind. They had haunted her since the night he had said them.

"I pray that you find what you're looking for..."

Now, as she looked around at the transformed apartment—at the work he had done—Gray chastised herself for the way she had treated him the day they had met.

Tony stood for a moment facing her. "Good night, Gray."

Just as he turned to leave, Gray fought past the lump in her throat. "Thank you." Her voice was shaky and pinched.

Tony turned around, but Gray could not bring herself to lift her eyes to meet his. To let him see who she really was . . .

A lost woman with a dead heart.

The seconds that passed could be measured by the loud, fast beat of Gray's heart, hot in her eardrums.

"You're welcome." The words were gentle, and Tony closed the door behind him as he left.

Alone in the living room, Gray sank into the soft, overstuffed cushions of the couch and let a single tear burn down her cheek.

8

White

"We got the record deal." Tony had felt detached as he spoke the words earlier that evening. "They want us in Nashville to record in June."

He stood back and watched his friends celebrate. The six men had gathered on the sidewalk outside the floral shop, ready to haul furniture into Gray's apartment. Tony had received the news earlier in the week, but he had been waiting until they were all together before he told the others.

This was it, the moment he had been waiting for. The years of writing and miles of travel to perform and hours spent refining their music; a culmination of events which had led them to this point in time. How many evenings or weekends had he spent at his construction job—blisters on his palms and a hammer in his hand—dreaming about this day?

So why wasn't he excited?

Tony had spent the evening lost in thought, unable to identify the root of his discontentment. Unable to snap out of his fog. Unable to feel.

Until she walked in the room.

"You?"

When her silver eyes met his, the fog was lifted and he felt a sudden pull back down to earth.

"You."

His thoughts were still on those silver eyes as he packed up the truck in the parking lot. Vince couldn't find his cellphone and Tony offered to go back upstairs to get it for him. He knocked on Gray's open door and told himself that he wasn't just searching for an excuse to see her again. But he knew that was a lie.

"Thank you." Tony could hear the internal struggle in her tone as she spoke.

Conflict. Reserve. Fear.

Agape, a soft voice whispered inside of him again.

"You're welcome."

Back out in the parking lot, Tony handed Vince his phone.

"We finally made it," Vince said with a huge smile on his face. "They want a record deal? Is this really happening?"

Tony nodded his head. "It's happening."

"This is it, man." Vince laughed. "This is the turning point. The moment it all changes. No more sleeping in the back of the van and touring statewide bars. It's going to be national shows on a tour bus before you know it."

Tony forced a smile. "The sky is the limit."

"I can't believe this is real," Vince said to himself. He shook his head and sighed. "Just a few more weeks and we're out of here. Have a good night, Tony."

The parking lot was dark and quiet after Vince pulled away. The cool night air felt somber and heavy. Tony took one last look up at Gray's apartment before he got into his Jeep and started the engine.

He wasn't sure he was ready to leave.

9

Black

The smell of whiskey tainted her breath as Gray snuck back in through her bedroom window. An alarm clock next to her bed flashed 3:15 a.m., and her three-year-old half-brother, Reese, was asleep in the bed across from hers. She was able to slip in and out of her window without waking her roommate. Gray stumbled into the hallway and caught her balance before she made her way into the kitchen for a glass of water and bag of Cheetos.

As she flipped on the light, Gray gasped. Her mother sat in a kitchen chair on the opposite side of the table, a cigarette hanging from her thin, wrinkled lips.

"Where have you been?" her mother asked, and the smoke blew from her nostrils like an angry bull ready to charge.

But Gray wasn't afraid of her anymore. After her father had passed away three years ago, Gray had been forced to move back into her old house with the woman who dared to call herself a mother, now of two children. Diana, the name Gray chose to call this woman, had received a large settlement from her father's life insurance carrier, contingent upon Diana raising Gray. If she ever laid a hand on Gray and was reported to the state, Gray would be taken away along with the settlement—a fact Gray never let Diana forget.

Gray rolled her eyes and stumbled to the cabinet where the cups were kept, if any were clean. With a coy grin, she retrieved a foggy glass and filled it with water from the tap.

"Out," Gray mumbled.

From the corner of her eye, Gray watched her mother clench and unclench her fist as she fought the anger.

"This is my house." Diana stood so abruptly that the chair she had been sitting in toppled over. "I make the rules, and as long as you live here you will follow them!"

Gray stared at Diana, who trembled with rage. There was a low grunt and then the sound of blankets being shuffled before Bill—the dark-haired adulterer and now live-in boyfriend and father of Gray's half-brother— steamrolled down the hallway while he mumbled a string of profanities under his breath. When he entered the kitchen, his eyes darted from his fuming girlfriend to Gray, who coolly sipped on her glass of water.

The veins in Bill's neck bulged, and in two large steps he was in Gray's face as he knocked the glass from her hand. She watched as it broke against the far wall of the kitchen. Unsure if it was an effect from the alcohol or weed, Gray felt as though she were having an out-of-body experience. In her mind, she floated up above the scene and looked down at Diana, who now stood at her boyfriend's side, screaming and waving her arms around above her head like a lunatic. Bill was an inch from Gray's face, his spittle on her cheek as he screamed obscenities and reminded her of how ungrateful and selfish she was.

She laughed.

But then, she no longer floated above them. She was there, in Bill's face as she laughed at his absolute lack of control. As she laughed in his face.

That's when Bill and Diana snapped. Bill grabbed her by the throat and slammed her to the hard tile floor, which knocked the wind from her chest. As she fought to catch her breath again, sharp pains echoed through her rib cage and her mother kicked her in the side. Before she had the chance to fight back, Bill had a handful of her hair wound around his cal- loused fingers, and he dragged her on her back from the kitchen through the living room and out to the concrete patio, where he kicked her down the front steps. She rolled for a moment and came to a blurry stop halfway into the overgrown garden that lined the walkway leading up to the front door. Something hit her in the back of the head and sent a ringing through her ears, followed by the sound of the front door being slammed shut.

Pain rang through her underweight body as she sat up, and Gray looked at the dresser drawer of her clothing that had been thrown at her, her clothes now scattered across the lawn. When she came to her feet, Gray pulled her cell phone out of her back pocket and dialed Audrey's number. Audrey's mom was rarely ever home and Gray frequently stayed over. She would rather crash on Audrey's couch and let Diana and Bill have the settlement than report them and live in a foster home.

The phone rang in her ear, and Gray touched the open wound on her cheek. As she walked toward the street, the banner that hung on the wall beside the front door caught her eye.

"As for me and my house, we will serve the Lord."

She spit the pool of blood in her mouth onto the banner and left her belief in God scattered in the dirt along with her laundry.

Gray sat on the back porch and looked out over the evening sky with a glass of whiskey in her hand. She thought about the night she had run away, if she could call it that—it wasn't like anyone chased after her.

"Gray?" Emma had walked outside, her car keys in hand.

Gray sat with her arms on the railing of the porch and her bare feet hung over the back. "Hi, Emma." Gray had tried to be more cordial, afflicted by guilt over her past treatment of Emma.

Emma took the greeting as an invitation and sat next to Gray. She eyed the glass in Gray's hand. This was the eighth time in two weeks Emma had seen Gray with a glass of golden bliss in her hand: Four times out on the back porch, twice when she answered the door of her apartment, once when Gray retrieved her mail, and once outside of the local bar, two blocks from their apartment building.

"How are you on groceries?"

The question threw Gray off. She expected Emma to say something like, "You know, you really shouldn't drink so much; it's bad for your liver." Or, "God hates drunks."

Gray considered her bare pantry. She was on her last two packets of ramen noodles and down to one last bottle of whiskey. "Pretty low, I guess."

Emma stood and tapped Gray's upper arm. "Let's go. I was just headed to the grocery store."

Gray could say no thanks, only to be further persuaded by Emma, who wouldn't let her sit out here and drink herself silly alone, or she could just go with the relentless woman. She did need more whiskey, after all.

With a stubborn groan, Gray stood and took the last gulp of whiskey before she turned for the back door. "Let me get my shoes and purse."

The ride to the grocery store was awkward with Christian music playing over the stereo system in the small car. Emma parked the car near the doors of the small grocery store, and the two headed inside. Like a good guardian, Emma made sure Gray grabbed herself a few fresh fruits and vegetables as they made their way through the produce aisle.

"Like it really matters how I eat," Gray thought.

But it kept Emma off her back, so Gray loaded her cart with apples, oranges, bananas, bell peppers, celery, peas, and carrots before she headed to the frozen dinner aisle. After she supplemented her cart with a broad array of junk food from salty to sweet, Gray found Emma in the pasta aisle with a box of whole-wheat spaghetti in hand.

Emma held up the box for her to see before she tossed it into her cart. "Do you like spaghetti?"

Gray shrugged. She eyed the cans of pasta sauce lining the aisle. "Sure."

Emma pushed her cart in the direction of the check-out lines. "Carla, Tiffany, and Vera are coming over Saturday night, and I'm making spaghetti. You're welcome to join us."

Gray ignored Emma's look of disapproval as she added a couple of bottles of whiskey to her cart. "Sure. Saturday night. I'll stop by."

Gray combed her bony fingers through her hair as they wheeled into line behind an older woman with two large bags of cat food. After she slid the plastic divider onto the conveyor belt, Gray pulled the bottles of whiskey from her cart. The cat lady gave Gray a frown and made a short but pointed cluck of her tongue before she turned to hand the cashier five coupons and a check for the remaining eighty-three cents.

"Oh, I forgot to tell you . . ." Emma slid a *Better Homes and Garden, Summer Edition* magazine back in with the others on the magazine stand. "We're having a summer kick-off party in a couple of weeks. You know, first day of summer coming up and all. It's kind of a big deal. Tiffany invites everyone out to the café, and we swim, barbecue, play volleyball and hang out. It's always a lot of fun."

The cashier began to ring up the overabundance of groceries that Gray knew would end up rotten before she even got halfway through the supply. "I don't know. You guys get together a lot. I don't have to be at everything."

Emma shrugged. "Well, I hope you come."

Gray covered her mouth and coughed. Like a good salesman, the cashier offered to point her in the direction of their vast supply of cold medicine and cough suppressants.

"No, thank you," Gray said as she loaded the plastic bags into her cart and eyed the exit. "It's just allergies."

"We also carry allergy relief—"

"I'm fine, thanks." Gray handed her debit card to the cashier, who rang her up while Gray pushed her cart out of the way so Emma could ring out.

A thin layer of sweat beaded across her forehead as she stood, waiting for Emma to checkout, and Gray brushed it away. The two bottles of whiskey taunted her. She shifted from one foot to the other and leaned her weight against the wall behind her. Gray considered opening a bottle right here in the middle of the store, but just before she could, Emma broke away from the counter and moved to the door.

When they stepped out into the cool, fresh air, Gray took a deep breath and steadied herself. Emma went on about the summer party, and Gray caught only bits of what she said as they unloaded their carts into the trunk of her car. When Gray slid into the passenger seat, Emma started the engine and then stopped mid-sentence as she caught a glimpse of Gray's face from the corner of her eye.

"Are you okay?" Her voice was strained with concern.

"Yes, I'm just a little warm," Gray said.

Emma turned up the air conditioning. They pulled into the parking lot of the apartment building and Gray unloaded her groceries and then tossed a casual "goodbye" and "thank you" to Emma. She carried her bags up the stairs to the back porch and into her apartment. As soon as the door closed behind her, Gray collapsed onto the floor of her kitchen. The bags in her hands burst open and sent apples, oranges, and TV dinners scattered in every direction across the floor.

Slouched over with her back against the door, Gray reached for the bag to her left, which now lay on its side. The contents of the bag called out to her.

Gray picked up one of the bottles of whiskey and twisted the top open. She steadied herself, and then put the glass to her lips. Minutes melted into hours, and after she ignored the knock at her door twice and put her groceries away, Gray slipped into bed alone, the bottle in hand.

"Forget them." Audrey slurred her words as she spoke. A small drip of beer ran down her chin as she took another swig from her beer can and leaned back on the old, plaid couch. She propped her feet up on the coffee table, which was scattered with packs of cigarettes and ashtrays.

"You can stay here." Audrey leaned over her current boyfriend, whose name Gray didn't even bother to get to know, and patted Gray on the shoulder. "I've got you."

Gray took a drag of her Marlboro. "Thanks, Audrey."

The taste of dried blood still lingered on Gray's lips. The effects of the alcohol from earlier that night had begun to wear off, and she silently watched the party around her. Audrey and her boyfriend had picked Gray up at the gas station down the street from her mom's house, and when they pulled into the trailer park where Audrey lived, Gray realized the party raged on inside. She just wanted to wash the blood off her face and go to sleep.

Audrey noticed the distant, tired look on Gray's face and set down her beer. "Gray, you're going to be fine. This is so much better. You're here most of the time anyways. At least now you don't have to stress about sneaking around. You can use my bathroom to get cleaned up and sleep in my bed. I'll sleep out here. You've had a long night."

Gray offered a reassuring smile to her friend before she got up and made her way down the hall to the bathroom, eager to wash away the day. The sound of the music and laughter was muffled through the closed door. As she undressed, Gray examined the bruises that riddled her body. A single tear slid down her cheek and stung her open wounds.

After a long, hot shower, Gray slipped into a T-shirt and shorts she had found in Audrey's dresser. She didn't have the money to purchase new clothes. Her after school job at the local retail department hadn't brought in much of an income, and her mom had taken most of her paychecks. Gray had only been able to stash away a few of her checks from her mom, and most of the money from those had gone to beer and cigarettes.

She would worry about it tomorrow. Tonight, she just wanted to rest.

Gray flipped off the lights and slipped under the wrinkled covers on Audrey's bed. The room was pitch black.

"I'm fine," she whispered into the darkness. "It's going to be fine."

10

Black

Reruns of *M*A*S*H* had run all day, and while Gray didn't care for *M*A*S*H*, it was a better choice than infomercials or the news. A roll of toilet paper sat on the coffee table in the center of the room. Gray coughed into a strand of the paper and tossed the crumpled trash into a plastic grocery bag she had brought into the living room earlier that day.

A soft knock at the front door interrupted a commercial for a non-profit asking for members to pledge a dollar a day to help feed children in a third world county. Scenes of tattered, makeshift homes and emaciated children rolled across the screen.

"It's open," she called out in a raspy voice.

"Gray?" Emma poked her head inside the door. "You don't sound well."

Gray waved a piece of toilet paper in the air in dismissal and turned her attention back to the TV. "It's just allergies. I've always gotten them pretty bad."

Hypochondriac, Audrey's voice echoed in her head. It was a word she'd heard often from her friend over the last few years.

"I'm sorry you're not feeling well." Emma glanced around the apartment. "I was hoping you would still be coming over for spaghetti tonight, but you stay home and get better."

Relief washed over Gray as she remembered Emma had invited her for dinner and realized she wouldn't have to come up with an excuse to get out of having to go. Her face must have been predictable because Emma grinned at her as she stepped back toward the front door.

"Don't look so happy about getting out of it." Emma laughed. "I hope you feel better soon. Let me know if you need anything."

"I will." Gray coughed into another tissue. "Thanks."

The front door closed, and Gray made her way into the kitchen to pour herself a glass of whiskey and grab a couple pills of ibuprofen. After she slammed the glass of whiskey, she set the empty glass in the kitchen sink and made her way back to the couch to snuggle under the comforter just as another episode of *M*A*S*H* came on. The picture faded as Gray slipped into a deep sleep.

A noise at the window woke Gray. As she stood up from the couch, her white comforter fell to the floor. The apartment had grown dark with the night sky. The only light was from the TV screen, which now showed the ten o'clock news.

"Emma?" Gray called and walked toward the kitchen where the noise had come from.

There was another loud clatter, and Gray jumped back, startled by the noise. The apartment grew silent again. Gray took another step forward.

"Emma? Is that you?"

The voice in her head told her to turn around, to run, that it wasn't Emma. But Gray's feet continued to bring her closer to where the noise had come from.

"Emma?"

As she stepped into the kitchen, a dark figure jumped from the corner of the room and grabbed her with a firm grip. With a loud scream, Gray fell forward, her stomach to the ground as the figure leaned over her, the voice of a man whispering in her ear.

"Emma's not here."

Panic gripped Gray at the familiar sound of his voice, and she clawed at the ground, fighting to get away, but the man held her down.

"There's no one to protect you this time."

Another scream tore from her throat, and suddenly, Gray was thirteen years old again. The man dragged her across the floor toward the broken kitchen window. She fought against him, but she was so young, so small, and he was much larger. The man hoisted her up over his shoulders and began to climb back out of the window. Gray clung to what was left of the window; the glass cut deep into the palms of her hands. She screamed and kicked, but the man wasn't going to let her go.

Blood poured from her hands, which lost their grip. She held on by her fingertips.

"Give up, Gray," the man said. "There's no one to save you."

Her fingers slipped, and Gray disappeared into the black of the night, held by her captor as she screamed. . .

A small scream slipped from her throat as Gray shot up, wide-awake. Her breaths came in quick bursts, and her eyes darted around the empty, dark apartment. Her hair was drenched in sweat, and her blanket lay crumpled on the floor next to the couch. The ten o'clock news was on the TV screen.

"It was just a dream. It was just a dream", Gray told herself, but she couldn't get her heart to slow down. She still felt the man's calloused hands on her skin, the heat of his breath on her neck as he spoke.

Gray rose from the couch and put on a pair of boots, grabbed her jacket, and tripped over the Tupperware of spaghetti Emma had left on her doormat as she ran out the door. The streets were still busy, and Gray steadied herself, slowing her pace so she wouldn't draw attention. She passed a couple who walked together, hand in hand.

She walked up away from the riverfront as she sorted through her thoughts and fought to push the dream to the back of her mind.

"A dream?" The man's voice taunted. *"Or memories?"*

"Hey, honey." A burly man stood next to his Harley and called out to her from outside the bar across the street.

She ignored the man's comment as she cut between two parked cars and crossed the street toward the bar. Gray pushed the door open and walked inside. She was greeted by the familiar smell of liquor and cigarette smoke. The sound of rock music and clinking pool balls sent a sense of calm over her raw emotions.

As she pulled herself onto a stool, the bartender approached. A man watched her from where he sat across the bar. She ordered whiskey and gazed back at the man in the corner. He looked to be her age or maybe a little older with jet-black hair, a clean-shaven face, and masculine build. With another drag of his cigarette, he stood and made his way over to where she sat.

"Do you smoke?" He offered his pack and lighter and settled into the stool beside her.

"I quit," Gray said as she took a cigarette, popped it between her lips and lit it.

"Devon," the man said with a smile, as he held out his hand.

Gray pushed the pack of cigarettes back into his extended hand and then turned her attention to the large plasma TV above the bar, which played *The Simpsons*. "Thanks for the cigarette."

The bartender reappeared and set her drink on a little, white napkin in front of her. Oh, how she'd missed this. The dim lights, the cigarette smoke that loomed like a dark cloud in the room, the little, white napkins under a glass of pick-me-up.

"Want another beer, Devon?" the bartender asked.

"Nah, I'll have what she's having."

She didn't look at Devon as she took another drag of the cigarette and let the smoke fill her lungs. Poison. She brought the drink to her lips and swallowed. The burn filled her mouth and ran down her chest into her stomach. Poison.

"You know what they say about beer before liquor, right?" she asked but didn't take her eyes from the TV.

Devon chuckled. "I guess I've built up my tolerance."

Gray threw back the rest of her drink and set the empty glass back on the napkin.

"If I buy you another drink, will you tell me your name?"

This time, Gray turned in her seat and let her eyes meet his, which were so dark they looked black in this lighting. "No."

A cocky grin pulled at Devon's lips, and he held his hands up in surrender. "All right, I get it. You're just here to relax and have a good time. I won't get in your way. Just let me keep you company for a while."

Gray turned back to the counter to flag the bartender. "America is still a free country. You can sit where you want."

When the bartender approached, Gray ordered another whiskey, and Devon insisted it be put on his tab. After the third, or maybe the fourth drink, Gray loosened up, and Devon was tuned into her state of mind.

The nightmare in her mind had begun to fade. The poison always works, Gray thought to herself as she took a drag of the second cigarette he had given her.

She smiled at the thought. Devon noticed the grin as he slammed the glass of whiskey in front of him.

"Oh, she's not made of stone after all," he teased.

Gray laughed. "Don't take it as an invitation."

After another round of drinks, Devon stood and extended his hand. "Join me for a game of pool?"

There was a moment of hesitation before Gray stood, the room spinning as she moved. They made their way over to the pool tables, and Devon cued the ball and took the first shot. He was good. Gray watched the muscles in his upper arms, shoulders, and back flex as be bent over to line the cue ball up with a trained eye.

"I knew this was a bad idea," Gray said as she took a clumsy step back and almost tripped over a man who played at the table next to them.

Devon caught her, his strong arm wrapped around her thin waist. "Whoa, careful," he cautioned before he apologized to the man she had knocked into. "What do you mean, this was a bad idea?"

She pulled herself from his arms, set the stick on the pool table, and held her hands up in the air. "I'm terrible at pool. And that's when I'm sober."

The bartender approached with their drinks. Devon took both as he stepped in close to Gray and handed her a glass. "How are you at dancing?" He nodded toward the small dance floor where a few couples danced to rock music.

Gray threw back her glass of whiskey, and then set the glass down on the counter beside them. Warning bells rang in her head. She had pushed herself this far a few times, and those nights had never ended well. This time, neither Audrey nor Tyler were here to nurse her back to health after she spent the night bent over the toilet. But she drank more frequently now than she had back then. Surely, she'd built up a tolerance.

Devon waited for her reply. Gray held out her hand, and with a large grin, he took it into his and led her out to the floor. The dance floor was small, and with the few couples that were already dancing, it was crowded. Gray was pressed against Devon as she moved, and she let her inhibitions go free.

"I think he's cheating on me." Gray sat with Audrey on the back porch of Audrey's parents' trailer. A guy they had graduated with was bent over the railing as he threw up in the grass. Audrey's parents had bought them beer for their high school graduation party, and Audrey still wore her graduation cap, twirling the tassel in between her fingers.

"What makes you say that?" Audrey didn't notice the guy leaving his dinner in her lawn. Her eyes were glossed over, and she wore a playful grin on her face. The same playful grin she always wore when she was drunk, no matter the topic.

"He's been gone a lot lately, and I saw a couple of messages on his phone . . ." Gray trailed off. "I don't know."

Audrey laughed and took another swig from her red Solo cup. "What do you expect, Gray? You and Tyler have been on again, off again since last summer and you're still holding out on him. The man can't wait forever. He's got needs."

Just then, the redhead Audrey was dating stumbled out onto the back porch and fell into her lap. "Come on, baby. Let's get out of here," he slurred.

"Okay, okay. Don't rush me," she hissed. Audrey stood and tossed her cup onto the ground, and then looked back at Gray. "Figure out what you want or cut Tyler loose. Just stop going back and forth. It's drama."

And with that, Audrey disappeared around the side of the house. Gray heard two car doors close, then the sound of an engine as it fired to life before she saw the taillights of Audrey's boyfriend's truck pull out of the trailer park onto the main road.

Audrey's words haunted her for the rest of the night. "What do you expect? You're still holding out on him . . . He's got needs . . ."

The chills ran up Gray's spine as the nightmare haunted her thoughts again. She pushed away from Devon and headed to the register to pay her tab. As the bartender rang up her tab, Gray asked for a pack of cigarettes.

"What did I do?" Devon walked up beside her.

The bartender returned with her receipt and the pack of cigarettes. Gray shoved them both into the pocket of her jacket and pushed past Devon toward the exit. "It's not you," she said over her shoulder as she opened the door.

The cool night air filled her lungs and she coughed. The street swayed, and she did her best to steady herself as she made her way down the sidewalk to the nearest intersection.

She had to get away. Gray couldn't go back to that apartment. He was there, waiting for her. The man.

Gray ripped the pack of cigarettes open and stuffed one into her mouth, lighting it up as she walked away from the small town. When she reached the other side of town, she needed a new cigarette, and as she reached into her pocket for the lighter, Gray lost her footing on the curb at a crosswalk and fell into the street.

A set of headlights filled her view followed by the screech of tires. The cigarette fell from her lips and burned her skin when it landed on her hand. The car stopped a foot from where she now sat in the street, and she heard a door open and close. A large shadow stepped in front of the headlights, and Gray lifted her hand to shield her eyes from the bright light as she tried to make out the figure.

"Gray?"

She moaned at the sound of the voice and let her hand drop from her face. "Hi, Tony."

11

White

Tony's heart was still pounding in his chest. What was she doing out in the street in the middle of the night? The accident had been a near miss. His shoes shuffled on the asphalt as he made his way over to help Gray to her feet. Her hair was disheveled and her face was pale. She was clearly drunk.

"What are you doing?"

Gray looked around the ground. "Well," she said as she peered at the ditch next to her, "I lost my cigarette."

With a sigh, Tony propped his arms around her to help her stand. "I'm sure you have another one."

As she stood, Gray wore a look of confusion for a moment before she dug her hand into one of her pockets. The smell of tobacco filled the air when she pulled the pack and lighter from her pocket and lit up another cigarette. The headlights of the Jeep illuminated the block around them as they stood in the middle of the street.

"Where are you going?" Tony looked around them. This side of town was quiet. There were no businesses for a few blocks, just a couple of small apartment buildings and a bank. "Your apartment is on the other side of town."

"Please don't talk to me like I'm an idiot." Gray pulled her arm from his grip and stepped back up onto the sidewalk. "I know where I'm going."

Gray took a few steps, headed in a direction toward town, and then turned around and began walking towards the riverfront.

"Clearly." Tony had his hands in his pockets as he considered his options. "Let me call Emma. She can come pick you up—"

"Absolutely not." Gray continued downhill toward the riverfront.

Tony watched her as she walked away. Gray stumbled into the street again, stood up straight, brushed herself off and made her way back onto the sidewalk. He shook his head. There was no way he could leave her here.

"Let me drive you home," he offered.

"I'm not getting in your car." Gray didn't turn around as she spoke to him. "I want to walk."

"Gray, please." Tony walked up beside her and took her arm into his hands again. "You shouldn't be out like this. I could have hit you. Or someone might . . ." he trailed off as he eyed the dark alleys around them. This wasn't the safest part of town. The local bar was a few blocks down the road, and any trouble their sleepy town experienced usually stemmed from that bar.

"Might what?" Gray prodded with a teasing grin. Laughter bubbled up until it burst from her lips with bitter intensity. "Someone might hurt me?" She laughed again and started to walk away.

"Gray." Tony's soft, blue eyes pleaded with her. If he left her here and something happened to her, he would never forgive himself. "If you won't let me take you home, then at least let me call Emma to pick you up."

"One Bible-thumper is enough for me to deal with in a night's time," she said over her shoulder as she walked down the street. "I don't need another, thank you."

Bible-thumper? Her disdainful words were like a arrows—sharpened, aimed and targeting his heart. Each one hit its mark with a jolt. Tony knew that the bow in her hands was created by past hurt and betrayal that had nothing to do with him, but he also knew that when she looked at him, she only saw a target. An enemy. And that, he realized, hurt him more than the blows themselves.

Tony had to quicken his pace to catch up to Gray on the sidewalk. Would she ever see past her preconceived notions about his faith to his heart?

Tony touched her upper arm and Gray pulled back.

"Don't touch me."

Another arrow. Another bullseye.

Tony pulled his hand back and held them both up as he spoke. "Let me walk you home then. I'll park the Jeep at the bank and come back for it after you're home."

Gray stopped walking to catch her breath. She bent over as a coughing fit seized her. When she looked up at him, he could see the fatigue. She stood still for a moment, her hands on her knees, and Tony wondered if she was about to vomit.

"Fine." She waved her hands in the air. Ash from the cigarette fell on her arm.

Tony parked the Jeep. They made their way down the sidewalk to the riverfront. The sound of the rushing water filled the night air. Gray puffed on her cigarette and the smoke rolled from between her lips. She stumbled again.

Tony walked beside her, his hands in the pockets of his jacket. He listened to the river and took in the familiar smell of cigarette smoke. He wondered how many nights he had spent walking this same path to his own apartment from the bar. It was a life that seemed so far behind him, yet at the same time, as familiar as yesterday.

One night in particular came to mind. It was a weekday, and the bartender had announced last call long before Tony was ready to leave. Most of the bar had cleared at that point, and he sat, unmoved, with a cigarette between his fingers and an empty glass in his hands.

"Come on, Jill," he slurred, holding up his glass, "one more. For a friend."

Jill shook her head from where she stood behind the bar, a dishtowel in her hand. "Not tonight, honey." Her voice had a sweet, southern drawl. "I think it's time to go home."

Tony slammed his glass down and threw his head back.

The bell above the door chimed, and he didn't have to look to know who was standing in the entryway.

"Hey, Vera." Jill's voice was stained with concern as she spoke.

Tony kept his head bent and his eyes on the empty glass, but he could feel his aunt Vera standing beside him.

"Tony, come on." Vera put her hand on his shoulder. "Let me drive you home."

He looked up at Jill. He was sure she had grown accustomed to this routine; calling Vera on his behalf hours after closing, Vera showing up to talk him into leaving, watching Tony stumble out the door beside her. Tonight, Jill's face looked worn and tired. She met his gaze for a moment before turning away. He snuffed his cigarette out in a glass ashtray and watched the embers flicker and die out.

Tony leaned back in his chair and pushed his empty glass aside. "Not tonight." He stood.

"Tony-"

"I said, not tonight!" Tony looked up at his aunt for the first time since she had walked into the bar. She was wearing her pajama pants and a heavy winter coat. Her hair was disheveled and her eyes puffy and red. He knew she had been crying.

The sight of her pity only further enraged him.

He shoved past her toward the door. "I'll walk. Go home, Vera."

Tony was no stranger to holding a bow and arrow of his own.

Gray took another drag of the cigarette and then flicked the ash onto the pavement of the sidewalk and cleared her throat. He glanced over at her, but she didn't turn her head.

"Guess your prayers didn't work." Her tone was bitter.

Tony was quiet for a moment. "Not yet, maybe. That doesn't mean I will stop."

Gray huffed. "You're going to be disappointed. God is good at disappointment."

There was a beat of silence.

"I haven't found that to be true." Tony kept pace with Gray as she trudged with unsteady footing. "The God I know is good at grace and love. He hasn't let me down yet."

"Save it, preacher." Gray took a drag of her cigarette. "This might shock you, but I grew up in church. There isn't anything you can say to me that I haven't already heard."

"Why would that shock me?"

Silence settled between them as Gray seemed to consider his question.

"I haven't always been like this . . ." the last word slurred.

"What do you mean?" Tony kept his eyes forward.

"You know, messed up." Gray motioned over herself as she spoke. She flicked her cigarette butt into the dark of the night and replaced it with another.

"Everyone is messed up," Tony said.

With a sharp chuckle, Gray waved her hands around. "Oh, right," she said. "I remember what they tell you. 'We're all sinners and Jesus is the only one who can save us,' right? It's been a while. I'm a little rusty." She laughed again.

"Something like that." Tony's voice was soft.

A car passed them, and Gray glanced over at Tony when the headlights illuminated their faces. Tony offered the driver a polite and common small-town wave. He recognized the truck and knew it was one of the local officers, Tim, probably on his way to clock in for the night shift. The street grew dark again and Tony walked on beside Gray, hands in his pocket, lost in thought.

He knew the source of the pain that had driven him to pick up a bow and arrow, but the woman standing next to him was a mystery. Like Tony, she shielded her pain, unwilling to let anyone close enough to see it. It had taken him years of being on the attack before he had let his guard down. How much time would Gray need before she would be ready to let the bow fall to the ground at her feet?

"Not everyone can be saved, preacher." Gray sounded winded as she spoke.

Tony cleared his throat. "Just because not everyone chooses to get into the lifeboat doesn't mean they couldn't be saved. It means they chose to stay in the water. The lifeboat is there either way."

Gray turned to face Tony, a lazy grin on her face.

"I heard that drowning is euphoric."

They walked another block in silence. Gray's breath was shallow and labored, no doubt from the ten cigarettes she had smoked in the last five minutes. Their pace slowed, and Tony watched as she flicked the half-finished cigarette out into the street and put her hands on her hips for support as she walked.

Gray was barely over five feet tall, and Tony's six-foot figure towered over hers as they walked down the street. He stole glances when Gray wasn't looking and studied her dark, wavy hair, pale, petite face, and dark style. She wore black leggings with a gray tunic shirt, leather jacket, and slouchy boots. The boots made her legs look even thinner than they were—just toothpicks that held her small figure up.

They walked past the bar Gray had come from, which now had the door open as a group of bikers hung outside, and classic rock music blasted from the jukebox inside. A man stood outside, a cigarette in hand, and Tony recognized him as Devon, a laborer Tony often worked with on the job. Devon threw up a peace sign as they walked by, and Gray laughed and shook her head. "I Love Rock & Roll" played, and as they walked past, Gray hummed the tune. This time, she caught Tony as he watched her.

"What?" she asked, an uncoordinated bounce back in her step. "You sing, don't you? Come on, you've got to know this song."

She sang the song and Tony was taken aback by how beautiful her voice was. A few of the lyrics were slurred and others incomprehensible, but her melody and pitch were perfect.

"Come on." She nudged him. "I thought you were a big-shot musician. You don't sing heathen music out in the street with drunks at two in the morning?"

"That's all right." Tony ducked his head to hide a smile. "I'll pass."

"Suit yourself."

Gray hummed as she fought her labored breathing for the next couple of blocks. As they grew closer to the block where she lived, the humming died off and silence settled over them again. Gray's face was pale and her eyes studied the ground in front of her as she walked. Every couple of steps, she would look up and her eyes would dart around before they shifted to the ground again as if she were watching for something.

Gray stopped and held her hair back as she vomited into the street. Tony gave her privacy. When she stood, her legs shook. At the door of the floral shop, Gray kicked at the ground.

"I know this sounds ridiculous, but can you come up with me and look around? Make sure no one is in there."

Tony looked up at the apartment's windows that faced the street. The lights were out, but he could tell the TV had been left on by the dim light that flickered from the other room.

"Gray," he hesitated, "I don't think that's a good idea."

Gray laughed. "Trust me," she said in an agitated tone, "it's not like that at all. But if you are worried about me coming onto you or something, go up there by yourself. I'll wait here."

With a heavy sigh, Tony pushed the door open and made his way up the stairwell to her front door. He picked up the Tupperware on her doorstep. The living room was quiet except for the sound from the TV, and Tony noticed the roll of toilet paper on the coffee stand and crumpled blanket on the floor next to the couch. He opened the closet door and peeked inside. Tony wasn't sure what Gray expected him to find, but he didn't want to have to come up a second time if she wasn't satisfied with his first investigation.

Her bedroom was empty. He walked to the kitchen, set the Tupperware in the refrigerator, and noticed the near-empty bottle of whiskey on the counter. Tony checked the bathroom before he locked the back door and checked that all the windows were secured and locked. When he came back down the stairs a few minutes later, Gray was seated on the doorstep to the flower shop, her knees pulled up to her chest as she waited.

"All clear," he said and stepped out onto the sidewalk. "No monsters in the closet or under the bed. There was a Tupperware bowl on your doorstep. I put it in your fridge."

Gray pulled herself up to her feet and took another nervous glance around.

"Thanks." Her voice was tired and worn. She stepped past him into the stairwell and then turned to close the door. "Goodnight, preacher." Her face was creased with a half-grin.

"Goodnight, Gray."

12

Black

"I don't have a swimsuit."

Gray stood in her doorway and ran her hands through her tangled hair as she stared back at six anxious eyes. The dreaded knock at her door had woken her from an afternoon nap, and as she rolled out of bed, she'd expected to find Emma on the other side of the six-paneled door. She hadn't expected Tiffany and Carla to be with her.

For the past five minutes, Gray had given them excuse after excuse for why she couldn't go to Tiffany's summer party, but they found ways around her lame explanations.

"We thought you might say that," Emma said with a big, obnoxious smile. "So Carla brought a few from her shop. One of them has to fit."

Carla held up four vintage-style, one-piece, halter-top swimsuits.

"And they're all black!" Carla pointed out with a smile.

Without a reply, Gray reached past Emma and snatched the suits from Carla's hand. She slammed the door behind her and marched to her bedroom to try them on. There was nothing that she could do to get rid of these people. Gray had come to Belle in search of a quiet, solitary place to stay for a while. She had never been more mistaken. Belle was anything but solitary.

After she found a suit that fit, Gray pulled a light charcoal sundress over the suit and pulled her hair back in a messy ponytail before she slipped on a pair of shoes, snuck a handful of whiskey shooters into her purse, and opened the door. The three women waited in the hall. She tossed the other three swimsuits to Carla and mumbled a halfhearted "thanks" as she followed the women down the stairs into the bright sunlight.

Tiffany and Carla rode together in Tiffany's car, while Gray slid into the passenger seat of Emma's car. The drive wound back through the woods and then through the familiar opening in the trees, which led to the café. A few signs stated the café was closed for a private event.

The parking lot was full, and Emma gave Gray a warm smile of encouragement as they pulled into the next open spot. "You'll have fun, I promise."

Gray forced a smile and pushed her door open, stepping onto the pavement. They walked together toward the café and Gray noticed a small group of people who stood off to the side of the front porch in conversation. She fidgeted with a wrinkle in her dress. Emma offered the group a "hello" and small wave before she stepped inside. After sliding a twelve-pack of Coca-Cola into the industrial-sized refrigerator, Emma directed Gray to the glass French doors, which led to the back patio.

The noise and chaos outside overwhelmed Gray. There were over two dozen people in the back of the café. Some played horseshoes, others volleyball, and a few sat around in lawn chairs in the grass or under the shade of the large, covered patio. She felt herself withdraw and searched out a place she could retreat to, unnoticed, to pass the time until she could return home.

Tony walked up beside Emma. "How did you get the vampire to leave her dungeon?"

Gray turned at the sound of Tony's voice. They locked eyes for a moment. She offered a sarcastic laugh, but it was followed by a genuine smile. He smiled back.

Two weeks had passed since the night he'd walked her home from the bar. She hadn't seen him, or anyone else for that matter, after that night. Emma had come and knocked on her door a few times, but she had ignored the sound as she sat in the otherwise quiet, secluded dark-ness of her apartment.

And now here she was, at Tiffany's party. Gray was sure by the surprised look on Tony's face that this was the last place he'd expected to see her. As much as she wished she were still at home, under her covers, his presence brought her a sense of calm and relief.

The sound of Emma as she cleared her throat cut through the silence that had settled between them.

"I'm going to go say hi to the Clancy twins." She stepped past Tony and made her way over to a group that stood near the white picket fence, which flanked the far side of the yard. Emma focused her attention on two identical male twins, both tall with sandy-brown hair.

"She's been trying to get Rick to notice her for months now." Tony nodded toward Emma. "Poor guy is clueless."

Gray took a step closer so she stood an inch or two from Tony. "Which one is Rick?"

"The one wearing the light blue T-shirt."

Someone across the yard called for Tony. Frank waved him over to where he stood next to the fence. Tony took Gray by the hand and pulled her along next to him. His skin was warm and soft under her fingertips. He seemed to suddenly realize that he was holding her hand, and let go as they approached Frank. Gray pondered for a moment on what the gesture had meant, but she was sure it had been an absent-minded act on his behalf.

The fence where they now stood was a safety measure so no one could fall down a steep twenty-foot drop, which led to the riverbank below. Frank pointed to Darren and Vince, who were about to jump off a small cliff on the other side of the bank into the rushing water below. Gray tried to focus on the scene, but her mind wandered back to the feel of Tony's hand in hers.

His motives had to have been innocent. Tony was a Christian. And Gray didn't have to look around to see that more than one pair of female eyes stole glances at him. She was sure he considered her arrogant, dingy, and a lousy drunk, not a compatible partner.

I'm not, she thought.

Darren and Vince jumped from the cliff and plunged under the river's current before they bobbed back to the surface. They fought to swim back upstream and reached the base of the cliff to begin the climb up the rock wall once more.

"Let's go down to the dock." Frank looked over and seemed to notice for the first time that Gray was there. "Hi, Gray."

He offered her a big, goofy smile and then looked past her. "Is Emma here, too?"

Gray noticed a tinge of pain wash across Tony's face. "Yeah, she's around here somewhere." He turned back to the river.

"Oh," Frank said in a soft tone when he noticed Emma, who was shamelessly flirting without reciprocation from Rick.

"Come on." Tony turned back to Frank and put his hand on his shoulder. "Let's go down to the bank."

Empathy settled over Gray as she saw the disappointment in Frank's eyes.

"Go ahead," she said and turned away from the two men. "I'm going to get a soda. I'll meet you down there."

Tony gave Gray a quizzical side-glance and then followed Frank down a narrow stone staircase, which led to the riverbank below. Once she could no longer see them, Gray turned and walked toward Emma, a new determination in her mind. Gray thought about Frank's casually styled, dark-auburn hair and easygoing green eyes, and wondered why the connection hadn't been made yet. When Gray approached the group, she caught the tail end of a discussion about deer season, a discussion she was glad she missed. Caught off guard by her approach, Emma greeted her and then did a quick introduction around the group. The names blended together and Gray forgot them, focused more on her task at hand.

"I was about to join Frank and Tony on the dock, and I was wondering if you wanted to come, too."

Three blonde, female heads turned at the mention of Tony's name.

Don't worry, ladies. You can have him, Gray thought to herself.

Surprise and excitement filled Emma's eyes as if she were flabbergasted by the idea of Gray encouraging a friendship. Gray was afraid she would see right through her intentions.

"Sure." She searched Gray's face before she gave up and turned to face Rick. "Would you like to join us?"

"That's all right, thank you," he said with a smile that dismissed the two women.

Emma's face dropped. "Okay."

When they walked away from the group, Gray watched Rick as he picked up a conversation with one of the blondes.

"Is it alright if I get a cola?" Gray hoped Emma wouldn't turn to see the flirtation behind them.

"Sure." Emma's mind seemed distant as she spoke.

Gray stepped into the kitchen and grabbed two cans of soda from the fridge. She popped one open, poured some of it out into the sink, slipped a shooter of Jack from her purse, and dumped its contents into the can. She met Emma at the door where she'd left her. Gray handed her the unopened soda and walked toward the small gate in the fence, which opened to the stairs.

"He's not that good-looking," Gray said.

Emma's face showed surprise and confusion. "Who?"

"Rick."

Emma stole a glance at the man who leaned in and laughed with the blonde girl.

"I guess you're right," she said with a sigh. "Obviously, the interest is only one-sided."

Gray shrugged. "You know what they say. 'There are plenty of fish in the sea.' I'm sure the right guy is just around the corner."

The walk down the staircase was steep and long, and when they reached the sandy beach, Gray had to catch her breath.

"Emma?" Frank jogged up beside them. "I thought you were. . ." He let his words trail off.

"Gray asked me to join her." Emma shrugged. "What are you guys up to?"

"Vince and Darren are about to jump again." Frank took her by the arm and walked with her toward the edge of the water. Gray watched the two of them as they stood together.

"What do you know? She has a heart, too." Tony walked up beside her in his blue swim trunks, wet from the river water. "Today is full of surprises."

Gray's eyes shifted to Vince and Darren as they took the plunge again, her expression flat. "I don't know what would give you that misguided impression."

Tony took the can of soda from her hands. "You didn't actually want a soda. That was an excuse."

Gray watched the guys swim back and start to climb again. "I wouldn't drink that if I were you. I only drink cola with Jack."

With a sigh, Tony handed the soda back. She took a gulp. The guys climbed to the top and pulled themselves onto the peak of the cliff, and that's when Gray made up her mind. She walked over to a shady part of the beach, set down her mixed drink, and pulled her sundress over her head, letting it fall beside a log on the riverbank.

"What are you doing?" Tony watched her as she walked toward the dock.

"I'm going to jump off the cliff." Her tone was even and flat.

Tony looked from the top of the twenty-foot cliff back to Gray. "That's really high up, you know. Looks even more intimidating from the top."

"I'm not afraid of heights." She walked past him.

He jogged up beside her. "Alright. I'll go with you."

Gray laughed. She stopped at the edge of the dock and turned to face him. "Then who will be down here to save me if I drown?"

A serious expression flashed across Tony's face. He took a step closer so that he was just inches from her ear.

"How much have you had to drink today?" He spoke in a tone only she could hear, and apprehension tinged his voice.

Gray laughed in response.

After a moment of hesitation, Tony shook his head and sighed. His attention turned to Vince and Darren, and he shouted for them to wait so he and Gray could climb up with them.

"All right, go ahead," he said to Gray, nodding toward the water.

"Are *you* afraid of heights?"

He kept his eyes on hers. "No, but I'm terrified of you."

With a grin, Gray jumped into the cool river water and felt the immediate, strong pull of the current. For a moment, she wondered if she had the strength to make the climb, but she pushed the thought to the back of her mind.

When she surfaced, Tony was beside her, and they swam together to the bottom of the rock wall. The rock was slick with mildew, and it took Gray a moment to find a decent foothold. As she pulled herself up out of the water and began to climb the wall, she heard Emma's voice from behind her.

"Wait, are you serious?" Emma shouted.

Gray ignored the comment and continued to climb, determined to make it to the top. The places of the wall that Vince and Darren had already used to climb were wet and slimy, so Gray had to find her own path using dry stone. Her fingertips gripped and her palms perspired as she put more distance between herself and the rushing river below. If she lost her footing, Gray would have to try and push herself off the wall so she didn't land on any rocks hidden under the surface of the water near the edge.

"You okay?" Tony asked from where he climbed a foot or so below her.

Unable to respond, Gray fought to save her labored breath for the oxygen her body needed. When she finished this, she was going to find someone here with a cigarette.

Her arms shook involuntarily at the strain of the climb. Sweat beaded across her pale forehead, and just before she considered giving up, she reached the top of the climb. Vince offered her a hand, but she refused and pulled herself up and over the edge of the rock. Tony came up right behind her.

"Are you okay?" he asked again, slightly out of breath.

Gray smiled and tried to hide her fatigue, but concern clouded Tony's eyes. He knelt beside her and put his hand on her back.

"Just lean back and catch your breath for a minute. This would be a bad place to pass out."

Gray leaned back, closed her eyes, and begged her airways to open. The blistering sun beat down on her. She felt the blood as it drained from her face and knew if she couldn't get a handle on herself soon, she would pass out. She needed that drink.

Gray heard Tony as he spoke to Vince and Darren. "Is there another way down?"

With a deep breath to steady herself, Gray sat up again. "I'm fine," she managed in a hoarse voice. "I just need a minute. Smoker's lungs, you know."

While she caught her breath, Darren and Vince showed Tony where the water was deepest and where they would want to aim to land. The two of them jumped once more, and Gray heard the splash of water a second later.

He studied her face.

"Are you sure you want to do this?"

Gray's breath had returned to normal. "I'm fine. Really. I'm going to do this."

She pushed herself to her feet and walked to the edge to look down at the river below. Darren and Vince had reached the bank and sat in the water as they watched Tony and Gray prepare for the jump. After a deep breath, Gray took a step back. She put her hand over her chest and felt her heart beating with a slow and steady rhythm under her fingertips. Gray stood for a moment and waited for the surge of adrenaline, for her pulse to quicken.

It never changed.

"Are you ready?"

Tony stepped up next to Gray. He showed her where to aim to land.

"Jump out as far as you can. Keep your legs straight and your arms at your side until you hit the water."

Gray playfully pinched his cheeks with her thumb and pointer finger so that his lips made a fish face. "Don't worry. This will be fun!"

When she released his face, Tony wore a slight grin and he looked out over the cliff again. "Whatever you say."

He got into position next to her but left enough distance between them so they wouldn't collide when they jumped.

"Three . . ." Gray looked at him. "Two . . ."

They both bent their knees and prepared for the leap.

"One!" She shouted, and they both jumped.

The wind blew against her face and whipped the stray strands of her hair around as she free-fell. Gray fixed her eyes on the dark surface of the water below as it grew closer. Just before her feet reached the surface, she sucked in a deep breath and stiffened her body. The sudden cold washed over her as she plunged below the surface. Her body was tumbled by the undertow, and it took her a minute to gain her bearings and swim for the surface. Just as she broke into the fresh air, her lungs seized, and she began to cough.

She kicked upstream, headed for the beach, a smile on her face. Tony swam alongside of her until the water was shallow enough to stand. They stood and stared at each other for a moment. Gray fought the urge to hug him out of excitement. She had never done anything like that before.

"Are you all right?" Emma ran to the edge of the dock.

Gray couldn't stop smiling. "I'm great. That was fun!"

"You sounded like you choked on some water." Emma's hands were at her chest. "Wasn't that you who coughed?"

"I'm fine." Gray peered up at the cliff again, astonished she had just made the jump. "My allergies are still bothering me a bit."

"Food's ready!" Tiffany called from the top of the stairs.

Emma returned to where Frank stood on the beach, and they walked together toward the stairs. Darren and Vince headed up the beach to join them.

When Gray turned back to Tony, he smiled. "You scared the crap out of me."

"Gave you a little more of a rush, didn't it?" She winked.

Tony shook his head. "I'd rather know I'm not going to be dragging a body out of the river than have a 'little bit more of a rush.'"

There was something in Tony's eyes as he spoke that Gray didn't understand. Back on the beach, she slipped into her sundress, and grabbed her can of soda before she headed to the stairwell. When she reached the bottom of the stairs, Gray could no longer see Tony. She bit her lower lip and began the tedious climb. Maybe this wouldn't be so bad after all. There was no harm in making new friends, right?

Her thoughts went back to Audrey. She imagined her as she sat at a bar somewhere in St. Louis and flirted with her next fling. That life had grown dull and wearisome: the parties, the nightlife, the overcrowded bars and clubs. She was sure Audrey had moved on and found a new close friend by now. After all, Audrey didn't attach herself to anyone.

Tiffany had set up about a dozen tables with chairs in the grass behind the café. The tables were covered in red and white checkered tablecloths. A few people had already been through the buffet line and sat on the far side of the yard with plates of hot dogs or hamburgers.

Gray got into line behind Tiffany and Darren, who held hands as they waited for the line to move.

"You scared me to death." Emma got into line behind her. "That looked like a lot of fun, though."

It's okay to make friends, Gray reassured herself and then smiled at Emma. "It was a lot of fun."

Emma studied Gray's face once again, noticing a change. Before she could say anything else, Frank joined them and started to talk about the party and how perfect the weather was for such an event. Gray let him procure Emma's attention and smiled to herself as she listened to the two of them talk and laugh with each other.

Gray added a hot dog and small scoop of potato salad to her plate and moved from the line to wait for Frank and Emma. They walked together to where Tiffany, Carla, Darren, Vince, and Tony already sat at a table overlooking the river. Gray sat beside Tiffany and took in the view of the golden evening sky over the river.

Tiffany addressed the rest of the group and announced the plans for the evening. While Tiffany spoke, Gray caught a glimpse of Tony as he watched her from across the table. He looked away, and Gray focused her attention back on Tiffany.

When everyone finished eating, Vince stood up and offered to take their plates.

"We should play horseshoes," he said as he collected the plate from Gray. "How are you at horseshoes, Gray?"

"I've never played," she confessed, a proud tone to her voice.

"Then you can be on Tiffany's team." Darren laughed and tickled Tiffany's ribs.

"And we'll still win." Tiffany stood. "Let's do it. Girls against guys. You guys in?" She directed the question to Emma, Frank, and Tony.

"Nah, you go ahead."

It wasn't until Frank declined that Gray noticed the strange exchange that seemed to pass between Emma and Tony. While Emma seemed to be on the offense, her face displaying a stern frustration—or maybe confusion—Tony looked distant.

The others noticed as well, and Gray followed Tiffany, Carla, Darren, and Vince as they left the table.

"I wonder what that was about," Tiffany whispered.

"I don't know." Carla looked as confused as Tiffany.

When they got to where the game was set up, the boys went into a lengthy and detailed explanation of how to play horseshoes, along with the proper scoring system. Gray tried to pay attention, but she could muster only so much false interest in a game she considered too Southern for her taste.

13

White

Back at the table, Emma had leaned in to look at Tony as she spoke.

"What are you doing?"

Tony cleared his throat and evened his tone as he pushed away his thoughts about Gray. "What do you mean?"

Emma crossed her arms and sat back in her seat. "Don't play me like that. I saw the way you were looking at Gray. The way you have been looking at her all evening."

Frank shifted in his chair.

Tony considered his answer. "I don't know." After a moment of hesitation, he met Emma's eyes. "Is it really so bad?"

With a sigh, Frank put his hands to his face and leaned back in his chair. Emma's face remained unchanged as she held his gaze.

"Is what really so bad? That you have feelings for Gray? Is that what you mean?" She kept her voice low and leaned back in her seat again. "Do you have feelings for Gray?"

The sky over the river was painted with hues of pink and gold as day began to give way to night. A few birds settled in the oak tree beside them to sing a harmonized lullaby to the setting sun. Tony breathed a heavy sigh and fought the answer that anxiously waited on the tip of his tongue.

"Yes. I think I do."

There was another grunt from Frank.

"Yes," Emma said flatly. "That really is so bad."

She leaned back in her chair. "Tony, you don't know anything about her. Why she's here. Her past. Her intentions. But more than all of that, she is obviously hurting. She needs a lot of help. You've seen how much she drinks." Emma held his gaze. "You can't save her, Tony. And if you pursue this, you could be a distraction that gets in the way of her healing. What if she falls in love with you and it doesn't work out? She doesn't need any more scars. She needs a friend."

His heart sank, and he cursed himself for getting caught up in his emotions. Gray's hopeless words had haunted him since the night he had walked her home from the bar. Each time he'd driven through town, he'd hoped to catch a glimpse of her as she walked down the street or see her through the window of a shop. Two weeks, and he hadn't seen her even once. No one had.

There was something about Gray, something that scared him to death and that he knew only God could change. She had stormed into Belle, cynicism and animosity built like a wall to keep everyone away. Tony saw past the wall to the beautiful, fierce, broken woman on the other side, and he irrationally cared for this person.

14

Black

Gray played a few rounds of horseshoes and the guys claimed victory over the women. She helped Carla pack the horseshoes back into a box. Emma, Tony and Frank were still seated at the table and Gray took the opportunity to sneak away while everyone was distracted. She walked down the tree line a bit until she found the path that led through the woods to the dock where she and her father had fished years ago. The path was a bit more overgrown and she pushed branches aside as she made her way to the riverbank.

Gray wasn't sure what she had expected to find when she got there, but when the woods opened and she stood at the end of the path, she was met by a vast nothingness. The dock was worn and weathered. The river had forged a new path and left yards of dry rock and dirt between where she now stood and the water's edge. The crickets were silent and the bullfrogs slept. She looked up to the sky. A fog had crept up and clouds had begun to gather. The stars hid. Not even a breeze roused as the earth held its breath. A shroud of gray encumbered a place that had once felt holy and alive.

She turned to watch the dark water flow and thought about the night in Belle with her father. Had she ever felt God? Even then as she sat on the dock with her father, and they stared up at the sky, had God been there with them? Or had she reached out into the darkness and grasped at the wind?

Gray began her journey back to the café and saw that Tiffany had lit tiki torches in the backyard. Emma and the rest of the group had gathered around the picnic table. The light of the tiki torches cast a warm glow on their faces as they laughed and talked with one another.

"Did you bring your guitar, Tony?" Carla asked as Gray walked up beside them.

"It's in the Jeep. I can run and get it."

With a nod of her head, Carla motioned toward the beach. "We have a small fire pit set up on the beach. We'll meet you down there."

Tony jogged off to get his guitar and Tiffany went to the kitchen to grab a pack of soda from the fridge while the others made their way to the stairway.

"Are you going to swim before it gets too chilly out?" Gray asked Emma. For a moment, she thought back to the tension between Emma and Tony at the table earlier that evening. She considered asking Emma about it, but decided it wasn't her place to pry.

They started to walk together towards the beach. With her usual smile, Emma looked up at Gray. "Of course! A little chill doesn't scare me. Each year, we'll have a bonfire and swim in the dark, and then they end the night with a big firework display."

Gray watched her footing as she descended the stairs and tried to keep pace with the others. Emma waited for her at the bottom of the stairs, and they walked over to the log. Emma slid her jeans off and pulled her tank top over her head, revealing a one-piece suit. Gray did the same, and they waded out to sit in the water together.

Carla and Tiffany stayed on the beach and lit a bonfire. Once the flames leapt from the piled driftwood, Tiffany sat in the sand and leaned against Darren. The light from the fire cast a warm glow on their faces and Gray took in the scene.

"Something changed in you tonight, Gray." Emma watched her friend.

Gray studied the winding path of the river. It reached a bend shortly downstream and carried on, out of sight. "What do you mean?"

"You're more . . . open."

After a long pause, Emma asked, "Why are you here, Gray?"

Gray wrapped herself back into her comfortable cocoon of distance. She shrugged her shoulders and offered a lazy smile.

"The beautiful scenery," she said as she looked out over the fog which now whimsically traced the surface of the river.

The faint sound of an acoustic guitar drifted through the air and caught her attention. Tony had rejoined the group and now sat by the bonfire. Their eyes met for a moment before Tony began to sing a melody Gray didn't recognize.

While Tony sang, Tiffany and Darren held each other more closely. Carla stood behind them and her body softly swayed to the rhythm. Emma and Gray sat together in silence, entranced.

Frank made his way to the riverbank and waded out to Gray and Emma, his movement sending ripples through the water as he walked.

"Emma," his eyes averted hers as he spoke. "Would you like to come sit with me by the fire?"

Emma looked at Gray, who offered a small nod. A big smile pulled at the corners of Emma's lips.

"I would love to join you." She stood up and took the hand he held out for her.

They walked away and Emma looked back at Gray, who winked at her. Gray watched from the river as the two of them sat close to each other, their connection clicking.

More people at the party made their way down to the beach. A few of them got into the river, others gathered around the fire or sat to chat on the dock. Chill set in and goosebumps began to spread across Gray's arms. She stood and walked ashore. The beach towel Emma had brought for her was draped across the log. Gray wrapped it around herself before joining the group by the bonfire. She sat in the sand behind Tony and listened to the music. High school stories were swapped between the group, and Gray smiled to herself while she listened.

As she sat on the outskirts of the circle of friends, Gray imagined what it would have been like to grow up in Belle. She imagined herself walking through the small halls of their high school, laughing with them, maybe even wearing denim jeans.

Maybe even happy.

"Come on." Emma came up beside Gray, took her by the hand, and pulled her to her feet. "The fireworks are about to begin."

They walked to the dock where Gray sat between Tiffany, Carla, and Emma, and they watched the sky south of them over the river. A minute later, the black sky erupted into an explosion of lights and color. Gray leaned back on her arms as she watched the display.

In all her life, she had never experienced a night like this. A few people jumped into the river to splash and play or just watch the fireworks from the water. The display ended, and the crowd erupted into applause. When the applause died down, Tiffany stood up next to Gray on the dock. As loud as she could, she addressed the people who stood around on the beach and in the river.

"Once again, I want to thank everyone for coming," she shouted. "You guys make this worth doing every year, and I am so glad to have you all here. Before we all go our separate ways, I want to end the night in a word of prayer. Summer is a time for family and travel, and I just want to ask God to bless and watch over each and every one of you. Thanks again for coming, and I look forward to doing this again next year!"

They bowed their heads, and Gray wished she could slip away unnoticed as she stared out at the water. Tiffany thanked God for His blessings and the gift of friendship and Gray shifted uneasily. It was strange to hear Tiffany talk so openly with God.

The prayer concluded and people stood to pack up their belongings. Frank met them by the fire pit and asked to talk to Emma alone. The dark cover of the night didn't hide the flash of pink in Emma's cheeks. The two of them split off and made their way to the stairs.

The quiet *thunk* of a guitar case as it closed pulled Gray's attention away from the new couple. Tony snapped the case shut and walked to stand beside Gray.

"Way to go." He nodded toward Emma and Frank. "It's been a long time coming."

Most of the crowd had cleared the beach. The fire had started to die down. Gray put her dress back on and gathered her things. Tony waited for her. The sand was cool and damp beneath her feet as they made their way to the bottom of the stairs. She stopped for a moment to slip her shoes back on. While they ascended the narrow stairwell, Gray had to walk in front of Tony so there was room for his guitar. She tried to keep pace with everyone else but had to stop halfway up and catch her breath.

"You really should stop smoking," Tony teased.

Gray punched his shoulder and gave a weak smile. "I already did," she said between breaths. "The other night was an exception. I threw what was left of the pack away the next morning. Not that I don't want a cigarette right now."

Her breath slowed, and she began the climb again. "These stairs are just ridiculously steep."

At the top of the stairs, Gray stepped to the side and leaned against the fence to allow Tony through. After he closed and locked the gate behind him, Tony stood next to Gray.

"We're headed to Tennessee to make a record in a couple of weeks."

The news took Gray by surprise. "How long will you be gone?"

"Two weeks, a month." He shrugged. "It depends on how well it goes."

Tiffany and Carla began putting out the tiki torches, one by one, until the only light illuminating the night was the light from the back patio. Tony and Gray made their way toward their parked cars in silence.

When they reached the parking lot, Tony finally spoke again.

"Can Emma and I come by Saturday afternoon?" His voice sounded nervous and high-strung. "I would like to get in to repaint your apartment before we leave, but I need to know what color paint you want. The three of us can walk down to the hardware store around the corner and look at paint swatches. That will give me the chance to pick up a few of the other things I'll need."

Gray caught sight of Emma as she waited beside her car and waved to her. "Sure, that sounds fine."

Tony walked with her to the car. "We'll be there around two. Does that work for you?"

"Don't you have a job?" Gray teased. "Seems like you're putting an awful lot of time into my apartment."

Tony smiled. "I'm a carpenter. Painting and fixing up houses is my job. Aunt Vera is paying me to paint your apartment. Emma's apartment also needs a few minor repairs and I'd like to just get it all done at once."

"Well, then," Gray smiled, "I'll see you Saturday at two."

15

Black

On her back porch, Gray took a sip from her can of beer. Dressed in a black sundress, Gray had left her hair down, and it tickled her shoulders as a breeze blew at the curly strands.

There was commotion in the hallway behind her, and the back door opened. Tony emerged, dressed in jeans and a white T-shirt. He eyed the beer in her hand and gave her a look of disapproval.

"What?" She drank the last of what was in the can. "It's after noon. And it's better than what I used to drink every day."

Tony shook his head and held the door open for her to walked inside.

"It's good to see you, too," she teased. After she pushed the door to her apartment open and tossed the empty can in the trash, Gray rejoined him in the hallway.

"It's good to see you." Tony smiled sarcastically.

The door to Emma's apartment was already open, and they both walked inside. Emma looked up from where she sat at her small, square kitchen table.

"Hey, guys! Sorry, just finished eating lunch." She stood, set her plate in the sink and then turned to hug Gray.

"See, now that's a proper greeting," Gray said and winked at Tony.

Before they left, Emma walked them through her apartment to show Tony a few areas needing attention: a chip in the tile, watermarks on the ceiling, caulking needing repair, a ceiling fan off balance, and a few other odds and ends.

"We need to get you a husband." Tony climbed the attic ladder to find where the water was leaking onto the ceiling. "Then you could start yourself a good, long honey-do list and take a little weight off my shoulders."

Emma laughed. "If I ever get married, we won't be living in this tiny apartment."

After a minute, Tony emerged from the attic, and dust covered the knees of his jeans. "Found the leak. I'll have to patch the roof until we can re-shingle it entirely."

Gray followed them outside. Tony dusted off his jeans. The summer air was light and breezy, and they made their way down the street.

"Frank asked me to go on a date with him tonight." Emma wore a wide smile.

"Really?" Tony smiled.

"Any pointers?"

Tony laughed. "Just be yourself. He asked *you* out for a reason."

With a long, drawn out groan, Emma threw her head back. "Twenty years of friendship, and that's all the advice you can give me?"

They rounded the corner to the hardware store. The store clerk directed Emma and Gray to where their paint swatches were kept while Tony took a cart and went to find the supplies he would need for both of their apartments.

Emma held up a swatch of a neutral tan color. "What do you think about this?"

Gray wrinkled her nose. "It's too brown. Maybe something lighter?"

She thumbed through the selection of neutral colors and thought about the way Emma and Frank had looked at each other while they sat beside the fire.

"Where is Frank taking you tonight?"

Emma smiled. "We're going to a tractor pull."

Gray laughed, and Emma joined in. "What? It's going to be a lot of fun."

"If you say so." Gray smiled at her friend.

"What about this?" Emma held up a pale, off-white swatch.

"That works."

After they settled on the shade, Emma and Gray walked over to the counter and waited for Tony. Emma made small talk with the clerk, who was a good friend of her father's.

A few moments later, Tony wheeled up behind them and began to unload his cart onto the counter. Gray handed him the paint swatch.

"This is the color we settled on."

Tony looked at it before he handed it back to Gray, and their fingers brushed.

"I think that will be a good accent color to the trim."

After they checked out, the three of them each took a couple of bags and left the cart by the door.

"So where is Frank taking you on your big first date?" Tony asked as he shifted a bag in his hand.

Gray held back the laughter.

"The tractor pull."

After a moment's hesitation, Tony realized she wasn't joking.

"I thought first dates were supposed to be romantic," he said with a smile.

"It could be romantic!"

"No—"

When they turned the corner, Gray froze in her tracks.

Tony and Emma stopped beside her and followed her gaze down the street to the parking lot in front of the floral shop twenty feet away.

"What?" Emma looked at Gray.

The blood in Gray's face drained and left her lips cold and tingling. She took a step down the sidewalk and then turned around the other way before she turned back again, unsure of where to go.

This can't be happening. This can't be happening, Gray thought as panic rose in her chest.

"What?" Tony asked this time.

Her eyes were glued to the 1972 black Ford Mustang parked a few feet away from them. The door of the floral shop opened, and a man with blonde hair stepped out into the sunlight. Gray couldn't bring her legs to move. Why was he there? The man started to walk toward his car and caught a glimpse of Gray as he slid his sunglasses back onto his face.

"Gray?"

He hesitated before changing course and walking toward her. With a side-glance at her friends, Gray stepped away from Emma and Tony and walked with the man until they stood next to his car.

"Tyler." She glanced behind him to make sure he hadn't come with Audrey.

"What's going on?" He looked past her at Tony and Emma, who stood on the sidewalk and tried not to intrude.

Gray watched her ex-boyfriend's face as he sized up her new friends from a distance, his gaze hidden behind his dark tinted sunglasses. The sight of Tyler caused anger to boil up inside of her—anger over who he was and what he had done, and anger over who *she* had allowed herself to become.

"How did you find me?" Her tone was flat.

With a bitter laugh, Tyler turned his attention back to her. "Samantha from your work gave me the address you had given them to mail your last check."

"That was kind of her." Gray spoke between gritted teeth.

"What?" His voice was raised. "You're upset because she told me where my girlfriend just up and moved to without even so much as a 'goodbye'?"

"I'm not your girlfriend, Tyler." Her voice was firm but calm. "We broke up *months* before I moved."

Tyler shook his head. He cleared his throat, moved closer to her and reached for her hand, which she pulled away.

"Look, Gray, I'm sorry. I was stupid. It won't happen again." He didn't bother to take the sunglasses off as he spoke to her. "This is crazy. Why are you here? I know we've been back and forth for the past five years and a lot happened during the times we weren't together, but I guess I always thought we'd end up working it out."

When she didn't respond, he turned away and threw his hands in the air out of frustration before he turned back to her.

"How can you just take off without even saying goodbye? After five years?" Tyler's tone dropped and he took her hand into his. "We talked about getting married. I just wanted to get a good job first, and maybe find a house so we could settle down."

Gray bit her lower lip, pulled her hand from his, and stepped closer to Tyler. Her face was inches from his and she spoke in a low tone so only he could hear. "Maybe Katie will marry you. Or Jen. Or Hailey. Or Rachel. Should I continue?"

Gray pushed past him. He tried to reach out to grab her, but she pulled her arm free. Out of the corner of her eye, Gray noticed Tony take a step closer and then stop himself.

"So this is how it's going to be?" Tyler shouted from where he stood next to his car as she walked toward her apartment.

Emma and Tony were still an earshot away, and Gray turned to look at Tyler again in hopes her attention would quiet his tone.

"Is this your new life? New boyfriend? New best friend?" With a nod toward Tony and Emma, he stepped back up onto the sidewalk. "I'm not the only one you hurt. What about Audrey? She called me, crying. After all we've been through, and everything Audrey's done for you, we're that easy to replace? Do you care about *anyone*?"

Gray shook her head and pulled the door of her apartment building open. She stepped into the stairwell and let the door close behind her, afraid to see all her secrets unravel in front of Tony and Emma. Afraid to see their faces. Afraid for them to see hers. A hot tear gathered in the corner of her eye.

"If they knew who you really were, they wouldn't want anything to do with you," Tyler shouted, his voice muffled behind the closed door. He turned his attention to Emma and Tony. "She's a fake. She's just going to use you and then disappear when you have nothing more to offer her. Just like she did to her own mother, just like she did to her best friend, and just like she did to me."

A moment later, Gray heard a car door close and the engine start. His tires squealed as Tyler pulled away. Gray waited until she knew he was gone before she jogged up the stairs and slammed the door closed behind her.

Once in the comfort of her bed, she buried her face in her pillow to muffle the sound and began to cry. A few minutes passed by before she heard the soft knock at her door. Gray pushed her blanket aside and reached under her bed for where she had stashed the remaining bottle of whiskey. She unscrewed the cap and threw the bottle back, chugging the liquid until she gagged. With the silver cap back on, Gray pulled her down comforter over her head and let her emotions loose. Her body shook as she wept.

A while later, the knock on her door subsided and the small apartment building grew quiet. The rush of the river could be heard outside of her windows, and Gray clung to her blanket as her tears soaked the pillow under her head. The light outside her window dimmed as night took over the sky and the streetlights flickered on.

"Hello?" Audrey yelled over the rock music as she walked into Gray and Tyler's apartment.

She walked over piles of clothes as she came around the corner and poked her head into the bedroom. "Loud enough?"

Gray sat up in her bed, pushed the blanket away, and put her hands on her spinning head. She found the bottle of whiskey and drank what was left. When the buzz settled in her mind, she walked to the window and looked out over the river.

Gray ignored her and continued to toss random outfits and dresses into a large, open suitcase sitting outside of her closet. Audrey went into the living room to turn the volume down on the stereo. When she returned to the closet doorway, she stared down at her friend, who was dressed in a towel and rummaging through her shoes.

"What are you doing?" Audrey's eyes wandered from her frazzled friend to the pile of clothes flung across the bedroom floor.

"Packing."

"What? You just moved in!"

Another dress was tossed onto the pile.

"Jake let me off work early. I walked in on Tyler with her, here, in the apartment, an hour ago. I told him to get out, that we are over, and that I'm leaving." Gray didn't look up as she tossed shoes, which missed Audrey as they flew by.

After a short pause, Audrey stepped into the line of fire and forced Gray to look up at her. "I'll help you pack. You can stay at my place until you get things figured out. Tonight we are going to take you out and get a few drinks into your system. Before the end of the night, you won't even remember what's-his-name."

"That's all we ever do." Gray slumped down onto the floor and rubbed her forehead to ease the stress. "Go out, drink ourselves to death so I can try to forget how messed up my life really is."

Audrey knelt beside Gray. "It's not that bad. You guys have officially broken up, right? And I'm not going to let you sulk around and then wind up taking him back again in six months like every other time before. Now it's your time. So get up, get dressed, let's drop this stuff off at my place, and then we will go out."

The memory echoed in her mind as Gray watched the night sky outside of her bedroom windows. The empty whiskey bottle hung from her fingertips. She took a deep breath and looked down at the bottle—an empty, fragile reminder of what her life had become.

Two hours later, they walked into Riff's, their favorite bar. The lights inside were dim, and the music was so loud the baseline pounded against Gray's chest. They made their way toward the bar.

"Hey, Victor," Audrey said in a sweet voice and leaned over the bar as she spoke. "We'll have the regular."

They waited for their drinks and Audrey took in her surroundings; her eyes prowled before they settled on a couple across the room.

"Guess who's here." Her head jerked toward the dance floor.

On the outskirts of the crowd gathered on the floor, Tyler danced with a beer in one hand and Katie in the other. Katie's narrow eyes met Gray's before she gave a coy grin and pulled Tyler closer.

"A Jack and Coke and an apple martini," Victor said and settled the glasses on the bar in front of the girls.

Audrey clinked her glass to Gray's. They downed their drinks and set the empty glasses to the side. As if on cue, Victor brought two more drinks to them.

"The two gentlemen at the end of the bar sent these."

A sick feeling ate at Gray's stomach when she thought back on that night. But like a freight train, there was no way to stop the memory as it barreled through her mind with a velocity and force that sent tremors down her spine. Gray collapsed to the floor, her hands on her head as she cried.

After she gave Gray a mischievous grin, Audrey turned to weigh the prospects. A blonde man with the build of a football player held up his draft beer and nodded at Audrey. He sat next to a man with a similar build but brown hair. Audrey repeated the gesture.

Gray rubbed at the glass in her hand. "What are you doing, Audrey? Don't leave me here by myself."

"By yourself?" Audrey grinned and eyed the guys again. "You're coming with me."

Terror rose in Gray's stomach. Gray pulled a pack of cigarettes from her purse, shoved one between her lips, and lit it up.

"Audrey, I can't do this," Gray said, her eyes drifting back toward the men. "Let's just go. I don't want to be here."

With a light smile, Audrey threw her hair back and laughed. "Come on, Gray. You're twenty-three years old. Don't you think you've been holding onto your virginity for a little bit too long? At this rate, you'll be forty before you give it up, and it won't be nearly as good by then. You're young. Live it up."

"Stop." The word came out harsher and more pointed than Gray had expected it to be. She shook her head at her friend. "You have no idea what you're talking about."

Ten years had passed, and still she couldn't bring herself to tell anyone. The secret festered in the back of her mind. She bit her lower lip and held the words back, unable to meet her friend's eyes.

"I was raped." Gray whispered into the dark of her room.

This was the first time she had allowed herself to say those words out loud, though they echoed through her mind every day. Like demons given a key, fear and shame were unleashed into the room to torment her, finally free of the cage she had kept them in for all of these years.

After a pause, Audrey shook her head. "No, I don't understand."

When Gray didn't respond, Audrey dropped her hands to her side. "Fine, just come with me and meet the guy. Have a few drinks. Get to know him. Show Tyler you can move on, too."

With a heavy sigh, Gray snuffed her cigarette out in an ashtray and let Audrey lead her to where the guys sat at the bar.

Introductions were made, though Gray never could remember what the brown-haired guy's name was. She slid onto the bar stool next to him and he ordered her another drink. Time seemed to lapse. Gray maneuvered through a shallow conversation and forced laughter at the stranger's unintelligent jokes. She tried not to think about Tyler.

Audrey laughed at something the blonde-haired man had said, and Gray caught a glimpse of Tyler as he stood on the other side of the bar. Katie was at his side, but he watched Gray, who looked away.

"Anyone else want a shot of whiskey?" Gray cleared her throat and flagged down the bartender.

The night wore on, and Victor continued to bring round after round of shots. Gray stopped counting each glass she downed. The other three laughed and fell over each other as they drank, but Gray was subdued, focused on the pain she still felt as she waited for the liquor to kick in to numb her mind. Her eyes drifted back to the dance floor. Katie and Tyler were now settled into the corner of the bar and Tyler caught Katie's lips in a kiss.

That was the moment when Gray snapped. Gray stumbled as she stood from the bar stool. The brown-haired man got up to catch her, his arm around her waist. He wore a thick cologne. Audrey laughed at the sight of her wasted friend.

"Wanna dance?" Gray's words slurred as she pressed herself into the stranger's chest, her breath against his neck.

Gray curled into a ball and cried harder now. She rocked herself and begged the memories to stop. But her plea was nothing more than a scream from the train tracks of her mind; a powerless cry for help in a moment where she stood frozen, unable to escape, and faced the train head on.

A glimmer of opportunity flashed in the man's eyes, and his hands slid a little lower as he led her out to the dance floor. The blonde and Audrey weren't far behind. The brown-haired man was at her side, his muscular arms wrapped around her as they began to dance. The alcohol began to take control, and the night increased in speed as everything whirled into a blur. The last image in Gray's memory was the look on Tyler's face as her thin legs hung over the brown-haired man's muscular arms while he carried her off the dance floor. Audrey was at their side, still laughing as they all walked out of the bar.

Vomit rose in her throat and Gray leaned over, throwing up on the hardwood floor beside her bed. Terror lurked over her in the darkness, and she fought to breathe. Her body withered as she continued to vomit and then collapsed with her head against the cool floor.

Gray woke in an unfamiliar car.

"Wait." *Panic rose in her chest at the realization of what was about to happen. The brown-haired man reached over and put his hand on her inner thigh as he drove.*

She realized Audrey and the blonde man were not with them. She couldn't do this. What was she thinking? She couldn't give him what he wanted from her.

"No, stop. Take me back," *Gray shouted as she reached for the door handle of his sports car.*

The guy came to a stop in the middle of the quiet street just before she got the door open. "Are you crazy?" *he yelled and slammed his fists on the steering wheel.*

"I'm sorry, I can't do this." *Gray tripped over her feet as she tried to get out and fell into the street.*

The guy cursed at her as he pulled his door shut and spun out. After she picked herself up and gained her bearings, Gray realized she was a few blocks from Audrey's apartment. She fell twice and bruised her knee as she walked through the dark, dimly lit streets of the city. Audrey's apartment was on the third floor, and Gray fell over and sat in the stairwell on the second floor before she continued to climb.

Her fingers trembled as she dug her keys from her purse and pushed the jagged metal into the deadbolt. Inside the apartment, she didn't bother to turn the lights on. She stripped away her clothes and stumbled into the shower to let the water run over her. With a heavy sigh, she closed her eyes and steadied her mind to keep the demon lurking behind her closed lids from escaping.

Audrey found her the next day naked, passed out, and sprawled across the floor of the shower as the water ran cold. An ambulance arrived shortly after. When Gray woke up in the hospital, she was alone, and Audrey was out at another bar.

Gray rocked on the floor and pounded the sides of her head with her fists as she held back a scream. The tears had drenched her cheeks and soaked through the collar of her dress. She vomited again, and loose strands of hair that had escaped her ponytail fell into her face.

The room spun out of control, and there was nothing Gray could do to make it stop. The memory played over and over in her head, picking up pace, until it whirled like a nightmare merry-go-round.

You know what you have to do, a voice echoed in the back of her mind. The same voice rang through her ears the day she returned from the hospital to an empty apartment. It was that day Gray had decided to leave St. Louis.

You can't make it stop. You can't run any longer.

Her body convulsed and Gray clung to the voice and begged for help, for a way out.

You know what you have to do.

On her feet, Gray looked out the window and watched the peak of the sunrise over the river outside, her eyes swollen and dry. Motionless, she watched until the sun overtook the darkness, and the town below her came to life. She felt as though she free-fell as she closed the blinds and made her way to the bathroom.

"I know what I have to do."

Gray opened the bathroom door, and her eyes found the razor sitting on the edge of the bathtub. Frozen in the doorway, she took a deep breath to calm her nerves.

There is no other way to stop it, the voice said. *There is no other way out. Haven't you had enough?*

At the side of the bathtub, Gray slipped out of her dress and let it fall to her feet before she leaned over to run the water. She stepped into the tub and left the plug open so that the water swirled around her feet for a moment before it disappeared down the drain. With a deep breath, she picked up the razor and stared at the glistening blade and she thought back on her life.

Every memory, every experience, all led to this moment. She closed her eyes and pressed her lips together as she pushed the razor into her skin. The burn spread as it pierced her flesh. She sucked a sharp breath in and tried not to cry out in pain as she dragged the razor down her forearm.

Gray had never intended to leave Belle. She had come here to die. This had been the plan all along. Her hands trembled as she stared down at the drops of blood now swirling around feet. She lifted the razor, closed her eyes, and pressed it to her arm again.

16

Black

"Gray?"

Gray's eyes shot open at the sound of Emma's voice in the living room. Panic rose, and Gray stumbled and dropped the blade as she rushed to close the bathroom door.

The door closed just as Gray caught a glimpse of Emma's soft, blonde curls. Her own pale, white face stared back at Gray in the mirror. She didn't know what to do next. She looked down at the blood dripping from her arm to the tile on the bathroom floor.

"I'm sorry, Gray," Emma said from behind the door. "I didn't mean to intrude. I knocked on the door, and when you didn't respond I got worried. You seemed really shook up after running into that guy yesterday. I could hear you crying last night. I just wanted to make sure you were okay."

"Seriously, Emma?" Her tone was harsh. "You're just going to walk into my apartment? Do you realize how messed up that is?"

"I'm sorry." Emma's voice was soft. "I know it's wrong. I just felt—"

The anger festered inside Gray.

"I don't know. I'm sorry."

Gray had to take a deep breath to calm herself. She cracked the door of the bathroom open just enough for Emma to see her face in hopes she could muster up enough sanity to look like she had it together. Emma was dressed in a sundress and flip-flops, with her hair and makeup done.

"I'm fine," Gray said. "Just taking a shower. You need to leave now."

The glow in Emma's face disappeared at the sight of Gray's pale, swollen face, and Gray knew there was no way she would be able to convince Emma to go.

"Gray, you look like you've been up all night," Emma said, her voice soft. "And it smells like vomit in your apartment."

"I'm okay, Emma, really." The blood started to puddle on the floor behind her and Gray knew if Emma didn't leave soon, she would pass out, and Emma would likely call for an ambulance and try to revive her. "I'm just going to shower and go to bed."

Emma searched Gray's eyes again, unconvinced. "Gray, I'm not leaving until you agree to come to church with me this morning."

"Okay, I'll meet you outside in an hour." She started to close the door.

"No," Emma said and put her hand on the door. "Church starts in twenty minutes. Shower and I'll bring you a change of clothes. The church is just down the street so if we hurry, we won't be late."

Gray slammed the door shut. "What is wrong with you?" She screamed through the door. Her head began to spin and she felt dizzy. Emma had to leave. "Get out!"

"Gray something isn't right. I'm not stupid!" Emma was quiet for a moment. "I'll go, but if you make me leave, I'm calling the police to come do a wellness check. I know you're not okay."

Falling on her knees to the floor, Gray put her hand over the cut, trying to stop the blood. She shook her head and fought back a scream. Gray cursed at Emma through gritted teeth and didn't care at all that it would upset her. She had no right to intrude.

A few moments passed and Emma didn't respond to the outburst. The old, hardwood floorboards creaked outside of the bathroom door as Emma shifted her wight on her feet. Gray knew she had been defeated. Emma wasn't bluffing. She would call the police for a wellness check if Gray made her leave.

"Fine, whatever," Gray hissed. "This is ridiculous. I'm being black-mailed into going to church."

Emma's tone remained even. "I'll get your clothes."

Gray was shaking as she stood. The blood had stopped. Gray pulled the shower curtain closed and turned the water on as hot as it would go. Steam filled the room and she sat on the floor of the tub and let the water run over her. When she stepped out from behind the curtain, Gray fumbled through the medicine cabinet for the first aid kit she had seen there when she moved in. She retrieved gauze wrap, a bandage, and medical tape to clean and wrap her arm. The first cut hadn't been deep enough to do any major damage.

After she cleaned up every trace of blood in the bathroom, Gray slammed the medicine cabinet closed, still angry about Emma's intervention. Emma had left clothes for her outside of the door, and Gray pulled the black cotton dress over her head.

She would finish what she had started when she got back home.

When she had slipped into the black flats Emma had left for her, Gray tucked her bandaged arm behind her, opened the bathroom door, and walked into the living room where Emma now stood.

"All right, let's get this over with," Gray mumbled and nodded toward the door.

Emma looked her over again before she made her way to the door and then out into the hallway. Gray walked to the coat closet, pulled out a dark gray hoodie, and slipped her arms into it before she followed Emma into the hall.

"A hoodie? It's like eighty-five degrees out." Emma said.

Gray didn't bother to respond as she closed the door to the apartment building behind her and pushed past Emma, headed in the direction of the large, white church down the street. Emma fell into step beside her, and they made their way to where a small group had gathered outside of the church doors, dressed in sundresses and silk ties.

Gray briskly walked past the crowd, pulled open the church doors, and stepped inside. A young man in a blue tie offered her a program, which she pushed away before she walked into the sanctuary.

The sanctuary of the church was well lit with a high, A-frame ceiling and exposed, dark, wooden beams under a row of skylights. Traditional pews flanked either side and led up to a large stage. Behind the stage was a large, wooden cross, and Gray rolled her eyes at the sight of the structure.

Cliché, she thought.

Gray plopped herself into the nearest pew. She pulled at a loose string on the cuff of her hoodie and avoided eye contact with anyone who might be watching her from the few clusters of people standing around the sanctuary.

Seconds after she had sat down, Emma walked into the church and sat next to her in the pew. A couple of people came over to talk to Emma before the service started, but Gray kept to herself, focused on the stage and the oversized cross.

A man dressed in dark jeans and an off-white button-down shirt stepped onto the stage, an acoustic guitar strapped across his shoulders. As he began to play, four other men walked onto the stage to settle behind various instruments, and it was then Gray realized this was Tony and his band.

The congregation made their way to their seats, and those who had been seated stood to join in worship. Gray sat in her seat and wondered how long the music and message would last. When her father was alive, they had gone to church together every Sunday. Gray's favorite part of the service had been the worship. The sound of the music evoked only anger in her now.

After a few songs, the congregation settled into their seats, the band stepped off the stage, and a silver-haired pastor got comfortable behind the pulpit. Gray itched to go home and make the memories and the pain stop once and for all. The minutes droned by and the preacher's words blurred into a quiet hum in the back of Gray's mind as she lost herself in a numb quietness.

". . . of the living dead."

The pastor caught her eyes, and his words tweaked her attention.

"The Bible says in the second chapter of Ephesians, verse one, 'As for you, you were dead in your transgressions and sins.' Apart from Christ, there is no life—no redemption. We go on along with our day-to-day lives, waiting for something to change, angry at the world for the hand we have been dealt, and desperate to feel something real and tangible. Desperate for anything that will bring us to life again."

Gray rolled her eyes and sighed.

"But what we don't realize is the answer is right in front of us, waiting to take us by the hand. Jesus says in John chapter fourteen, verse six, 'Jesus answered, 'I am the way and the truth and the life. No one comes to the Father except through me.' He says that to find true life we have to give Him the broken, shattered pieces of what's left of us. Give him our problems, fears, and worries. To live, you must first die. You have to kill the part of you that is fighting to control what we have no power over. How many times have you tried to fix your own life? How many times have you wound up standing there, in front of the mirror, looking at the same person as yesterday? How many times have you seen the pain staring back at you? How many times have you tried to escape, to leave it all behind? How many times have you felt like there is no way out of this cage? There is no hope? There is nothing we can do to save ourselves. But Jesus offers us life, if only we will give him ours."

It's time to die. Lose your life, Gray. The voice was as faint as a whisper in the back of her mind.

The throb in Gray's head grew worse. The preacher's eyes met Gray's again for a moment before they moved on. It was enough to sear into Gray's consciousness. Images from the night before flashed into Gray's mind: the flashbacks from her life in the city, the memory of waking up alone in the hospital bed. The stale taste of alcohol filled Gray's mouth.

Lose your life, Gray.

Frustrated, Gray stood up and made her way down the aisle and out of the sanctuary. After she passed the front desk, Gray leaned into the heavy doors of the church. Stepping out into the bright sunlight, the doors swung shut behind her, and Gray made her way into the empty street. Her pace quickened as the preacher's words echoed in her mind.

"Gray!" Tony called from behind her as he stepped out from the church, Emma on his heels. "Gray, where are you going?"

She spun around to face him, and Gray threw her arms out in frustration as she motioned toward the church building. "I don't need this!"

"What do you mean?" Tony asked calmly. He stopped in the street next to her, but Emma stood by the door to the church and didn't speak.

"Any of this!" Gray shouted. "I don't need you and Emma constantly babysitting me, intruding on me like I'm an irresponsible child. And I definitely don't need your God."

Tony took a step back. "Everyone needs God, Gray."

"No. Maybe this works for you, but I don't need someone standing behind a podium and telling me how to live my life. What has that man ever had to deal with? What does he know about God? Did God take his father and leave him to fend for himself with an alcoholic, abusive mother? Where was God through all of that? God has never been a part of my life before, so even if He did exist, why would I want Him to be a part of it now?" The tears burned down her cheeks, and Gray hated herself for crying.

Tony bowed his head and stared down at his hands. When he spoke, his voice was gentle. "Jesus loves you, Gray. He wants to be a part of your life. He wants to heal those wounds. He wants you to live and to stop hurting."

Anger burned deep inside of Gray's chest. She took a few steps away from Tony, her thin hands clenched into tight fists. "Do you know how ridiculous you sound? I don't need *Jesus* to save me. I don't need a crutch. I can do this alone." She turned to walk away. "The way I've been doing it for the past ten years."

"Gray," Tony called after her.

"Tony," she heard Emma's voice say, "let her go. Just give her some space."

Gray ignored them and broke out in a light jog as the tears came faster. When she reached her apartment, she slammed the door shut so hard the floor beneath her shook. She slammed her fists into the closed door and a scream of pure anger tore through her throat. When she could scream no longer, she kicked the door and threw herself into it, angry at herself for going with Emma.

Out of breath, Gray collapsed onto the floor, her back against the unharmed piece of wood. She struggled to catch her breath and the words from the morning echoed in her ears.

Everyone needs God, Gray.

To find your life, you must lose it.

Then a strong voice rang through her memory as clearly as the day her father had first spoken the words.

In moments like this, I can feel God.

"Dad," Gray whispered in a broken, raspy voice.

I can feel God.

"Why did you leave me?" She screamed into the empty apartment. "Where was God when I was alone for all those years?"

We're never alone, baby girl. In moments like this, I can feel God.

"Dad!" Gray cried out, her voice tormented. She sat against the door, her forehead against her knees and her hands on her head as she wept.

I feel like I could just reach out and touch His face.

With her eyes closed, Gray imagined she was back on the dock by the river with her father and reached her hand out in front of her to search the empty room. When she opened her eyes and saw her outstretched hand grasped at only air, Gray dropped her hand and threw her head back. The sobs shook her body as she let all the pain and anger wash over her.

"Oh, God," she screamed. She fell over onto the floor and tore at the bandages on her arm. For hours, she wept until she felt lifeless.

"Save me." Her voice was a whisper. "Please save me."

17

Black

A wind chime rang above the door of the floral shop and, as Gray stepped inside, the smell of freshly cut flowers lingered in the air. Music played over a small radio behind the counter. The shop was empty, and Gray crossed the hardwood floors and peeked around each corner as she made her way to the back of the building.

"I'm out back." Vera's familiar voice sang out from a room behind the counter.

Gray made her way behind the counter and stepped into the doorway marked *Employees Only*. The room was dark, and to the right of the open doorway was another door, cracked open with sunlight that peeked through and spilled onto the floor. Gray pushed the door open and stepped out into the garden the deck to her apartment overlooked.

Vera was on her knees bent over a rose bush, pruning shears in one hand. She looked up from where she sat and slid her thin-framed glasses from her eyes with a smile.

"Good morning."

Her voice was always soft and inviting. Gray took another step into the garden, the gravel crunching below her feet.

"I brought you the check for June's rent."

The check in her hands, Gray waited as Vera slipped the gardening gloves from her hands and stood to brush the dirt and mulch from the knees of her jeans.

"My husband is always telling me I need to get one of those kneeling pads to keep my jeans nice, but a little dirt never hurt anyone." She brushed off the last bit and then walked over to join Gray and took the check from her extended hand.

Vera accepted the check from Gray and her eyes momentary lingered on the corner of the bandage, which protruded from the hem of the shawl Gray had used to cover her arms before she left the apartment.

Gray was taken back by the beauty of the flowers and greenery of the garden. The scent of honeysuckle and lilac filled her senses.

"Which is your favorite?" She nodded toward the heart of the garden.

"Plant?" Vera looked around her at the rose bushes in bloom. She moved to a couple of wicker chairs set up in the corner of the garden under the deck in the shade. They both settled into the cushioned seats, and the sun shone through the cracks of the deck above them to cast a low light on the section of the garden surrounding the chairs where they sat.

"Have you ever heard the story of Job?" Vera asked.

"Job?" Gray looked confused.

"From the Bible."

At the mention of the Bible, Gray grew distant.

"Job was a man of God, strong in his faith," Vera began. "The Bible says he was honest inside and out, was totally devoted to God, and hated evil with a passion. He was also very wealthy and influential."

A hummingbird stopped at the feeder hanging below the deck in front of them, and Gray admired its beauty as she watched it closely.

"So then one day, Satan comes to God, and God asks him if he has noticed Job's devotion. He points out how upright Job is. Satan retorts, telling God Job is only faithful because he has never experienced hard times, never truly suffered. Faith must be easier for those who have it easy, right?"

Gray's eyebrow rose as she considered her words to Tony the day before.

"Satan attacks Job, taking his wealth, the lives of his family, his home, everything from him. Even through his mourning, the Bible says that Job falls to the ground and worships God, even when he had lost all that he had. Job says to God, 'Naked I came out of my mother's womb, and naked I will depart.' He never doubted God, even in his suffering."

As Gray considered her words, she met Vera's eyes, in search of truth and sincerity.

With a small smile, Vera continued with the story. "So Satan theorizes that Job only remained devout because he would do anything to save his own life, but that he would turn his back on God the moment his health was in jeopardy. Satan strikes Job again with terrible sores from head to toe that itch and ooze so badly, Job takes a piece of broken pottery to cut at his own flesh. His wife turns her back on him, condemning Job for his faith and cursing God, but even still, Job holds firmly to his belief, never doubting God's faithfulness.

"Job's friends hear of what has happened to Job, and they come to his house to mourn with him. As they sit together, his friends are convinced that these things are happening to Job because he did something wrong. So they continually criticize Job and beg him to repent, saying that God is cursing Job. Even still, Job holds to his faith."

A soft wind blew at the chimes hanging around where they sat, and Gray watched the flowers sway in the breeze. "So, what happened next?"

"Job can't take it anymore. He questions the injustice of why God allows wicked people around him to prosper while other innocent people suffer. Why do bad things happen to good people? He curses himself and wishes he had never been born. But just when all seems lost, a thunderstorm gathers on the horizon, and out of the storm, God, in all His glory, speaks directly to Job and his friends.

"God tells Job He was always in control, even when it didn't make sense to Job. The God who hand-painted the sky and formed the mountains in the palms of His hands knew of Job's life and his sufferings and had never forgotten him. He asks Job and his friends who they are to question His will and purpose, for only He can see the bigger picture. He turned Job's life around after that, giving Job more than he ever could have dreamed of. And Job had a new understanding of life. How precious it is, how quickly it could change, and how each moment belongs to God and isn't ours to own."

"It doesn't seem fair that he had to go through any of that."

Sadness washed over Vera's face. "We live in a broken world. This isn't meant to be our home. It will never be perfect."

"That just seems like an excuse," Gray said with a shrug. "God still allowed it to happen. He took everything from Job. For what? To prove a point?"

"Maybe." Vera took a deep breath in. "Or maybe it was to use Job's story to show the world that no matter how broken your life is, you are never forsaken. Maybe it was to show the world how beautiful healing can be. To help others who have walked through suffering and feel alone. To help us all learn to lay our pride aside and accept that our wisdom is limited and our lives are not in our control, but we can rest because the same God who breathed into darkness and created light is the same God who walks beside us."

Silence fell between them as Gray digested Vera's words.

"You asked me about my favorite plant."

Vera nodded at a small magnolia tree planted in the center of the garden. "While Job is suffering, he curses himself saying there is more hope for a tree than for him. If you cut a tree down, it's a matter of time before water will bring it to life, and it will sprout again.

"Many years ago, a tornado came through Belle, and it completely uprooted a magnolia tree in the backyard of the old house where I had grown up, tearing both the tree and the house to shreds in the process. I cut a small shoot off of the fallen tree and kept it in a mason jar of water until roots formed, and then I replanted the tree here. It's my constant reminder of Job's story and that no matter what I may face, there is always hope because the God who set the earth into motion is always here with me. He loves us more deeply than we can ever understand,

and though we don't always see that love in the circumstances of our lives, His love never ends, and He will never let us go.

"I lost everything in that tornado." Vera closed her eyes for a moment as she thought back. "I watched many people suffer. I started a community garden to help us all heal and work through it together, to give us an outlet, a place of beauty and restoration. That garden inspired my business. And I met my husband because of that storm. Isaac had volunteered with a church out of town to come in and rebuild the homes lost in the storm. He lived six hours away. Our paths may have never crossed if it hadn't been for that tornado. That storm brought suffering, but it also brought our town closer together and changed the direction of my life."

A moment of silence passed before Gray stood and laughed with a light smile. "You could have done the sermon at church yesterday."

Vera smiled. "The pastor is my husband after all." She winked at Gray.

"Of course he is." With another soft laugh, Gray said her goodbyes and then headed up the steps of the deck to the quiet retreat of her apartment to consider Vera's words more deeply.

18

Black

"For in this hope we were saved . . ." Romans 8:24
Love, Vera

The note was scribbled in fine cursive on a light pink Post-it note and stuck on top of a package wrapped in brown, recycled paper sitting on Gray's doorstep. Gray had tripped over the gift when she left to check her mail, and she sat on the edge of her bed now, the unwrapped package in her lap.

Brown paper fell to the floor as she pulled it from the box, piece by piece. Gray opened the box and peeked through packed tissue paper at a leather-bound Bible. Forty-five minutes passed by as Gray stared at the book in her lap and a mix of fear, anger, and excitement passed through her in waves.

The Bible reminded her of the leather-bound Bible her father had owned. Each morning when Gray woke up, her father had sat at the kitchen table with a coffee mug in one hand and his Bible in the other. He had always called his morning readings "breakfast for his soul." For Christmas one year, he'd bought her a pink girl's Bible, but Gray hadn't seen it since she left her mother's house eight years ago.

The leather cover was soft as she ran her hands over it, and Gray let the box and tissue paper fall to the floor next to the wrapping paper as she picked the Bible up. She flipped the pages open and searched the index for the book of Job.

While she read, she stopped at a passage and pulled her journal out from under her bed. After she opened to a blank page, Gray scribbled down the words of Job.

Job 10:19-22

"If only I had never come into being or had been carried straight from the womb to the grave! Are not my few days almost over? Turn away from me so I can have a moment's joy before I go to the place of no return, to the land of gloom and utter darkness, to the land of deepest night, of utter darkness and disorder, where even the light is like darkness."

Lowering her pen, she let the words echo through her mind.

"Where even the light is like darkness."

19

Black

Gray rummaged through her bare cabinet and found a fresh produce bag tucked away in the back. The smell of mold blew into her face as she peeked inside. Gray wrinkled her nose, twisted the bag closed, and tossed it into the trash. She resorted to another pack of ramen noodle soup for breakfast and decided she would use her evening for much-overdue grocery shopping.

There was a knock at the front door, and Gray closed the microwave door and pushed the start button before she walked to the front door. Tony, Frank, Vince, and Darren stood in the hall and held paint cans, brushes, drop cloths, and rollers.

"Right on time." Gray opened the door wider and invited the group inside.

Emma had been by the night before to remind her that the guys would come by today to repaint and do general maintenance on both the apartments. Pete and Jim were across the hall in Emma's apartment to inspect the leak in the roof further.

"We have another load to carry up." Tony set the five-gallon paint can and brushes down in the corner of her living room. His eyes didn't meet hers as they spoke, and Gray thought about their last confrontation. "If you don't mind moving whatever furniture you can into the center of the room, we can get the big stuff later."

Gray waited for the four men to set down what they carried and disappear down the stairwell again before she turned to retrieve her soup. She added the packet of seasoning and blew at the noodles.

"Chicken or beef?"

A whisper of a smile was on Tony's lips as he walked into the kitchen with two more drop cloths and paint rollers. Gray studied his face and wanted him to meet her eyes, but he never looked up as he moved across the room.

She stirred the soup. "Shrimp."

"A hoodie when it's ninety degrees outside, and shrimp soup for breakfast." His tone teased her.

Gray looked down at the gray hoodie she had dressed in once again to hide the bandage that still wrapped her arm. She shrugged her shoulder, mostly to herself, as Tony walked from the room.

Once she had finished eating her soup, Gray joined Tony and Vince in the living room where they covered her furniture. As she stood in the corner, she watched Tony, who was dressed in a pair of dark blue jeans, leather work boots, and a plain white T-shirt. The muscles in his jaw flexed as he and Vince lifted the couch and moved it to the center of room.

"Vince," Frank called from Emma's apartment. "You're good with leaking pipes. Come and take a look at this."

Vince left the front door open as he joined the others in Emma's living room. Gray caught a flicker of a glance her way before Tony motioned toward the bedroom.

"Can I get a hand in here?"

She walked with him into the bedroom where he made his way to the end of the bed and bent over to grip the metal frame beneath the box spring.

"Take a hold of it on the other side. We're moving it about a foot away from the wall, but I don't want the legs to scratch the floor."

The muscles in her arms strained as she lifted the bed and moved with Tony; her breath caught in her chest as she tried to muster more strength. The bed hit the floor with a heavy thud when they reached the center of the room. Gray stood upright, taking a deep breath. A soft *thunk* caught her attention, and as Gray looked up, Tony bent over and retrieved the Bible and journal that had fallen out from under her pillow.

He set the journal back on the bed and stared down at the Bible. Tony turned it over in his hands and ran his thumb over the *Holy Bible* inscription across the binding.

Gray reached across the bed and snatched the Bible from his hands along with her journal. She felt his eyes on her as she walked from the room, opened the coat closet in the living room, and tossed the books onto the shelf inside.

Heat rose from her chest to her neck as embarrassment and frustration washed over Gray. The conflict building inside her whirled under her skin, and Gray bit her lower lip so it wouldn't quiver. For so many years she had hated God. She wasn't sure if she was ready to let go of that grudge, and if she could ever forgive or trust Him.

When she returned to the bedroom, Tony poured paint into a roller pan. His eyes met hers for a moment, still guarded.

"Don't get too excited, preacher." Gray shifted her eyes. "It doesn't mean anything."

Frank and Vince walked in through the front door, deep in a discussion about a popular band as they entered the bedroom and brushed past Gray. Relieved for the distraction, Gray slipped into the living room unnoticed while the guys continued to talk about riffs, chords, lyrics, and performance, unaware of the war raging in her heart.

Frank picked up a paintbrush and ignored a comment Vince had made about the band's drummer being the best he had heard in mainstream music. "I'll cut in around the trim if you roll."

Vince picked up a roller and shrugged. "I hate cutting in. I would much rather use the roller."

"No way, man."

Gray listened as the pair began a new argument. She smiled at the guys and imagined that this is what it would have been like to have grown up with brothers. For a moment, she thought about Reese. His twelfth birthday was next month. Reese was three when Gray had left, but she thought about him almost every day, wondering if he was safe and if her mother ever hurt him. Guilt tore through her as she thought about how she had abandoned him, but she had been naive and young when she left. Maybe this year she would send him a birthday card and gift.

". . . and Gray can paint the living room."

The mention of her name caught her attention. Tony motioned to her with his paint roller as he talked to Vince.

"If we split up like that, we can get the apartment done in half the time," Tony continued. "I know you hate to cut in, but we can rotate out after each room."

Vince shook his head—his long, straight, brown hair tossed by the motion—and slunk into the living room where Gray stood. He chewed at his lower lip while he picked up a paintbrush and opened a fresh can of paint. Gray waited for orders as Vince stirred the paint.

"Can you bring me a roller tray from over there by the door? You'll also want to grab a roller for yourself." His voice was soft as he spoke to her.

Tony poured the paint and then showed her the best way to get paint evenly across the roller. The room fell silent as she took the roller from his hands and began to roll the paint over the dingy walls.

Hours ticked by as Gray worked beside Vince. Conversations drifted from the benefits of latex paint versus an oil-based paint to the band's trip to Tennessee in the morning. They all took a break for lunch, which Emma made for them. While the rest of them ate, Frank drove home to pick up a small radio to listen to in Gray's apartment as they completed the second coat of paint. Gray listened to classic rock music for the next couple of hours as Frank, Vince, and Tony critiqued each band.

When Gray rolled the last wall of the bathroom in her apartment, her shoulders, arms, and hands ached, and she had barely spoken a dozen words since the work had begun six hours ago. She picked up the roller and paint tray and walked into the kitchen where Frank rinsed paintbrushes out in the sink.

"Rollers and trays go outside," he said, looking up at her as she entered the room. "Tony and Vince are rinsing those with the hose."

"Thanks." Gray made her way through the back hall to the covered deck and down the steep staircase. The summer heat was in full blast, and the humidity clung to her pale skin as she stepped into the sunlight.

Tony and Vince were on the other side of the garden behind the floral shop. A long, green hose had been pulled over to where they stood, and they were both bent over a stack of paint trays and rollers. Gray set her tray and roller with the rest and made her way back to the apartment. Frank had disappeared and left clean, wet paintbrushes to dry on the edge of the sink. Gray heard Emma's playful laughter faintly across the hall, and she was sure Frank had joined Emma, Pete, and Jim while they wrapped up the repairs they had been working on all day.

Gray smiled at the sound of her friend's laughter, and she pulled her hoodie around her thin frame. Frank and Emma seemed to be good for each other, and she wondered again why the connection hadn't been made sooner. Then again, they had been friends since childhood, and it's often difficult to view someone in a new light after so many years.

The furniture in the living room was still pushed to the center of the room and covered with drop cloths. Gray pulled the covers away, folded them, and set them on the floor next to the front door. All her windows were open to air out the strong smell of fresh paint, and she stood for a moment to listen to the sound of the river's quiet gurgle. The radio was set up on the floor of her bedroom, and soft worship music played in the background. Gray recognized the song as one the band had played at the church service on Sunday morning.

She pulled the drop cloth from the couch and folded it in her arms. She heard the back door open and close. Tony came around the corner, his arms and pants speckled with paint. He stood in the doorway for a moment after he entered the living room and looked at the drop cloth in Gray's arms.

"You don't have to do that." He motioned toward the cloth. "We'll go through and get them all before we leave."

"It's all right, I don't mind." She finished folding the cloth and set it on top of another next to the front door.

Tony hadn't mentioned anything about the Bible falling from her bed, and Gray had spent most of her day confused about why she even still had the Bible.

They began to move the furniture back into place.

"Emma is going to barbecue for everyone tonight." Tony didn't look up as they moved the dresser. "You should eat with us. It's been a long day."

"Sure, that sounds good."

In the living room, they moved the entertainment center and TV, and Tony looked up at her as he bent over the coffee table. Gray followed his movements.

"I'm sure it was torture to have to listen to this stuff for the past hour," Tony said and nodded toward the radio, which played a slow worship song.

They lifted the table. "No," Gray said with a strained voice. Her breath came in quick, small bursts. "You guys were playing some good stuff earlier—the classic rock. I really don't like this worship music, though. It's too contemporary for my taste."

The table was set back in its place and Gray stood to catch her breath for a moment.

"What kind of music do you prefer?" Tony walked to the couch.

"I like alternative rock and indie music, mostly."

The front door burst open, and Frank knocked into Gray as he stumbled into the apartment and slammed the door shut behind him. Breathing heavily, he turned to look at Gray with a large grin on his face.

"I am so sorry," he said as he glanced over his shoulder at the door. "Are you all right?"

"I'm fine."

"It's stupid, really." He stood and guarded the door as he spoke. "Emma was on the back porch near the barbecue pit, and Vince and I thought it would be funny to dump a pitcher of water over her head. She retaliated by chasing us into her apartment and hosing us down with the kitchen sink faucet. I ran in here because I knew she wouldn't mess with your apartment."

"It's okay."

"The food is ready, if you guys want to go grab a bite. I can finish up in here." Frank turned the lock on the front door. "Give Emma some time to cool off."

"Thanks." Tony walked up beside Gray.

Together, they walked to the kitchen and Tony opened the back door for her. The door to the deck was open, and before Gray pushed the screen door open, she heard the sound of laughter.

The smell of hamburgers made her mouth water as she stepped outside. A buffet line had been set up on a fold-up table from Emma's apartment, and Gray added potato salad and green beans to her plate next to a small cheeseburger before she settled into her favorite spot on the deck in front of her apartment window.

Emma laughed with Vince, who was soaked with water. Gray watched the way they talked casually and comfortably. Gray had been an introvert growing up, and light conversation had never come naturally for her. More often than not, she would be tucked away in the corner of the lunchroom at school as she watched the world around her.

"May I join you?" Tony lowered himself next to Gray. They sat together and watched the group on the other side of the deck.

"Thank you for everything you did today." Gray met his eyes. "The apartment looks much better."

"You're welcome."

His smile revealed straight, white teeth. For a moment, Gray wondered if he'd ever needed braces. As she tried to imagine what he would look like with braces, he laughed and dipped his head to catch her attention.

"What?"

Gray blushed as she realized she had been staring at his teeth. "I was trying to picture you with braces."

"Never had them."

Of course not, Gray thought. Still, in the back of her mind she thought of Tony as a socially awkward teenager with braces and an imperfect life, just like herself. She thought, in some other universe, maybe they could have had something in common.

Everyone settled in to eat. Frank had poked his head out from the back door, determined he was safe, and found his now-usual place next to Emma. The two of them shared a quiet conversation between bites, and Emma wore a look of sadness.

"Why does Emma look upset?" Gray took another bite of her cheeseburger.

"We're leaving tomorrow morning for Tennessee to record. It will be at least a month before we're back." Tony played with the potato salad on his plate. "Frank's pretty disappointed. He and Emma were just starting to hit it off. He's afraid the time away might change things between them."

"No." Gray turned her eyes to the couple again. "Emma really cares about him. I can tell. Nothing will change."

The sun played on her skin as Gray leaned back against the brick wall and looked out over the garden. She thought about the morning she had sat with Vera and listened to the life of Job. The leaves of the magnolia tree rustled in the light breeze, and the small burst of life reminded Gray of the hope Vera had spoken about.

"When did you get a Bible?" Tony's voice was casual.

Gray looked down at her hands as she thought about the past week and the long, sleepless nights she had spent curled up in her bed as she read the frail pages of a book she despised. A hunger seemed to grow inside of her, and no matter how much she read, Gray longed to read more. She searched to find a flaw, something to justify her hatred for God. She needed to prove herself right. But the more she read, the more she felt a small light grow inside her, and it threatened to burn her from the inside out.

Hope.

"What is hope? A beacon that burns in a lifeless land," she had written in her journal the night before, *"and calls out across the darkness to bring the ghosts safely home."*

"Vera gave it to me last week."

Tony nodded, but didn't take his gaze from the garden.

"And yes, I have been reading it."

"And?"

Gray thought back on the stories she had read in the Old Testament books: David, Job, Solomon—all people she had come to be familiar with. The night before she had read the New Testament letters that a man named Paul had written to churches he had helped to start.

"And I've found the Bible is full of stories of broken people crying out to an infinite Being. It's like the ultimate tragic, Greek play." She set her plate down. "You had God Who is absolutely perfect and Who created a perfect, beautiful world. Then you had humans, Adam and Eve, who defied Him in the garden."

Tony nodded his head, and Gray continued. "Adam and Eve's desire to be their own gods caused separation between them and God, forcing their exile from the Garden and introducing physical death and suffering into the world. After that, the Bible is filled with stories of people who tried as hard as they could to fix what could never be undone—to be in unity with God again—but were never able to live a perfect life. You constantly see the struggle between humans defying God to take control of their own lives, and then realizing that nothing they do apart from Him brings them peace or joy. God wanted to fix the wrong we had done, and He sent Jesus, who is His Son—a perfect being. We were so blind, lost, and confused we couldn't even recognize Him, the true Love of our lives, the One sent to save us, our Creator, and out of anger, jealousy, and spite, we beat and murdered Him. All because He didn't meet the standards of what we thought He should be.

"But Jesus saw past our anger, our pain, and our cruelty to the true heart of the matter. So even though once again we had turned our backs on Him—once again we had rejected Him—He took all of the wrong we had done, all of the pain, all of the anger, all of the cruelty onto Himself and accepted our punishment and shame. He died, but through His death we were given life. Three days later, He overcame death itself, giving us eternal life and the strength to walk in the light of God, becoming one with Him again."

She met Tony's eyes.

"It's the ultimate love story."

Tony searched her eyes. "But you don't believe it."

"No." Gray didn't break his stare. "It's an eloquent, far-fetched story. How could a loving God send people to Hell in the first place? The same people He cared so much about that He would sacrifice His Son? And how could He allow so much wrong in the world? So much evil?" She looked away. "Bad things happen to good people every day."

The wind played with the leaves of the small magnolia tree.

"Close your eyes," Tony said.

When Gray met his eyes, Tony nodded out toward the garden, and Gray turned to look out over the expanse of flowers once again.

"Close your eyes." His voice was soft.

With her eyes closed, Gray's once bright and vivid world became black.

"Adam and Eve wanted the power and wisdom God had, so they took control and broke the perfect world He had created specifically for them in a failed attempt to become what He is. They didn't trust that God had created them perfectly. Their doubt and defiance and rejection created a black cloud in His perfectly clear, blue sky. That cloud is called 'sin' in the Bible, which creates a barrier between us and God. He is so perfect and so holy, and we had made ourselves and our world to be flawed. He could no longer walk the earth side by side with us as He once did."

As Tony spoke, the image of his words filled her mind: the perfect garden, God walking beside man as He once did, and the dark cloud rising on the horizon.

"Over time, we continued to push God away, frustrated He didn't fit the mold we wanted Him to fit. Frustrated that He didn't do the things we wanted Him to do. Our emotions of selfishness, entitlement, and hunger for power overwhelmed us. Murder, lust, and greed all began to corrupt us, and the black cloud thickened. Soon we could no longer see God or feel His presence. We had blotted Him out."

The dark scene of a desolate, black world filled Gray's mind.

"Keep your eyes closed and think about how dark your vision is right now, Gray. Now open your eyes."

A bright and colorful world filled her view again, and Gray felt almost overwhelmed as she took in the sight of the beautiful garden and clear blue sky.

"I've heard it said once that darkness is the absence of light. Like darkness, evil is the absence of God in our world. Behind the cloud of separation that we have created, God's light is still there, as bright as the day, wanting to be seen and felt again." He held his arms out under the sun's rays. "God does not *want* bad things to happen. Bad things happen as a result of our separation from God—a separation we create, like continually polluting the sky. The world is not perfect and will never be perfect again until Jesus's second coming. Yes, good people fall victim to this sick, broken world each and every day, but God gives us hope. He may not always calm the storm around us, but the faith we have in knowing that He is always there, shining bright, just on the other side of the clouds, gives us the strength to stand and face the wind. He is our hope and our guiding light, not the creator of our pain and suffering. Your closed eyelids prevented you from seeing the light, but the light was always there."

Gray considered his words. She thought about what she had read and compared it with what Tony told her.

"Maybe it does all sound far-fetched." Tony shrugged. "The validity of it is for you to decide for yourself. But Jesus came to give us hope. Not a hope that nothing bad will ever happen on this earth or that Christians won't have to deal with the evil of the world we live in and helped to create," he met Gray's eyes, "but hope that even in the darkness of this world and the thickest storms, we will have an eternity in the sun when the storm passes. The storm isn't the end of our story. This earth isn't all there is, and what awaits us on the other side is far greater than any suffering we face here."

After a moment, Gray sighed.

"Okay." She stood. "That's enough heavy talk for today."

Tony stood and took the paper plate from her hand. "I'm glad you're reading and asking questions."

Gray shrugged her shoulders and pulled at the hoodie. "Like I said, don't get too excited, preacher." She turned and walked back into the apartment.

The next morning, Gray sat in her room alone, journal in hand and Bible beside her as she looked out at the sun rising over river below. A mix of emotions tore through her, and she was weary from wrestling with herself. How much longer could she hold on to the hatred and bitterness?

Her mind raced through the past few days—everything she had read, everything she had heard, everything about the Bible that she had researched. Irritated and worn out from a restless night pouring over Tony's words, she resolved to end her inner torment and throw the Bible away.

Gray ran her hand over the soft binding again. An image of her father sitting on their front porch, watching the sunrise with his Bible in hand came to Gray's mind. She lifted the book and flipped through it, letting the sound of the soft rustle of the delicate pages fill the room. When the last page settled, the image of her father faded away, and Gray was left sitting alone in her empty bedroom. She snapped the book closed, stood, walked into the kitchen, and opened the trashcan.

The leather-bound Bible felt heavy in her hands as she stared down at it and told herself to throw it away, but her fingers didn't move. Her anger grew, and after a few minutes passed by, she stepped away and tossed the Bible onto the table instead. Her biblioclasm would have to wait for another day.

20

White

The sunrise colored the sky with hues of purple, gold and orange as Tony loaded his bags into the back of Frank's van. The crisp smell of rain lingered in the morning breeze and the air was cool enough to raise goosebumps on his arms.

"This is it," Darren said as he walked up beside Tony. "This is the moment when everything changes."

They had all met at Vera and Isaac's house to pack the van and head out to Tennessee.

"I baked you boys some cornbread and cookies. Snacks for the road. They're in the van." Vera hugged Tony.

"What about that infamous homemade lemonade?" Tony asked, his arm around her shoulders.

Vera scoffed. "Of course. But you better get to it before Frank does. He'll drink it all."

Tony chuckled. He thought back to the many evenings he spent as a child out on the back porch next to his aunt Vera, sipping lemonade and listening to stories from her childhood.

Vera leaned her head on his shoulder. "I'm proud of you, Tony."

Tony cleared his throat to ward away his rising emotions. He kissed his aunt on her forehead. "You and Isaac have always been there for me. Thank you, Aunt Vera. For everything."

Vera wiped a tear from her cheek and laughed softly. "Love you, son."

She squeezed his arm one more time before she walked away.

Isaac prayed with the men before they dispersed and began to say their goodbyes. As Darren kissed Tiffany goodbye and Frank wrapped Emma in a hug, Tony looked out over the sunrise again.

The morning dew had covered the tall grass of the fields surrounding Vera's house in a whimsical silver dust that shimmered under the warm light. A couple of bluebirds landed on a fence post nearby and shook the sleep off their wings. Tony breathed in a deep breath and smiled.

Deep within him, Tony felt the gravity of this moment. He filled his lungs with the cool country air one last time. There was almost a hesitation in his step as he turned to walk to the van. When the door closed behind him and he settled into his seat, Tony knew he was leaving a part of himself behind. He knew that the man who just stepped into that van was not the same man who stood next to the fence post to take in the sunrise moments ago. He knew that he might stand in that exact spot again someday in the future, but he would never be the same; Belle would never be the same.

Tony's friends and family gathered on the sidewalk and waved their last goodbyes. The van pulled away, leaving a trail of dust along the gravel path as they parted ways.

21

Black

Gray slipped into the crowded church unnoticed and ran her hands down the seams of her dress as she kept her eyes low to avoid the side-glances from strangers. Worship had already begun. Gray spotted Emma's blonde curls and made her way down the church aisle to step into the pew beside her.

Emma moved to make room for Gray, and her wide eyes brimmed with surprise as they caught Gray's gaze. Gray ducked her head and turned her attention to the stage. Tony and the rest of the church band were still in Tennessee. A man who sang with a soft Southern drawl and played an acoustic guitar led worship as his wife joined on the piano.

The music concluded, and Pastor Isaac took the stage and spoke about faith. The musician and his wife concluded the service with a song. A quiet murmur stirred as the small aisle between the two rows of pews filled with people. Gray anticipated the excitement that would be there to greet her as she turned to face Emma.

"I am glad you came this morning." Emma's eyes beamed.

"Thanks." She twisted her fingers together and thought about all the questions racing through Emma's mind, questions Gray herself didn't understand the answers to. Why was she here?

Gray took a deep breath. For weeks, she had argued with herself about coming to church with Emma. Part of her was curious. Part of her longed for friendship. But above any other reason, the more she read and sought out answers with an open-mind, the more she thought she should at least give God a chance to prove He was real. Last night, she had resolved to give church another try.

"Gray." Vera's soft voice broke through her thoughts. Vera made her way from the front of the crowded church and looped her arm with Gray's. "I have to introduce you to my husband."

They weaved their way toward the foot of the stage where Pastor Isaac stood and spoke with an older couple. His dimples showed as he smiled. The couple each gave him a friendly hug goodbye before they walked away. The woman stopped and shook Vera's hand as they passed and wished her a good day.

"This must be Gray." Pastor Isaac stepped closer to his wife. "It's nice to finally meet you."

"You too." Gray bit the inside of her cheek. Could he see her doubt and bitterness—her distrust for the God he served with diligence?

Isaac's eyes were a soft brown, and his face wore smile lines that creased his skin as he spoke. "I'm sorry we haven't met up to this point. I have heard many good things about you from Vera. I may be a decent preacher, but I'm a lousy business- or handyman, so I have next to nothing to do with the apartment or floral shop. I was blessed to marry such a versatile woman." He winked at Vera.

"The apartment is great. Belle's a beautiful town, and everyone has been welcoming to say the least." She smiled and caught a glimpse of Emma, who waited for her near the back door.

"I'm glad to hear it." Isaac's eyes smiled with his upwardly curved lips. There was so much of Isaac that reminded her of her father . . . his happy disposition and the twinkle in his eye as if he was on the edge of his seat and wanted to share some great news with you.

"Vera and I would love to have you over for dinner sometime. She cooks a mean steak." He nudged Vera as he spoke. "Just let us know if you ever want to drop by."

"I will, thanks." Gray wanted to end the conversation on that note. She nodded toward Emma, who spoke with a silver-haired woman by the back door. "I better get going. It was very good to meet you, Isaac."

Isaac smiled and nodded his head as he took his wife's hand into his own. "We're happy to have you."

With a small wave, Gray glanced back at the pastor and his wife. She saw Vera kiss him once as they talked together, hand in hand, smiles on their faces. Gray thought back on the story Vera had told her about how she had met Isaac, and Gray smiled to herself before she followed Emma out the door.

When they stepped into the sunlight of the hot afternoon, Emma slid a pair of sunglasses on and walked beside Gray down the street.

"Would you like to come over for lunch? Tiffany and Carla are coming over. We take turns having lunch at each other's houses each Sunday afternoon. Today we're having tacos, and then we are heading to a children's home in Rolla to play games with the foster kids there for the afternoon."

"Sure."

As they approached the doorstep to the stairway of their apartments, Emma's eyes betrayed her curiosity and desire to probe. Emma pursed her lips together, and let her hands fall limp at her sides with a sigh. She held the door for Gray. "So we'll see you for lunch?"

Gray nodded her head and stepped in behind Emma, taken aback by Emma's self-control. "I need to change first, and I'll be over."

"Sounds good. See you then." With another smile, Emma walked up the stairs.

A large white envelope in Gray's mailbox caught her eye. The unfamiliar return address did not include a name. Gray tucked the envelope under her arm and fished for her keys as she walked up the stairs.

Once inside her apartment, she tossed the envelope onto the couch. After she changed into a pair of leggings and a long, white, linen shirt, she let her hair down and fell into the soft, overstuffed cushions of the couch. She took the envelope in her hand and pulled the tab to tear it open. Inside was a piece of paper and something in bubble wrap. Gray read the note first.

Gray,

"The light shines in the darkness, and the darkness has not overcome it." John 1:5

I thought you might enjoy this CD.

-Tony

Tony's handwriting was in block letters across the CD case. *CHRISTIAN MUSIC.* When she flipped open the case, the names of the individual songs and bands were written on the inside of the case. Gray ran her finger over the writing, and a small smile teased her lips. She was sure she wouldn't like it. Christian music was worship music. As far as she knew, it came in two styles; contemporary or hymns. But she stood up from the couch and slipped the CD into her stereo.

Gray settled back into the chair. The CD began auto play, and the first song was a woman who sang with a little more of a rock edge. Gray looked at the CD case where the titles and bands were printed: "All Around Me" by Flyleaf.

Gray was surprised again when the next song came on, and she liked it as much as the first. She thought about the work Tony had put into the CD, choosing songs he knew she might like.

At the end of the CD, Gray felt a twinge of disappointment there wasn't more. She turned off her stereo and made her way to the closet. As she retrieved her hoodie, Gray made a mental note to thank Tony next time she saw him. She caught the sound of muffled voices in the hallway. Gray opened her front door and met Tiffany and Carla, who greeted her as she stepped into the hallway.

"I'm so glad you're joining us," Tiffany said, as Emma opened her front door.

The three of them stepped inside the apartment and were greeted by the smell of Mexican rice, beans, and salsa.

"Mmmmm." Carla closed her eyes and savored the smell. "Emma makes the best homemade salsa. I hope you like spicy food."

"I love spicy food."

Tiffany smiled at Gray. "You'll fit right in then."

A bowl of tortilla chips and salsa sat out on the table in the kitchen, where Emma stood over the stove and browned ground beef.

"Help yourselves," she said over her shoulder.

"Don't mind if we do." Tiffany picked up a small plate and scooped a handful of chips before adding salsa. Carla was close behind her. Gray helped herself to a plate and followed the girls into the living room where they settled onto the couch. She scooped her first helping of the salsa onto a chip and took a bite.

The fresh flavors of tomato and cilantro hit her first, followed by a pinch of garlic and the burn of the jalapeño peppers. Carla had not exaggerated when she had said it was the best homemade salsa.

"The guys are going to be so jealous." Tiffany spooned another helping into her mouth. "They join us for lunch every once in a while and always ask for Emma's salsa. It's been a while since she's made it."

Emma emerged from the kitchen and wiped her hands on a towel. "Well, I get my ingredients from the farmer's market, and I haven't had a chance to go out that way in a while."

Tiffany pulled out her cell phone from her purse and tossed it to Emma. "Take a picture. I'll send it to Darren. He'll be so mad."

The three girls posed—each holding up their plates of chips and salsa with big smiles on their faces—and Emma snapped the picture. She tossed the phone back to Tiffany and announced the tacos and burritos were ready.

As they ate, they talked about the sermon earlier that morning and the women filled Gray in on their regular service projects at the orphanage. They smiled and laughed together as they shared stories with Gray about the children and their weekly experiences. For the first time since she had moved, Gray felt like she was free to make friends, no matter the danger she might put her heart in.

She was learning to trust people again, and that was the best feeling she'd felt since the day her father had died.

22

White

Hundreds of miles away, Tony sat in the living room of Vince's Aunt Kayla's home and leaned his head back against the couch to stare up at the popcorn-textured ceiling. They didn't have to stay in a hotel while they were recording, but the monotony of their visit had begun to wear on Tony. They had spent the first leg of their trip meeting with the record label and hashing out the details of their contracts. The week had been spent either in the studio going over the same songs repeatedly, or in Kayla's living room staring at the plasma TV mounted on the wall.

Tony heard a light sigh, and Melody, Kayla's daughter, flopped onto the couch next to him. She had spent a lot of time with the guys since they had arrived and had even tagged along to the studio a couple of times. Last weekend, she had gone with Vince and Tony to see a movie, and they had stopped at a small ice cream parlor for a few sundaes on their way home. Melody was lighthearted and funny. She made Tony laugh until his ribs hurt as they had walked home. It was the first time in months since Tony felt normal.

Melody was a couple of years younger than Tony, and her strawberry-blonde hair was cropped short, which framed her thin face and brought out her light-green eyes.

"You look as bored as I am." She elbowed his side.

"How could you tell?"

Melody was quiet for a minute. "Do you want to throw a football in the backyard? I'm pretty good. St. Louis Rams were talking about drafting me last year." She winked.

Tony's stomach sank at the thought she might be coming onto him, but he was also caught off guard at the small tinge of excitement at the idea. The two of them had gotten along well since they came to stay at Kayla's house. Melody didn't live with her mom—she rented an apartment near the Christian university she attended as she studied to be a youth pastor—but she had been at her mom's house often during the days the guys had been in town.

"I wouldn't brag about the Rams trying to draft you." Tony laughed. "I heard they'll take anyone at this point."

He stood and stretched as he turned off the TV.

Tony followed Melody through the kitchen to the back door and Vince looked up from where he sat at the kitchen table, a bag of Doritos in his hands. "What are you guys doing?"

The other four guys looked up and eyed the football tucked under Melody's arm.

"We were going to toss a ball around." Melody held the ball up, a wry smile on her face. "How about a game of football?"

Almost in unison, all five men stood up. "We're in."

A half an hour later, they had divided into two teams; Jim, Peter, and Vince versus Tony, Melody, Frank, and Darren. Jim's team was up by a touchdown. Tony gathered his team into a huddle and decided to fake a pass to Darren but have Melody run it in with Frank guarding her. The huddle broke, and they went for the play. Tony snuck the ball to Melody, and she ran as fast as she could for the tree line that marked the end zone. Before the other team had realized what had happened, she threw the ball down and waved her arms around for a victory dance.

Tony ran up beside and, without thinking, he scooped her up in a hug that lifted her off her feet and swung her around. When he set her back down, Melody caught his eyes. Tony took a step back and cleared his throat as he tossed the ball to Jim.

"Ready for round two?"

Tony walked back to their side of the yard and gathered his thoughts. Had he crossed a line he hadn't meant to? Why wouldn't he have feelings for Melody? She was beautiful, and they had a lot in common. But for whatever reason, Tony didn't have feelings for Melody. Any feelings he did have—he was ashamed to admit—stemmed from boredom, and for that reason, he had to steer clear of her.

Behind him, Tony heard Darren's phone sing out a love song that was set for when Tiffany called or messaged him. Tony stifled a laugh.

"Oh, man," Darren moaned as he looked down at the phone in his hand.

"What?" Frank came up beside him and looked down at the phone. His face dropped. "Are you kidding me?"

Jim, Peter, and Vince jogged up and the phone was passed around. Tony looked over at Melody, who stood next to him. He thought he should pull her aside later to talk to her, and an awkward knot in his stomach formed.

"Tony, look at this." Frank held out the phone.

"What is it?" Tony stared down at the picture on the screen.

"Emma finally made her salsa, while we're all out of town!" Frank threw his arms up in the air. "I've been begging her to make that for months!"

"What salsa?" Melody asked. She stepped in closer to Tony and looked from his face to the picture.

The guys went into a lengthy explanation about Emma's homemade salsa, but Tony wasn't listening. His heart was in his throat as he looked down at the smile on Gray's face and the plate in her hand as she sat on the couch next to Tiffany and Carla. There was something in her eyes that hadn't been there before. Resolve? Optimism? Whatever it was, Tony found hope in what he saw, and something deep within his chest ached to be home. But he was in Tennessee, and as he stood and stared down at the beautiful, strong woman who had taken their small town by storm, he prayed for Gray.

The football game picked back up, and Tony's team won by a touchdown. Tony stood out in the backyard and wiped the sweat from his forehead with his T-shirt when Kayla came to the back door and called them in for a late lunch. Jim and Darren argued about plays as the group headed for the back door.

"Tony," Melody came alongside of him and placed her hand on his arm. They stopped walking, and Tony's heart picked up speed. The last half of the football game had been awkward with Melody, as she stole glances at Tony between plays. But her gaze wasn't the same as it had been. He no longer saw excitement in her eyes but a curious sort of pain.

The same gaze was now locked onto his face as the guys disappeared into the house and left the two of them outside alone. Tony shifted his feet and cleared his throat.

"Okay, I'll just come out and say it." Melody held her hands up in front of her. "I like you. Since the first night you guys arrived, you caught my eye. And I felt like we had kind of hit it off and the feelings might be mutual."

With a soft sigh, Tony dropped his head. "Melody."

"No, wait," she said and closed her eyes for a moment. "Let me finish."

She took a deep breath.

"But at the same time, I felt like you might not have the *same* feelings for me that I did for you, and I wanted to hang out today to get to know you better. I was hoping to feel you out and see where you stood, and maybe take things to the next level if I was wrong." Pain clouded her eyes, and Tony bit his lower lip.

"Then Darren got that message, and I watched your face when you looked at the picture. It all became very clear at that moment. You don't feel the same way about me because there is someone else back in Belle, isn't there?" The look in her eyes seemed to plead to him to say no as she held on to some kind of hope she had been mistaken.

A million thoughts washed over Tony at once. What was he doing? He was about to pass up an opportunity to spend time with a well-grounded, beautiful woman because he had feelings for a mixed-up, hurt woman who had stormed into his life, angry at the world. Gray hadn't wanted anything to do with Tony or his friends. She might spend more time with Emma, Tiffany, and Carla, but there was no way to tell if she cared for Tony or if she ever would. After all, she had left a serious relationship back home and made it clear Tony was not her type.

Then there was the issue of her faith, which Emma and Frank reminded him of. And they were right. How could Tony live a life with a woman who hated the very Being that Tony centered his life around?

Melody waited, her eyes locked onto his. He inhaled and took a step back.

"Melody, I am so sorry." Her gaze shifted to the ground. "I never meant to hurt you or lead you on."

Unsatisfied with his answer, Melody asked, "You care for someone else, don't you? One of the girls in the picture. I saw the look on your face when Frank showed the phone to you."

Tony shook his head and took another step away. "Melody, look . . ." he trailed off, unsure of what to say as he sorted through his own thoughts and emotions,

"Ah, I get it." Melody tilted her chin up. "You can't be honest with me because you're not being honest with yourself."

Her words cut into him and made him defensive. He let the words sting.

"How long has it been? And she doesn't even know." Melody laughed. "She probably hasn't even shown any feelings for you, but here I am, pouring myself out to you, and you're holding back for someone who doesn't even know you care for her. I don't get it, Tony. Why are you holding back? I know I wasn't wrong. There is some kind of attraction in your eyes when you look at me. And the way you hugged me earlier. We have fun together. I don't get why—"

Tony put his hands up and cut her off as she spoke. "Because I love her."

There. He had said it. The words hung between them and Tony felt ashamed for admitting them out loud. He had to be losing his mind.

Love.

He had fought the idea for the past two months, chalking his emotions up to fleeting sentiment born of loneliness and desire. But the harder he fought against his heart, the more the truth revealed itself. For a reason he couldn't fully explain, he loved Gray, even if she never changed. He had prayed for her every night since he had driven her home from the carnival, and deep in his heart he knew God was working in her life.

It was crazy, and it was ridiculous, and it didn't make sense, but Tony knew he loved Gray.

The words had slapped Melody in the face, and she stood stunned.

"I'm sorry, Melody." He dropped his gaze.

A small breeze teased Melody's short, strawberry-blonde strands, and when he looked up she held his gaze. Her eyes were a mix of sorrow and anger.

"Tell her."

She turned to walk inside and left Tony out on the patio to wrestle with the truth. Half an hour passed as he sat, stared out at the yard, and argued with God. Why did he feel this way if he could not express it? But the more he prayed, the more he felt that Gray was in a time of healing right now and what she needed the most was a friend. He had faith the time would come. Until then, he had to wait and pray.

23

Black

The children's home was smaller than Gray had imagined. A nonprofit organization had purchased an old, two-story schoolhouse built in the early 1900s and converted it into the children's home. As Gray followed Emma up the walkway, she noted the welcome sign hung by the door, and a large garden wrapped around the front of the building.

Emma held the door open for Gray. The smell of freshly baked cookies lingered in the air, and the sound of children's laughter drifted from the back of the home.

"Hello, hello!" Emma called out, and a woman who looked to be in her forties poked her head around a large, wooden staircase in the hall.

"Emma!" The woman emerged from behind the stairs, her plump hands held out. "We are always so happy to see you. This is their favorite part of the week."

"Thank you." Emma embraced the woman when she approached before she turned to face Gray. "Mrs. Hattie, this is Gray Wilcox. She recently moved to Belle from St. Louis."

The cheerful woman took Gray's hands in her own and smiled. The woman's hands were soft and warm, and her round, freckled cheeks squeezed her brown eyes into crescent moons when she smiled. Her hair was brown, streaked with gray.

"We are so blessed to have you with us today, Gray." Mrs. Hattie released her hands. "You can call me Rose. My husband, Matthew, is out back playing basketball with the boys."

"I'm happy to be here."

Rose told them about their week as they walked to the back of the house. Rose explained how she and Matthew could never have children of their own, and how God had put it on their heart to start this ministry. Since they had purchased the schoolhouse seventeen years ago, they had seen over seventy children walk the halls of their home. The building and their state license allowed for them to have ten children in the home at a time, and with the help of volunteers, they were able to keep the home functional and orderly.

"The children just finished lunch," she explained and smiled at Gray as she held the door open for her. "Every meal, a volunteer from the church comes over to help cook, serve food, and clean. They form as much of a relationship with these children as we do."

They continued their walk to a set of sliding glass doors at the end of the hallway on the far side of the home. A little girl with red hair caught her eye. The girl sat tucked away close to the wall at the top of the stairs, a brown bear in her hands. She couldn't have been older than seven or eight, and the look of loneliness in her eyes made Gray want to rush up the stairs and take her into her arms.

Gray made a mental note to ask Rose about the little girl later and followed the others outside. A basketball court was set up on the right side of the large, secluded backyard, and a line of picnic tables and benches flanked the other side. A group of three little girls sat on the picnic benches, and when they caught sight of Emma, they all stood and rushed toward her, arms open wide.

"Emma!"

Their little voices carried in the warm summer air. Emma, Tiffany, and Carla each took their turns to hug the girls before they introduced them to Gray. A moment later, six young boys bounded up; one of the boys carried a basketball in his hands. After all the children had said their greetings and been introduced to Gray, they settled into the grass around Emma, Carla, and Tiffany.

Gray stood next to Rose and Matthew and watched as Carla told the children the story about Jonah and the whale. When the story concluded, Emma produced a large, smiley face parachute from her bag and walked with the children into the center of the grassiest part of the yard. They sat around in a circle, and each took a corner of the fabric. Emma had games and different activities to do with the parachute, and Gray watched the children laugh and enjoy themselves.

Out of the corner of her eye, she saw the little redheaded girl poke her head out of the back door, the teddy bear still in her hands. Rose turned to follow Gray's gaze.

"That's Sylvia." Rose nodded to the girl. "I have been praying twice as hard for her."

The girl made her way out of the house and sat on the far edge of a bench at a picnic table to watch the other children from afar.

"Why? What's the matter with her?"

With taut lips, Rose said, "No one here has been able to connect with her. Her mother was a heroin addict, and they lived most of their lives homeless on the streets. When Sylvia was four, her mother died of an overdose and a police officer found Sylvia scrounging for food in a nearby dumpster." The woman's eyes misted over again. "No one was sure how long Sylvia had been left in that alley alone to sleep next to her dead mother."

Too choked up to continue, Rose waved her hand in the air and excused herself as she gained composure. "I'm sorry."

Gray thought about the horror Sylvia had been exposed to from such a young age. The image of her as she ate food from the garbage made Gray's stomach turn and brought tears to her own eyes.

"After that, it was discovered that Sylvia's mother carried the HIV virus, and that Sylvia had contracted it at birth. The first foster family she lived with looked at Sylvia like a diseased, contagious dog. She was removed from the home when she was six after her foster brother told the social worker about how their foster mom would make Sylvia shower multiple times a day with the water so hot it left her skin red, dry, and cracked. She wasn't allowed to eat with the rest of the family or go outside and play for fear she might fall and cut herself, exposing her blood. Sylvia rarely left her bedroom. They also found out that the family had not been properly treating the virus with medication, and it had developed into AIDS.

"When she came to live with us last year, so much damage had already been done. She has been in intense counseling and therapy, but she loathes herself and even the volunteers who come through the house keep their distance, ignorant of the disease and how it can be contracted. The disease can't be contracted through sweat, saliva, or tears as most people think. The only way for a person to contract HIV is to come in contact with a specific few types of bodily fluids from an infected person. And even then, it's not as easy to contract as most people believe. As long as people know about her disease, she will face a world of loneliness and misunderstanding. She may never be able to love a husband or live in a world without judgment and condemnation. It's sad."

The story was more than she could bear, and before Gray could regain control of herself, a tear slid down her cheek. Rose put her hand on Gray's back and let her have a moment. After a few minutes, Gray gathered her composure and wiped her cheeks with the backs of her hands. Turning away from Rose, Gray made the walk across the neatly kept yard to the table in the shade where a lonely, hurt girl sat and clung to her bear.

When Gray knelt in front of Sylvia, the girl was taken aback at first, shying away. But as she looked at Gray and studied the tears in her eyes, something in Sylvia's expression changed. Recognition resonated. They stared into each other's eyes without a word. Both Sylvia and Gray knew they were looking in a mirror. Each of them faced a lonely, hurt girl who longed for someone in the world to love her.

In one swift motion, Gray scooped the girl up and held her in a close hug as both of them cried. Sylvia clung to Gray; her tears soaked the collar of Gray's shirt and wet her hair. Gray didn't fear Sylvia's tears.

In that moment, something inside of Gray broke, as if all the walls she had built up around herself had fallen to pieces and left her exposed. As she wept with this little girl, Gray fully understood once again what it meant to love and to be loved. All at once she saw the ways God had been synchronizing the history of her life as stepping stones to lead her to this moment. She saw one piece of the story He was writing into her life. She saw a part of His purpose in using her pain to bring hope to this little girl. She saw one ray of light break through the clouds, and she was blinded by His glory.

Gray welcomed the comfort of the embrace of another damaged soul, another innocent child who had been dealt an unfair hand and had to carry the sins of another in her blood as she lived what was left of her life.

24

Black

Tiffany's Independence Day party was the talk of the town for weeks prior to the event. The Sunday before the big party, the guys had been expected back, but the record had taken longer than anticipated to complete. Tiffany was an emotional wreck after another church service without the worship team, or more specifically, Darren. After the sermon, Emma, Carla and Gray stood together in the foyer of the church with Tiffany. She broke down in tears for the third time that morning when she received a text message from Darren that said they would miss the big event. Tony had gotten sick and lost his voice earlier that week and it had put recording on hold until he had fully recovered.

Tiffany cried and dabbed at her tears with a tissue. "I miss him so much. We have never been apart this long."

Emma comforted her friend, but Gray could see the sadness Emma was trying to mask in her own eyes. She wondered if Frank had been right to be concerned about the distance putting a strain on their budding relationship.

The scene replayed in Gray's mind as she walked through the grocery store later that week and gathered a few items she had offered to bring for the party. Gray worried about how the night would go if Tiffany was in shambles over Darren's absence.

She stocked her cart with four bags of chips and headed down the soft drink aisle. As she passed the liquor aisle, her hands trembled and she stopped to eye the rainbow of glass bottles lining the shelves. Gray had stopped drinking a couple of weeks ago. Emma had to stay the night with her through the worst of the withdrawals. Gray trembled as the images from the night flashed through her mind: sitting over the toilet throwing up, sweating uncontrollably, and shaking and convulsing in her bed.

And then there was the cottonmouth.

The cottonmouth was the worst, and it returned to her now as the glimmer of the halogen lights beamed off the bottle of whiskey. Beads of sweat dotted her forehead, and Gray turned her cart in the direction of the aisle.

What could it hurt, after all? She had sobered up. She could drink with restraint now, right? She would just get a little something to slip in her cola later that evening and lighten her mood for the party a bit. A lot of people drank socially, even Christian people. There was no harm.

The tremors increased and she was barely able to keep her hands on her cart. She mustered every bit of strength in her being and thought about her life and the direction she was going.

"God, help me," she whispered between gritted teeth as she forced her cart forward and past the liquor aisle to the soda.

People did drink socially, even Christian people, and they were able to keep control. But Gray was not one of those people.

Gray loaded her cart with two cases of soda and headed for the checkout. At the checkout, the sweat danced down the back of her neck as she fought the urge to return to the whiskey. The tremble in her hands had lightened a bit, and she held the cart to try to steady them.

The whiskey could not help her anymore. The pain and emotions the alcohol masked were too much to numb. She was learning to deal with them without drowning her sorrows in a bottle. Gray had come to Belle because this is where she had shared her last good memory with her father, and she thought about what her father would think as he watched her cling to a bottle and throw up on the floor of an empty apartment.

"Is this all for you?"

Gray hadn't realized the cashier had finished ringing her up and now watched her as Gray stared at the liquor aisle behind her.

"Yes."

Gray pulled her debit card from her pocket and swiped the card. She loaded the bags of groceries into her cart. The account her father had set up for her with his life insurance policy had a monthly withdrawal limit, which was the reason her mother hadn't been able to drain it.

Each month, his trust fund deposited an allowance into her personal checking account. Her mother had been furious with her when she found out Gray had taken her off the account the day of her eighteenth birthday. Diana had waited for Gray in the dark parking lot of the retail shop where Gray worked, and after Gray had locked the doors of the store and walked to where her Cavalier had been parked, Diana knocked Gray out cold. When she woke up, her car had been keyed and the windows smashed in.

"Thank you. Have a nice day." The cashier handed the receipt to Gray, who stuffed it into one of the grocery bags and headed toward the exit.

The automated doors to the grocery store slid open, and a rush of warm air washed over her as she stepped out into the parking lot. Once outside, Gray took a deep breath. Immediately, the tremors calmed and the cottonmouth subsided.

When home, she had a decent lunch, good nap, and fresh shower. Gray retrieved a box from her closet, which contained a deep red, vintage-inspired sundress Carla had designed for her to wear tonight. Red wasn't a color Gray gravitated to, no matter how dark the shade, but Carla had been elated when she handed Gray the box. Carla had done a great job matching Gray's style. Gray didn't normally wear halter dresses, but this went well with the vintage look.

There was a soft knock at her front door just as Gray finished with a light touch of makeup in front of the bathroom mirror. She slipped a loose strand of hair behind her ear and hurried to where Emma waited for her in the hallway between their apartments. Emma wore a red, white, and blue sundress in the pattern of the American flag with white flip-flops. The two of them rode together to the café.

It took three trips to unload the car, and by the time Gray settled into a chair on the back patio, her breath was labored and sweat trickled down her neck. She was lost in a thought about how out of shape she was when a familiar face caught her eye from across the yard.

Tony walked up the stairwell that led down to the river.

Gray's heart skipped a beat, and her breath caught in her throat as a smile spread across her lips. Tony was distracted as he spoke to a person out of view. Gray was about to stand to walk in his direction when Tony stepped away from the stairs and Gray could see that the person beside him was a petite woman with cropped red hair. Gray was sure she had never seen this person before, and the smile froze on her face as she watched the two joke with each other. The woman elbowed Tony in his side, and he flinched as he laughed.

Gray looked away. A tight knot formed in her stomach at the thought of Tony flirting with the woman, and the jealousy surprised her. But the way she felt didn't matter. There wasn't a doubt in Gray's mind Tony wasn't attracted to her. He cared for her soul and wanted to win her over for God's Kingdom like a good Christian. He approached his mission in a less obnoxious and close-minded manner, but his intentions shouldn't be mistaken for anything other than him fulfilling his religious obligations.

The truth was Gray could never be the kind of woman Tony needed or deserved. Even now, she was broken—ruined. No amount of prayer or reading could undo what the last ten years had destroyed. Deep down, she was still Gray, the scarred girl from St. Louis who could never let a man into her heart.

Her thoughts wandered back to St. Louis. Had truth rung in Tyler's words when he'd said she had replaced him and Audrey? The way she felt for Tony was different than the way she had felt for Tyler. When she'd met Tyler, the way she felt for him had ignited quickly. He was five years older than Gray. Tyler was handsome and outgoing, the life of the party. At the beginning of their relationship, Gray and Tyler had spent every possible moment together, almost obsessively. Their on again, off again relationship was wild and unpredictable, built on lust and rebellion.

The way she felt for Tony, however, seemed to morph within her like a caterpillar. Her feelings had started out strange and unfamiliar and then found a protected place to nestle within her heart where they could transform into something altogether new. Now, the emotions she felt toward him took her breath away with their delicacy and splendor as the layers of protection she had hidden them behind began to break open and the colorful wings of love started to appear.

And like any other unwanted pest, Gray would have to find a way to squash the attraction before it carried her away.

"You've been staring at the soda in your hand for the past five minutes."

His voice caught her off guard and sent a jolt of unwanted emotions coursing through her veins. When she looked up, Tony stood beside her, a smile on his face. But there was something else there, something that hadn't been there before he left for Nashville. Was it confidence or perhaps happiness?

Love.

Tony was in love with the red-haired woman. Gray understood the look when she read his eyes. All the time she had spent in bars people-watching while Audrey danced the night away with a stranger, Gray had studied that look on the faces of countless women— women at the bar to find their soul mates as they stared into the eyes of men who were there to find a thrill for the night. Gray knew the look very well. Her heart sank again, and she chided herself. Tony could love the petite woman with red hair if he wanted to. There was no connection between them, and there never would be.

Tony laughed and stepped closer. "I'm gone for a month and I don't even get a 'hello'? What are you thinking about? You look like you're lost in outer space."

Gray blushed and ducked her head. "Nothing. I was just surprised to see you." She nodded toward the woman, who stood near the picnic tables next to Vince and Jim. "Who's the new girl?"

The words spilled out of her mouth, and blood rushed to her cheeks. Unable to look Tony in the eye, Gray fidgeted with the hem of her dress. There was a long, uncomfortable pause. Gray was sure Tony had caught on and found her little crush on him to be amusing. When his silence overwhelmed her, Gray met his eyes again, and she froze with disbelief.

There wasn't laughter or teasing behind his clear, blue irises, but a deep longing and hope. Her head spun when he studied her face and searched her eyes. She felt exposed as she sat before him, her thoughts and feelings out in the open for him to read.

He didn't break her gaze as Tony took a step closer and leaned in so he was inches from her face. "That's Melody. Vince's cousin and Jim's new girlfriend."

His reply caught her off guard and tore her from the trance. She looked from the short, dark-haired Jim to Melody and back to Tony. "Jim? But I thought . . ."

She trailed off. What difference did it make what she thought? She was wrong. Tony didn't love Melody. Fear swept over Gray, and she pulled away from Tony in an effort to steer herself away from a dangerous road she knew she couldn't travel.

"Gray."

Her name sounded perfect on his lips and her eyes were drawn back to his.

"Walk with me."

Before she could stop herself, she slipped her hand into his as he helped her out of her chair and they made their way across the yard and down the stairwell to the rushing river below.

25

White

The feel of her hand in his radiated up his arm as Tony settled into the sand on the far end of the beach. This part of the beach was raised and overlooked the water. The sight of Gray in the chair on the patio with her soda can and red dress caused his heart to skip a beat.

The last few weeks in Nashville were strange. He had wrestled with himself about Gray for the first two nights after the football game and then spent the next five nights talking to Frank about her and one night praying and coming to peace with himself. He loved Gray, and he made the decision to give his feelings to God and trust He would change her heart. Until then, Tony had to wait on the sidelines as he prayed for and encouraged her however he could.

Melody had disappeared for the first week after the football game. Then she began to come around again. The attraction between her and Jim didn't spark until the last week they were in Nashville, the week they weren't even supposed to be there. Jim and Melody agreed not to enter into a serious relationship for the time being since distance was a factor, but Vince had offered to let her stay with him for the remainder of the summer, and she jumped at the opportunity.

They had arrived in town late last night, and Tony had stayed with his aunt and uncle, too emotionally and spiritually worn out to go home to an empty house. Vera had a home-cooked meal ready for him when he pulled in her driveway at 10:30 p.m. He was grateful for the hot meal and rest until he started to receive reports about Gray. For most of the evening, Isaac and Vera's conversation centered around how much Gray had changed. Vera mentioned Gray had attended church every week and gone with Emma every week to see the children in Rose's Children's Home. She also volunteered full time throughout the week to clean and cook at the Children's Home.

Tony tossed and turned all night in the spare bedroom as excitement and fear battered his emotions. He thanked God for Gray's change of heart but didn't want to be quick to chase her and set her back. Tony could never live with himself if his relationship with Gray wound up hurting her. When he rolled over and sank his head into his pillow a little after the sun came up, Tony once again handed the way he felt over to God.

Then, when Gray stared across the yard at Melody, jealousy in her eyes, a switch had flipped in Tony's heart. Before he left, Gray had begun to question faith, but had started down a path she had made it clear he was not invited to join her on. Now, after he had spent the last month in prayer for her and confessing his feelings for her to his closest friends, Tony had come home to find that not only had Gray given her heart to God, but God had changed her heart about Tony.

And now here they sat, side by side by the river. Tony felt comfortable sitting beside her, and he fought the urge to take her hand into his again. He was not going to push anything.

"How was your trip?" Gray was the first to speak.

As he met her silver eyes, he searched again for a sign from her that her feelings for him were real, but a fog now hid her emotions.

"Long." He sighed, leaned back on his hands and looked out over the river. "And it wasn't what I expected. I thought we had the songs down, but once we were in the studio recording, we kept finding flaws or new ways to enhance the notes or lyrics. It was a lot of repetition, and it burned me out quick. Definitely different than performing live. Then I got sick and felt like I was holding everyone back. I spent a lot of time praying about why God had called us there and if we had made our decision out of the desire for fame or because we were truly seeking after His will. After that, we had a renewed sense of purpose and energy. I'm excited about the finished results."

Calm settled between them, and once again, Tony was struck by how comfortable he felt with Gray. They sat together with the evening sun glistening on the river's choppy surface and listened to the rush of the water. Tony memorized Gray's features as she gazed out over the small cliff. The golden sunlight added a shimmer to her pale skin, and her petite nose drew his eyes to her deep red, delicate lips. For a moment, he wondered what it would be like to kiss her.

Gray blushed and laughed when she caught his gaze. She pushed Tony and wrinkled her nose at him as she spoke. "Didn't your mother ever teach you that it's rude to stare?"

With a soft chuckle, Tony turned his attention back to the water. He picked up a soft stone, turned it over in his hand, and studied it as he rubbed his thumb over the jagged edges. Another minute passed by.

"It's going to be hard to leave again in February." Tony tossed the rock out into the rushing water below.

"Leave again?"

While his heartbeat in double time, Tony caught Gray's eyes with his. At this moment, she was transparent. Fear, worry, and disappointment screamed out of her silver hues. The answer he searched for stared him right in his face.

Gray cared for him, too.

After he cleared his throat, Tony turned away to keep from giving into the temptation to wrap his arms around her, confess his feelings, and promise never to leave again. He found another stone and tossed it into the water.

"Yes, we're going on tour as an opening band for a well-known musician from New York."

Tony thought about how his career—his dream—was about to take off. The tour and record label came once in a lifetime, and they had caught their break. But now Tony wanted to stay here in the sleepy town of Belle to lead worship music for the church. What was Gray doing to him? How had he gotten so caught up in his feelings for her?

"How long will you be gone?" Her voice was taut.

Tony leaned back on his hands and released a deep sigh. When he leaned back, his head was inches from her shoulder and the smell of her shampoo drifted in the warm air around him. "Two months."

The look on Gray's face changed, and as sorrow and anguish colored her tone, she turned to him and said one word.

"Stay."

Her eyes pleaded with him.

At that moment, it was like a dam of emotions broke loose inside of him. Her lower lip quivered as she stared back at him. The weight of her own emotions was more than she could bear, and Tony wondered if, in that moment, she had realized for the first time how she felt about him. Before he was able to stop himself, his hand brushed her cheek. His voice was caught in his throat, and the touch was the only comfort he could offer.

The way her skin felt under his fingertips sent waves of electricity down Tony's spine. He steadied himself and dropped his head as his hand fell to his side.

"Dinner!" Tiffany shouted down to the groups that had gathered on the beach.

Tony still felt the warmth of Gray's skin against his fingertips.

Gray regained her composure and her clear, silver eyes studied his face for a moment before she smiled. He stood, brushed his hands off, and helped Gray to her feet. They walked up the stairs and Tony kept his fingers looped in hers.

The group sat together at a picnic table for dinner, and the men shared stories from their time in Tennessee. Occasionally, Melody would interject with an outsider's view of the story being told, and everyone would laugh at her interpretations. While Melody corrected a story Jim told, Tony stole a glance at Gray, who held a sort of sadness in her eyes.

After dinner, Carla gathered the group to play volleyball, boys versus girls. Melody fit in well, as she eased into a friendship with Tiffany and Emma without effort. Tony watched from his group huddle as Gray stood with the other women but kept a reasonable distance as they conspired together. Even now, Gray didn't click with Emma, Tiffany, and Carla in the way Melody did. The difference between the two women was palpable, and as Tony watched the scene before him, he only loved Gray more for it.

Gray would never fit in like Melody because Gray was unlike any other woman Tony had met. She was quiet and reserved, but beneath her pale skin burned a fire that would consume all it touched when she let it free. Gray was deep and intelligent—erratic but restrained. To study her would be to try to predict the weather. She was calm and beautiful but fierce and uncontainable. Only God knew Gray Wilcox, and Tony prayed that someday he would be given a glimpse through His eyes.

26

Black

The men beat the women at volleyball, and after they exchanged high fives and congratulations, Gray made her way back to the picnic table. Her glass of lemonade had created a puddle of water from the condensation on the cup, and the liquid was warm on her tongue, ice long ago melted. She settled into a chair next to the table, took another drink, and watched Tony.

Tony was in a conversation with Pete, his face relaxed and a smile on his lips. As she studied him, she was sure of one thing; she was in love with Tony Reese. She didn't care to think beyond how she felt in this moment. In this moment, she would simply be in love.

But what about tomorrow?

The voice crashed through her mind, and Gray bit the inside of her lip as her stomach turned to knots.

What about tomorrow?

Tony fell into the chair next to Gray. "What are you thinking about?" His eyes studied Gray's face.

Gray smiled and shook her head. "Nothing entertaining."

Tony considered her answer for a moment and decided not to press her. "I'm going to grab something to drink. Would you like anything?"

"Sure, I'll have whatever you're having."

Tony stood and Gray noticed how quiet it was around them, with only a handful of people scattered around the yard.

"Where did everyone go?"

"You really were deep in thought about something, weren't you?" He smiled. "Most people went down to the beach to swim before the fireworks."

Tony retrieved a couple of sodas and they walked together, hand in hand, across the lawn to the stairwell that wound down to the beach. The sound of music being played over a speaker system grew louder.

"Did you bring your guitar?" she asked.

Tony stepped down onto the beach and turned to help Gray off the last step. "No. I had different plans for the night."

The group was at the far corner under the shade provided by the cliff above them. Tiffany lay on her stomach on a beach towel in the sunlight, sunglasses on and tanning lotion in her hand. Darren sat next to her and said something to her that made her smile. Tony and Gray settled into the sand next to Emma and Frank, who were in a conversation with Melody and Jim.

As the evening sun began to set, Gray leaned against Tony, her head on his shoulder. She studied the group, and a smile teased her lips. Emma had linked hands with Frank, Jim studied Melody from the corner of his eye, Darren was now lying on his back in the sand next to Tiffany, and Pete had gravitated to Carla and was deep in a conversation with her about forest life in South America. Vince sat next to Pete and contributed to the conversation when asked.

Gray thought about how she had almost allowed herself to miss out on the company of this group of friends. They had loved her from the moment she walked into Belle, using every opportunity they had to express that love. They had been given the cold shoulder or been turned away, and yet they had still reached out to her, unwilling to watch her suffer. With her eyes closed, Gray breathed in the warm summer air, thankful God had sent her this group of friends at a time in her life when she had needed them the most.

A slow song came on over the radio, and one by one, each couple stood and made their way to the dock to dance. Gray felt the muscles in Tony's shoulder tense, and she knew what he was about to ask.

"Gray, will you dance with me?" His voice was quiet, nervous.

Gray smiled. "Yes."

He took her hand into his, and they made their way across the sand to the dock. Tony held her close and wrapped his free arm around her waist. The sun had begun to set as he took the lead and danced with her under the fading light. Gray didn't recognize the song, but that didn't alter the moment. Lost in the soft melody, Gray leaned her head against Tony's chest, and she could hear the faint thump of his heartbeat.

What about tomorrow?

The thought threatened her composure, echoing through her mind and constricting her throat. Gray pressed her face into Tony's shirt and allowed herself to feel safe and at home in his arms. She fought to force the thought away.

Tony's lips pressed against her forehead again, and he rested his cheek against the top of her head as they swayed to the music. The warmth of his embrace chased the taunting voice from her thoughts, and Gray smiled, her arms on his chest as the song concluded.

Today I love Tony, she thought. Tomorrow I will still love Tony, and that's all I need to know for now.

The song ended. Tony and Gray stood motionless, transfixed in each other's embrace. Tony was the first to move, and he walked to the edge of the dock to sit and let his bare feet dangle in the water below. Gray watched him for a moment, unable to move. With a deep breath, she walked over and sat next to him and let her feet sink into the cool river.

"What's wrong, Gray?" His eyebrows were creased, and worry strained his face.

Gray swallowed past the lump in her throat and fought the rising fear. "What do you mean?" She brushed her feet through the water.

Tony didn't speak for a moment, and then he shook his head to look up at the sky and then back at Gray. "I don't know. I just feel like there is something you aren't saying. Something that scares you."

Tomorrow, tomorrow, tomorrow . . . the words screamed in the back of her mind.

Gray shook her head.

Without a word, Tony lay down, his back against the hard wood of the dock, his eyes fixed on the sky above them. Gray watched the water, her thoughts on the day. How had they gotten here? Here she sat, contemplating her feelings and what they meant in regard to a relationship, in regard to her life.

Love.

With Tony here next to her, she wondered how she had ever even believed that what she had with Tyler was anything close to love. She let a small puff of air escape her lips and lay back on the dock next to Tony, her arms folded across her stomach. Peace and a sense of freedom washed over her as she stared up into the clear sky. Why get wrapped up in the worries of tomorrow? Gray was learning to trust God, and she knew that as long as her eyes were on Him, she didn't need to worry about what tomorrow held.

Emma approached them. "We are all about to go for a swim. You should join us." Emma winked at Gray, a playful grin on her lips.

"Thanks, Emma." Tony stood and then helped Gray to her feet.

They made their way back at the café and Gray retreated to the women's restroom to change clothes. She left her hair down but teased it in the mirror before she left the bathroom. Tony had been waiting outside the door and when Gray took a step toward him, their hands easily looped together and they fell in step beside each other.

Lantern lights sat in clusters around the sand, and a bonfire had been lit on the far side of the beach. Music played over the speaker system, and as Tony led Gray to the dock, Tiffany announced the fireworks would begin in a few minutes.

Frank and Emma were in inner tubes, which had been tied to the dock. Tony slid into the water next to them and stayed where he could stand to keep from having to fight the current. Gray slid in next to Emma and laughed nervously as she swam over toward Tony.

"It's a little nerve-wracking to swim at night," Gray mumbled as Tony pulled her up next to him. "You never know what rocks—or snakes—may be hiding beneath the surface."

"So far, we've never had any serious accidents," Frank said, his hand linked with Emma's. "Most people are pretty cautious."

A younger man jumped from the cliff and hit the water with a loud splash. A hum of disapproval washed over the crowd. Frank turned in his tube to face Gray.

"I said *most* people."

A loud whistle filled the night air, and a firework burst into a colorful array of light above them. Tony pulled Gray close enough that she could rest her head on his chest. The fireworks display lit the night sky, its various flashes of color reflecting off the river's surface.

For the second time in her life, Gray stared up at the night sky next to a man who treasured her heart. As the fireworks concluded and everyone began to swim again, Gray and Tony stayed together for a moment, cherishing the night and the relationship that had begun. The stars took over the night sky, and Gray thought back to the night when she sat feet away from where she was now and looked up at the same beautiful sky above her.

27

Black

Tony opened the front door for Gray and she stepped into Vera's modest, country-style home, fighting reluctance in her mind. A week had passed since the Fourth of July party, and Tony had come by the apartment to invite her to Vera and Isaac's house for dinner three nights ago. Since then, she had spent her time cooped up in the apartment alone, contemplating their relationship and the risks involved. She could sense the doubt rising, the fear taking root. The walls of self-preservation being built back up.

Gray genuinely loved Tony. Unlike in her past relationship, Gray didn't love him with lust or out of a desire to have someone affirm her value and worth. She had discovered that her love for Tony was a blossom off the tree of her faith, a creation that stemmed from the love she had for God. But she was concerned she could never give Tony what he wanted; she would never be the companion he would need.

Her thoughts consumed her as she watched Vera walk down the hallway of the two-story home. "Good evening." She opened her arms and embraced Gray. "I'm so glad you came. We're happy you finally took us up on our offer for dinner." Vera winked at Gray and squeezed her hand.

A brown leather couch and loveseat were seated around a large fireplace. The decorations were rustic and southern, and Vera invited Tony and Gray to sit down.

"What can I get you to drink? Soda, lemonade, water, or juice?"

Gray settled onto the couch next to where Tony had sat down. "I'll have lemonade, please."

"Me too. Thank you."

When Vera left, Tony slipped his hand over hers. "The same fear is in your eyes again today."

Gray looked away.

Tony's thumb rubbed the back of her hand and he sat back in the chair. "Don't worry. I'm not going to pressure you. If you want to talk to me about it, you know I'm here. I'm not going to *tell* you that you don't have to be scared. I would rather show you."

With a deep breath, Gray tried to let her fears dissipate, but they still threatened to choke her.

Vera entered the room carrying two glasses of lemonade. She set the glasses on coasters on top of a large, wood coffee table in front of the couch and then settled into the loveseat across from them.

"Isaac is grilling the meat and veggies now. I let him know you are here." Vera shot Tony a glance that Gray didn't understand, but Tony did. He ducked his head and cleared his throat.

"Your home is beautiful." Gray admired the modest decor.

"Would you like an official tour?" Vera asked.

"I would love to see the rest of the house."

As Vera showed Gray their home, Tony slipped out onto the deck with Isaac. When Vera and Gray joined them, the two men sat at the large, glass patio table. Isaac stood to greet Gray before he returned to his station next to the barbecue pit.

The house sat on two hundred acres, and Gray saw the wooded part of their property from where she stood. The deck overlooked an expansive backyard followed by a small barn and pasture enclosed with a white fence. Two horses stood out in the pasture, grazing.

"This is only part of the porch," Tony stood close to Gray. "The porch wraps around the house. It offers a three-sixty view of the property. In my opinion, the porch is the best part of the house."

They walked together hand in hand around the house. The woods shrouded the house and offered shade and privacy. The front porch had four wicker chairs lining the wall. Live potted plants and fern hanging baskets added to the southern charm.

"You're right." Gray imagined sitting out in the chairs at night, a small blanket over her lap as she stared out into the dimly lit yard. "The porch is the best part of the house. The whole house is beautiful and very welcoming."

"Food's ready!" Isaac called around the corner.

The two of them made their way back to the deck.

"I thought it would be nice to eat outside since the weather is so beautiful today. Is that all right?" Vera set her glass on the patio table.

"That sounds great." Gray set her glass next to Tony's, and they helped Vera prepare the table while Isaac served the meat and vegetables. In a moment, the table was neatly set and a basket of rolls sat in the center of the table, covered with a cloth to keep the buns warm and soft.

"Vera makes the best homemade bread." Tony held Vera's gaze for a moment as he pulled Gray's chair out for her.

"He says that because he was here when I first started trying to make my own bread." Vera laughed and took a seat next to Isaac. "We went through many bad batches before I got it right."

Tony sat next to Gray. "Yes, but it was well worth it."

Isaac blessed the food, and Vera served everyone their plates. The dinner conversation was casual and relaxed, and the four of them sat at the table long after the food was gone. When they stood, Gray helped Vera clear the table, and they washed the dishes together as Tony and Isaac cleaned the grill.

Isaac was a reserved man. He was soft spoken and seemed to prefer to observe rather than lead in conversation. During dinner, Gray had noticed that, while he often remained silent, when Isaac did choose to speak, his words were well thought out and carefully chosen. When Isaac spoke, people listened because his words held power. As she helped Vera with the dishes, Gray thought about how light conversation didn't come naturally to her, and she envied Isaac's demeanor. She rinsed the last dish, put it on the drying rack, and excused herself to the restroom.

In the bathroom, she stood in front of the mirror for a long time and stared at her reflection. Today she had chosen to wear a black, cotton dress, her hair pinned back. The woman who stared back at her wore a look of concern and worry, her eyebrows creased and lips pulled tight. Gray's hands trembled.

"I haven't been down to check on them since this morning." Isaac was speaking to Tony when Gray returned.

"I don't mind riding down to take care of them." Tony put his arm around Gray's waist when she approached.

The gesture made her want to lean into him, feel his arms around her. His embrace always had a way of making her feel secure.

"The food is in the cooler on the back of the four-wheeler." Vera joined them as Isaac spoke. "Thank you, Tony."

"No problem."

The exchange ended, and Isaac took Vera's hand and walked inside but left the patio door open, closing the screen door instead. The cool summer night's air was refreshing, and the sounds of bullfrogs and crickets filled the air.

"Vera and Isaac breed chocolate labs, and their dog just had a litter five weeks ago. I offered to ride down to check on them and feed them for the night." Tony moved away from the rail and offered his hand. "Would you like to come with me?"

Gray had never ridden a four-wheeler before. "Of course."

They walked around the deck to a small stairway off the side of the house. A red four-wheeler was parked next to the porch, the key in the ignition. Tony slid in first and started the engine. Gray was relieved she had chosen to wear a dress short enough not to have to hike it up as she straddled the seat but long and full enough to keep modest as she sat behind Tony.

"Don't we need helmets?" Gray had to raise her voice to be heard above the engine.

Tony chuckled. "I'll drive safe. Just hang on."

The two of them made their way across the backyard and rode along the fence line towards the barn. A large chocolate lab ran alongside the four-wheeler. The horses made their way toward the barn as well.

The barn was well kept. Inside, there were two stalls to one side and a tack room off the other. Two wooden benches lined the wall opposite the stables, and large double doors were open to the pasture beyond. In the open doorway, a gate blocked the horses from entering the barn. Both horses stood on the other side of the gate, and one whinnied as Tony approached.

"This is Mabel." He ran his hands along the horse's face. Mabel was a white horse, and she nuzzled Tony as he gave her attention. "And this is Brute."

The horse deserved the name. He was taller and more thickly built than Mabel. Tony unlatched the gate and led Brute to the nearest open stall. After both horses were in their stalls, he checked that they both had food and water.

Gray stood by the door and watched Tony at work.

"Would you like to pet them? They don't bite." He smiled.

"Sure."

She cautiously approached Mabel's stall and stroked the horse's muzzle.

"She's so soft." Gray ran her hands along Mabel's face.

"Have you touched a horse before?"

Gray shook her head.

Brute snorted and pawed at the stall door with his hooves.

"Just wait, she'll visit you, too." Tony laughed. "They get jealous."

Brute poked his head between the bars and let Gray rub along his face and behind his ears.

"They are beautiful."

Brute pulled his head back into the stall to get a drink of water. Tony walked to the tack room, and when he opened the door, six brown puppies bounded up to them.

"That's Mama over there." An adult dog stood from where she lay on a bed of straw in the corner of the room and greeted them. "The dog running alongside of us earlier was her mate, Bear. And these are their puppies."

Gray knelt and let the puppies jump onto her lap and lick her arms. "They're adorable."

A row of water and food bowls hung from the wall, to keep them out of the dirt and debris. Tony filled each bowl and checked the water. Gray sat in a bench against the wall and watched the puppies play. Tony sat next to her, and Mama made her way over to him and then placed her head in his hand. He petted her, and she wagged her tail in response.

"I've never had a dog." The little bundles of energy played around Gray's feet. "I didn't know they were this energetic as puppies! I thought they were cuddly."

"It takes them a couple years to really settle down."

One puppy sat off away from the rest of the group and watched its siblings as they played. Tony shook his head. "That one has always been different. Isaac didn't think he would make it the night the litter was born. He's always been the runt, and his energy is much lower than the others. They will have a harder time finding a home for him."

"Poor guy." Gray watched the puppy as he lay down in the straw, content to sit back and watch the fun.

"I think he'll be all right." Tony took the puppy into his hands. When Tony sat back down next to Gray, the puppy curled up in Tony's hands, appreciating the warmth and attention. Gray stroked the puppy's head, behind his tiny ears. The puppy stretched and licked Gray's fingers as he lay in Tony's hands.

"He's sweet." Gray rubbed his belly as one last treat before Tony set him down. "I think he'll be all right, too. No one can say no to that adorable face."

When they stepped out into the cool night air, Gray wrapped her arms around her waist to conserve heat. This time the ride back to the house was much cooler, and Gray was thankful to hold onto Tony. The four-wheeler rolled to a stop next to the porch, and once inside the house, Vera looked up from where she sat, cuddled up on the sectional couch next to Isaac watching television. "There is chocolate cake on the counter. Help yourself. Milk is in the fridge."

"Thank you."

Tony and Gray washed their hands in the kitchen, and then Tony cut Gray a piece of cake before serving himself. Gray poured them both a glass of milk. Tony took his plate and glass and headed out to the deck. They settled into patio chairs overlooking the backyard.

"This is how I imagined your life growing up." Gray motioned around her. "Having it all. Nice house, home-cooked meals with dessert. Family blessings before the meals. The perfect, conventional family."

Tony didn't speak as he sat next to her.

Gray set the plate on the table and sat back in her chair. "I can't imagine what it would have been like to grow up in a home like this. After my father died, I lived with my alcoholic, abusive mom and her boyfriend until I was sixteen. That's when I moved in with Tyler. Nothing was normal after my father passed away."

"What was he like?" Tony's voice was soft, and he took her hand into his.

"You would have liked him. My dad was a Christian. And not just the kind that goes to church on holidays. He loved God and it showed. He never cursed or raised his voice to me, even when I pushed him to the limits." Gray laughed. "He was a doctor and started a clinic in the city for people with low income or who couldn't afford health insurance. After he found out my mom was abusing me, using drugs, and having an affair, he left her, and we moved to the city together. We lived together in the city for seven years before he died, and those were the best seven years of my life."

A smile graced her lips. "He did the best he could, you know? My mom didn't want anything to do with us, so he played the role of a mother and a father, which was hard for him, especially because he spent so much time at the clinic. But we never missed a church service, and he read the Bible with me every night before bed. On the warm summer nights, we would sit out on our porch swing, and he would read to me. Those are some of my favorite memories with him."

The crickets chirped in the distance, and the night breeze picked up. Gray shivered and rubbed her hands along her arms.

"I'm going to take these inside." Tony collected the plates and cups before he stood. "I'll be right back."

Gray sat alone on the deck in the dark night. She thought about her father and how seldom she spoke about him. Tyler had never asked her about her dad, and she wondered if he even remembered his name. She heard Tony say something to his aunt and uncle before the screen door slid open again.

When he walked up beside her, he held out a large, zip-up hoodie. "I'm sure it will be big on you, but it will keep you warm. It's mine."

"Thank you." Gray put the hoodie on and Tony's rustic, earthy smell engulfed her.

"Would you like to see Vera's garden?" The darkness hid Tony's face, and Gray nodded, following Tony's lead while wrapped in his hoodie.

28

White

Tony and Gray cut across the lawn to a small stone path. Solar-lit garden lights cast a faint glow on the path, and a small pergola guarded the entry to a manicured and expansive garden. Stonework had been added for dimension, and in the center of the garden was a small pond. Vines wound up the trunks of the surrounding trees, and honeysuckle's sweet scent filled the night air. In the light from the full moon and the few garden lights along the path, Tony stopped to point out the wildflowers and rosebushes.

"This is Vera's passion."

"It's beautiful." Gray's voice was just a whisper.

Tony led Gray over to a patch of grass next to the pond where the hill made a slight incline.

"This is my favorite place. I used to lay here at night and try to count the stars." Tony held out his hand to help Gray sit before he lowered himself beside her. The pond reflected the stars off the glassy surface. Tony took Gray's hand into his.

"Your hand is shaking." His voice was soft.

"There is so much you don't know, Tony." Her voice cracked as she spoke. "The closer I move toward you and your family, the more I am terrified of hurting you. Of hurting myself. I tried for so long to stay away and not make any friends, to not grow close to anyone when I moved, but you guys made it impossible." She laughed. "You are perfect, and you deserve someone who—"

Tony interrupted her as he pulled her closer. "Gray, you're not any worse than me. Everyone makes mistakes. Everyone has scars."

Gray's laugh carried no humor. "Even you?"

A frog jumped into the pond and sent a ripple across the surface. Tony lay back into the soft grass, his arms behind his head as he stared up at the sky. "Even me."

The tone in his voice was a mix of sorrow and anger, and Gray didn't speak.

"My life isn't what you think it is, Gray." Tony's kept his eyes fixed on the sky above him. "Haven't you ever wondered where my parents are?"

He glanced at her for a moment before he continued.

"My mom got pregnant young. I've never met my dad. I was told he lives somewhere in Canada now." His voice was pinched as Tony fought the bitterness that seemed to always be waiting for him, just beneath the surface. "I lived with my mom, but she was a career-driven woman and didn't want a kid to hold her back. I spent most of my childhood visiting my grandparents, my aunt and uncle, or in daycare. When she got a promotion traveling monthly from California to Paris for a big-shot designer, it was just the excuse she needed to unload me. Vera and Isaac offered to let me stay with them for a weekend. A weekend turned into a week, a month, a year, and I never left. I see my mom once a year around Christmas."

"I'm sorry." Gray touched his arm. "I just assumed..." she trailed off.

Tony put his hand on hers. He rarely spoke about his childhood, but most people in town already knew. Nothing makes headline news in small town gossip like a woman abandoning her son to chase big city dreams.

"Vera and Isaac loved me like parents, but I went through a bout of rebellion my senior year. Isaac didn't think I was ready to go on a trip to Florida with my friends for spring break that year, so I snuck out in the middle of the night and met up with my friends. We drove down together, and by the time Vera and Isaac realized I was gone, we were checking into our hotel. I thought—" He sat up, his head in his hands. Shame washed over him in waves. "I was just angry at the world. No matter how much Vera and Isaac loved me, I felt the rejection of my parents every day. I thought I was an adult, and I could make my own decisions, decisions I thought would make me happy, make me feel independent."

Tony shook his head and cleared his throat. "So my friends and I spent the week on the beach, soaking up the sun, surfing, and drinking every night until we threw up. The last night we were there, there was a big party, and a girl I had met on the beach invited me back to her place. One thing led to another, and when I woke up in her hotel room the next morning, I barely remembered the night before. I was in a serious relationship with a girl from school that hadn't come on the trip with us. I cheated on her that night. The entire drive home, I was hungover, and I knew what I had done. I decided I wasn't going to tell my girl-friend. I wasn't going to tell anyone."

Gray didn't speak, she just leaned her head onto his shoulder.

"I kept in touch with the girl in Florida for a few weeks after we got back, mostly because I felt guilty for using her. But then one day she just stopped answering my calls."

Tony struggled with his emotions. He felt sick to his stomach. Gray looped her arm around his waist. The light breeze rustled the leaves of the trees around them, and Tony regained his composure as he stared out into the woods around them. "I found out the night I graduated that she had gotten pregnant and had an abortion. She called me, crying, and after she told me what she had done, she asked me not to contact her anymore and said she was changing her number."

Speaking the words out loud was like a bucket of cold water emptied over Tony. A rush of emotions consumed him.

"I never heard from her again. My girlfriend found out about every-thing and she hated me for what I had done. She moved out of state for college and never spoke to me again. That summer was the worst of my life. I was just like my father. I felt like had made an irresponsible, selfish decision and then abandoned my unborn child and left my mess for that girl to have to face alone. It still haunts me to this day."

A tear slid down Tony's cheek. "I'll never forget the pain in her voice when she called. I know it's not my right to look in from the outside and judge her for that decision. I used her, got her pregnant, and then abandoned her. I can't imagine what she was going through. And I hate myself for the agony my actions caused her."

The tears were falling steadily now. "But I can't help but think about the baby. Was the baby a boy or a girl? What would life be like now if he or she had been born? What kind of a father would I have been? I think about that baby every day.

"I spiraled out of control for a while. Drank a lot." Tony thought back on all the late nights Vera had to pick him up from the bar. "But Isaac and Vera were always there, loving me through it."

Tony and Isaac had spent many evenings walking the tree line beside the garden, talking about life. One evening four years ago, the weight of the shame became too much, and Tony sat on a bench with Isaac, yards away from where he sat now, and broke down. He told Isaac everything, and with a tear in Isaac's eye, his uncle embraced him. Tony had spent the last four years focusing on his music and getting his life together. Relationships had been far from his mind, and he never could have imagined in that moment—sitting on that bench next to his uncle— that he would be lying here tonight next to a woman that didn't fear the dark shadows of his life.

29

Black

Under the night sky, lying in the grass, Gray held Tony in her arms and a tear slid down her cheek onto his T-shirt. She could hear the pain in his voice when he spoke about his past. She felt ignorant for assuming that he had never experienced pain or trauma. Her mother may have abandoned her, but her father had not left by choice. She couldn't imagine the rejection he felt from the willful absence of both of his parents. Gray knew what it was like to allow trauma to fuel her decisions, and she knew what it was like to carry the weight of the shame from those decisions. Her heart broke for Tony.

"What changed?" Her voice was tender.

"When I was twenty-one, I felt exhausted. I felt like I couldn't run from it anymore." He paused for a moment and then wiped the remaining tears from his cheeks. "I gave my heart to Christ and asked Him to undo the mess I had made of my life. I always loved music, and when I got more involved in the church, I became closer friends with Vince, Darren, Pete, Frank, and Jim. We formed the band, and I devoted myself to using music to reach people who are hurting. We used to travel to the city twice a month and play in bars, but the travel expenses became too much."

"That *was* you." Gray sat up and looked at Tony. "You used to play in the bar by my apartment, Riff's. I thought I recognized your music, but I assumed it couldn't have been you."

Tony nodded his head. "We stopped coming to the city last year and decided to focus more on a record deal so we could afford to travel."

All of those nights spent drunk with Audrey and Tyler as Gray fell over herself and let Tyler manipulate her; all of those nights Tony stood a few feet away, close enough to touch as he sang to her, his words calling her to a true and fulfilling Love. The realization was more than she could bear.

Gray lay back into the grass. The full moon hid some of the stars in its luminous light, and Gray closed her eyes as she sketched the scene into her mind. All of that time and Tony was right there. How could she have missed him?

"If only I had known then . . ." her voice trailed off.

"Your past doesn't scare me," Tony said. Gray held his gaze as he spoke. "If anything, it makes me care for you more deeply. You've been through hell, and it didn't break you."

Tony reached out his hand and stroked Gray's cheek. "I love you, Gray."

A small tremor ripped through Gray, and her heart rate doubled. She fought to keep her breath steady as she closed her eyes and let the words sink in. Joy filled her heart, but pain and regret also tore at her.

"If only I had known," Gray whispered. "You were right there all along. If only I had known what I could have had and who I could have been. If only I had known how dead I was and how much more was waiting for me—standing right in front of me. I wish I could have run into your arms the first night you ever played at the bar. Can you imagine? What if we *had* bumped into each other there? What if we had struck up a conversation? What if we. . ." The pain and sorrow for what she had missed because of the choices she had made was more than she could take.

"It wasn't the right time. You're here now." Tony's voice was quiet. "God had a plan all along."

His words echoed through her mind. *You're here now.* She had been so foolish to keep him at bay for so long. God gave her this love and this chance now, and she had almost ruined it out of fear.

"I love you." Her voice was a coarse whisper. "More than I have ever loved in my life and in a way that I never imagined I could love. I love you, Tony."

Tony brought his hand to her face and traced her jawbone with his thumb until she leaned closer. He brushed the hair from her face as he leaned down, and his lips met hers. The kiss was tender. After a moment he pulled away and kissed her forehead once as his hand brushed her cheek. Gray moved to rest her head on his chest, and she listened to the steady thump of his heartbeat, thanking God for each beat He gave her with Tony.

Unsure of how much time had passed by, Tony was the first to move. He ran his hand across her back. "We should make our way to the house."

The lights inside had been turned down, and Vera and Isaac were still on the couch, the television now off and a Bible open between them.

Everyone said their goodbyes, and Vera invited Gray to come by whenever she wanted a home-cooked meal. Gray climbed into the Jeep, still wearing Tony's hoodie. The drive to her apartment was quiet, but Tony's hand held hers between shifting gears.

When they pulled up to her apartment, Tony cleared his throat.

"I think I should stay in the car."

Tony would always be a gentleman, and she would never want to put him a situation that would compromise his integrity. She trusted him more with each passing moment.

"That's okay." She opened her door and then turned back to face him. "Thank you for everything. Tonight was very special to me. Your family is wonderful."

"Thank you for spending the evening with me." Tony reached out and brushed her cheek again.

"Good night." Gray stepped out of the Jeep, and then stopped at the bottom of the stairway to wave before she disappeared inside.

30

Black

Sickness washed over Gray, and she spent the day in bed in a vain attempt to try to keep the room from spinning as she moved. The curtains were drawn, and her down comforter was pulled over her head. Under her pillow, her cell phone buzzed. She had turned the ringer on silent earlier that day, and Tony had called once already.

His name flashed across the screen now as she stuffed the phone back under the pillow and hit the ignore button. No doubt he was wondering why she hadn't come to church that morning. Two months had passed since the day at Vera and Isaac's house. Tony had met her at church every Sunday since then, and they sat together when he wasn't leading worship. They spent every weekend together with Tiffany, Darren, Emma, Frank, Carla, Pete, and Vince. Melody and Jim didn't hang around with them much, and Gray wondered if Melody and Tony had shared more than he had let on while they were in Tennessee. There was something about the way Melody looked at Gray when she and Tony were together, something that left Gray feeling uneasy.

Every Sunday after church, Tony and Gray would go to the children's home, and they had made plans to bring them ice cream this afternoon. Last week, they had taken the whole group of children to the city park. The next morning, Gray had started to feel sick, like she had caught the flu.

After they had left the children's home last week, they had driven home together and sat in the Jeep outside of her apartment to talk. They decided to set boundaries for their physical affection. The way they felt for each other was passionate and intense. The more time they spent together, the harder it had become to preserve each other's integrity.

Gray stared out the window of the Jeep and remembered the constant pressure from Tyler to take their relationship to the next level. She was happy to be in a relationship where she felt loved for who she was, not for her sexuality.

Tony ran his thumb along Gray's palm and watched her. "What are you thinking about?"

She looked down at their hands together and frowned. "Tyler."

Tony stiffened beside her. "I'm not sure how I should take that."

"I was thinking about how different the relationship was. The constant pressure and expectations." She met Tony's eyes. "I never slept with him."

Tony seemed puzzled. "But I thought you lived together."

"Don't get me wrong," Gray studied her hands as she spoke. "We crossed some boundaries, but—"

She stopped to think of how to explain herself. "But when he tried to touch me or be intimate with me, I would shut off."

She cleared her throat. "I'm sorry if that's too much information."

"How did he take that? I mean, I just can't imagine a man who is not a Christian and, from what you've told me, isn't the most selfless man, dating someone off and on for five years without having sex."

"At first, it wasn't an issue because he was so much older than me and he was afraid my mom would accuse him of things because she was angry that I left. But as soon as I turned eighteen, there seemed to be this expectation. For a while, he would get really angry with me, called me names sometimes, and even tried to force me once when he was drunk."

Anger flashed across Tony's face, and his grip around her hand tightened.

"But then all of the sudden he didn't care anymore, and I couldn't figure out why. Then I found out he was cheating on me. He had been for a long time with a lot of women. That kind of became our pattern. We would date for a while, he would get bored with me and find someone new, we would break up, and eventually he would come around again and we'd start the cycle over. Honestly, I was upset but it was also almost a relief. I didn't feel obligated anymore. I think he kept coming back because he saw winning me over as a challenge and because my trust fund helped pay his bills, and I kept taking him back because my relationship with him is all I ever really knew of love after my father passed away. As warped as that love actually was, it was still more love than I had felt from my own mother."

The conversation echoed through her thoughts now. Gray usually met Tony for lunch at least once throughout the week, but she had been sick, and the more time she spent cooped up in her apartment fighting the illness, the more time she had to think about their relationship and where it was headed. The dark distance and fear she had kept at bay for so long crept back into her life like a fog, and it was increasingly easy to ignore his calls or Emma's knock at her door.

Her phone vibrated again, and this time she shut it off and fell back to sleep.

- - -

The week had carried on with little improvement. By Wednesday, she was able to drag herself out of bed to eat something. She sat at her kitchen table eating a bowl of ramen noodle soup, when there was a soft knock at her front door. Guilt wrung her stomach as she thought about the times she had ignored Emma over the past week and half, and Gray steadied herself and made her way to the front door.

When she opened the door, Tony stood on the other side.

"Tony." Surprise and alarm stung her tone. The surprise wasn't as much directed at him as the chocolate lab puppy he had tucked under his arm. "What are you doing?"

Sadness and hurt crossed his face at her less-than-loving welcome. "Can I come in?"

Gray looked past him into the hallway for a moment before she opened her door. Tony moved past her into the apartment, and she closed the door behind him. At least she had showered this morning and slipped into an oversized pair of sweatpants and a sweatshirt. Gray sat on the couch. Tony stood by the door for a moment before sitting beside her.

"What are you doing here?" She tried to hide the unjust frustration in her voice.

Tony shook his head while the puppy lay at his side on the couch. "I haven't seen you in almost two weeks, and you are treating me like I'm an annoyance. You haven't answered my calls. You haven't answered the door when Emma came by to check on you. The children's home called Emma when you didn't show up for over a week. I was worried, Gray."

"Worried?" Anger and defensiveness burned through Gray like a fierce fire.

Tony considered his words carefully. "I was worried you had falling back into old habits."

Gray crossed her arms. "What do you mean, 'old habits'?"

Tony leaned back in the couch, defeated. "I was just worried about you, Gray. That's all." He rubbed his forehead, took a deep breath. A beat of silence followed before he spoke again. "I came by to make sure you're alright and to give you this dog. You seemed like you really liked him, so I took him home and I've been working on training him. I was going to surprise you with him last Sunday."

Fear dug its nails deep into her heart. "I don't want a dog." Her voice was pinched and tight. "And don't try to change the subject. Why were you so worried? Did you think I had skipped out of town like I had in

St. Louis? Or that I was locked up in the apartment drinking all day? You still see me as—"

"Stop!" Tony stood to his feet.

Gray's arms dropped to her sides and regret filled her heart as she saw the intense pain in his eyes.

"Do you want to know what I was so worried about, Gray?" His voice was trembling. Before she could respond, Tony reached out and took her left arm into his hand and pulled her sleeve back. Her forearm was held out for them both to see. The scar from the cut had never fully healed, and a dark-purple, jagged line marked her skin now.

"You think I never noticed? The day we painted your apartment, I noticed the bandage, and I knew what it was." He released her arm, and she pulled the sleeve back down and crossed her arms again. When Tony spoke, his voice was lower. "I was terrified that reliving your past with me that afternoon in the Jeep had tapped into emotions you weren't ready to face yet and that you could have been lying in a pool of blood in your bathtub."

The puppy whimpered and sat up from his place on the couch, confused by the tension in the room.

"Forgive me for caring if you were dead or alive."

In one swift motion, Tony swept the dog into his arms and headed out the front door. It closed with a thud behind him. Gray melted into the couch and held her head in her hands as she wept. She pulled her sleeve back and ran her finger along the scar. Some days she wished she had been able to finish the attempt, but then she would read or pray and be filled with a sense of purpose and security.

Not today. Today she looked at the scar, and the last person she wanted to talk with was God.

31

White

The puppy slept soundly in the passenger's seat of the Jeep as Tony headed down the backroads. Belle hadn't changed much over the years and he knew the path of each hidden dirt road. The weather was beginning to change, and the leaves of the oak trees and maples were turning to vibrant shades of orange and red. A breeze swept through their branches and the leaves flickered, like rows of fiery torches guiding his path, as Tony drove to clear his mind.

The look of disappointment on Gray's face when she opened her front door to see him standing at her doorstep flashed through Tony's mind.

When Tony hadn't heard from Gray, he wasn't worried at first. He knew she had been feeling sick and assumed she just wanted to rest. But after another week had gone by, his concern grew. When Emma mentioned that she hadn't seen or heard from Gray either, a terrifying feeling came over him. He pushed the thoughts from his mind. Another day passed with no word. Tony had tossed and turned in his bed, restless and unable to sleep.

On his drive to her apartment, his mind couldn't help but wander to images of finding her lifeless in her bathroom. He had to fight the panic as he steeled himself for that possibility.

Gray hadn't seemed depressed lately. Sure, some days, she seemed a little distant, but it hadn't been anything alarming. But he had seen the scar on her wrist. Tony went over their conversation in the Jeep in his mind and couldn't put the pieces together. He couldn't convince himself that she would do that. He couldn't convince himself that she wouldn't reach out to him if she struggled with those thoughts. But what other explanation could there have been? Why would she just disappear?

He wracked his brain for answers but kept coming back to that image in his mind.

When she answered the door, a flood of relief washed over him. He wanted to throw his arms around her in that moment, hold her close. But the look on her face kept him from moving.

Your father left you. Your mother left you. They all leave eventually. The words were the subtle voice of insecurity that haunted him.

Tony shook his head and gripped his steering wheel tighter. He knew there wasn't truth behind those words. He didn't understand why Gray was pushing him away and it hurt, but he knew there was more to the story than he could see in that moment.

He knew Gray. And Tony knew that whatever she was going through, she needed the space to face it alone. He would respect her privacy.

The puppy woke and turned his head to Tony and let out a whimper.

"It's alright, buddy," Tony said, petting the dog with his free hand. "It's not you. She just isn't ready yet. Give her time."

32

Black

Another week went by, and the sickness passed. Gray still felt weak, but Emma had come by and asked her to join her for grocery shopping, so she mustered up energy. Before they went to the store, Emma took Gray out to lunch, and Gray told her about her past struggle with depression. Emma prayed with her and after they brought their groceries home, Emma invited Gray over. They spent the rest of the day together watching movies and eating ice cream.

At the end of the day, Gray felt stronger than she had that morning, and she read her Bible at home that night. Tony remained in the back of her mind. She still couldn't bring herself to call him. She was ashamed of the way she had behaved toward him and afraid she had done irreversible damage to their relationship over the last few weeks.

The truth is that Gray was damaged by her past, in more ways than one. And as much as she loved Tony, she knew that ending their relationship was the right thing to do. If she loved him, how could ask him to be there for her when she knew deep down, it would only end in pain? No man could bear her burdens for her, and what loving woman would put that weight on another person's shoulders?

Loving Tony meant letting him go.

The next morning, Gray woke up early enough to meet Vera under the porch for her morning cup of coffee. Fall came like a soft whisper over the small town, and the temperatures outside were chilly. The surrounding trees had turned beautiful shades of auburn, gold, and orange. Vera talked about the upcoming events at church and Isaac, but Gray noticed she was careful not to mention Tony. She was sure Vera knew about their argument and the way Gray had treated her nephew.

When the coffee was finished, Vera smiled at Gray and patted her hand. She let her know she and Isaac were praying for her and that they had missed her at church and hoped she was feeling better. Vera went to work inside the flower shop, and Gray made her way up the stairs into her apartment. More than ever, she missed Tony and longed to pick up the phone and talk with him for hours like they used to, but she knew they would never talk like that again.

If only he knew everything... she thought.

He wouldn't love her if he knew the real reason why she had never slept with Tyler. If he knew that intimacy with a man terrified her and even the idea of it sent her into a panic attack.

Gray knew she needed to tell Tony about the night her father died, but she couldn't bring herself to face that time in her life yet. It was a night she never relived by choice, and no matter how strong her faith had grown, the fear still lived dormant in the back of her mind.

The next two days dragged by uneventfully, and that Friday night, Gray sat awake in bed, her Bible in her lap, staring out her bedroom window at the river below. She used to spend her Friday nights with Tony. The last Friday they had spent together they had gone on a double date with Emma and Frank to eat dinner at a local burger joint before they headed to the theaters to catch the latest late-night movie. Tony and Gray shared popcorn and a soda, and she had thrown popcorn at him when he made fun of her for getting choked up at the end of the movie.

Gray ached to feel his hand in hers again and to hear the sound of his laughter. As she sat cross-legged on her bed, lost in memories, there was a soft knock at the door. Butterflies filled her stomach, and she jumped out of her bed. Gray glanced at the clock. It was just past ten o'clock.

After she checked her reflection in the mirror, Gray moaned. She was in a pair of thick leggings and an oversized knit shirt she had purchased from Carla's store, but her hair was a mess, and she looked haggard. A quick pinch on her cheeks added a little blush, and then Gray ran her hands down her shirt in an attempt to gather her composure. Gray took a deep breath before she opened the door.

"Surprise!" Carla, Tiffany, Emma, and Melody stood in the hallway.

Gray's heart sank, and she was sure her smile had faded also, but she couldn't prevent the reaction.

Emma cast her a knowing glance, then bypassed the moment with a step into the apartment. "We have come to kidnap you."

"Kidnap me?" Gray's eyes lingered on Melody for a second too long. Melody had decided to transfer to a college closer to Belle and rented an apartment five miles outside of town.

"Yes." Emma took both of Gray's hands into her own. "We are having a wild girl's night, and you are coming with us whether you want to or not."

Gray sighed and leaned her head back, thankful for the break away from her misery. "No, I want to. Please, kidnap me."

Tiffany went through Gray's closet. She pulled out Gray's thick wool coat and matching black woven boots. "You'll want these. It's pretty cold out there."

"Out there?" Gray looked at Emma, confused, while Tiffany pulled the coat on over her and then added an orange scarf from the closet. With Tiffany's guidance, Gray slipped her feet into one boot and then the other.

"You'll see."

Before Gray could gather more information, the four women swept her out of her apartment, making sure to lock up behind her. Carla and Melody chatted as they walked behind her down the narrow stairwell; Tiffany and Emma snickered in front of her. In a rush, they all packed into Melody's mid-size SUV, and it was then Gray noticed the toilet paper, cooler, and dodgeball in the back of the car.

"Where are we going?"

Melody slid behind the wheel, and Gray caught a cold glare from her in the rear-view mirror.

"We are going to park to play an intense game of kickball," Emma's voice sang the words. "Then we may go out and vandalize one or two people's homes."

"Vandalize?" Gray studied Emma's face to see if she was serious. Destruction of personal property was the last thing she expected from Emma.

"You've never toilet papered someone's house?" Tiffany looked at her, awestruck.

Gray shook her head.

"It's not as bad as it sounds," Carla said from the passenger's seat. "We only toilet paper our friends. It's more like a running joke between us."

A moment later they pulled into the city park, and Melody parked the car on the far side of the baseball fields in the darkest area she could find.

"The park is closed after dark," Emma explained as they unloaded a cooler from the trunk. Carla grabbed the dodgeball, and they made their way to one of the fields.

Carla agreed to be the pitcher for both teams since there were an uneven number of girls. Tiffany and Melody were on a team together, and Emma and Gray were the opposing team. Tiffany and Melody were up to kick first, and Melody sent one straight to Gray, who caught it mid-air. Melody was automatically out, and she shot Gray a sour look before she returned to her place next to Tiffany. The first round was over after Tiffany kicked a home run. Emma was the first up to kick, and Gray retrieved a soda from the cooler as she waited for her turn. By the fourth inning, Gray and Emma were up five runs, and Melody's patience for Gray seemed to wear thinner by the moment.

Just as Gray stepped up to home plate, Tiffany shouted, "Cops!" from where she stood in the outfield. The five girls ran and gathered under the seclusion of a tree near the parking lot, but it was too late, and the police car rolled to a stop in front of them.

Emma stepped forward as the window rolled down.

"Emma, are you guys at it again? You know the park closes at dusk." A man's voice carried from the dark car. The dome light inside flicked on, and a man who looked to be around their age was dressed in his uniform as he smiled from behind the steering wheel. "I don't know why you guys even bother trying to hide. You're not discreet. It's not like you'd get in trouble anyways."

"We can pretend we're walking on the wild side, can't we?"

The officer laughed. "I can write you a ticket for trespassing if you want."

"No, thank you."

"I'm sure this isn't the only event you have planned for the night." The dome light flipped off in the officer's car. "Just stay out of my yard tonight, okay?"

"We have gotten you too many times by now, Tim," Emma joked. "You're safe."

Emma waved as the officer rolled his window up and drove away.

The game resumed with Gray up to kick. With a good run, Gray kicked the ball and sent it high into the air, but the distance was lacking. Melody homed in on the ball and caught it after it bounced off the grass. The two women ran full speed for first base, and at the last minute, Melody collided with Gray with a force that knocked the wind out of her.

Tiffany, Carla, and Emma were at her side as Gray shoved Melody off her. In one quick motion, Gray rolled to her side and pushed herself to sit up, her body cramping in pain. Gray shoved Melody again. "What's your problem?"

"It's just a game," Melody said.

"No, don't pretend like it's not more than that. I'm not oblivious to your attitude toward me. You have a problem with me, and you need to get over it. I haven't done anything to you."

Melody shoved Gray back out of her face. "Me get over it? Get over yourself! You're miserable, we all know it because you're constantly walking around with a chip on your shoulder and your sad puppy dog eyes trying to act tough and cold. It's getting old! You hide behind this poor, tormented girl mask and use it as an excuse to treat your friends like trash. I'm sorry I'm the only one in this town willing to say it," she shouted at Gray. "You have this amazing group of friends who love you and you had the chance to be with a great guy and you just used him and then discarded him! Do you have any idea—"

At the realization of what she had said, Melody stopped herself and sat back in the grass. "You don't deserve him." Her voice was low. "You don't even care enough to fight for what he's trying to hand over to you on a silver platter. It makes me sick."

Silence fell over the group as they stood over the two women. The anger drained from Gray's blood, and regret filled her heart instead. The longing for Tony's presence overwhelmed her again, and without a word, Gray pushed herself to her feet, brushed herself off, and headed toward the cooler. Emma walked with her, while Carla and Tiffany stayed to help Melody to her feet.

"What she said—that's her opinion. None of us feel that way. I hope you know that." Emma said once they were earshot from the other girls. "Are you okay?"

"I'm fine. It's not a big deal. I just want to drop it. I'm not mad at her or anything." Gray retrieved another can of soda from the cooler. She popped the top open and drank the contents.

Emma nodded her head. "Okay. Let's call it a game and grab something to eat."

At the mention of food, Gray's stomach growled. "That sounds good." She offered Emma a weak smile.

Emma hugged Gray and then started to walk back to the field.

"Emma?"

She stopped and looked at Gray.

Gray's voice caught in her throat. "I know I'm not always a good friend. I'm sorry. I care about you guys a lot, and..." her voice trailed off.

Emma smiled. "I know. We all love you. No one who truly knows your heart is judging you or holding anything against you. Not a single one of us."

A few minutes later, they all loaded their stuff into the car. Melody came up to Gray and stared at the ground. "I'm sorry for my attitude. It wasn't mature and I apologize. What you do with your personal life is your business. It's just hard . . ."

"I know." Gray fidgeted with the tab on her soda. "I had a feeling you cared for him more than you let on. I'm sorry, too."

When their eyes met, Melody nodded her head twice before she turned away and slid into the car behind the steering wheel. Once the cooler was packed, Gray slid into her seat next to Emma, and they headed for the twenty-four-hour diner on the other side of town. They filled their stomachs with greasy burgers and fried food and plotted their toilet paper attack, settling on Darren as their victim. Darren had never been toilet papered before because Tiffany had always protected him, but tonight she felt especially affable, and everyone else they thought of had already been victim more than once. Melody remained withdrawn and rarely added to the conversation.

Melody followed Tiffany's directions and wound through the back roads before the SUV came to a stop on a small gravel road. There wasn't a house in sight, and Gray wondered out loud about this as Emma passed out rolls of toilet paper.

"We park far enough down the street that we can't be detected, but close enough that it's not a far run if we get caught." Tiffany stuffed rolls of toilet paper into her shirt.

"Get caught? What happens if we're caught?"

Tiffany shrugged her shoulders. "We've had people spray us with their hoses or chase us in their car. One guy shot at us with his paintball gun. It depends on the person, I guess. It's all in good humor though."

"Yea, sounds like it." Gray took the toilet paper Emma handed her. "So, what do we do if someone comes outside?"

"Run for the car."

Carla turned in her seat, her arms loaded with toilet paper. "Ready?"

"Ready," the other women answered. Gray just stared down at her toilet paper.

They all crept out into the dark night, and Gray fell in step behind Emma down the gravel drive. The trees opened to a large yard with a log cabin built away from the road. Emma, Tiffany, Carla, and Melody went to work, unraveling their toilet paper and tossing the rolls over trees and bushes. Gray papered the bushes around the house. Adrenaline pumped through her veins as more time passed by and thoughts of paintball guns being shot at her filled her mind.

Tiffany and Melody waited at the far end of the yard, out of toilet paper. Gray jogged up beside them as Emma and Carla finished the rolls they had. With a glance out over the yard, Gray stifled a laugh. The lawn looked eerie as strands of toilet paper swayed in the wind from the tall trees lining the yard. Emma wound toilet paper around the railing of the front porch when a dog inside of the house barked. A light flicked on, and Carla and Emma dropped their rolls and bolted.

The front door swung open, and Darren emerged into the porch light wearing nothing but his boxers. "Tiffany! You are going to help me clean this in the morning!"

Once Emma and Carla had caught up to them, all the women ran down the street, headed for their car. They all piled inside, and Melody turned the key, the engine coming to life. As her headlights turned on, they saw Darren as he ran barefoot down the gravel road. He had pulled a pair of shorts on but had forgotten shoes.

With a squeal, Melody threw the car into drive and cut the wheel hard, making a U-turn in the middle of the street, and they sped away, leaving Darren in their dust, shouting after them.

The women laughed the rest of the drive home. They all clamored up the stairs to Emma's apartment and crashed on the makeshift beds

Emma had set up in the middle of her living room. As she settled under her covers, Gray felt joy and peace for the first time in weeks.

33

Black

The church hosted an annual Fall Festival at the park on the last Saturday of October, which happened to be Halloween this year. Gray lay in her bed and stared at the costume that Carla had made for her. The lingering exhaustion from the flu had returned, full force, and she willed her body to move. The costume was a medieval dress with lace trim and matching black boots.

Gray debated whether she should attend the party. More than the residual effects of illness hindering her, the thought that she might see Tony at the party made Gray nervous. It was easy enough to avoid Tony at church when she slipped in just after the service started while he was on stage leading worship and left as soon as the service ended while he was on stage leading the closing song. But she knew he would be at the party tonight, and she didn't feel ready to face him. The more time went by, the more she needed concrete answers to give him before they met again. She needed to be able to tell him the truth, and that was something she couldn't bring herself to do yet.

The fear of that night haunted her thoughts, and she decided going to the party was less terrifying than staying home alone with the demons threatening to break loose. Gray sat up, dizzy. She sank into bed again and decided to take a nap before she left. As she drifted off to sleep, the shadows in her mind crept forward and called to her.

"*Gray . . .*"

"*Gray . . .*"

This time it was a woman's voice.

"*Are you here to see your father?*" *the secretary asked from behind the sliding glass window. The window had information about the small doctor's office taped across the glass along with other pages about co-pays. Gray always found it strange because her father ran a practice for low-income people without insurance and rarely asked for payment.*

"*I'm just waiting for him to get off work,*" *Gray said.* "*He's driving me to my volleyball game.*"

The woman smiled. "*I'll let him know you are here when he is finished with his current patient.*"

"*Thanks.*"

A song by Garth Brooks played over the small radio, which sat on the counter near the window. Gray hummed along with the song as she flipped through the stack of magazines left on the coffee table in the center of the waiting room. Settling on Vogue, *Gray sank into a chair near the office door. Only then did she notice the man who sat on the other side of the room. A small shiver ran down her spine as her eyes caught his, and he looked her figure over slowly.*

Gray shifted in her chair and turned away from the man. The minutes ticked by before the door leading back to his office swung open, and her father stepped into the waiting room. A smile lit her father's face at the sight of his daughter, and she jumped to her feet, running over to meet him.

"*I'm sorry, Mr. Forrester, I'll be with you in one moment,*" *her father said to the man sitting in the chair across the room.*

Mr. Forrester.

Mr. Forrester.

Mr. Forrester.

The name echoed through her mind, and Gray jerked awake in a cold sweat. Her hands trembled as she stumbled out of bed. She had to get out of the apartment. Her alarm clock read 11:30 p.m. Her heart sank at the realization she had missed the party, and she was left to face her demons alone. Gray grabbed her phone and fell to a crumple on the floor. She pulled her knees to her chest as her eyes darted around the room.

She punched the only number she could think of into the keypad and pressed the phone to her ear. It rang eight times before Tony's voicemail picked up.

"Tony, it's me. I—" Her voice cracked as she spoke, and she hyperventilated. She tried to calm herself and pushed herself up to slide her feet into a pair of boots. She pulled her jacket on before she ran out into the hallway and stumbled down the stairwell. She was halfway to the door before she thought about Emma. After she ran back up the stairs, Gray knocked on Emma's door. When no one answered, she ran down the stairs out into the street. Emma's car wasn't parked in its usual spot, and the lights were still off inside the apartment.

Gray instinctively headed in the direction of Tony's house. He lived on the other side of town, but she would walk all night to get there if she needed to.

As she walked down the street, Gray heard the crowd from the bar bursting with life, hosting a party of their own. The cottonmouth returned and turned her tongue to sand as she thought about her nights in the bar. Her hands still trembled from fear, and she paused on the sidewalk. She fought the urge to throw a Jack and Coke back and let the contents numb her mind. A minute ticked by as Gray fought her desires before she settled on stepping inside to buy a pack of cigarettes. Though she had given up smoking, she reasoned it was okay if she just had one or two to calm her nerves. Tobacco was better than buying the drink she craved.

A wet T-shirt contest was in full swing, and a group of men stood around the women on the bar, as they cheered them on. Gray leaned past the men to the bartender.

"I just need a pack of cigarettes."

The bartender stared at Gray with a grin on his face. "Didn't you read the sign?"

"What sign?" Gray swallowed her frustration, shouting above the music.

The bartender pointed to a sign taped to the bar. Gray's eyes skimmed the sign. Free drinks for women who participated in the least-dressed costume contest.

"You're a little overdressed, aren't you?" He winked.

Gray ground her teeth together. "I just need a pack of cigarettes." She tossed a fifty-dollar bill at him.

The man disappeared for a moment and returned with the pack, her change and a Jack and Coke. Her mouth watered.

"Compliments of the man across the bar. Lighten up." The bartender disappeared again.

Gray saw Devon as he raised his glass toward her, a cocky grin on his face. She stared at the drink for a minute before she settled into the empty bar stool. The tremble in her hands worsened, and her mouth burned with desire. The flashback replayed in her mind, pushing her over the edge.

What did it matter anyway?

She threw the drink back and felt the alcohol burn as it ran down her chest. Ripping the cigarettes open, she stuck one in her mouth.

"Need a light?" Devon leaned over her and offered her his lighter.

Gray thanked him as she lit her cigarette, and then handed the lighter back to him.

"It's all right, hang onto it. I've got more."

His eyes were bloodshot, and Gray dropped the lighter on the counter next to her. She handed the bartender more cash, and he refilled her glass. The effects of the liquor worked quickly, since she had been dry for so long and hadn't eaten all day. She took another drag of her cigarette.

Devon leaned in toward her. "So, are you going to tell me your name this time?"

"No," she said and threw back another glass.

"Ouch." He laughed and told the bartender to put the next drink on his tab.

"I have a boyfriend."

It wasn't a total lie.

"Then he's a terrible boyfriend. Where is he now? You are obviously upset." Devon slurred his words.

Gray ignored him and finished her drink. She slid the bartender cash and ordered a shot. After a shot of Jack, Gray took a break, sitting back on her stool, smoking her cigarette. The scene blurred by in a mix of country music and bar fights as the night wore on. She had one more drink and Gray was about to gather her things to leave, when a popular country music song blared over the speaker system. One of the girls on the bar knocked a man's drink over. The man swore and demanded she buy him a new drink. The scene amused Gray, and she laughed and shook her head.

The room spun, and Gray knew she had pushed herself too far. Her hands out in front of her, she steadied herself on the bar.

"Here." Devon held her pack out for her. Gray snatched the pack from his hands, shoved another cigarette into her mouth, and fought to steady her hands enough to light it. Once again, Devon leaned in, taking the lighter and flicked it to life. Gray took a puff of the cigarette as he lit the end and then handed the lighter back to Gray.

"Thanks," she mumbled, unable to keep her head together. She had to get out of there before she passed out or threw up. Gray stood and held onto the bar for a moment to steady herself before she walked to the door.

"Wait." Devon stumbled to his feet and followed her outside. The door closed behind them. Gray stumbled down the street and tried to keep her feet under her.

Tony's house. That's where she was going, right? Was this the right direction? Or was it the other way?

"You can't leave yet. You still haven't told me your name," Devon said as he stumbled along behind her.

Gray waved him off, about to step out into the street, when Devon grabbed her hand and pulled her toward the back of the building. Gray struggled against him. Her cigarette fell from her hand as she fought to free her arm. "What are you doing?"

He pushed her against the wall and leaned into Gray as he spoke, a big grin plastered across his face. "Come on. I know you're just acting tough to drive me crazy. It's working. Do you know how often I have thought about you since the last time you were here?"

"Get off me." Panic exploded through Gray's mind, but her thoughts were clouded by the alcohol, and she couldn't free herself from his grip.

"You don't have a boyfriend." His breath was hot against her cheek as he spoke. "If you weren't interested, you would have left the minute I approached you in the bar."

He pushed her coat open and ripped the strap of her shirt, exposing her bra. His hands touched her, and a deeper fear set itself free from the shadows of Gray's mind. Gray fought to release herself from his grip, her nails digging into his face, but Devon's strength overpowered her uncoordinated body.

"You like it rough, hu?" Devon mumbled and laughed as he fumbled with her bra. "You want it and you know you do. You were begging for it. I could see it in your eyes."

Gray couldn't breathe. She couldn't scream. Terror coursed through her veins and her vision began to tunnel.

No. No, no, no, no, she screamed in the back of her mind. Why couldn't she speak?

Just before Gray thought she might pass out, she was loose from the man's grip. Her hands went to her chest, and she pulled her jacket over herself as she stumbled away. Everything in her mind told her to run while she had the chance, but she couldn't pick herself up off the sidewalk.

She heard a man grunt. Her eyes followed the noise. Someone had pulled Devon off her, and the man now held Devon by the collar of his shirt. With a swift movement, he threw Devon to the ground and watched him clumsily pick himself up and curse as he scurried off to the bar.

When the stranger turned, Gray's vision blurred, but she knew who stood in front of her.

34

White

"Tony?"

Tony helped Gray to her feet and looked her over for any signs of injury. "Are you okay?"

Gray dropped her gaze, unable to meet Tony's eyes. She nodded her head.

You can't even look at me, Tony thought. *Give me something here, Gray. Even just a glance. Anything!*

But Gray stood in silence, her head down.

Tony's breath was heavy, and a mix of anger and fear caused his hands to shake. He held his arm around Gray's waist and walked her beside him to his Jeep, which was parked in the middle of the street, engine still running. After he opened the passenger's side door, Tony lifted Gray into the seat and slammed the door shut behind her.

He wanted to punch the Jeep. He wanted to scream. He wanted to follow Devon back to the bar and knock his teeth out. He walked to the driver's side door, took a deep breath and tried to steady his anger.

Once he slid in behind the wheel, Tony slammed the Jeep into gear and pulled a U-turn, heading away from town. Silence rocked the air between them.

"How did you—"

"Stop." His tone was strong and forceful. "I'm not ready to talk."

Gray leaned closer to him and touched his arm with her hand. "Tony, please."

He glanced over at her and then turned his eyes back to the road, another wave of anger swelling in his chest. "Your shirt is torn."

Gray's jacket had come open, and she pulled back into her chair and wrapped the coat around her more tightly. Tony pulled over on the side of the road, unable to keep his composure. He jumped out of the Jeep and paced.

The past few weeks had been agony. He wanted to reach out to Gray, but he knew she needed space. His heart had leapt in his chest when he saw he had missed a call from her. But then he heard the fear in her voice as he listened to her voicemail. Tony called her back and she didn't answer. When he got to her apartment and she wasn't home, he knew something was wrong. He started driving through town, and that's when he saw Devon, forcing Gray back into the alley behind the bar as she was trying to leave. He saw the panic in her eyes.

A loud and tormented scream tore from his chest. When he finished, he knelt on the ground with his head in his hands. Gray opened her door and ran to him.

His cheeks were stained with tears. "What were you thinking? What were you even doing there?"

"I don't know what happened." Gray fought to put the words together between her own tears.

"I got your voicemail, and I drove to your apartment. When you didn't answer the door, I started driving around town looking for you." Tony sucked in a sharp breath of air. "Then I saw . . ." Sobs shook his body again. "Are you okay? Did he hurt you?"

Gray shook her head.

"Why didn't you wait for me? I called you right back, Gray. I would have come to get you."

Gray couldn't control her tears. She lowered her head. "I don't know. I didn't think you would come. Not after our fight."

Tony cried harder. Reaching out, he pulled Gray into his arms and held her against his chest.

"I only went in for a pack of cigarettes," Gray mumbled as he held her. "Then the bartender handed me a drink, and I couldn't stop. I told that guy I wasn't interested, but he followed me out. It's my fault, it's all my fault."

Tony held her until he regained his composure. When his breathing slowed, he touched her chin, tilting her head to his face. "What happened in that alley was not your fault. He made the choice to come after you."

Gray buried her face in Tony's chest and wept. He held her as she cried. When she stopped, Tony stood and helped her up.

"Are you okay?" He brushed the hair from her face and pulled the jacket more tightly around her.

Gray nodded her head.

"Okay, we're going to get you a cup of coffee and take you to the hospital." Tony reached past her to his door.

"No," Gray reached out, her hand on his arm. "I'm not going to a hospital. I don't need a hospital. I'm fine. He just tore my shirt."

Tony searched her eyes. "Gray, he assaulted you. At least let me take you to the police department to file a report."

Gray shook her head. "I'm not going to a hospital. I'm not going to the police. I'm fine, really."

He wrapped his arms around her again and held her. What if he hadn't gone out looking for her? A shudder ran down his spine.

"Where do you want to go?"

"I was walking to your house." A tear bubbled in the corner of her eye and then trickled down her cheek. "I just wanted to see you. I don't care where we go. I just can't go back to my apartment."

Tony walked with Gray back to the passenger's side, opened the door for her, and helped her inside. They headed back into town, and Tony stopped at a truck stop. When he returned to the car, he held a T-shirt and two cups of coffee. He handed Gray the shirt and she slipped it on over her torn shirt.

Pete had crashed on Tony's couch after the Halloween party, so he couldn't bring Gray to his place. Once she was dressed, Tony pulled back out onto the road and drove across town to the only place he could think to go, Marie's Café. The parking lot was empty. Gray sipped her coffee, letting it warm her. When the cup was finished, Tony walked around to the passenger's side and opened the door for her. Together they walked into the dark night, as Tony led the way along the over-grown river access path to the abandoned dock.

The wood was worn and weathered, and Tony held Gray's hand as they walked to the end. Together they stood and looked out over the river. The surface of the water was barely visible in the cover of the night.

"I'm sorry, Tony."

Tony closed his eyes and ducked his head. "Gray, I have never been more terrified in my life. I thought—"

"You thought he was going to rape me."

Tony's shoulders slumped, and he stared out into the darkness, head hung low. "Yes."

A drawn out silence settled between them.

"Tony, I haven't been open with you." Gray rubbed the palms of her hands down her pants as she spoke. "Something happened to me, something I have never told another person about before. I've been keeping—" she stopped as she choked back the tears. "I've been keeping a secret for eleven years, and it's eating me alive. I think you should know."

35

Black

Gray held Tony's gaze for a moment before she turned away. Gently, he guided her to sit next to him on the dock, and they looked out over the water.

"I told you that my father died when I was thirteen." A tornado of memories spun through Gray's mind. She closed her eyes and fought the emotion that threatened to keep the truth away. Gray had never wanted to confront this night in her past, and now as she stood at the door to her heart, the clouds swirled around her, and she stared out into the eye of the storm.

"Earlier that day I had come to the clinic after school to see my father." Gray sucked in a sharp breath as the man in the waiting room sat on the other side of her mind, a crooked grin on his face. "There was a man in the waiting room, and something about him didn't sit right with me, but I didn't know." The tears fell as Gray's composure crumbled.

With her hand in his, Tony rubbed the top of her fingers with his thumb.

"It was exactly three seventeen in the morning. I remember because when I heard the sound at my window, I looked at the alarm clock next to my bed." The tears fell harder now, soaking the collar of the T-shirt Gray wore. "The man from the clinic had followed us home that evening and waited outside of our house. At three seventeen, he climbed in through the window of my bedroom. The weather was cool, and I had left it cracked so we wouldn't have to run the air conditioning."

Gray shook her head as she tried to shake the memory free and pull herself out of this nightmare. "Sometimes when I sleep, I see the dark figure slowly standing up, towering over my bed. I couldn't scream, couldn't move. I just remember thinking this couldn't be real, it wasn't happening. It was just a bad dream. Then the man was over me, his hand covering my mouth. He smelled—" Gray stopped, closed her eyes and tried to hold the vomit down. "He smelled like beer, car grease, and sweat. And I knew then that it wasn't just a bad dream."

Her lungs shut down, no longer willing to cooperate with her, and Gray brought her legs to her chest, holding her knees as she fought for air. Tony knelt beside her and rubbed his hands along her back as he waited for her to calm.

"Gray, did he rape you?" Tony's voice was soft, and the words were spoken into her hair as he held her. Her body withered at the memory.

"I was only thirteen." She shook as the fear became as real to her in that moment as it had been eleven years ago.

Tony's muscles tensed, and he sucked in a sharp breath. She could feel his heart pick up speed in his chest. Gray clung to Tony, terrified to open her eyes, terrified the man would be standing on the dock beside them, here to take the last of her life from her.

"After he was done, he pulled a switchblade from his pocket." Her tremors increased, and Gray's teeth clattered while she spoke. "When I saw the blade, I panicked, and as I tried to fight him off, I knocked a lamp off my nightstand. The man had the blade to my throat when my father burst into the room."

Gray stopped speaking and stared down at her hands. "I will never forget the sheer terror on my father's face when he saw me."

The tears streamed from her eyes, and her breath came in short, violent bursts. "My father charged at the man and he let me loose. I tried to warn my father, I tried to protect him, but it was too late. I saw him stab my father before he turned back to me. I screamed, fighting to move past him, to get to my father, but he pushed me back down on the bed, turning the knife against my skin. Then I heard a groan, and the man turned around just as my father stumbled to his feet. He was caught off guard, and my father was able to knock the knife from his hands. Turning the blade on the man, my father cut a main artery under his arm. He was dead within seconds."

Gray's cheeks warmed with shame at the memory of that night. "I couldn't do anything except sit on my bed screaming. I can't help but think . . . I can't help but think that if I hadn't knocked into the lamp, or if I could have thought clearly enough to run to the phone as soon as I was freed from his grip, that maybe . . ."

Her sobs echoed through the night as she remembered her father, his lips pale and his night shirt soaked in blood as he stood over the body of the man who stole her innocence, the man whose life her father had been trying to save only hours before.

Gray put her hand over her mouth as she relived the rest of the night. "My father's face was so pale, Tony. There was so much blood. But he stumbled over and picked me up. He carried me to our neighbor's house. The police and an ambulance showed up minutes later, but it was too late."

A warm hand touched her shoulder. "He bled out on the neighbors' couch while I was passed out. He had been stabbed in the stomach." Her words were distant and void of emotion. "I didn't get the chance to tell him how he was the only person in my life worth living for. I couldn't tell him how much I loved him or beg him to hold on for just another minute, that help was on its way."

Tony remained motionless as he knelt beside her.

A humorless laugh gurgled from Gray's dry throat. "I've spent the last eleven years of my life angry at God and disgusted with myself."

An icy shiver ran through her soul.

"I can't explain what it's like to watch someone you love give up his life and die for you." She looked away. "He was a better person than I could ever be. If God is all knowing, then He already knew who I would become and the direction my life would take. He knew my father's death had been in vain. So why then? Why would he let my dad die in my place? How could He let that happen to a man who loved Him and literally gave his life for Him? God should have let me die and spared my father."

The tears blurred her vision, and she closed her eyes, letting them spill down her cheeks. Images of her father filled her memory: the time he cleaned her skinned knee after she fell off her bike when she was five years old; when he carried her from the house the night he left her mother; his smile when he threw her a birthday party; the sight of him walking in the front door in his blue scrubs after a day at the clinic; his voice as he sang and worshiped at church; and his strong hands in hers as he prayed with her at night before bed.

"He was murdered by a man he was trying to help." Gray balled up her fists and pressed her temples until her head ached. "None of it makes sense."

For an hour they sat on the bridge clinging to each other, lost in an undertow of anguish, held below the surface. In many ways, they were the same. Wave after wave, the current of life held them under as both of them cried for their pasts and what had been robbed from them. Both of them abandoned children who needed love and an answer to why the world could be so ugly.

The sun was rising over the river when Gray dried her cheeks on the shoulder of her T-shirt.

"You deserve life, Gray." His words were a whisper in her ear. "You can't live the rest of your life haunted by death. Your father gave his life for you so that you could live. If only for him, you have to let go of the anger. It's suffocating your soul."

Gray's shoulder shook under Tony's arms, and he held her more tightly.

"God didn't do this, Gray. I believe that deep down, you know that. The world is an ugly place, and Satan robbed us both of our childhood.

If you spend the rest of your life angry at God, then you are chasing away the only light left in your life." He leaned in closer to her ear and ran his fingers through her hair, brushing it from her tear-drenched cheeks, his words a breath against her cold skin. "Don't let the darkness win, Gray."

Gray let his words sink in, and for the first time that night, she felt as though she could breathe. She inhaled and let the oxygen fill her lungs and bring life through her veins. She gulped the air in, the tears choked back as her soul inhaled and pulsed to life. There was comfort in Tony's arms as she faced the rising sun and let the warmth of the rays touch her. A single tear coursed down her cheek and tickled her chin before it fell to the river below.

"It's time to let go, Gray." Tony didn't move. "Let go of the fear. Let go of the anger. Let go of the shame. You deserve to be free."

Her chin trembled. She looked up at the dusk sky, and with a deep cry she expelled all of the anger and bitterness from her being. Her hands shook, and her heart pounded hard against her chest. She cried out until there wasn't a breath left in her body, and her head fell limp into her hands. With her breath as short gasps of air, Gray let the peace fall over her.

"I forgive You."

The words were whispered into the air. They were the only offering she had to give, and as she sat on the dock and looked out over God's creation, they seemed an insignificant and meaningless gift. But as she spoke the words out loud, she felt her soul rise for the first time, and she knew somewhere, somehow, a perfect, holy, infinite God had heard her and breathed life into her lungs.

36

Black

Winter approached with blistering winds and ice storms. On Christmas Eve, Gray sat in the windowsill of her apartment next to a single, lit candle and gazed out over the frozen river. In her lap was her journal, open to an entry she had written the Sunday following her encounter with Tony. Their relationship had mended, and they were drawn closer than before.

The chocolate lab whimpered and nuzzled Gray's feet as she read her journal.

"Good boy, Rooster."

She had adopted the puppy, and he had proved to be a comforting companion. Three weeks after he came to live with her, she settled on the name Rooster because every morning at 7:00 a.m., he would jump into bed with her and nuzzle her cheek until she woke and took him for a walk.

On some evenings, Tony would come by, and they would walk hand in hand, Rooster at their side, through the heart of the small town. Those were some of Gray's favorite moments. Tony always had a good story to tell or comforting words to ease away her fears from the day. The two of them shared a bond Gray knew few people experienced in life, and Tony had been in the audience the Sunday she had asked to be baptized.

With a deep sigh, Gray pulled the knit throw around her and leaned back against the wall. She had poured herself into the children's home, and she and Rooster spent almost every day there. Most days she would help clean and cook while the children played with Rooster, but every once in a while she led the children in crafts or games or sat with them to help with homework.

On one cold, windy day, Gray sat with Sylvia at one of the desks, Sylvia's math homework spread out in front of them. Her eyes seemed glossy and distant, and Gray pushed the papers aside and touched the child's hand for a moment.

When Sylvia looked up, her eyes were wet, and her chin trembled.

"Am I going to be an orphan forever?" A large tear spilled down her cheek. "Nobody wants me because I'm sick."

Gray pulled the girl into a hug. "You know what, Sylvia?"

The girl sniffed the tears back.

"I felt like an orphan for a very long time too." Gray offered a sad smile, brushing Sylvia's hair behind her ear.

"What do you mean?" She wiped her cheeks dry.

"My dad died when I was young. And my mom wasn't really around. I spent a lot of years with a big hole in my heart, and I tried to pretend other people could make me happy—like my friends. I even thought that if my dad hadn't died and my mom had been there for me, then I would have been happy." The other children were going about the living room, unaware of the conversation. "But I think the truth is, all of us are a little lonely and lost. Only God can fill that hole in our hearts. He is our Father, and without our Godly Father in our lives, we are all like orphans, in a way. But none of us are truly alone. Ever. No matter what. All we have to do is remember He is with us and love Him and give Him our entire hearts so that He can patch up that hole."

She touched the child's cheek. "No matter what, you are God's child. You're never alone. And you will always have a Father who loves you."

The conversation played in the back of Gray's mind now as she watched the sleet fall. The road outside of her apartment was empty, and the streetlights flickered to life under the cover of the dark clouds. Gray exhaled onto the glass, causing it to fog with perspiration.

Every Sunday, Emma and Tony would go with her to the children's home. At least twice a month, the others would join them. They all got together to throw the children a Thanksgiving party complete with a large turkey and four-course meal. For once in Gray's life, she felt like her life had purpose and meaning.

Her cell phone rang and pulled her from her thoughts. With a smile, she pushed the talk button and pressed the receiver to her ear.

"Hello?"

There was a soft hum on the other end of the line. "I love hearing the smile in your voice when you answer my calls."

The sound of Tony's voice washed over Gray, and her smile widened. "Don't let it get to your head."

"Too late." Tony chuckled. "So, what are you doing this dreary day?"

Legs crossed as she sat on her bed, Gray watched the ice fall and create icicles outside her windows. "Watching the sleet fall and waiting patiently for Santa Claus."

He hummed again. "I hate to be the one to tell you, but there is no Santa. Just a beautiful miracle born in a manger."

"Oh, right," Gray rolled her eyes. "I must have forgotten."

"The weatherman said the precipitation is supposed to continue for another few hours, then turn to snow and go all night. We should have four or five inches in the morning."

Gray pursed her lips together as she considered what that meant for their Christmas plans. Isaac and Vera had invited Gray to spend Christmas with them. Tony's mother had flown in and was staying the night at Vera and Isaac's house.

"So," Tony continued, "what if I came to get you and Rooster? We could go out to an early dinner before the weather really gets bad, then you can stay here at Vera and Isaac's with us tonight. I'm worried that if I wait, I won't be able to make it out in the morning to pick you up."

The smile returned to her face. "That sounds perfect."

"Good." Gray could hear a car door open and close on the other end of the line. "Because I'm here."

Gray looked out her window at the Jeep that was now parked in front of her apartment. She heard the door to the stairwell open and close. "Now? But I'm not ready."

"Better hurry."

After she hung up, Gray rushed to the closet and pulled out a duffel bag. She retrieved her black, velvet dress, which she had bought from Carla just for the occasion, and tucked it in the bag with her dress shoes. There was a soft knock at her front door.

Gray hurried to the door. Tony stood in the hallway, his hair damp from the falling sleet. He was dressed in a white button-down shirt and jeans, his thick brown coat hanging open.

Without hesitation, Gray threw herself into his arms, not minding the cold, wet water that dampened his coat. Tony wrapped his arms around her as he stepped into the apartment. Gray thought about how much she loved the way she fit perfectly in his arms, though she stood shorter than him. After a moment, she stepped back and closed the door as Tony made his way over to the open closet door.

"I just have a few more things to pack." Gray scooped up the bag and walked to her bedroom. "Help yourself to a glass of water if you're thirsty. I'll just be a minute."

She closed the door behind her and went to her dresser to pack her undergarments and then retrieved a pair of black wool leggings and a gray sweater dress to change into. She decided to leave her hair down, teasing it a bit before slipping into a warm pair of socks and boots.

"I'm ready," she said when she opened the door.

Tony smiled at her from where he stood next to her couch. His hair was still speckled with beads of sleet that shimmered in the light as he stepped closer to her. He ran his fingers through her curls and pulled her close before his lips met hers.

"You're beautiful."

Gray's lips tingled, and the warmth spread to her cheeks and sent an electric current through her veins. Tony kissed Gray again. Her knees became weak, and Gray pressed herself into his tall, lean frame, yearning to be closer to him. Tony reacted to her movement and pulled her more tightly to himself. Gray's hands wound around his neck, into his hair. A million alarms rang in her head, but Gray couldn't hear them over the heartbeat which pounded hard against her chest.

Tony's hands were around her waist as they moved to the couch. Gray pulled at his coat until it fell on the floor behind them. The sound of the soft *thunk* on the hardwood floors broke through both of their minds, and slowly, Gray pulled away and took a step back.

"Tony. . ."

Tony looked down at the floor and ran his hands through his hair. His breath hadn't yet slowed, and his muscular physique was more easily seen through his shirt without the coat. Gray had to look away as her heartbeat calmed.

"I know. I'm sorry." Tony's words were quiet.

Gray met his eyes, a small smile on her lips. "Me too. Now let's get out of here quick."

Tony smiled, picked up his coat, and called Rooster as Gray slid past him to the closet to retrieve her black wool coat. A minute later, they stepped out into the cold winter air, as Rooster followed behind them. Tony looped his arm around hers as they made their way through the sleet to the parked Jeep.

"Be careful, it's slick."

Tony opened the passenger's side door for her and helped her step up into the cab. When Gray was seated, he closed the door and let Rooster into the back before he made his way around to the driver's seat. The Jeep rumbled to life, and they were greeted with warm air as Tony backed out onto the street. They drove for twenty minutes before they found an open restaurant on the outskirts of town. The parking lot of the small pizza parlor was packed with cars. Tony parked and cut the engine.

"I'm sorry about earlier." His gaze held hers as he spoke. "I should have known better, but I let my emotions get the best of me. I know your past and your fears and I never want you to feel pressured around me or afraid or uncomfortable. I'm sorry if that was a trigger for you."

"Tony, it's not like that. I'm not scared. It's different with you." Gray considered her next words carefully before she spoke. "We're both trying to take this slow and not compromise each other's integrity. I don't want us to have any regrets. I want to do this the right way and keep our integrity intact."

Tony kissed Gray's forehead. "Me too. The moment got away from me and I'm sorry for putting you in that position."

Gray bit her lower lip. Her motives and reasoning were not solely pious. Gray was attracted to Tony with a deep intensity, and she wanted to give him every part of herself. But her convictions weren't the only reason she had pulled away.

Tell him. The voice was quiet and firm in the back of her mind, and Gray pushed it aside and ignored what she knew was right.

"It's okay." She swallowed hard. "I'm sorry, too."

A lazy grin played on Tony's lips, and he ran his hand down her cheek. "Ready for some pizza? I packed a few heated blankets in the back for Rooster. We won't be gone for long. He will be all right."

A heavyset woman met them at the door and ushered them to a small booth in the corner of the restaurant. The small parlor was packed with families out to eat before their big Christmas dinner the following day. As they ate, they talked about past holidays with their families, and Tony shared more with her about his mother.

Gray's stomach was in knots as she thought about meeting his mother later that evening. The impression Gray had of Tony's mother, Gina, didn't reflect a warm and welcoming woman. Gina sounded like the higher-class version of Gray's mom: cold-hearted and selfish.

Tony squeezed her hand. "You have nothing to worry about. I'll be there with you."

The car ride home was quiet as Tony drove over the glazed roads, his brow furrowed and lips taut as he concentrated. The snow fell as they pulled into the driveway. A new, red BMW SUV was parked in front of the garage, and Tony pulled in beside it.

"That must be her rental car," he said. Tony winked and let Rooster out of the back, and they walked together up the porch stairs. Vera met them at the door.

Inside the house, a fire was lit. Isaac sat alone in the family room and warmed himself next to the flames. Vera took their coats before ushering them into the family room and taking Rooster to the basement with the other dogs.

"Your mom got here about half an hour ago." Vera's voice was soft and understanding. "She wanted to freshen up. She's upstairs in the shower."

Tony nodded his head and turned his attention to the crackling fire.

A decorated Christmas tree had been erected in the corner of the room near the fireplace. Gifts lay under the tree, and the smell of cinnamon and cedar lingered in the air. Gray closed her eyes for a moment and imagined what it would have been like to grow up in a house like Vera and Isaac's.

The sound of footsteps down the stairs caught everyone's attention, and Tony stood as his mom entered the room. Gray was intimidated by Gina's presence. Tony's mom was tall and thin, with unnaturally tan skin and smooth, long, blonde hair. She wore an all-white pantsuit with a silk shirt and flawless makeup.

Gina tossed her head, and her hair fell behind her left shoulder as she smiled a perfect, white smile. "Tony."

Tony closed the gap between them and hugged his mother. "Mom."

Gray stood, unsure of what she should do next.

"Let me look at you." Gina pulled back, her hands on Tony's arms as she looked him over. "I like how you're styling your hair now. And I heard that you were in Nashville making a record."

Gray saw Tony's shoulders stiffen a bit.

"Yes, we were in Nashville over the summer."

Gina stepped back and put her hands together and brought them to her lips as she smiled. "My son a hotshot musician. I'm sure the pay is decent. Not as much as what it would be if you had pursued law like I had suggested. You've always been so intelligent and well spoken. I know you would have done well for yourself if you had gone to college."

After he cleared his throat, Tony stepped to the side of Gray and slipped his arm around her petite waist. "Mom, this is Gray. Gray, this is my mom, Gina."

Gray smiled, unable to look Gina in the eye. "It's nice to meet you, Ms. Reese."

Gina looked her over, her face seeming to say that Gray fell short of her expectations, but she mustered a smile nonetheless and took Gray's hand into hers. "It's nice to meet you, Gray."

When Gina released Gray's hand, it fell limp at her side. An awkward silence fell over the group, and Vera stood to announce she had dessert ready for anyone interested. They all made their way to the kitchen, and Gina picked up a conversation with Tony about her current investments in stocks and the possibility of planning a family vacation to Hawaii.

The evening droned by, and everyone ended up crashing on the couch in the great room, watching *It's A Wonderful Life*. When the movie concluded, Isaac excused himself to check on the fire, and Vera offered to show Gray to her room so she could unpack and shower.

37

White

Tony watched as Gray followed Vera from the room, and they disappeared up the stairs. The moment they were out of sight, his mother let out a heavy sigh and Tony's jaw tightened because he knew what would come next.

"So how did you meet?" His mother's tone was void of emotion, almost bored.

Tony met his mother's gaze, determination fixed on his face. "She rents an apartment from Vera."

Gina scoffed. "You mean one of the old apartments above the floral shop? She lives in one of those?"

"Yes." His voice was even.

"What does she do for a living?"

"She's a volunteer at a children's home." Tony never shifted his eyes from his mother's.

"Volunteer?" Gina laughed. "The apartment makes more sense now."

Tony leaned his head back against the couch.

"Tony, I'm only looking out for you." Gina squeezed his arm.

He wasn't reassured.

After a moment, his mother relaxed, eased closer to Tony, and changed her tone. "I'm just disappointed because there is a woman I work with that I was hoping to introduce you to. She saw a picture of you on my desk and asked about you. Her name is Susan, and she's a very prominent model in California. She does a lot of bikini and underwear modeling, if you know what I mean."

Tony didn't flinch.

"Anyway, I told her I was flying out for Christmas, and I was going to talk to you about coming back to California with me for the company New Year's Eve party. Tony, she's a gorgeous girl, her parents both went to—"

"Stop." Tony sat up and ran his hands down his face before he stood. "I'm in love. I want to marry her, Mom. I'm not interested in coming to California or meeting Suzanne."

"Susan." His mom's eyebrows were furrowed, which showed the few wrinkles that marked her smooth face.

"Whoever." Tony sighed. "I'm not interested."

"Marry *her*?" Gina scoffed. "You can't be serious. This is a small town, Tony. There is so much out there that you haven't even seen or experienced yet."

The soft sound of footsteps could be heard on the stairs, and Gray came around the corner a moment later, dressed in cotton leggings and an oversized sweatshirt. Her hair was still damp and her face fresh and glowing. She paused when she entered the room, unsure of what she had interrupted. Tony stood and walked over to her.

"Do you guys need a moment?" Gray searched his eyes.

Those eyes. Those silver, piercing eyes had a way of searing his soul. He brushed a stray string of hair from her cheek and kissed her forehead.

Yes, he was going to marry this woman.

"No, my mom and I were just catching up."

"Excuse me." Gina stood and walked past the couple. "I'm going to bed."

She disappeared up the stairway, and Tony let out a deep sigh. The two of them sat together on the sectional couch in the quiet great room. Gray pulled a throw blanket over their legs and leaned into Tony, her hand on his chest. He kissed her forehead and stroked her hair.

"I love you."

His words were soft and reassuring. Gray smiled.

"I love you, too."

Vera walked into the kitchen a moment later to retrieve a coffee mug from the cabinet. "I'm making some hot chocolate. Would you guys like a cup?"

"Sure." Tony smiled at his aunt. "Is there Cool Whip?"

Vera laughed. "Of course."

She went to work, making four mugs of hot chocolate topped with Cool Whip as Gray and Tony sat on the couch, entranced by the snow and lost in the moment. With a sly smile, Vera poured their glasses and brought them over, and set two on the coffee table in front of the couch.

"You two should take the horses for a ride tomorrow. They haven't been out in a while." Vera sipped her hot chocolate.

"I've never been horseback riding before." There was hesitation in Gray's tone.

"What?" Tony laughed. "Is that fear I hear in your voice? Gray Wilcox, afraid of something?"

Gray rolled her eyes and elbowed him. "I didn't say I was afraid. I just said I've never been before."

"They're well trained horses," Tony reassured her.

"As long as you show me what to do first. I don't even think I know how to get into the saddle."

Tony squeezed her arm. "Give it a try. If you don't like horseback riding or if you're too nervous once we get moving, we can turn around and head right back. Promise, I won't leave your side."

"Great." Vera smiled. "Breakfast is at eight. You guys can go after that. It will give you time to get a good ride in before lunch."

With a smile, Vera disappeared down the hallway into the family room with the remaining two mugs of hot chocolate. Tony took a sip from his mug. He closed his eyes and let the evening wash over him. Despite his mother's obvious disapproval of Gray, tonight had been one of the best evenings of Tony's life. When they finished their mugs of hot chocolate, the two of them sat together and watched the snowfall out the window. Tony ran his hands through Gray's hair as he counted the many ways he loved her. Minutes ticked by until eventually Gray fell asleep on his chest. He kissed her forehead, savoring the memory.

How much better could tomorrow be?

38

Black

Snow covered the lower half of Gray's window when she woke, and the smell of bacon and eggs caused her mouth to water. Gray pushed the thick comforter aside.

Rooster stirred from where he slept in the corner of the room.

"For the first time, I'm awake before you, Rooster." She patted his head.

Vera had let her borrow a pair of riding pants and a shirt. Gray slipped into them now, pulled her hair back into a loose ponytail, and stepped out into the hallway. Rooster was on her heels as they headed down the stairs to the kitchen.

Isaac was in the family room, bent over a fresh stack of wood in the fireplace, a lighter in his hand.

"Merry Christmas." He smiled and waved the lighter in the air. "Soon to be a warm Christmas."

"Merry Christmas." Gray smiled and then turned to walk down the hall.

When she entered the great room, Tony sat at the island, a cup of coffee in his hands while Vera set dishes out on the dining room table. Tony looked up, set his mug down, and turned in his chair so she could sit next to him.

"Merry Christmas." His eyes were warm and exultant.

Gray blushed under his gaze as she sat on the stool next to him. Rooster settled onto the floor beside her.

"Would you like something to drink?" Vera finished setting out the plates and stood on the other side of the island. "Coffee, milk, or orange juice?"

"Coffee sounds great. Thank you."

Tony took Gray's hand into his own as he bent over and rubbed Rooster between the ears with his free hand. Gray watched the dog's mouth hang open under Tony's touch. Rooster sat up when Gina entered the room and stopped when she saw the dog.

"In the kitchen? While we're eating?" Gina waved her hand at the dog.

Tony called to Rooster, who stood and walked down the stairs to the basement without complaint. Satisfied, Gina approached the island and requested a cup of coffee. Her thin fingers tossed her hair, and she settled into a chair before she noticed Gray. Gina's smile seemed forced as she tilted her head up a notch and stared down at Gray.

"Good morning."

Gray smoothed her shirt with her hands and then turned to her cup of coffee. "Good morning, Ms. Reese."

Isaac walked into the room after getting a fire going in the fireplace, and they sat down at the table to eat. When breakfast was finished, Isaac retrieved his Bible, and they all sat together as he read the Christmas story out loud. Gray imagined a perfect, all-powerful God being born in human flesh as a baby. Jesus knew what lay ahead. His human existence entered the world humbly and left the world brutally.

Across the table, Gina sighed and rolled her eyes as Isaac concluded and closed his Bible. Vera ignored her sister's antics and Gray and Tony helped Vera carry dishes to the sink. When the table was cleared, Tony kissed Gray's forehead.

"Are you ready?" He nodded toward the barn.

A smile veiled her concern, and Gray hugged Tony back. "Yes, let me just get the boots from Vera."

Tony let Rooster out of the basement as Vera fitted Gray into her riding boots. Gray and Tony slipped out the back door, Rooster on their heels.

- - -

Mabel had been gentle and slow with Gray. The ride through the woods was breathtaking and beautiful. Snow covered the ground and trees, and icicles hung from the branches, glimmering as they caught the morning light. Tony rode next to her with Rooster following beside them, every once in a while checking out a rabbit hole or following the scent of a squirrel.

When they got back to the barn, Tony dismantled the horses' gear and set Mabel and Brute out to pasture before he checked that their water hadn't frozen over and their feed was full. They rode up the hill on the four-wheeler, but this time Tony stopped at the basement door to let Rooster in and dry him off before they rode up to the house and walked in together through the mudroom.

They cleaned up and washed their hands in the sink. Gray was lost in thought. The whole morning had been nothing short of magical. But the holidays always made her miss her father.

Tony flicked water at Gray, breaking her silence. She laughed and splashed him back and then grabbed the towel from the rack, which left him to drip dry. Gray ran for the kitchen but wasn't fast enough. Tony caught her and used her shirt to dry his hands as they both laughed.

When Gray looked up, Gina sat at the island. She cleared her throat, stood, and walked out of the room.

Tony shrugged his shoulders. "Do you know what sounds good for lunch?"

"What?"

His smile widened. "Grilled cheese sandwiches and tomato soup. Want to help me make them?"

Gray smiled. "Grilled cheese and soup for Christmas lunch? Let's do it."

They went to work, buttering slices of bread and adding cheese before grilling them. Gray made the soup and set the table. After all the food was finished, Tony called everyone in to eat.

Isaac and Vera enjoyed the meal, but Gina noted that she hadn't eaten a grilled cheese sandwich since she was a child. Tony ignored the comment, and the rest of the meal was spent with Gray telling them about their morning ride through the woods.

The afternoon slowed down, and Gray decided to shower and take a nap. When she woke, the sun was lower in the sky, and the smells from dinner rose from the kitchen. Gray slipped into her velvet dress and black shoes, adding a pinch of makeup and teasing her curly hair before making her way down the stairs.

Tony sat in the family room next to the fireplace, dressed in black dress pants and a gray button-down shirt with a black tie. He smiled and patted the seat next to him. Rooster sat on the floor in front of the fire, and he stood as Gray walked into the room. When she sat next to Tony, Rooster nuzzled his head against Gray's hand as he begged for attention.

"How was your nap?" Tony kissed her cheek.

"Refreshing." Gray looked around at the empty room. "Where is everyone?"

Tony hugged Gray. "They are in the great room, talking. My mom said some pretty nasty stuff to Vera after you fell asleep, and they have been deep in conversation since. I read for a while, took a shower, got dressed, and came down a few minutes ago to find them still talking. It's better if I'm not there. I add kind of a . . . strain on the relationship between my mom and Vera."

Gray cuddled against Tony and felt the warmth of the fire on her face.

"This has been the best Christmas I have had since my father passed away." Her words were a whisper in the empty room. "Thank you."

Tony ran his fingers through her hair.

Twenty minutes passed before Vera called them to dinner. The meal was delicious, and Isaac and Vera were lost in stories of Christmases past, sharing memories that made Gray laugh until her ribs hurt. Gina remained quiet and withdrawn throughout the meal. When everyone finished eating, and the stories came to an end, Gray and Tony offered to clean up.

Together they unloaded and loaded the dishwasher, and then hand-washed the remaining dishes, keeping most of the water in the sink. As Gray hung the hand towel on the oven, she thought about what her life could look like with Tony, ten years down the road. Washing dishes together at night before bed, sharing stories at the table about their family holidays, snuggling up beside the fireplace and kicking their feet up after all the work was done.

"Time for presents!" Isaac called from the family room.

Gray followed Tony to the family room, and they settled onto the couch next to Gina. Vera handed out gifts, and when there was nothing left beneath the tree, they all began to open what they were given. Gray had brought Isaac a gold-plated bookmark inscribed with *1 Corinthians 13:13 And now these three remain: faith, hope and love. But the greatest of these is love.* With his gift was a note from her.

Pastor Isaac,
Thank you and Vera for teaching me about faith, hope, and especially about love.

For Vera, Gray had given her a vase of roses, handmade from music sheets of Vera's favorite songs.

Vera,
Thank you for showing me that not every flower looks the same and not every petal has to wilt.

Gray nervously rubbed her fingers together as Gina opened her gift from Gray. By request, Carla had designed and handmade intricate, silver bangle bracelets for Gina, each with a different but correlating pattern. When Gina opened the box, she froze as she stared down at the bracelets inside. After a moment, she smiled and slipped the bracelets onto her arm.

When her eyes met Gray's, her lip quivered, and her cheeks blushed. "Thank you. They are beautiful."

Gray smiled, and Gina turned her attention back to the bracelets. With a gentle nudge, Tony elbowed Gray and winked at her.

Gray got a devotional book from Vera and Isaac, and she waited to open Tony's gift, which was so large it sat at her feet.

Tony opened his gift from Gray. Four tickets to the upcoming concert of his favorite band fell into his lap along with a note.

Tony,
Thank you for bringing music into my life.

Tony's eyes met Gray's. "These are front-row seats."

Gray smiled. "You said you had never gotten the chance to see them live."

Tony hugged her. "You know you're coming with me." When he pulled away, he nodded toward his gift to her. "Open it."

All eyes on her, Gray leaned over the large gift and ripped at the wrapping until it tore. On the large box under the paper was a picture printed and taped to the box, displaying what was inside.

Gray gasped. "A porch swing?"

"You are always sitting on the back porch, so Vera and Isaac chipped in to buy this for you. A guy who lives down the street handmakes them." Tony put his hand on Gray's back. Tears were in her eyes.

"My dad used to sit with me on the porch swing at our house and read Bible verses to me." She ran her hands over the picture as the memories flooded over her.

Gray hugged Tony, burying her face in his chest as she fought the tears. "Thank you," she whispered into his shirt.

Once her emotions were in check, Gray turned to Isaac and Vera. "Thank you guys so much."

"Thank you for your gifts, Gray." Vera held the note to her chest. "They were all very meaningful. I will treasure these always."

Gray's heart felt so full that the warmth it created flowed through her veins and radiated from her skin.

When Vera finished cleaning up the paper, Gina excused herself, pulling Vera aside into the great room. Isaac put on his boots and coat and went outside to check the roads.

In the quiet of the family room, Gray said, "Thank you, Tony."

Tony gently kissed her on her lips.

Isaac stomped the snow off his boots when he came inside.

"The roads have been plowed and salted. You should be fine. Just drive slowly."

Gray stood, heading up the stairs to retrieve her bag. When she came back down, Tony had already loaded her porch swing into the Jeep and brought Rooster up from the basement. Vera and Gina met them at the door, saying their goodbyes before Gray and Tony stepped out into the icy wind, Rooster on their heels.

When they arrived at the apartment, Tony offered to hold on to the porch swing until he could come by to hang it for her. Stepping into his arms, she let him hold her for a long moment.

"I got you something else." Turning to her duffel bag, Gray pulled out a long box, which was wrapped with a matching bow. "Don't open it until you get home."

Tony smiled. "Okay."

Standing on her tiptoes, Gray planted a light kiss on Tony's lips before walking to her door. Gray turned to look back at Tony who stood by the car, his gift in hand. Giving him another smile, she disappeared into the stairwell, Rooster right behind her.

39

White

Tony had agreed to stay at Vera's house for the duration of his mother's visit. When he returned to Vera's after he dropped Gray off at her apartment, the house felt a little less like home. He drank hot chocolate with Isaac, Vera, and Gina and watched a movie about the Christmas story. Tony fell into bed later that night, the gift on the pillow beside him. When the house was quiet, he opened the present. A note was taped to the box.

So you think of me while you're away.

Removing the lid, Tony pulled a handmade guitar strap from the box. The strap was soft, black leather. Tony noted how well-crafted it was and knew Gray had to have spent a lot of money to have it made for him. The verse Matthew 4:16 was inscribed in calligraphy down the middle of the strap.

"The people living in darkness have seen a great light; on those living in the land of the shadow of death a light has dawned."

Tony ran his fingers along the verse. For all of his life, his music would be his mission, bringing hope to the lives of those like Gray—like himself—lost in the shadows. He thought back on the day they had met. He had spotted her from the stage where he had been performing as she had approached his friends, Emma at her side. He hadn't thought much of it at the time. Vera had mentioned a young woman moving into town, and he assumed this stranger with Emma was the newcomer. Then, she just stumbled right into his path. Tony thanked God every day for bringing Gray into his life.

There was a soft knock at his door.

"Come in."

Gina opened the door and stepped inside the room. She stood in the doorway, silent for a moment.

"I wanted to say I'm sorry." She fidgeted with the bangle bracelets that Gray had given her. "For everything."

Tony moved over on his bed and she accepted the invitation to come and sit next to him. He wasn't sure what to say. He had forgiven his mother years ago, but the pain he felt still had a way of rising over time. It was a constant struggle to keep giving his hurt to God. A struggle he was sure would continue for many years to come.

"When I started down this career path, I swear my heart was in the right place." Gina's voice quivered as she spoke. "When your father left me, I felt so rejected. Worthless. And I had to prove to myself and to the world that I was capable."

She dabbed at her nose. "I thought that if I was successful, I could give you a better life. I wouldn't just be another small-town girl who got knocked up and left with a kid. I wanted more for you than this town had to offer."

Tony thought back on his childhood in Belle. All the summer days playing in the creek and catching crawdads, the summer evenings chasing fireflies, the autumn outings at pumpkin patches, and the cold winter days making snowmen and sledding. These were memories he treasured. Belle felt like home to him. He wouldn't have wanted to be anywhere else.

But his mother had different needs and desires. She had spent her life in these fields. Her family had been poor, her father an alcoholic.

He knew from stories his aunt Vera told him that Gina and Vera had often been picked on by other kids growing up because of their social status. They often spent their weekends working the fields with their father, who was a farmer and had inherited the land from his father. Tony doubted that his mother shared similar childhood memories to his in this town. He understood why she needed to leave. And from this perspective, he was almost glad she hadn't taken him with her. Tony never would have been happy in the city.

"My desire to provide and prove that I could make something of myself—that I could make it alone—became addicting. The more success I earned, the more I wanted." Gina shook her head. "And I sacrificed everything for it."

Tony put his hand on his mother's shoulder. "I forgave you a long time ago, mom. I love you. I always will."

Gina hugged her son, and Tony held her for a moment. When she pulled away, she dabbed at the corners of her eyes and then gently laughed to herself.

"It's embarrassing to cry." She cleared her throat and then smoothed out the wrinkles from her shirt. When she turned to face Tony again, she put her hand on his arm. "I like Gray. She seems like a wonderful person. I'm sorry for misjudging her."

Tony smiled. "Thank you, mom. I love her."

Gina stood. "I can tell. I see it in your eyes when she's near you. I can hear it in your voice when you speak about her. It's the kind of love most people only experience once in a lifetime."

She walked to the door and paused for a moment before turning back around. There was a tear on her cheek when she spoke.

"Don't ever let her go."

40

Black

Rooster stood at her feet as Gray dabbed the makeup on her face in the mirror. Tonight was the big New Year's Eve party at Marie's Café, and Emma would be at the door ready to go in a few minutes. Gray had spent the last hour showering and pinning her hair into a fancy updo for the occasion.

Every New Year's Eve, Tiffany hired a famed chef from St. Louis and held a ball to raise money for a local support group for widows. Gray wasn't sure how much the cost per plate was because Tony had paid for her to go with him, but she was sure it was expensive by the way everyone else talked about the event.

A deep ache spread across Gray's abdomen, and she held her side for a moment as she caught her breath. She was not going to miss the party tonight, no matter how ill she felt. Carla had made a silver, silk A-line dress for Gray, and the back of the dress had a deep plunge that came together just above her hips with a large, loose bow. Gray felt out of her element as she slipped into the gown. She put on a pair of silver flats and took a deep breath to steady herself.

There was a soft knock at the door, and Rooster sounded two warning barks before he came to Gray's side. When Gray opened the door, Emma stood in the hall, her makeup and hair done. She wore a red sequined dress, her coat in hand.

"You look beautiful!" She smiled.

"So do you."

Gray grabbed her long, wool winter coat before she held up her dress so it wouldn't get wet in the snow as she fell in step behind Emma. On the drive to Marie's, Emma talked about the upcoming tour and how much she would miss Frank. Gray pushed her emotions aside, determined to enjoy the night.

When they arrived, a valet parked their cars as two men in suits ushered them to the front door. The large wooden doors opened, and the café had been decorated, ceiling to floor, in red roses. Candles lit every surface in sight, and a four-piece band played on the stage on the far side of the room.

Emma caught sight of Frank and disappeared. White silk banners hung along the ceiling, and the curtains were open to the dark, snowy night. While she looked up at the banners, Gray felt a hand on the small of her back, and she closed her eyes and let Tony put his arms around her waist and hug her from behind.

"You are the most beautiful woman I have ever seen." His voice was soft in her ear.

Gray spun around, admiring Tony in his three-piece black suit and silver tie. "You don't look so bad yourself." She smiled and winked.

"Would you like anything to drink?" He nodded toward where the drinks were served.

"No, thank you." Tony brushed his thumb along her jaw.

"Would you like to dance?"

Gray didn't blink. "Yes."

With his fingers entwined in hers, Tony led Gray to the dance floor where a few other couples had gathered. He held her close while they swayed to the music.

"I love you." He whispered the words into her ear. "Since the day we met, I knew there was something different and unequivocally beautiful about you, Gray."

He looked Gray in her eyes, and she wondered if he could hear her heartbeat.

"I will never love another woman as deeply as I love you."

Unable to breathe, unable to speak, Gray's eyes were frozen onto his, and the music faded, its beauty muted by his words. "I love you, Tony."

Gray lost herself in the moment. Tony loved her. She loved him more deeply than she ever imagined she could love. They were here together, dancing their way into the New Year in perfect unison.

Tomorrow.

The voice taunted her. The pain in her abdomen pulsed and grew stronger with every beat. Tony spoke again, but this time, Gray couldn't hear him. Her head screamed, and nausea twisted her stomach. A sharp pain shot through her gut, followed by a burning sensation, and Gray knew something was wrong.

You always knew tomorrow would come, Gray.

She excused herself when the pain intensified, and Gray had to stop at a table, her arm gripping the back of a chair with white knuckles. Tony was at her side, his hand on her back as she doubled over. He spoke inaudibly, and she tried to wave him off, tell him everything was okay, but the pain increased, stealing her breath.

No, not now, Gray thought. Please, God. Just one more night.

Black specks filled her vision. Gray fell to her knees and covered her mouth as she vomited, her lungs in a desperate fight for air. Emma and Frank were at her side along with Tiffany and Darren. Tony leaned over her as he spoke to them, but she couldn't understand what he said.

When he knelt in front of her, Gray fought to see him as her vision faded. One thing was unmistakable—shock and fear shone through Tony's blue eyes. He mouthed her name as he looked at her dress, his face white as a sheet. Gray followed his gaze.

The last image in her mind before she passed out was the sight of blood down the chest of her gown.

41

White

Tony sat quietly beside the hospital bed, still dressed in his suit, as he stared down at the princess-cut diamond ring in his hand. He looked over at the blood-soaked silk dress, which had been cut into two pieces by the paramedics and now sat crumpled in a chair next to Gray's bed. With a sigh, his head fell into his open hand while the other hand closed the velvet box and tucked it back into the pocket of his jacket.

Movement caught his eye as Gray turned her head, her silver eyes on him as she awoke. Tony was able to notice features in Gray now that he had neglected to see before, features that concerned him. Her body was too thin, her bones protruded from her pale skin, and dark circles lined her eyes, eyes that now met his. Realization filled her expression, and Gray looked away, fighting tears.

"You weren't referring to your experience with your father's death when you said you swore you wouldn't enter another hospital unless you were on a stretcher, were you?" Tony asked, not looking up.

"No."

His eyes shifted to hers, and he studied her face.

"How sick are you?" Tony's voice was unsteady, and he wasn't certain he wanted to know the answer.

Gray looked down at the IV in her left hand. The steady beep of the heart monitor counted the seconds that passed by. In the hallway, a nurse rushed by the room, her voice indistinct.

"I'm dying."

A lone tear ran down Gray's cheek. Tony leaned back in his chair and took a deep breath to control his emotions.

"I'm sorry." The words were a hoarse whisper as the tears fell. "I never meant to fall in love."

Tony stared at the wall, unable to comprehend Gray's words.

"I should have been honest with you." Her words broke as she sobbed. Gray wiped at her tears and looked down at her hands. "I never finished telling you the story about the night my father died. I wanted to tell you, Tony. I wanted to so bad, but I was scared of losing you and ashamed of myself. I was selfish. I couldn't lose you . . .".

When her voice returned, it was a soft whisper. "I wanted to tell you."

Tony ran his hands down his face, refusing to believe it was as bad as she was making it out to be. There was an answer . . . a way to fix this.

"Gray, there is nothing you could ever say that could make me leave. No matter what." He took her hand into his. "Tell me."

Gray's lip trembled.

"I have AIDS."

Like a soda can being crushed, Tony's world imploded around him as the pieces fell into place. A hot tear slid down Tony's cheek. "From the rape?"

Gray nodded her head.

"No." Tony shook his head. "People don't die from HIV anymore. No, they would have found the virus in time. Didn't they run tests during the rape kit?"

"No one knew I had been raped." She drew in a sharp breath and released it. "You are the first person I have ever told."

Tony couldn't speak.

42

Black

Gray's mind was unable to focus, unable to accept the words she had to say, the truth that she could no longer run from.

"I'm dying."

She had never said the words out loud before, and they seemed even more terrifying here, now, as Tony sat beside her. Gray balled up her fists, pressed them against her eyes, and cried. "I found out about a year ago. The night I found out, Tyler and I had gotten into a fight and Audrey had talked me into going to a bar with her and hooking up with a guy. But I freaked out and made him drop me off on the side of the road."

Gray was in the car with the man from the bar once again as the night played back in her mind.

Gray woke in an unfamiliar car.

"Wait." Panic rose in her chest at the realization of what was about to happen. The brown-haired man reached over and put his hand on her inner thigh as he drove.

She realized Audrey and the blonde man were not with them. She couldn't do this. What was she thinking? She couldn't give him what he wanted from her.

"No, stop. Take me back," Gray shouted as she reached for the door handle of his sports car.

The guy came to a stop in the middle of the quiet street just before she got the door open. "Are you crazy?" he yelled and slammed his fists on the steering wheel.

"I'm sorry, I can't do this." Gray tripped over her feet as she tried to get out and fell into the street.

The guy cursed at her as he pulled his door shut and spun out. After she picked herself up and gained her bearings, Gray realized she was a few blocks from Audrey's apartment. She fell twice and bruised her knee as she walked through the dark, dimly lit streets of the city. Audrey's apartment was on the third floor, and Gray fell over and sat in the stairwell on the second floor before she continued to climb.

Her fingers trembled as she dug her keys from her purse and pushed the jagged metal into the deadbolt. Inside the apartment, she didn't bother to turn the lights on. She stripped away her clothes and stumbled into the shower to let the water run over her. With a heavy sigh, she closed her eyes and steadied her mind to keep the demon lurking behind her closed lids from escaping.

Audrey found her the next day naked, passed out, and sprawled across the floor of the shower as the water ran cold. An ambulance arrived shortly after. When Gray woke up in the hospital, she was alone, and Audrey was out at another bar.

"We ran some tests, Miss Wilcox." The doctor held a chart in his hands. "You have HIV that has progressed to AIDS. Your CD4 counts are dangerously low. With how far it has progressed, I can only assume you've been living with this virus in your system, undiagnosed and untreated, for years. Without the proper treatment, the damage the virus has done to your immune system has made you extremely susceptible to other diseases. Not treating your HIV left you vulnerable."

The doctor cleared his throat and looked down at the paperwork in his hands. "You have cervical cancer. The chances of getting this specific type of cancer are much higher for women who have AIDS and are not receiving proper treatment."

Gray absorbed the news.

"I know this is a lot of information to take in. But I'll need a list of anyone that you have had a sexual relationship with. They will need to be notified of your HIV status and tested."

"There's no one."

Gray looked around the empty hospital room, and realization dawned on her.

There was no one.

As the doctor went into the seriousness of her illness, treatment options, and her prognosis, Gray made the plan in her mind. She would leave St. Louis. She would find somewhere to go and die alone in peace. No one would know about her sickness. No one would ever know her secret.

There was a long pause as Tony absorbed the news.

"There has to be something we can do, right?" He took her hand into his. "I mean this isn't the eighties. No one dies from AIDS anymore. Science these days is so advanced, there has to be some way to treat it or prolong your life. What about doing one of those special studies? There has to be something . . ."

Gray faced him with bloodshot eyes. "There is nothing we can do. I am going to die. By the time they found it, my counts were very low. They told me that if I started on anti-retroviral treatment for the AIDS right away, there was a chance they could bring my white blood cell counts up high enough with enough time to treat the cancer before it spread. They couldn't start me on chemo or radiation until my white blood cell counts were higher. And the cancer was already stage three and proving to be aggressive. I didn't have much of a chance. I was miserable and alone. I didn't want to live any longer. I didn't want to spend whatever time I might have left getting treatment after treatment. Have you seen the side effects of chemo?" Tears filled Gray's eyes. "And they couldn't even promise me that it would work. I didn't want to die that way."

She looked away. "I just wanted to die. On my own terms. I was tired of holding on. I never thought . . ." her voice broke.

Tony lowered his head in defeat. "So, what are you saying?" he whispered. "I have to just watch you die?"

Gray touched his head, and he looked up at her. She sobbed, and he took her hand, pressing it against his cheek before kissing her palm. Her body shook as she cried, unable to control the tears. Tony stood, nudged her over in the bed, and made enough room for him to lie next to her. He wrapped her in his arms and let her cry, her face buried in his chest.

"I'm so sorry," she sobbed. "I never meant to hurt you. I tried to stay away from everyone. I didn't want it to happen this way. I'm so sorry."

"Shhh," Tony whispered to her. "Don't say that. You are the best part of my life, and you always will be no matter the length of time you are in it." He buried his face in her hair and whispered in her ear. "I will never regret falling in love with you."

They lay together in bed as the clock turned to midnight, the rest of the world celebrating the welcome of the New Year. They drew strength from each other's embrace.

Tony slept next to Gray through the night. The doctor came in the next day and explained that the cancer was now considered metastatic cervical cancer—stage four—and had spread to other regions of Gray's body including her lungs. Her white blood cell counts were dangerously low because of the untreated AIDS, and her body simply had no chance of fighting off the cancer. The amount of time she had left was uncertain.

The news shattered Tony's composure, and after the doctor excused himself, Tony clung to Gray's failing body and wept.

Nurses were in and out of the room for the rest of the night, but Tony never let Gray out of his arms. Hours passed by, and as they lay in each other's embrace. Gray ran her fingers through his hair. She traced the curves of his face with her fingertips. They watched the sunrise outside the large, hospital window, and Gray wondered how many sunrises she had left with the man beside her.

43

Black

Gray settled onto the leather couch in Pastor Isaac's study. Her eyes ran over the numerous books on the bookshelves. Vera closed the door to the study and sat next to Gray on the couch. Isaac settled into the armchair across from them.

"Have you read all of those?" Gray nodded in the direction of the bookshelves, which covered the entire wall behind Isaac's large oak desk.

"Yes."

Gray looked down at her hands as they quivered. The shake had begun at the hospital, and as her exhausted days wore on, the shake became constant. Her heart sank at the realization she would never have the opportunity to read that many books in her lifetime.

"How are you holding up, Gray?" Pastor Isaac's voice was soft and understanding.

A humorless laugh whispered from the back of Gray's dry throat. "I'm hurt and confused."

Isaac and Vera waited for her to continue.

"When I started reading and I gave my life to Christ," Gray said as she thought back on the past year, "I felt different. I had peace and an energy I couldn't explain. I knew that no matter what happened to me, no matter if He called me home the next morning or a year from then, God had a plan for my life. If He didn't choose to heal me, I had faith that He had forgiven me and that I was in His hands now."

Gray sighed and leaned back in the couch. "I never doubted He could heal me if He chose to. Then, when Tony came along and I realized . . ."

The tears stung her eyes and she tried to hide her emotion. "When I realized how much I love him, my life just kept getting better and better. The closer I drew to God and the more time I spent at the children's home and with Tony, I felt . . ." she searched for the right word, "I felt alive. And I truly believed that God had healed me."

She wiped the tears from her eyes and met Pastor Isaac's gaze.

"He has healed you, Gray." His words were soft.

Like a bolt of lightning, understanding struck her. For the past few days, she had been so focused on what she hadn't been given that she overlooked all that He had given her. In a very real way, God had given her life.

"And He may still choose to heal your disease." His words were soft. "You are still in His hands, and God has a plan for your life, even though it looks like an ugly, painful mess right now. Only God can see the bigger picture. We have to take comfort in knowing that no matter what happens, our story doesn't end at our grave."

Gray considered Isaac's words. "I know you're right. Honestly, I am fine with whatever God does with my life. I'm not scared of death. I'm worried about Tony." Gray knew Isaac had similar concerns.

"Tony is a strong man." Vera put her hand on Gray's arm. "You have to trust God with your relationship with Tony also. You have to trust that God knows what Tony can and cannot handle, and that He would never push Tony past his limits. God has a plan for him through all of this as well."

Isaac moved his hand to his chin and cleared his throat. "Tony told me they are still going on tour next week."

A million needles pierced Gray's skin as she thought about Tony leaving, and she fought the urge to scratch her neck. "I told him to go. He wanted to cancel, but he can't put his life on hold and miss this opportunity for me."

The snow had melted, but the lawn and surrounding trees were bare as winter moved forward, full force.

"After all, when I pass away, I will only have been a short breath in Tony's life."

With a gentle and understanding sigh, Vera touched Gray's cheek. "I don't believe that's true, Gray. I don't believe it's true for anyone who has had the opportunity to get to know you and see your heart."

Gray met Vera's soft green eyes.

"You are fearless, Gray. And you have a passionate heart that cares for others more than you care for yourself." A tear slid down Vera's cheek. "You give me hope and ignite a desire in me to live my life as fearlessly and passionately as you have been. I have never met anyone as beautiful and influential as you."

"We are here to support you in any way that you need." Isaac leaned forward in his chair, his elbows on his knees. "And we want you to live in the apartment rent free. Finances are not a burden we want for you to carry right now." His voice was low, his tone even. "You're not alone, Gray. You have never been alone."

Peace washed over Gray, and the three of them spent the last minutes of their time together praying for Gray and the future God had in store for her. When they finished praying, Gray silently thanked God for giving her Isaac and Vera. Without her friends in Belle, death would have long ago engulfed her, body and soul.

On the ride back to her apartment, Gray thought about the last two weeks and how different everyone's reactions were than she had expected. They didn't chase her out of town with pitchforks, ignore her, or whisper behind her back. Her friends embraced her and brought them all closer together.

The rest of her evening was spent in bed, asleep. Now while she slept, she played the worship CD Tony had made for her. When she considered how much of her days she spent in bed, depression and loneliness would settle in, but the music helped to take the edge off. She liked to wake to her favorite songs greeting her. Pastor Isaac had also given her the entire New Testament on CD and she would rotate them out.

The sound of a power drill stirred Rooster, waking Gray. Her clock read a little past 8:00 p.m., and Gray pushed herself out of the bed. She slipped on a pair of wool boots and pulled a wool shawl around her arms before she followed Rooster as he made his way to the back door where the sound came from. The door to the porch stuck in the cold weather, and Gray had to jerk the handle with force before it opened.

When she stepped out into the cold night, Tony looked up from where he stood at the far side of the porch. Rooster wagged his tail as he jogged over to greet Tony. Tony set the drill down to pat the dog on his head.

"Did I wake you?" He eyed the porch swing box at his feet.

"It's okay. I've been asleep too long." Gray moved closer. "What are you doing?"

Rooster trotted off down the porch stairs to the backyard. Tony pressed the drill to the ceiling of the porch and drove a screw in, which fixed the hook in place. "I've been putting this off and I figured I should come by and get it done before I have to leave."

Gray watched as he pulled the swing from the box and untangled the chains before he carefully hung the bench. When he finished, he sat in the bench, waited for it to hold his weight, then began to rock. With a smile, Gray walked over and sat next to him, the cold air pinching her cheeks.

"I don't have to go, Gray." His words were tormented as he looked out over Vera's winter garden, withered and dead under a layer of ice.

Gray let the motion of the swing carry them away. For a moment, it was spring, and the garden was coming to life again. The smell of honeysuckle carried in the air, and Gray was healthy. She and Tony sat on the swing together, laughing and drinking lemonade.

The vision faded.

"Yes, you do." With a heavy sigh, Gray thought about the torment of the months to come without Tony. "I just keep thinking about how you were right there at the bar in St. Louis. You had the answer. You brought God to my doorstep and I was too self-involved to hear."

Gray took Tony's hand into hers and traced his fingers—studying every calloused fingertip, each crease in his knuckles. "Your music is different, Tony. It has purpose and life. You bring hope to people just like me. I am not going to stand in your way."

Tony's chin quivered. He leaned forward, kissed Gray and then wrapped his arms her, pulling her close. His body was warm and she felt safe in his arms.

"Do it for me." Her voice was a whisper. "If there is one thing that I want more than life, it's to see people like me find hope. You're music—your message—brings people hope."

The swing creaked as it glided, carrying two broken spirits.

"Then come with me, Gray." Anxiety pulled at his vocal cords. "We can put you and Emma up in a hotel. It's a lot of traveling and time on the road, but we can work it out. We could . . ." He sighed.

"You know I can't." Gray closed her eyes, and let a single tear slip down her cheek. "I'm not strong enough."

Tony clung to Gray and buried his face in her hair as he cried. His shoulders shook and his chest tightened as he fought the tears.

"Wait for me, Gray." Tony's voice cracked as he spoke. "Please wait for me."

The feel of his cotton shirt under her skin was a comfort to Gray as she wrapped both of her arms around his torso and wept. She prayed God would give him the strength to bear what lie ahead.

"I promise. I will be here, waiting for you."

They sat outside together until Gray's body shook with chills. Tony walked her and Rooster to her door, kissing her once more before saying good night.

The next morning, Gray made herself a cup of coffee and walked out to the porch with Rooster to enjoy the steaming brew on her new swing. Etched in the wood was the reference to their verse, Matthew 4:16, next to a heart encompassing both of their initials.

Tony had also added a cushion to the seat of the bench, and Gray set her coffee on the floor next to her and lay on the cushion. After she set the swing into motion, she lay there, with her eye on the carving, running her fingers over the letters repeatedly. This became her morning routine.

The evening before Tony left, they went to the children's home and then Tony brought Gray home and made her dinner. When they finished eating, the two of them sat on the couch, the Bible open in Tony's lap as he read to her. Gray was nestled under his arm, comforted by his embrace and the encouraging words he read out loud.

They had decided not to see each other the day Tony left, knowing the departure would be hard for both of them to endure. When evening rolled around, Gray lay awake in bed, as she clung to her cell phone and fought herself to keep from dialing his number. Deep down, she knew the phone call would make this harder on them both.

There was a knock on her door, and Gray sat up, relieved for the distraction. Emma stood in the hall, and tears stained her cheeks. Gray knew this was hard for her and Frank, too. They had drawn closer together over the past months, and Gray saw the pain in Emma's eyes every time the tour was mentioned.

"Would you like to go out to dinner with me?" Emma's words were dry and cracked.

"Sure. Let me get my shoes."

The two of them ended up at Marie's Café, and they sat together for hours as they enjoyed their meal and sipped on hot coffee. They shared stories of Tony and Frank. Emma had known Tony since childhood and had a bank of memories to share about them growing up. When they stood to pay their bill, Gray was laughing so hard her ribs hurt.

"Thank you, Emma." She put her hand on Emma's arm. "I really needed this."

Emma smiled. "Me too."

When they arrived back home, Emma sighed when she looked up at the empty apartments. "Gray, I've been thinking."

Gray waited for her to continue.

"What if I come stay with you? I work full time, so I wouldn't be in your hair, plus I can keep my apartment, just move my bed and a couple of things into your spare bedroom. I think we would both enjoy the company." She paused for a moment and her tone shifted to a somber key. "Plus, I could help you with whatever you need."

A crooked smile tugged at Gray's lips. "I think that would be nice. I could definitely use the company. When you're sleeping away almost sixty percent of your day, life becomes quite lonely and depressing."

The next day, Isaac came by to move Emma's bed and dresser into Gray's spare room. Over the next few weeks, Gray fell into a routine of sleeping while Emma was at work so that she could be awake by the time Emma got home. Tony called Gray each morning and evening. Sometimes they would be on the phone together for hours. Other times Gray only had the energy for a quick check-in. Vera would drop by every few days and she always brought with her fresh flowers to brighten up the apartment. Emma helped Gray with the housework, went with Gray to the grocery store, and cooked dinner almost every night. They took turns walking the dog, and in the evenings, they would crash on the couch together with a bowl of ice cream and a good movie. Emma's presence in the apartment brought joy and hope into Gray's life again.

44

Black

One chilly morning, Vera picked Gray and Rooster up to take them to the children's home like she always did on Wednesdays. Tears glistened in Gray's eyes and Vera was concerned.

"Will you come in with me? We won't be staying today." Her lower lip trembled.

"Sure." Vera put her hand on Gray's shoulder. "What's wrong?"

The tears spilled from her eyes as Gray shook her head. "I'm fading fast, Vera. I'm in a lot of pain." Gray looked out the window at the children's home. "I don't want Sylvia to see me get worse. It would only scare her."

Vera thought about Sylvia and understood Gray's concern. The little girl had been filled with hope and joy since Gray had started volunteering at the home. To watch Gray deteriorate in the hands of the same disease that afflicted Sylvia would devastate her.

They walked together into the children's home, and Gray spoke with Rose privately before she found Sylvia in the corner of the living room playing with her dolls. Gray knelt beside her and put a hand on Sylvia's shoulder.

"Are you going to play dolls with me today, Ms. Gray?" The little girl's wide eyes were beaming, and Gray's heart sunk in her chest.

"No, sweetheart. I'm not staying today. I won't be able to come back anymore to play dolls with you." Gray kept her eyes in Sylvia's.

"Why not?" The girl set her dolls on the floor.

Her heart hurt. "You know how sometimes people get sick?"

Sylvia's eyes dropped to the floor. "Yes."

"Well I'm sick, Sylvia. And you know how when you have a fever or a cold, sometimes it makes you sleepy? My sickness is different than a fever, but it's making me sleepy a lot right now, too." Gray fought to keep the tears at bay.

The tears trickled down Sylvia's cheeks as she met Gray's eyes. "Did I make you sick? My foster mommy said that if I touched someone, I would make them sick."

Gray pulled Sylvia into her lap and held her in a hug. "No, Sylvia. I was sick before I came here. You made me better."

Sylvia used her sleeves to wipe at her eyes as she looked up at Gray. "Then why do you have to leave?"

Gray set Sylvia back down on the floor in front of her. "I don't want to leave. I want to stay here and play dolls with you every day. But my body is very tired, and it needs to rest."

Vera watched from a distance as the girl reached up and wrapped her arms around Gray's neck.

"But guess what?" Sylvia pulled back and looked Gray in the eyes as Gray spoke. "I have been putting in extra prayers for your new mommy and daddy and God told me He has someone special picked out just for you."

Sylvia's eyes lit up. "Really?"

"Promise."

"When do I get to meet them?" Sylvia rocked back on her knees.

Gray stood up. "Very soon. Just keep praying."

Her tiny arms wrapped Gray's legs in a big hug, and Sylvia smiled ear to ear. "I will. And I'll pray that you get better too, Ms. Gray. That way you can come to my new mommy and daddy's house to play dolls with me."

Gray choked back the tears. "Thank you, sweetheart."

After she said goodbye to the rest of the children and let them play with Rooster one last time, Gray and Vera drove home in silence.

Vera offered to stay with Gray until Emma got home. She helped Gray into bed. "I'm so proud of you, Gray."

Vera walked to the living room, but the door to the bedroom didn't close all the way behind her. Gray couldn't sleep, she tossed and turned in her bed. Her mouth was dry and it was hard to swallow. She stood to retrieve a cup of water from the kitchen, but when she got to her bedroom door, she could hear Vera's voice in the living room as she spoke on the phone.

There was determination in Vera's tone. "What do you think about adopting a child? Her name is Sylvia."

Gray crept back to bed, a smile on her lips.

She slept the rest of the day, and her body convulsed with shakes worse than before. By the time Emma got home, Gray's lips were dry and cracked and her voice nearly gone. Emma brought her a large glass of ice water and gave her the pain medication the doctor prescribed. The medication took the edge off the pain, but it also made her drowsy. She fell back into a deep sleep and it was dark outside when Gray's phone rang and woke her.

"Hello?" Her voice was weak, just above a whisper and she fought to open her eyes.

"Hi." Tony's voice was soft and low, and it sent an immediate wave of energy through her heart. "How are you feeling?"

"I'm doing all right."

There was a long pause on the other end of the line, and Gray knew he had seen through the lie.

"Tell me about your day," she said in a breathless, raspy voice.

There was a faint sigh on the other line. "The concerts are amazing. The headlining band has been great. They really have a heart for music. We have learned so much from them over the past month."

Behind the excitement, Gray heard the anxiety and fear in his voice. "Be thankful, Tony. This is an answer to your prayers. Thank God for what He has given you."

Tony exhaled. "I would gladly give this up if only He would answer another one of my prayers."

Gray closed her eyes for a moment in a silent prayer.

"I'm sorry." Tony's voice was saturated in agony. He cleared his throat. "Tell me about your day."

Gray smiled faintly. "My day was fabulous," she said, and her grin grew wider. "Today, you and I went for a walk."

"Oh yeah?"

"Yes." Her thin fingers pulled the blanket more tightly around her before Gray continued. "I was asleep in bed and you woke me. You asked me if I wanted to go with you, but you wouldn't tell me where we were going. You said it was a secret. We drove for miles down back-country roads with the top down on the Jeep, enjoying the fresh spring air."

"So where did I take you?"

Gray fought the fog that hindered her memory of the dream.

"We went to Vera's garden. It was alive with spring, and the soft grass was wet with dew." Gray fought to keep the memory in her mind. "I can still smell the fresh flowers and hear the pond, like it actually happened."

"What are you talking about? It did happen. I just dropped you off." Gray could hear Tony's smile in his voice. "What happened next?"

Gray laughed to herself as she remembered the dream. "I felt so alive. Like God was standing right there with us. So, I walked out to the middle of the garden amongst all the flowers, and I reached my hands out to the open sky. With both arms open and the sunlight warming me, I danced. Isn't that silly? Right there, in the middle of the garden, with you watching me. I held my arms out to God and I danced, and I physically felt Him embrace me, just like my father used to hold me when I was a child."

When she had finished speaking, Tony was quiet for a moment. "Well your day definitely beat mine," he said.

Gray's body was giving in, and she fought back sleep. "Do you think it could happen?" she asked as her voice grew faint.

"What?"

"That God could reach down from heaven and hold me," Gray replied, her voice above a whisper.

After a moment of hesitation, Tony choked out in a weak voice, "Yes. It could happen."

When Gray didn't respond, Tony said, "Close your eyes and I'll be there in a moment to pick you up again. Tonight, we're going to have a candlelight picnic under the stars."

As she slipped from consciousness, Gray whispered, "Sounds perfect."

"Gray?"

"Yes?" She forced her eyes to stay open.

"I will always love you."

"Forever?" Gray murmured.

His voice quivered. "Forever."

Gray shifted in her bed. With a gentle hum, she closed her eyes, and fell into a deep sleep with the phone still pressed to her cheek.

45

White

Hundreds of miles away, Tony sat on the edge of his hotel room bed and listened to Gray's shallow breaths, unable to bring himself to end the call. A tear slid down his cheek and spilled onto his hand. Without bothering to pull back the covers, Tony collapsed into the bed and cried silently. His body shook, his throat swelled, his eyes burned, and his pillow was drenched, but he still could not bring himself to hang the phone up.

Anger rose in his chest. How could this happen to her? He thought back on the night they spent by the river. Sorrow and anger washed over Tony as the image of Gray reliving the night of her father's death entered his mind. He thought about the emotions she had walked through life alone with for so many years.

She was a child. How could You let her face this alone?

The questions screamed inside of him. In the still of his quiet hotel room, as Tony clung to the phone and listened to the woman that he loved slip away, a voice as soft as a whisper echoed through his heart.

I will never leave you nor forsake you.

Hours ticked by before Tony fell asleep with the phone pressed to his ear. In his last moments awake, he listened as the love of his life breathed uneven gasps, terrified that each breath Gray took might be her last.

46

Black

The full moon reflected off the black, choppy surface of the water. Tree frogs chirped in the woods around them, joining a symphony of crickets. Occasionally, a bullfrog would give a bass vocal input to perfect nature's song. Gray turned onto her back to look up at the stars. Jack lay down next to her, his arms folded behind his head, and they both silently watched the sky.

"Wow," Gray whispered, transfixed by the glistening lights which floated carelessly above them.

Unlike the populated city where Gray had grown up, there was not enough skyglow in Belle to blot out the magnificent display of stars, which presented itself before them now. The Milky Way wound through the ebony sky like a ribbon of a million Christmas lights strung above them.

"We're never alone, baby girl." Jack closed his eyes and inhaled a deep breath of the cool, moist air. The scent from the cedar trees along the river carried through the breeze. "In moments like this, I can feel God. It's like we could just reach out and touch His face."

With her eyes closed next to her father, Gray focused in on the sounds around her: the crickets and frogs, the wind as it combed its graceful fingers through the branches of the trees, and the gentle sigh of the river as it moved beneath them. The cool night air kissed her cheeks as the breeze picked up and sent a small shiver down her spine. While her eyes were still closed, Gray reached both her hands out to the sky above her. Her fingertips longed to touch something real. She believed for a moment that God was there, reaching His hands down from Heaven, His fingertips disguised as the gentle caress of the breeze against her open palms.

47

Black

Gray woke up alone in her room, and the sun shining outside her window indicated mid-day. Her body was drenched in sweat and her body quivered. Every time she awoke, her body ached more than before she had fallen asleep.

A wave of nausea took over Gray, and she leaned over the side of her bed, to vomit into a pail Emma kept beside her bed. Those who cared for her took extra precautions to avoid contracting her illness, which included wearing protective gear when they cleaned up her bodily fluids. Gray still feared for her friends, and she thought about them now as her body heaved in an effort to rid herself of the pain that afflicted her. When the room stopped spinning, Gray wiped her mouth with a tissue and remained motionless, as she stared down at the vomit inside of the light green pail. Her pulse slowed, and she pushed herself from the bed to make her way to the restroom. The water tasted bitter as she rinsed her mouth. Gray peered into the mirror, terrified of the person that met her eyes.

There were deep, black circles carved into the pale, fragile flesh under her eyes, and her hair had grown thinner from the lack of nutrition her body received. Wasting syndrome, the doctors called it. Gray's lips were dry and cracked, and her cheeks sunken in. Her thin fingers touched the mirror and she traced the outline of the reflection, her hands running down the cheek of the ghost which stared back at her. A large tear began to bubble up in Gray's eye, and she turned away from her reflection, unable to bear the sight of herself any longer.

The clock on the microwave in the kitchen 5:10 p.m. in bold, red numbers. Gray grieved the loss of the day as she slipped into the shower. Once she had finished showering, she pulled on a lightweight cotton dress, not bothering with her thin, tangled hair. The front door opened, and Emma walked into the apartment, her arms loaded with a sack of groceries.

"I'm sorry I'm so late." She bustled into the kitchen and set the sack on the kitchen table. "I got caught up at work, and I knew we were low on groceries, so I had to stop by there on the way home."

Gray was looking at her friend, but she couldn't see Emma. The room was suddenly dark. Her head began to spin.

"Emma?"

That was the last thing Gray remembered before waking up in a hospital bed. Emma was by her side. She looked at her friend. The day that Emma knocked on Gray's door—the first day they met—Emma had a lightness to her. Her bouncing curls. Her bright smile. She exuberated warmth and joy. Now, as Emma sat beside her staring out the hospital window, her friend's hair was flat and disheveled. Her eyes looked tired and worn.

"What happened?"

Emma turned in her seat, glad to see that Gray was awake. She took Gray's hand into her own.

"You passed out. When you got here, you were running a high fever. Emma was silent for a moment. "They think you're having an allergic reaction to the anti-retroviral medication. They are taking you off it."

"The medication for the AIDS? The medication to increase my white blood cell counts?"

Emma nodded her head. "They said they can try a different combination." Her lower lip quivered. "But they also ran your counts. Your counts haven't improved much."

A tear slid down Gray's cheek. "No. I don't want to spend my days like this."

"I know."

Silence settled between them.

Emma stood, but Gray could see the tears in her eyes. "I'm going to let the nurse know you're awake."

The worst part of dying is watching how it affects those around you. Gray reflected on this truth as she watched her fatigued friend rise to her feet.

Once Emma had left the room, Gray stood from her bed. She couldn't spend another moment in a bed. Tears threatened to fall, and she inhaled a sharp breath to force them away.

The wheels of her IV stand squeaked as she made her way down the hallway of the hospital. She walked by the doorways of other patients. One of the doors she came to was open, and an older, silver haired woman lay in the hospital bed. Four of her family members stood beside the bed, weeping. Gray looked away as she passed by, but the sounds of their agony followed her down the hall.

She reached the small chapel at the end of the wing. Gray pushed the heavy double doors open and stepped into the sanctuary. There was a stained-glass window on the far wall and dim light spilled through, casting a colorful glow against a small wooden cross on the makeshift altar in the center of the room. In the soft light, Gray saw a man in a motorized wheelchair on the other side of the room. His head was bowed, and as Gray walked closer, she noticed first how thin the man was and then that his limbs were twisted unnaturally. Sinking into a pew a few rows back from the man, Gray bowed her head in prayer.

With her eyes shut, Gray tried to focus but was unable to get past her doubt and anger fueled thoughts.

Why are You letting this happen, God? I gave You my faith and my life, and it seems that things have grown worse. Where are You in this storm? Don't You see me? Why do You allow me and those I love to suffer?

Gray leaned back in the pew, frustrated. She didn't want to speak with God. Instead, she chose to focus on the intricate design of the stained glass window—each piece heated, colored, cut, carefully chosen and soldered into place to create a masterpiece.

"Beautiful, isn't it?" The man's quiet voice ripped Gray from her focus. When she turned her head, the man still had his eyes closed, and she wondered if he had spoken to her.

"I'm sorry?"

"God's supernatural patience. It's beautiful, isn't it?" The man opened his eyes and turned his electric wheelchair so he could face Gray. "I'm Daniel." His voice came in thin wisps through his labored breaths. "I didn't mean to startle you."

With her attention back on the flame, Gray let the anger burn within her. "I don't know anything about supernatural patience." Her voice was tired and worn as she spoke. Gray closed her dry eyes for a moment, gathered her frustration, and forced it back. "My name is Gray."

Daniel was quiet; his eyes were still closed. Gray noted the kippah perched on top of Daniel's thin, brown hair. When he opened his eyes again, there was an overwhelming sadness reflected through the dark brown irises.

"I'm sorry, Gray." Daniel's voice wavered with his genuine apology. "Would you like for me to pray with you?"

Taken back by his boldness, Gray looked down at her hands before she met his eyes again. "No. God can't hear my prayers."

Her words seemed to pain Daniel, as if her bitterness was directed at him personally. This time when he met her gaze, his eyes revealed a small flicker of hope.

"'For I know the plans I have for you, declares the Lord, plans to prosper you and not to harm you, plans to give you hope and a future. Then you will call upon Me and come and pray to Me, and I will listen to you.' This is just one of God's promises to us from the book of Jeremiah."

Anger rose in Gray's chest. "Then why am I still dying? Why is He allowing it to destroy everyone I care about?"

Daniel's face remained calm as he spoke. "In Isaiah, a man named Hezekiah became terminally ill. He prayed to God to give him a second chance, and God let him live for another fifteen years. Hezekiah was not healed, but God did give him more time. I believe He hears us, and answers our prayers, although sometimes not in the way that we want or expect."

Hot tears boiled down Gray's sunken cheeks, and she bent her head down and cried into her thin, bony hands. Gray's shoulders shook as she wept, gasping for air between sobs.

"It's okay to cry," Daniel said, his voice kind. "In Psalms, it's written that God keeps our tears in His bottle. He loves you, Gray. He knows you're hurting, and He cares."

The minutes passed by as Gray tried to pull herself together. As her weeping began to quiet, she reached for the box of tissues at the end of the pew and wiped her tears. "How do you know so much about the Bible?" Gray asked through a stuffy nose.

"I have cerebral palsy. I've been immobile since I was born. My family couldn't care for me, so I have lived in nursing homes for the past fifteen years. Most of my days are spent reading God's word. His word is all I have." Daniel smiled. "It's all I need."

"I wish I had your faith," Gray said, sitting back in the pew.

"What about you, Gray? Why are you here?"

Gray looked down at her deteriorating hands. "I have a progressed form of AIDS. I'm going to die."

Daniel frowned. "We all die, Gray. But not all of us live."

Gray didn't speak.

"I have HIV." He looked down at the Bible in his lap. "Due to my health, I've had more surgeries than I can count, including blood transfusions. During one of the transfusions I received in 1987, I contracted the virus. I've been on anti-retroviral treatment for years."

With a heavy sigh, Gray studied him. A man sat before her who had been born with a broken body, encountered several painful procedures, and contracted a deadly disease from one that was meant to save his life.

"How do you still believe when you have been through so much?"

A moment passed before Daniel spoke. "In Ephesians, Paul wrote that because of His great love for us, God, who is rich in mercy, made us alive with Christ even when we were dead in our own transgressions. It is by grace we have been saved." Daniel smiled. "Though my body is dying, Gray, I'm alive in my faith."

Another large tear bubbled down Gray's cheek. "I don't feel alive. My body gets weaker every day, and my faith seems to be dying with my flesh."

"I have a message for you." Daniel's brown eyes locked onto Gray's as he spoke. "Strengthen what remains. You may feel like your faith is dying away, but you can keep Christ alive in your life. You have no power over your body. You cannot tell your heart to keep beating or force the AIDS from your blood. You cannot prevent your flesh from dying. However, you can keep your faith alive and live through Christ. Don't let your dying body kill your soul."

Gray felt as if there was a piece of the puzzle she had missed, and Daniel had put the last piece in place. She now saw the whole picture.

"Can I pray with you?" Daniel asked again.

Gray nodded her head this time.

Daniel closed his eyes and prayed in a soft, awestruck voice. "Lord, we come before You now, two broken bodies, and ask for Your strength. For You have said in the book of John, 'Peace I leave with you; my peace I give you. I do not give to you as the world gives. Do not let your hearts be troubled and do not be afraid.' Give us Your supernatural peace, Lord, Your supernatural patience through these hard times. Awaken in us Your Spirit, so that we may live even now, as we face death. Thank you for every day that You give us. Thank You for every breath that we breathe. I pray these words in Christ's holy name. Amen."

Unable to move, Gray's head remained bowed, and a single tear slid down her already tear-stained cheek. When she raised her head to meet Daniel's gaze, he smiled.

"Thank you." Gray's voice was hoarse.

"You're welcome."

Without another word, Daniel turned his wheelchair and left the sanctuary. For the next hour, Gray was on her knees at her seat. She was released from the hospital later that day and Emma drove her home. As she slipped under her covers, Gray thought about Tony, a hundred miles away, and wondered what God was doing with his heart.

48

White

Tony sat on the small couch of the tour bus, his acoustic guitar leaning against the cushion next to him. Darren, Vince, Pete, and Jim were asleep on the bunk-style cots in the back of the bus, and Frank sat in a chair across from him watching a movie. Tony's heart ached for home as he stared out the window at the headlights and taillights that rushed by through the darkness.

Emma had called him to tell him that Gray was in the hospital and she relayed what the doctors had said about Gray's medication and treatment. Emma had asked Tony not to tell Gray that she had called. Gray hadn't wanted him to worry or cancel the tour to rush home.

There wasn't much time left. God had been preparing Tony for Gray's death the last few weeks, and after the conversation with Emma on the phone, Tony knew it wouldn't be long now. He thought about the night together on the porch swing.

I promise. I will be here, waiting for you.

Tony let the pain settle in his heart. How selfish had he been to ask that of Gray? The thought of her clinging to a sick, broken life awaiting his return kept him awake at night and riddled the sleep he did get with nightmares.

The time was coming when Tony would have to let go and give Gray to God. The glass window cooled his forehead as he pressed against it. Tony wanted to cry, but the pain was deeper than a tear could express.

I can't, Lord. I want her here with me. I'm not ready to let her go . . . The discord consumed Tony's mind.

The selfishness of his attitude made Tony sick to his stomach. Would he rather keep Gray here, on the earth with all of its trials and hardships, rather than allow her to be in heaven with a God who loves her more deeply than Tony could imagine? Would he rather watch her suffer than let her be in peace?

You can heal her, God. I know that You can. The thought tormented Tony.

Then as soft as a whisper, a voice spoke in Tony's heart.

But what if I don't? Will you still love Me? Will you still trust that My will is just and good?

The words were arrows that pierced Tony's soul. If Gray passed away, could he live a life serving the God who let her die? If she suffered a cruel, painful life until the final breath, would he trust that God was still in control?

The bus hit a bump in the road, and his guitar shifted and fell against his leg. The custom-made leather shoulder strap caught his attention. Tony studied the inscription.

"The people living in darkness have seen a great light; on those living in the land of the shadow of death a light has dawned."

What was it Tony had told Gray that afternoon on the porch after they had painted her apartment?

Darkness is the absence of light. Like darkness, evil is the absence of God in our world. Good people fall victim to this sick, broken world each and every day, but God gives us hope. He may not always calm the storm around us, but the faith we have in knowing that He is always there, shining bright, just on the other side of the clouds, gives us the strength to stand and face the wind. He is our hope and our guiding light, not the creator of our pain and suffering.

The memory was a clear picture in his mind, and Tony considered his words. That day on the porch, he had felt as if God had been the one speaking, not him, as if God told Tony the exact words to say to heal Gray's heart. Now, Tony was the one in need of healing.

She knew. Tony's eyes widened at the revelation. The day on the porch, Gray knew she was sick. She knew she was dying. She wasn't only referring to her painful life and the cruel hand she had been dealt as a child; she had been talking about her disease. And after all of that, she still chose to trust God and give Him her heart.

And now, with a healthy body and the answer to his dreams and ambitions at his fingertips, Tony doubted the God that Gray trusted. Guilt squeezed at his stomach and tore at his heart. How selfish he had been. God did not do this to Gray, and Tony knew that God's heart was broken as He watched His child suffer though this life. But Tony had been too wrapped up in his own hurt and blame to understand God's pain.

Frank turned off the TV and stood to stretch. "How are you holding up?"

With a sigh, Tony looked out the window again. When he turned back to Frank, he knew what God wanted him to do.

"I think this is going to be our last show. I think it's time to go home."

Frank gave a nod of his head and put his hand on his friend's shoulder. "Okay. Let's go home."

Tony breathed a sigh of relief.

The guitar strap was still in Tony's hand and Frank noticed the inscription.

"She really is something special." Frank's voice wavered. "It's like God sent her to us to teach us more about His love, how to cherish every moment, and how we should love others. She's our own angel in disguise."

Tony considered Frank's words. He was right. Gray was sent to them for a purpose. If she hadn't been sick, she never would have come to Belle, and he may never have met her. Though a tornado seemed to be tearing through his life, Tony saw God amongst the rain, guiding them to safety. Tony had to trust God could take a terrible storm and use it for His honor and glory.

Hope. There was always hope.

49

Black

Her days grew shorter, and Gray had shed another five pounds. Carla had fashioned an entire new wardrobe to fit her shrinking size. This afternoon when she awoke after a daunting sixteen hours of sleep, Gray could barely move. More than the physical pain that cramped her muscles, the depression from the time she spent confined to a bed made it harder to face each day.

There was a soft tap on her bedroom door, and Emma entered the room, sitting on the edge of Gray's bed and running her fingers through Gray's hair.

"How are you feeling today?"

Emma had shed a few pounds of her own, and Gray knew it couldn't be easy to watch a friend suffer. She was grateful for Emma's care and support, but she felt like a burden to her friend.

"My body doesn't hurt as much today," she paused, looking out the window at the clear spring sky, "but my heart hurts more."

Emma ran her hand down Gray's bone thin arm, and then patted her hand. "What do you say we get out of here tonight? Rest up for the rest of the day, then I'll fix you a good dinner and we can get in the car and just go. Enjoy a beautiful spring night out."

A smile tugged at the corners of Gray's mouth. "Sounds wonderful."

Emma patted Gray's hand again before standing. "Good. Now let me bring you lunch and a bottle of water before you sleep again."

Gray drank most of the water but was unable to eat the sandwich before she fell back to sleep. When she awoke that evening, Emma had hung one of the new, white, linen dresses that Carla had made for Gray on her bedroom door handle.

Forcing herself up, Gray sat at the edge of her bed for a moment until her head stopped spinning. The hardwood floors felt cool and rough under her bare feet. The pajamas she wore fell silently to the floor and she slipped into new undergarments. The bones in her hips protruded unnaturally, and her ribs were easily seen. Gray wrapped her bony arms around her torso as she fought the tears, knowing the end was near.

After she slipped into the dress, Gray joined Emma in the kitchen where she prepared dinner. Two plates were set at the small table, and they sat down to enjoy the meal together. Gray was able to hold down more than she had at lunch, and she packed an extra bottle of water in her purse before they headed out the door to Emma's car.

The cool, crisp, spring air sent pleasant goose bumps up Gray's arms and she closed her eyes, enjoying the sensation. A full moon lingered in the clear night sky, and the rushing sound of a full river filled the air.

"It's beautiful outside." Gray held her hands out and felt a gentle breeze.

"What do you say we ride with the windows down?" Emma winked.

Gray slipped into the passenger's seat and rolled her window all the way down.

"Where are we going?"

Emma rolled the other three windows down before she pulled out into the street.

"I don't know. How about we just drive and see where the road takes us?"

Soft music played on the radio in the background, and the rush of air against Gray's face made her feel full of life again. She needed to be out of the apartment, enjoying herself. With her hand out the window, she let the wind comb between her fingers as the car pushed forward through the night.

"That sounds perfect."

They drove for twenty minutes through winding roads. Emma would point out a house or a street and tell stories about childhood memories. Gray closed her eyes as Emma spoke, leaning her head against the headrest and imagining that she, too, grew up in a close-knit community.

When Gray opened her eyes, she realized they were within a mile or two of Vera and Isaac's house. A longing filled her chest, and she leaned forward in her seat as her eyes searched for the small gravel drive that led to their home.

"Can we stop to see Vera and Isaac? It's been so long since I've been to their house."

Emma turned on her high beams to more easily spot the turn. "I'm sure they are still awake and would welcome the company."

The car pulled into the gravel driveway and bumped along until the trees cleared and the country-style home Gray had grown to love was in view. Her heart sank at the sight.

"All of the lights are off." She leaned in closer and examined the home. "Even the porch lights. I don't think they are here."

Emma nodded at the parked SUV in the driveway. "Their car is here."

The two girls got out of the car and stood in the driveway for a moment.

"Wait." Emma moved to the side of the house and Gray followed. "What's that?"

She nodded to the small pathway that led along the side of the house to Vera's garden. Small garden lanterns lit the path and were the only lights to be seen. Emma led Gray along the path. Lanterns hung from stands that lined each side of the path creating a fairy-like atmosphere.

They passed under the pergola and stepped into the garden. Gray's heart missed a beat. The entire garden had been lit with candles and lanterns. Even the pond had been adorned with floating candles. As her eyes swept over the sprouting flowers and the magnificent display of light before her, a movement near the edge of the pond caught her eye.

Tony stepped out into the middle of the garden, wearing a white button-down shirt and jeans. The sight of him brought Gray to her knees, and Emma was at her side, holding her arm as Gray began to cry. Emma released Gray's arm as she stepped away and the familiar feel of Tony's hands on her face brought Gray's eyes to meet his. Tony knelt in front of her, her face in his hands and a smile on his lips.

"You didn't think I would back out on our candlelit date under the stars, did you?" He brushed a tear from her cheek.

Gray fell into his arms as she wept and laughed at the same time. When she pulled away, Emma had left and they were alone in the garden.

"I didn't think—" Gray's voice broke, overwhelmed by emotions. "I didn't know if I could hold on."

Pain flashed through Tony's eyes, and he cradled Gray in his arms. "It's okay. I'm here now and we are going to enjoy tonight together."

50

White

The soft grass was damp, but Tony didn't mind. He lay next to Gray, her arm on his chest and her head against his shoulder as they admired the sky. He had just prayed for them, and they sat in silence now, the infinite universe that God had handcrafted on flawless display above them.

"Come to Nashville with me, Gray." His words were soft and quiet. "I talked to our producer and he pulled some strings. I want to record a song with you. Just us two. Any song that you want."

Gray smiled. "When?"

"This week. I already talked to Emma and Frank. We can all drive up together and stay in a hotel."

The urgency didn't have to be stated; they both understood that time was limited. Tony thought about the trip and the time that Gray had left.

"Okay." She pulled herself closer to him. "But only if we can stop in St. Louis on the way. There are a few things I have to do."

"What song would you like to sing?" Tony had considered a million possibilities when he had first come up with the idea, but then decided that he wanted Gray to choose on her own.

Gray shifted so that her back was against the grass, her face to the sky. With a gentle laugh, she spread out her arms above her head.

"When I was a little girl, I used to lie on the pavement of our driveway and stare up at the sky, just like we are now." The memory brought a smile to her face. "I would spread out my arms and legs and feel the weight of gravity against my body, holding me down against the earth. I would imagine that the earth just stopped spinning, and I was able to float away, into the endless sky."

Tony closed his eyes and imagined that he was free, his body weightless in the air above them.

"It's strange, isn't it?" Her voice was soft. "How we're all stuck to the ground. But we all just keep trudging around, never taking a moment to stop and think about what it would be like to be free, floating around the universe without anything holding us back."

The cool breeze carried with it the sweet smell of spring and Tony saw Gray shiver. He wrapped his arms around her. For a long time, they sat together and imagined that they were free to wander the universe as they pleased.

Gray broke the silence. "There's this worship song Carla played for me on a CD, 'Sweet Surrender.' The woman who wrote it, Kayla Massey, was a friend of hers and has a story like mine. She walked away from her faith, but found that God had been there all along, loving her through it. She wrote the song and recorded herself singing it, but she passed away shortly after."

Gray shivered again and Tony rubbed her arms.

"Kayla had such a beautiful voice, such an amazing gift. She could have been signed a record deal someday. Her song deserves to be heard."

Tony studied Gray's eyes, amazed by the heart of woman before him. With a smile, he kissed her and pulled her closer.

"Will you dance with me?"

Gray laughed. "There's no music."

"We'll make our own."

Tony took her hands into his own and helped her to her feet. They walked together to the middle of the garden. Gray stepped into his arms and he held her. Slowly, they began to sway, and Tony sang with a quiet voice into Gray's ear.

He may not have tomorrow with Gray. Tony didn't understand why this had happened to her. But Tony had this moment, and he finally understood that more than he could ever love Gray, God loved her, and there was no one that Tony trusted more with her heart. Tomorrow, he may have to let Gray go, but tonight God had given him another memory to share with her, and Tony would hold her close and make this memory count.

51

Black

The back seat of the large, spacious passenger van was comfortable, and Gray slept for most of the drive to the city. The rented vehicle was roomy enough to accommodate the four adults, featuring two second-row captain's seats and a third-row bench seat long enough for her to lie comfortably in.

When they arrived at their hotel in the heart of the city, Frank checked them in while the others loaded their luggage onto a rack to be wheeled in. Tony had reserved two adjoining rooms, one for Emma and Gray to share and the other for Tony and Frank. The Arch and Mississippi river could be seen in the distance from the large windows in the rooms.

While the others went to lunch, Gray took a nap. The day before they had left for the trip, Gray had called her mother and Audrey. Audrey hadn't answered or returned her calls yet, but Diana had agreed to meet with Gray later that evening. Five o'clock rolled around, and Tony knelt beside the bed and ran his fingers down Gray's cheek, summoning her to wake.

With drowsy eyes, she focused on his face.

"We are supposed to meet your mom in an hour." He stood and set a carry-out bag on the nightstand next to her. "I brought you dinner."

Gray pushed herself up and moved the pillows behind her back. "Thank you."

Tony sat in the reclining chair next to the window and studied the view as Gray ate what she could manage. When she was finished, he cleared away her plate and brought her a glass of water before helping her out of bed. Gray walked with Tony down the quiet hall of the hotel to the elevators.

"Where are Emma and Frank?"

Tony pushed the down button for the elevator.

"They are making it a big date night, exploring the city for the evening and then going out for a late dinner." One of the elevator doors opened and they stepped inside. "I think he is going to propose tonight."

The statement caught Gray off guard, and she turned to Tony with wide, excited eyes. "Really?"

He smiled.

With her hands on her mouth, Gray absorbed the news, and laughed in excitement. "I'm so happy for them."

Tony wrapped his arm around Gray. "Me too."

The car ride was long, and Gray pulled at the skirt of her dress. Today would be the first time she saw her mother since the night her mom knocked her out in the parking lot of her workplace all those years ago. Gray was glad Tony had agreed to join them. Once they arrived at her childhood home, the memories with her mother poured into her mind, and Gray fought to focus, pushing her anger away.

As they stood on the small concrete patio, Tony knocked on the front door. The screen on the door had been torn and now hung to one side, and the banner that read "As for me and my house, we shall serve the Lord" still hung next to the door, tattered and bleached by the sun. Gray looked away from the banner as her mind recollected the night that she left. Her mind reeled, taking her back to that night again, and she was lying on the concrete sidewalk, drunk, bruised, and bleeding.

The front door opened and in the dark doorway stood her mother dressed in a cut-off T-shirt, jeans, tangled hair, and a cigarette in her lips. A slur of curse words were mumbled under her breath as Diana squinted to see her daughter in the sunlight

Diana opened the screened door. She cursed under her breath again. "You don't look good."

Tony and Gray stepped past Diana into the house, and Diana let the screen door close behind them. She invited them to sit on the couch. A TV talk show was on the small television, and Gray didn't see Bill in the living room or kitchen.

"Hi, Mom." The last word was hard to get out, as Gray peered into the eyes of the aged woman in front of her.

"Hi." Diana sank into a beat-up armchair across from the couch. Tony and Gray took their seats on the couch. "So, what's the big news? You wouldn't have called if there wasn't some big news to share." Diana took another drag of the cigarette and blew the smoke from the corner of her mouth. "You pregnant?"

Gray shook her head. "No, I'm not pregnant."

Diana swore again and laughed to herself. "Good. You scared me. I am not ready to be someone's grandma."

Gray bit the inside of her lip. Her mother would never have the opportunity to be a grandparent to any of Gray's children. Gray had never considered allowing her mother back into her life, but now the decision wasn't hers to make.

"When was the last time you saw your brother?" Diana let another puff of smoke from her lips.

"Reese? It's been eight years."

"Reese!" Diana called in a hoarse voice down the small hallway of the home, which led to the room that Gray and Reese had once shared. "Reese, get in here!"

Diana huffed, pulled another cigarette from the pack and lit it. "He hasn't been the same since his dad left four years ago."

A moment later, shuffling footsteps could be heard in the hallway. A nearly teenage boy stood in the entrance to the living room. His hair had grown long, just covering his eyes, and he slouched as he stood, hands in his pockets. The boy who stood in front of them had little-to-no resemblance to the smiling three-year-old that Gray had known.

"Reese come sit down in here with us." Diana motioned to the armchair next to her. "This is your half-sister, Gray. I bet you don't even remember her."

"I remember a little." Reese shuffled over to the seat and collapsed, his hands in his lap.

"You look so different." Gray studied her brother. "You're all grown up now."

"If you had been around, you might have noticed sooner."

The comment cut Gray's heart. How many times had she thought about Reese, wondered if he was all right or if her mother had treated him the same way she had treated Gray? How many times had she wanted to call him or stop by, but didn't out of her own pride and cowardice? She had left Reese to fend for himself because she was too wrapped up in her own pain to care.

"You're right." Her words were soft and quiet. "I'm sorry."

Diana cleared her throat, sat forward in her chair, and motioned to Tony. "So, who is this young man?"

Gray's cheeks blushed when she realized she hadn't introduced them yet. "Sorry. This is Tony, my boyfriend. He plays in a band in Belle. They actually just got their first record label."

"It's nice to meet you." Tony stood and shook Diana's hand.

When Diana settled back into her chair, she took another drag of her cigarette. "Enough with the small talk, Gray. You came for a reason. If you aren't pregnant, and he isn't your fiancé, then why are you here?"

Gray studied the dust on the blinds, as she gathered the courage for what she had to do next. Tony put his hand on Gray's knee, and she took a deep breath before she said, "I'm sick."

The words hung in the air for a moment, darkening the room.

"Well that's obvious. You look terrible. But you didn't have to come out here to tell me you caught a bug." Diana laughed. She took another long drag of her cigarette.

With her eyes closed for a moment, Gray prepared herself for the impact. "No, Mom. I'm dying. I have AIDS. It happened the night of the—"

She couldn't bring herself to say the word.

"From the night that Dad died. I didn't know until it was too late." Gray paused, the hot tears burning her eyes. "I'm dying."

The cigarette hung between Diana's motionless fingers. For a long time, Diana sat and stared at her daughter, the words sinking in.

"You're . . ." The ashes from her cigarette drifted to the floor. "You're dying?"

Gray nodded her head.

Diana's jaw set, and she took a long drag from her cigarette. Her hands trembled, and Gray wondered if she was angry or sad. Reese sat in silence, an engraved frown on his face.

"I haven't seen you in years." Her mother's voice trembled and she didn't look away from the window. "You just stroll in here one day to tell me you're dying?" She took another drag. "How long have you known?"

Gray closed her eyes, and let the few tears fall. "Just over a year."

Diana sucked in a sharp breath. "Just over a year," she mumbled between gritted teeth. "Well I'm glad you could find the time to come by and tell me. How long did they give you?"

A long silence followed before Gray could find the courage to continue. "Not long."

Diana's head collapsed into her trembling hands. No tears came. No sobs shook her. Gray knelt in front of her mother. With both of her hands on her mother's free hand, Gray bowed her head as she spoke. "I am so sorry, for everything. Over the past year, I've gotten to know God like I never knew Him before, and I've forgiven you. No matter what you or Bill did to me, I shouldn't have treated you the way that I did. I shouldn't have left the way I did." The tears spilled down her cheeks. "And I should have told you as soon as I found out. You're my mother."

Reese shifted in his chair.

"Get out." Diana's voice was quiet and raspy, and she didn't move her head from her hand as she spoke.

A fresh batch of tears sprang into her eyes. Gray looked up at her mother, unable to see her eyes. Before she stood to leave, she held more tightly to her mother's hand and spoke the words she had never spoken before to her mother. The words that she knew, now more than ever, that she meant.

"I love you, Mom. Please remember that."

Gray leaned forward and kissed the top of her mother's head.

When she and Tony walked out the front door, Reese sat crouched over in his chair and Diana still hadn't moved. As they pulled out of the small neighborhood onto the main street, Gray let the emotions go, her head in her lap as she cried. For the past three days she had imagined a hundred different ways the encounter with her mother might have gone, and all of them had ended with the two of them embracing and telling each other how much they loved one another. None of them had ended this way.

Tony directed the car to the side of the road. He put it in park and leaned over to take Gray into his arms as she cried.

"It's okay, Gray." Tony stroked her hair. "You did the right thing. Your mother is feeling the weight of her guilt right now. She loves you. I promise that she will realize it someday."

The tears subsided, and Tony wiped her cheeks. "You are an amazing woman. I am so proud of you, Gray. I know that you love your mother."

"I just thought," Gray looked down at her hands, "maybe I could share my faith with her, and she would see in my heart how much I care about her. And maybe she would change."

Tony held Gray's gaze. "Don't underestimate God, Gray. Your mother can still change. You did."

Gray nodded her and decided to trust God with her mother's heart. Tony rubbed her back with his hands.

"You ready to go back to the hotel?" He brushed her hair from her face.

"Yes." Gray sat back in her seat, buckling her seat belt.

Tony pulled the van onto the road again, and they drove together as the sun set over the highway. Gray thought about Emma and Frank and wondered where they were or if Frank had proposed yet. She imagined the look on Emma's face when he presented the ring and heard her laugh as she said yes, and he slipped the ring on her finger.

Absently, Gray rubbed her ring finger as her thoughts drifted to Tony. What would it have been like for him to propose? Would he have gotten on one knee? What would the ring have looked like? Would she have said yes?

A smile warmed her cheeks. Yes. Gray would have married Tony if she had been well. They would have had a small ceremony, then taken off on a destination honeymoon. Three years later they would start a family, and Rooster would sit out on the front porch with them as they watched their children play in the front yard. Fifty years from now, Gray would be wrinkled and Tony would have hair in his ears, but they would love each other more strongly than she could imagine even now. Because that's how true love goes; it isn't constant, it grows with each new year, bringing two people closer together.

"What are you thinking about?"

She blushed. "I was thinking about Emma and Frank. Do you think he has proposed yet?"

"Probably." Tony checked the clock. "He said he was going to take her to the top of the Arch and propose at sunset."

Gray couldn't wait to get back to the hotel to hear the news and see the look on her friend's face as she showed off the ring. The van pulled into the hotel parking lot thirty minutes later, and Tony came around to open the door for her, offering his hand as she stepped out. Together they walked up to their rooms, but when Gray opened the door, the room was empty.

"Frank isn't in our room, either." Tony ran his hand across Gray's shoulders and kissed her cheek. "There is a rooftop restaurant in the hotel. Are you hungry?"

Gray gave a half smile. "Sure."

They took the elevator to the top floor. When they stepped out, a hostess greeted them and brought them to a seat with a view of the Arch and riverfront. The bright city lights gleamed against the dark night sky. Gray soaked up the moment as she stared out over the view. All the years that she had lived in St. Louis, she had never enjoyed a view like this before.

"It's beautiful."

Tony smiled and nudged Gray's knee with his own. "You're beautiful."

The waitress came over and they both ordered a dessert; Gray ordered cheesecake with chocolate and strawberries, and Tony ordered a double rich chocolate cake with ice cream on the side. The candle at their table flickered in the light breeze, and Gray let her mind wander back to the life that she and Tony may have shared.

When she was finished with her plate, Gray pushed it to the side and propped her elbow on the table, and her gaze met Tony's. He offered her a smile and took her hand in his.

"I love you." His voice was strong and sure.

Gray fought the questions in her mind. Was Tony so fiercely in love her because she was dying? Would he have proposed to her if she had been healthy? Or was their future life her fantasy alone?

"Did you ever think about our future before . . . you found out?"

Tony sighed. "All the time."

Gray put her other hand on his. "Would you have married me?"

The question hung in the air for what seemed like an eternity before Tony reached into the pocket of his jeans and laid a platinum, solitary diamond ring in the middle of the table, just under the candlelight. Gray's breath caught in her throat as she stared down at the ring. Bringing her hand to her mouth, she didn't dare touch the ring.

"When?" Her voice was a quiet whisper, barely audible over the noise of the busy restaurant around them.

Tony let his despair show. "I was planning to propose on New Year's Eve. I've been carrying it around with me since. It's comforting and a terrible reminder all at the same time. But it makes me feel like you're close."

A tear fell from her eye onto the table. The ring was beautiful. Gray closed her eyes and imagined Tony, whisking her off someplace quiet during the party on New Year's Eve, maybe out to the back deck to look over the snow-covered trees. Standing behind her with his arms around her to keep her warm, he would pull the ring from his pocket, slipping it onto her finger as he proposed.

When she opened her eyes, Tony's gaze seemed as tormented as her own. "I would have said yes."

She knew his heart was breaking for the future they had lost, the future that had never been given to them.

"I want you to have it."

Gray looked down at the ring. "I can't, Tony. It belongs with you."

Gray's hand hovered over the ring, and she closed her eyes for a moment, letting the visions of their future go. "This ring is a part of our story. It's a symbol of our love, and I want you keep it. To remember me, and how much I love you."

The waitress came to clear their plates, and Tony paid their bill. Tony stuffed the ring back into his pocket and they walked to their rooms. Emma and Frank still weren't back.

They sat on a small loveseat next to the window. The room was still dark, and for a long time, neither of them moved. Then Tony took the ring from his pocket, slipping it onto Gray's ring finger. The ring was loose, but she was sure it would have fit before she had lost so much weight. Tony lifted her hand to his lips and kissed her ring finger.

Two hours wore on, the two of them sitting in each other's embrace as Gray stared down at the diamond on her finger. When Emma's voice could be heard in the hallway, Gray sat up and Tony straightened himself out. Running her fingers over the ring once last time, Gray slipped the diamond from her hand, bringing it to her lips and kissing it before handing it back to Tony.

Tony brushed his hand along Gray's cheek and tenderly kissed her lips. "I love you."

With her eyes still closed, Gray breathed in, savoring the moment. "I love you, too."

The door to the hotel room burst open, and Emma walked in the entryway. She flipped on the lights, spotting Tony and Gray before turning back to the hallway. "Frank, they are in here."

Frank walked around the corner, joining Emma, his arm around her waist and a smile on his face.

"Guess what." A giddy laugh escaped Emma's lips and before either of them had a chance to guess, she practically jumped in the air, announcing their news. "Frank proposed! We're getting married!"

Gray stood, joining her friends. Emma hugged her, laughing with excitement.

"Congratulations." Gray smiled. "Let me see the ring."

Emma held out her hand and revealed a gold ring with a round-cut diamond set between two sapphire stones. Gray took her hand in her own and holding it up in the light, examined the ring.

"It's stunning." She tossed a grin to Frank and winked. "Well done."

"Thank you."

Tony walked up behind Gray, his hand on the small of her back. She was sure he was feeling the same ache as she was at the news of their friends. It was harder for Gray to celebrate with Emma now that she knew what she had missed out on three months ago.

"Congratulations, man." Tony's voice masked his sadness well.

The smile never left his face as Frank kissed Emma one last time for the night. "We better be getting to bed."

"Yea." Emma looked back down at her hand, then up at Frank. "I love you."

"I love you, too." Frank kissed her hand. "Good night."

"Good night."

Momentarily looping his fingers in hers, Tony squeezed Gray's hand as he brushed past her, exiting with Frank. When the door closed behind them, Gray turned to where Emma now stood by her suitcase, a pair of pajamas in her hands. As the two of them changed clothes, Gray listened as Emma described the night, starting with their exploration of the city, to dinner, and ending with his proposal at the Arch and then a carriage ride along the riverfront.

Once she was settled into the covers next to Gray, Emma let out a content sigh.

"I love him so much, Gray."

Gray smiled, enjoying her friend's excitement. "I know you do."

Emma turned over and studied Gray for a moment. "He told me about that day at the café, you know. And how you secretly set us up."

Emma looked down at the white comforter. "He liked me for four years before that. Four years. And he never had the courage to tell me. I was so caught up in my own head that I never even noticed." She looked up again and smiled. "And I may have never noticed if it hadn't been for you, Gray. Frank was about to give up, and I don't blame him."

With a half-smile, Gray leaned back in her pillow. "I'm sure you would have come around. You guys are great for each other, and you would have realized it on your own eventually."

After a momentary pause, Emma laid back in her pillows, flicking off the light. "Maybe so. But either way, I'm glad you helped me along. Who knows how long and how much heartache we both may have suffered in the process."

The room grew quiet, and when Gray was sure Emma was asleep, she turned over on her side, looking at the loveseat where she and Tony had been sitting. Closing her eyes, she pictured the ring on her finger again, feeling the cool metal against her skin.

Next to her, Emma slept, her engagement ring on her finger while Gray lay awake, tormented as she thought about Tony in the other room, their engagement ring in the pocket of his jeans.

52

Black

"No, Gray."

Her mother's laughter filled Gray's memory. When Gray opened her eyes, she was three years old, sitting cross-legged in the backyard across from her mom. Diana was smiling, her wrinkles gone, her hair shiny and full of life, and her eyes sparkling under the sunlight. Back then, her mother had been a different person. Before the drugs.

"Like this." Holding the wand in front of her lips, Diana blew into the wand, bubbles filling the air around them.

Picking up her own wand, Gray imitated her mother, but she blew too hard and the soapy water ran down her hands. Diana laughed again and flicked the water at Gray who laughed in return.

"Don't worry, you'll get it someday."

Gray watched as her mother blew more bubbles, and they floated effortlessly into the sky. Gray held out her hand and tried to capture one of the bubbles, but it popped when her small fingers touched it.

"Bubbles are free," Diana said before releasing more into the air. "You can't catch them."

Once she was on her feet, Gray stumbled over to her mother and sat in her lap. She looked out over the bubbles that danced mysteriously in the wind. Diana touched Gray's nose and smiled. She dipped the wand and held it in front of her daughter.

"Would you like to try again?"

Gray puckered her lips and let out a smooth, short breath. A single bubble broke away from the wand and joined the others. With a proud smile, Gray looked up at her mother who kissed her cheek.

"See, baby. I told you that you could do it."

Gray woke from her sleep in the back seat of the van. The memory of her mother drifted away, and Gray pushed herself up, peering out the window. Unsure of where they were, Gray looked around the van. Emma was sitting in the passenger's seat asleep, and Frank was driving. Tony was in one of the second-row captain's seats, reading a guitar magazine with headphones in his ears. Her movement caught his attention.

Tony removed one of the earbuds and smiled at Gray. "Good morning."

Gray smiled back at him. "Good morning. What time is it?"

Tony checked his watch. "Almost two thirty in the afternoon. We are almost to the hotel now."

They had left the hotel in St. Louis at 8:00 a.m. and limited their stops along the way so they could check into the hotel in Tennessee around 3:00 p.m.

"We're early." Gray smoothed her shirt down and brushed the hair from her face.

"Frank is a bit of a lead foot." He set the magazine on the floor of the van before unbuckling his seat belt and moving to the back seat next to Gray, taking her hand into his own.

Tony's skin was smooth and warm, his hand engulfing her tiny fingers. The sight of his olive-toned, muscular hand against her pale, thin hand made her feel her weakness more intensely.

Time was fragile, and the cracks that would shatter her life were spreading more quickly with each day that passed. Any moment now, her body would shut down and the pieces of her life would come crashing in, leaving a dangerous, broken mess for those she cared about to clean up behind her.

"I love you, Gray. No matter what, I will always love you." Holding her more tightly, he leaned his head against hers. "And nothing can ever make me regret loving you."

53

Black

The next day when Gray sat next to Tony in the recording studio, a microphone in front of her face, she thought back on that moment in the van. Gray had done nothing to deserve or earn Tony's love. He chose to love her for who she was.

While they had set up in the studio earlier, Gray thought about Kayla Massey's story and how similar Kayla's journey had been to her own. Gray intimately identified with the words that Kayla had written. She wondered out loud if she could do Kayla's song justice.

Tony had knelt beside her and took her hand. "You were right about this song. It deserves to be heard. Kayla deserves for it to be heard. And there isn't a shadow of a doubt in my mind that you are the one who should carry that torch, Gray. God used Kayla's words to bring hope to you, and He is now using you to continue this legacy and carry hope to others."

Now, as Tony began to play his acoustic guitar, Gray waited for her cue just as they had practiced together, but her mind wasn't on the cue or the recording studio or even on the unbelievable man sitting next to her. For this one moment in time, she closed her eyes and focused on Christ. And for this one moment, she was in His presence, standing before Him as a broken human being.

For the wages of sin is death. The verse echoed through her mind. Then like a soft whisper, His voice filled her heart. *But I have come so that you can live, truly live, forever.*

Gray's breath caught in her throat, and she let the emotions flood her veins.

She heard her cue and Gray let the presence of God surround her as she began to sing a worship song for Him. The words flowed from between her lips as her heart's melody, and all at once she was taken away into another world where death wasn't a shadow to chase her, and she could freely love as she was loved.

> *I've got a fire burning in my soul*
> *The kind of love that only sinners know*
> *Everybody cleaned of every sin*
> *The revelation begins within*

Her heart raced as the song picked up. Words took on a new form to express the truth of her life. Tony's voice joined hers and they sang together

> *'Cause there is glory in Your name*
> *There is salvation in His way*
> *Face to face with God*
> *Amazing grace comes from the right*

As Tony strummed his guitar, Gray silently thanked God for His love for her, and as she kept her eyes closed, staying with Him in that moment, her shame, guilt, and pain seemed to melt away. Here she was, standing before her Creator in all of His glory, and being Gray was good enough. The emotion was more than she could bear.

> *'Cause when I'm standing in Your light*
> *Even the darkest days seem bright*

And when I go astray
You shine Your light and guide my way

Gray imagined God reaching down and taking her into her arms. Like a daughter reaching to her father, she felt His embrace as she sang to Him.

I know they're gonna wonder
What kind of spell I'm under
Yeah, they might say I lost my mind
Yeah, we all do and it's alright

Blinded by my own fear
Not sure what my purpose is here
Running circles through a house of mirrors
You shine Your light and the image is clear

Summoning what strength she could, Gray opened her eyes and let the passion and emotion of the song carry her away.

'Cause there is glory in Your name
There is salvation in His way
Face to face with God
Amazing grace comes from the right

With his voice in the background, Gray saw Tony's lips as they moved, worshipping with her, their voices a perfect harmony. Both of them sang together, emotions unchecked.

I want to serve You
I want to learn You
I want to walk in Your shoes

Closing her eyes again, Gray savored the moment as the song concluded.

I want to serve You

54

White

The hotel where they stayed had a restaurant with a large patio where Tony and Gray now sat, overlooking the brightly lit streets in the heart of the city. Frank and Emma had gone to visit with Vince's aunt before they left town the next morning, so Tony had taken Gray out for a romantic dinner. The city was quiet on this cool, Thursday night, and the restaurant was all but empty.

The waiter came over and refilled their coffee mugs before disappearing back inside. Tony sat with his chair next to Gray and his oversized coat around her thin body. The cool spring breeze nipped at the both of them.

Sitting open on the table next to them was the Bible that Vera had given Gray. Gray had asked if Tony would read it to her since her eyesight was getting worse. For over an hour, Tony had read passages from the book of Galatians aloud. Occasionally, Gray would stop him so they could talk about something the apostle Paul had written in the book.

Gray picked up her mug of coffee and took a sip.

The steam rose around her face and Tony longed to kiss her. "You were perfect today."

Gray gave him a sarcastic grin.

"No, I'm being serious." He chuckled, adjusting himself in his chair to reach his own cup of coffee. "I am glad that you agreed to come and do this with me."

"Me too."

Tony knew Gray had more say but she held back. He took a drink of his coffee and set the cup back down on the table, running his fingers through her hair. After a moment, Gray shifted in her chair.

"I'm sorry for the time I wasted holding you at a distance. Specifically, after we fought about the dog. I was scared, and I didn't want to hurt you or anyone else. And now," she touched his face as a single tear slid down her cheek, "I realize that I was only causing more hurt by wasting what little time we did have together instead of treasuring it. I'm sorry."

Tony thought back on the time they had spent apart. Unaware of her illness, he had given her the space she seemed to have wanted, and now looking back, he wished he had fought his way back into her life sooner.

"I'm sorry, too."

Their coffees grew cold. Within his chest, Tony's heart was breaking. In a few minutes, he would have to walk Gray to her room and say goodnight, counting down another day until he would never get to sit with her in his arms again. The close of each day marked a step closer to what was inevitably lurking in the shadows of tomorrow. Grasping onto the last straw of hope he had, Tony spent every night before bed on his knees, begging God to let Gray live, to give her another day's breath on this earth.

"Will you keep reading to me?" Gray's voice was quiet and hoarse, tearing Tony from his thoughts. He knew she was on the verge of sleep.

"Yes." Tony set the leather Bible in his lap and opened the pages to the book of Psalms where he began to read to her. Long after her breathing slowed and her eyes had closed, Tony continued to read, unwilling to let the day come to an end. When he came to a passage in the fifty-sixth chapter of Psalm, he read the words out loud to himself for a second time.

"'You number my wanderings, put my tears into Your bottle. Are they not in Your book?'"

God knew his pain and heard him every time he cried out. Gray slept peacefully against his chest, and he buried his face in her hair.

For one more night he would cry out to God and plead with Him.

"You promise," Tony whispered, his voice lost in Gray's hair. "You promise in Your word that all things work together for good to those who love You. I have to trust that no matter what, You understand what's best for Gray. If that's a full life on earth, I promise to love her and cherish her for the rest of my life. If that's an eternity with you starting tomorrow, I promise to love and worship You and to be thankful for the time You have given me with her, even though I don't understand."

Gray stirred, and he moved so that she could more comfortably sleep against him. Tony let go of his emotions, giving them up to God, knowing that there was nothing more he could say. Reaching into his pocket, he retrieved cash to leave on the table for the waiter, and then lifted Gray into his arms. Her head leaned against his shoulder, her warm breath on his neck as he carried her to the hotel room she shared with Emma.

Emma and Frank were not back to the hotel yet. Tony opened the door to the room and tucked Gray into bed, pulling the covers over her. He left the lights off and retreated to a small reclining chair in the corner of the room. Tony watched Gray sleep, the unsteady rise and fall of her chest reminding him of her constant frailty. For one more night, Tony let himself cry. His soul longed for a miracle and he took faith in the knowledge that God understood his pain and loved him so much that at this moment, He was reaching down from His Heavenly throne, collecting each tear that fell from Tony's trembling chin.

55

Black

Two weeks had passed since their return from Nashville, and each day seemed worse than the one before. Gray was confined to bed, too weak to stand, and her eyesight was reduced to a massive blur of lights and color. Her days were filled with coughing fits, headaches and bouts of nausea, her nights filled with fever, chills and sweats. In every way, she knew her body was failing her.

Still, every day her friends would come to be with her, reading to her and encouraging her, and Gray used every opportunity to encourage them also. This morning, Vera sat next to Gray's bed and read to her from the New Testament with the warm spring breeze blowing through her open bedroom windows and Rooster cuddled up in bed beside her. Gray silently thanked God for the beautiful day, and for Vera who kept a vase of fresh flowers in Gray's room.

Vera set the Bible on the windowsill and took Gray's hand into her own. "How do you feel today?"

"The nice weather and scent of your flowers help." Her voice had become hoarse, and it was difficult to speak above a whisper.

Vera leaned her head against Gray's hand and said a silent prayer. Gray touched the top of Vera's head, understanding her friend's pain.

"I'm okay, Vera." Gray smiled. "I know it's hard to understand, but I really am okay."

Vera touched Gray's cheek. "I know you are."

There was a soft knock on the door and Tony stepped inside of the bedroom. Rooster stirred beside her. Vera patted Gray's hand once more before she stood and left the room. Tony sat in the bed next to her.

"You're the only person I recognize before you even speak." She didn't turn her head. "It's strange. I know you are here from the moment you walk into the apartment."

Tony leaned his head against her chest and listened to her heart beating. Gray brought her hand to his head, running her fingers through his hair as the spring breeze filled the room again.

"Is it hard, not being able to see?"

Gray was quiet for a moment. "Sometimes. There is a lot that I miss. But I still have the smell of Vera's flowers, the sound of the river just outside, the warmth of the sun through the windows, and the feel of your skin against my skin . . . your hair between my fingers."

Tony kissed her lips and Gray savored the moment.

There was a knock at the door, and Emma poked her head inside, concern in her tone as she spoke. "There's someone here to see you, Gray."

Tony kissed her cheek once more before standing and making his way to the door. Rooster jumped from the bed and followed at his heels.

Gray focused her eyes on the side of the room that she knew the bedroom door was on, but she couldn't make out a figure in the dark shadows. A person wearing heels walked across the room and sat in the chair next to the bed. She could make out a woman's figure. She had long, dark hair.

"I don't believe it."

A mix of emotions washed over Gray, but her surprise was stronger than all the others. "Audrey?"

"I ran into your mom at a bar. She told me everything."

Gray blinked, unsure of what to say.

With a heavy sigh, Audrey shook her head, unable to grasp the reality of Gray's condition. "When you came to St. Louis, I ignored your calls.

That night when I got home, I listened to your voicemail, but I was so angry with you for leaving that I didn't call you back."

Audrey shifted in her seat. "Tyler told me he came up here to see you and you had a new boyfriend and friends and you wouldn't even talk to him. I mean, when you left, I was terrified. I didn't know what the heck happened to you. Then Tyler tells me he found you in some other town, making new friends and I was hurt and confused . . . and angry."

She paused. "I'm sorry, Gray."

"I'm sorry too, Audrey." Gray's voice quivered. "I should not have left the way that I did. I wasn't trying to hurt you."

A tear dropped onto Gray's hand and she knew Audrey was crying.

"How long do you have?"

Gray gave a half smile and sighed. "A day. A week. Who knows? But not much longer."

More tears began to fall. Reaching her hand out, Gray touched Audrey's forearm, offering a small smile to help deflect some of the shock she knew her friend must be feeling. Another knock at the door interrupted the moment, and Emma brought in a small tray of food, setting it on the table beside the bed.

"Lunchtime." Her voice was soft and low.

Unable to manage more than a liquid diet, Gray's meals consisted of a glass of water and a cup of chicken broth or tomato soup.

"Audrey, you can stay as long as you want." Gray pushed herself up in the bed as Emma stuck a straw in her soup and then handed Gray the mug. "I understand if you don't want to hang around. I know it's difficult to see me like this."

Audrey watched Emma as she helped Gray eat. "No, I want to stay. I don't have any plans for the day, and I wanted to see you."

She stood from the bed.

"May I?" Audrey was speaking to Emma this time.

"Of course."

A moment later, Gray heard Emma leave the room. Audrey sat beside her again and lifted the straw to Gray's lips. When Gray had finished eating, Audrey set the cup back on the nightstand and tucked her friend's hair behind her ears. She touched Gray's cheek.

"So, tell me about the past year."

56

White

Needing a breath of fresh air, Tony walked Rooster to the pizza parlor to pick up lunch for everyone while Gray spoke with Audrey.

"You were right there all along." Gray's words in the garden drifted through his mind. *"If only I had known . . . I wish I had run into your arms the first night you ever played at the bar. Can you imagine?"*

Tony paid, taking the pizza and sandwiches and heading for the door. Rooster rarely needed a leash, and he sat obediently outside of the restaurant door, his tail wagging when Tony approached. He licked Tony's hand and then fell into step at his heel as they made their way back to the apartment.

Tony thought back on his time at Riff's Bar and if he remembered seeing Gray from the stage. How could he not notice her? His mind ran through all the possibilities. What if he had noticed her? Would he have stopped to talk to her after a set? What would he have done if she had been with Tyler? Could he have changed the ending to this story?

No.

Tony stopped on the sidewalk, bringing his hand to his mouth and fighting back the vomit. In the pit of his stomach, Tony knew that even if he had noticed Gray, even if he had tried to talk to her in the bar, her life wouldn't have been different today. Gray had come to him in her own timing. Neither of them could change the course that their lives had taken.

He approached the apartment building, still lost in thought. Tony opened the door and began ascending the stairs, Rooster bounding up the stairs beside him. The voices of the women inside could be heard from the hallway, and he steeled himself, preparing to face Audrey again. He opened the door to the apartment and stepped inside.

Audrey and Emma were perched on the loveseat, and Vera was in Gray's bedroom, her head bent in prayer. Tony set the food on the kitchen table. A small moan echoed through the apartment from Gray's bedroom, and Tony left the food, and walked toward her. Vera ran her hands along Gray's cheek. Gray's face was twisted in pain.

When Vera looked up at Tony, tears flooded her soft green eyes. Pursing her lips together, she closed her eyes for a moment to regain her composure. Vera bent over and kissed the top of Gray's head before she left the room.

Tony touched his forehead to Gray's as he stroked her hair. Tears slid down her bony cheeks as the pain of the convulsions rocked her body. Gray groaned and writhed as fought back the urge to cry out.

Minutes ticked by. Tony held her, letting her cling to his arms for strength. When Gray's grip let up and she laid back into her pillow again, Tony took her hand into his and massaged her palm. Working his way down through her arm, he watched as her face relaxed.

"I want it to end."

The words cut through his heart like a knife. For a moment, his fingers froze on her forearm. Tony leaned in closer to Gray and touched her face. Her gaze shifted in his direction. He stared into her hazy, lost, silver eyes but there was no recognition reflecting back at him.

A tear slid down Gray's cheek.

"I can't do this anymore, Tony." Her words were spoken softly, but everyone in the apartment seemed to stiffen. "I just want to die."

"You're so strong, Gray." His voice was trembling. "You have been through so much. I've never met anyone as strong as you."

Gray's lower lip trembled. "I don't feel strong."

Climbing into the bed next to her, Tony took Gray into his arms and let her cry into his chest. Her entire body shook in his arms. He fought back the tears. The tremors started again, seizing her muscles and she cried out in anguish. Gray leaned into Tony's chest and buried her face in his shoulders. He held her more tightly.

In the other room, Audrey stood. "I'm sorry." Her face was pale and her hands trembled. "I can't."

Without another word, she opened the front door and disappeared into the hallway. The door closed behind her.

After a moment, Gray's convulsions stopped. Her breathing slowed and she grew limp in his arms. When Tony looked down, Gray was fast asleep, her face taut. He lay with her in his arms until they had both fallen asleep. A few hours later, Vera woke him and encouraged him to eat.

Tony slid his arm from under Gray's frail body and stood. Gray didn't stir. Vera sat in the chair beside Gray's bed, and Tony looked down at her, unable to bring himself to walk out of the room.

"She needs you to be healthy and strong, Tony." Vera's voice was soft.

Tony nodded his head and walked out of the room. Emma was asleep on the couch when Tony passed by her. He washed up before eating and as he stood in front of the sink, he peered into the mirror. His face was worn and pale, his facial hair overgrown and unkept.

God was not going to save Gray's life.

57

Gray

Tony's hands trembled as he held the phone to his ear. He was sure the early morning call must have woken Vera. She and Isaac had gone home the evening before to try to get some rest and to check on Rooster, who had been kept at their house for the past few days.

"Is it time?" Vera's voice was soft and somber.

"Get here soon." It was all Tony could manage. He hung up the phone.

When Vera and Isaac arrived shortly after everyone else. Carla and Tiffany sat on the couch, their heads bowed in prayer. Emma was at work in the kitchen, organizing several Tupperware containers of food with Melody, who was at the sink washing dishes. Frank and Jim sat motionless at the table, staring down at the plates of egg and bacon in front of them. Just out of the kitchen window, Darren, Pete, and Vince stood on the back porch, watching the dark, cloudy morning sky.

Tony sat next to Gray's bed, her hand in his, but he could hear everyone's voices as they spoke.

"How is she?" Vera asked as she approached Emma.

"Not well." She reached into the dish drainer for a clear, square Tupperware dish and matching purple lid. "Tony is with her now."

Gray's labored breath could be heard from the bedroom, and the sound seemed to darken the already dreary apartment. Emma's chin trembled as she turned to Vera. "It won't be long."

An hour passed. Darren, Pete, and Vince came inside, but no one else seemed to move.

"Please God, I'm not ready." Tony's prayer was a coarse whisper. He held Gray's hand to his cheek. "Please."

When Tony emerged from the room, his eyes were red and puffy, tears still fresh on his cheeks. Dark circles were under his usually cheery blue eyes, and his cheeks were sunken in.

"She's sleeping right now." Defeat tainted his voice when he spoke. "Can someone else—" he broke off, bowing his head, crying for a moment, "—can someone else sit with her? I need a moment."

Vera and Emma took Tony's place at Gray's bedside. They left the door open as they prayed over her. Isaac walked with Tony to the back porch. Tony sat on the floor of the porch overlooking the garden below. Isaac lowered himself to sit next to Tony.

The streets of the small town were desolate. In the next two hours, people would be waking up, getting ready to start their daily grind, oblivious to the soul the world was about to lose. The warm wind blew fiercely, bringing a cold front that the weatherman said wouldn't last more than a week. The magnolia tree below bent and creaked under the unseen force.

"Tell me what you're feeling, son."

Isaac's words were soft and understanding, and all at once, the shell Tony had created to protect his heart burst into fragmented pieces. In an instant, Tony crumbled, bringing his fists to his face as he let lose. He cried out in agony as he felt his heart being ripped from his chest. Isaac held him, the same way he had all the times Tony had fallen as a child and came running to his uncle, arms wide open, just wanting to be held and rocked.

With his eyes closed, Tony listened as Isaac cried out to God. "Hold us, Father. We all need Your loving embrace right now."

When the tears subsided, Tony sat up and wiped his cheeks. The sun was just beginning to rise.

Isaac took Tony's hand. "This is not the end."

For the next three hours, Vera and Emma read passages of scripture to Gray as she slept, and everyone listened, drawing comfort from the words.

Gray woke a little bit after nine o'clock in the morning. Tiffany brought her a glass of water with a straw. With protective gear covering her hands and clothes, Vera carried Gray's bony body to the restroom and helped her wash her hands and face, then changed her into a white linen dress. Carla also slipped on a pair of gloves as she changed the sheets and pillows on Gray's bed while she was in the restroom. When Vera carried her back to the room, they all helped her get settled comfortably in the bed.

Once she was settled in again, Tony came into the room and sat in the chair next to her bed. "I love you, Gray."

A small smile lit Gray's gaunt cheeks. "I love you, too."

The minutes ticked by, and each person rotated, taking turns reading to Gray from her favorite poetry books or passages from scripture. Tony sat at her side and held her hand. The day wore on but the sky seemed to grow darker beneath the cover of heavy, black clouds.

Thunder sounded in the distance, and Gray turned her hazy eyes to the windows of the bedroom. A warm breeze brought the smell of rain. Sitting up a little higher in the bed, Gray rubbed Tony's arm with her bony fingers.

"Will you carry me to the porch swing?" A small smile played on her lips.

Tony stood. "Sure."

He took her into his arms and lifted her frail frame from the bed. Her body was light in his arms, and he held her close to himself. As he walked through the living room and kitchen, he fought back the tears. Holding her, he could feel the sharp bones of her ribs and spine protruding under the cover of her delicate skin.

Once they were outside, Tony lowered himself onto the seat of the swing and kept her in his arms. He rocked the swing and stared out over the garden below. Gray kept her eyes closed, listening to the approaching storm, imagining the dark clouds and flashes of lightning.

No one followed them outside. Through the kitchen window, he could see them gathered in prayer together in the living room. The sky was growing darker by the second and flashes of lightning could be seen in the distance. Light green spring leaves were uprooted from the budding branches of surrounding trees and scattered in the intense wind. The smell of rain lingered.

Gray quivered in pain, and he ran his hand up and down her side in a feeble attempt to warm her cold skin. He could count her bony ribs with his fingertips.

"I'm not shivering because of the temperature," Gray said in a quiet voice.

The swing rocked delicately as he watched the distant storm clouds roll in. The chains of the swing groaned as the two of them glided back and forth.

"I remember when you surprised me with this swing," Gray said. "It was that day, surrounded by your family, celebrating the first Christmas since my father passed away, that I understood selfless love."

Tony stopped swinging. The reality of her words weighed on him. He sighed, wondering if the love they shared added to her fear and agony in facing death. If they hadn't fallen in love, would facing the grave have been easier for her? Would she have let go sooner, not dragging out the pain and suffering? The thoughts haunted him at night.

"I don't regret it," she whispered, not lifting her head from where it was nestled against his chest. "Every minute more I get to spend with you is worth every ache and pain this sickness burdens me with. You have shown me what life is. All the friends that I have made in this town have given me life. You brought me hope and love when I was lost, alone, and confused."

Gray's words pierced him, and he felt as if the life had begun to drain from his body. Tony hunched over her head, overwhelmed with guilt and desolation. He could not save her. He could not take away her pain.

No one should have to endure the pain that Gray was experiencing. She was so beautiful, so innocent, so sick. His tears fell on her thinning, unruly curls. He began to sob harder, clutching the hem of her skirt in his hand as he wept.

Gray clung to Tony's trembling body and she also began to weep. He wished he could absorb her illness, take it upon himself so that she could be free of its effects. How many times had he prayed for God to relieve her of the disease? How many times had he offered himself in her stead?

The swing methodically swayed.

The storm grew closer, and a crack of thunder caused the ground beneath them to tremor. Lightning bugs were bobbing in the sudden darkness of the backyard. Tony watched the lightning reflect off Gray's silver irises. He ran his thumb down her sunken cheek, then across her cracked, dry lips.

"You are so beautiful," he whispered to her before tilting her chin up and kissing her.

A smile tugged on the corners of Gray's lips as she kissed him back.

"I've always loved storms." Gray's glossy eyes were turned to the horizon. "They are so powerful. It's exhilarating to witness their strength. The dark clouds, heavy wind, thunder, and lightning. Being that close to something so powerful makes me feel like I can be strong, too."

"How so?" Tony asked, his cheek pressed against the top of her head.

She listened to the roll of thunder in the distance. "I'm not sure. It amazes me that God can hide that kind of strength in something as gentle and delicate as a cloud and then unleash it in such a dramatic display of fury and strength that even the earth trembles. It gives me the hope that somewhere inside of me, He has hidden that same strength and is waiting to unleash it."

The wind picked up and the dark clouds swirled above them, overcoming the sky with authority.

- - -

Gray could feel her body failing. She leaned her head against Tony's neck and silently prayed, God, be with him.

Her father's words echoed in her mind.

"We're never alone, baby girl. In moments like this, I can feel God. It's like we could just reach out and touch His face."

Gray let herself be carried away to another time. She was a little girl again, lying next to her father on the dock, the starry sky brightly lit above them.

"It's like we could just reach out and touch His face."

With her eyes closed next to her father, Gray focused in on the sounds around her: the crickets and frogs, the wind as it combed its graceful fingers through the branches of the trees, and the gentle sigh of the river as it moved beneath them. The cool night air kissed her cheeks as the breeze picked up and sent a small shiver down her spine. While her eyes were still closed, Gray reached both her hands out to the sky above her. Her fingertips longed to touch something real. She believed for a moment that God was there, reaching His hands down from Heaven, His fingertips disguised as the gentle caress of the breeze against her open palms.

Gray smiled at the memory.

"God's hand." Through her blurred vision, she saw a sudden flash of lightning. "A storm reminds me that God Himself, in all of His might and wonder, is reaching His own hand down, trying to wake us up, to tell us He is still here."

The wind whipped her hair around her face, and Tony smoothed it back. Vera and Emma joined Gray and Tony outside, sitting in wicker chairs beside the back door. Streetlights flickered eerily along the empty cobblestone roads. A raindrop fell from the sky, pinging against the tin roof of the porch. A few seconds passed and more drops fell, faster and faster until the rain poured down steadily. A burst of lightning lit the sky, followed by a loud blow of thunder, rattling the porch and pounding against Grey's chest.

Gray looked up at Tony, bringing her hand to his face.

"Can you carry me down the stairs?"

Tony searched her face, confused. Vera and Emma wore concerned expressions and he fumbled for a response. Vera gave him an understanding nod, and Tony braced himself for what was to come. He tenderly held her in his arms as he stood, his movement slow and graceful. Vera and Emma also stood, their faces a mix of emotions as Tony carried Gray down the rickety back stairs of the porch. Once they reached the bottom of the stairs, Tony stood with her cradled in his arms under the protection of the deck and he watched the rain pounding into the grass, bending the frail blades.

"Let me stand." Gray's voice quivered.

Tony tightened his grip on her, starting to object, but Gray interrupted him.

"Tony," she said with a steadier voice. "Let me stand."

His arms clung to her for a few seconds, unwilling to let her go. Burying his face in her hair, he kissed her cheek one last time before he set her on her bare feet.

Her weak legs shook, and she focused to steady them. The rain was falling harder now, and she brought her useless eyes up to the clouds, searching the dark sky for strength.

Emma and Vera watched from the top of the stairs, their hands hiding their open mouths as Gray took a feeble step out from under the protection of the deck, crossing the line into the rain. Both women rushed down the stairs to stand beside Tony. The commotion caught the attention of Carla through the kitchen window, and she came running out onto the porch followed by everyone except Isaac, who remained in the bedroom, praying.

It's time.

The voice was a soft whisper, but it shook Tony to his core. He fell to his knees in the grass, his body unwilling to move as he watched the scene unfold before him.

- - -

Unaware of the attention she had drawn, Gray continued to walk across the grassy lawn, the mud seeping between her toes as she took each step. The cool rain was running down her face and sending chills down her spine. Gray took another step, then another, each one growing stronger as she made her way to the middle of the garden. A clap of thunder pounded against her chest and she turned her face back up to the sky.

The storm was above her now and repeated flashes of lightning lit the dark garden around her like a strobe light, each flash filling her limbs with courage. She reached out her hands and touched the tip of one of the branches on the magnolia tree. She knew she was in the center of the garden now. With a smile, Gray lifted herself to her tiptoes, her hands stretching toward Heaven as her fingers yearned to harness just one touch of the storm's invigorating strength.

The wind picked up and rain crashed hard against her body, soaking her linen dress. With her eyes closed, she swayed back and forth as the wind swirled around her. Overwhelming joy burned inside of her and her heart pounded wildly against her chest, yearning to break free. Her fingertips tingled, and an intense strength coursed through Gray like an electric current from her soul. Swaying freely, her arms lifted, palms out, as she danced before God. A strong and powerful scream tore through her chest as she sprang up and down in sheer exhilaration.

In this moment, she was free from the earth's pull, and she was staring into the face of God.

When her strength was spent, she stood and gazed toward Heaven. Gray pushed the wet hair from her face and allowed the cool rain to run over her bony cheeks.

- - -

Tony's breath caught in his throat as Gray stood in the center of the garden, her arms outstretched while the rain drenched her upturned face. She turned to him and there was a look of peace in her silver eyes. He knew in that moment that despite her failing sight, she could see him. Tony held her gaze for a moment and a single tear slid down his cheek.

But as suddenly and mysteriously as the light had appeared within her eyes, they became dark again. Gray collapsed to her knees in the grass.

Tony ran out to her and scooped her up into his arms. The others remained standing where they were, unable to move. Tony held Gray's drenched, cold body close to himself as the storm picked up with full intensity. The howling wind and heavy rain masked his agonizing cries as he held her lifeless body, her silver eyes still open, unblinking as they stared up at the unruly clouds above.

Epilogue

The storm has passed. Rooster is now asleep at my feet as I hold my empty coffee mug. The rain has left an array of crystals shimmering in the light of the rising sun.

For many years, I had done all that I could to repress the memory from the day that Gray left this earth. For many years, I fought hard against reality and truth. In the end, I realized that reality may not always be sunshine and happy endings, but even the darkest storm eventually gives way to blue skies.

The day Gray passed away was not the end of her legacy. Audrey attended Gray's funeral with Diana and Reese. Diana spent four hours in the cemetery after the funeral as she wept and clung to Vera who eventually convinced her to enter a rehab facility nearby. Reese came to live with me while his mother was away. He remained in my care until he graduated from high school, with honors.

Diana completed rehab a year after her daughter's death and still lives in Belle. Six months after her release, she convinced Audrey to enroll in the program. Today, Diana is the head over a program at our church for rehabilitated addicts and has changed the hearts of many women who share her struggle. Audrey joined her in her ministry after she completed the rehab program. Diana still carries the weight of the pain and guilt over her treatment of Gray and from having given up what little time she had with her daughter, but her testimony has been a tool that has prevented other woman from making similar mistakes.

A month after the funeral, Vera and Isaac adopted Sylvia. With proper treatment, her HIV remains under control, and she has been able to enjoy a life with little sickness. Now that she is older, she helps her mom in the floral shop every day after school and still talks about her memories with Gray. Gray was the first person to see Sylvia as another human being instead of a broken spirit.

As I'm sure you have assumed, Emma and Frank were married. Emma insisted that Gray would be her maid of honor and she carried a small trinket with Gray's picture in the bouquet that Vera made for her. Tiffany and Darren's wedding followed shortly after Emma's.

Carla moved to St. Louis and opened her own boutique. She does well for herself, and I see her frequently. She married a professional mountain climber and they bought a vacation home in Colorado. We have all been invited to join them for Thanksgiving in Vail this year.

Jim moved to Tennessee to be closer to Melody, and we rarely see either of them. The rest of the band stayed together. We have recorded five albums, four of them going platinum. The EP with the song "Sweet Surrender" performed with Gray is still one of our most downloaded songs. To this day, I wear Gray's guitar strap when I play. The strap is a constant reminder of my purpose, and it keeps me grounded.

As I close my eyes, I imagine Gray sitting in the chair beside me, running her hands over Rooster's soft fur. Her hair is long and flowing, her body fully restored and eyes bright. She's sipping a mug of coffee and smiling at me, our engagement ring on her finger next to a wedding band.

Why would I share such a disheartening story, you ask?

I have learned that the world is a dark and ugly place, but just as God has placed stars in the night sky to guide a lost sailor safely home, He has also placed people in our lives to light the way along our journey. Gray will forever be the most brilliantly shining star in my sky. She taught me through her own example that life doesn't end in the wake of death. She taught me how to hope. She taught me not to fear the storm, but to dance in the rain.

Though Gray no longer lives, her light lives on through the legacy that she left. Her story deserves to be told. Her light deserves to be held high, for all the world to see.

When you close the cover of this book and put it back on the shelf to collect dust or pass it along to a friend, my prayer is that you realize how fragile and fleeting our lives on this earth can be. I pray that you think about Gray the next time you hear the roll of thunder as a storm draws in over the sky.

Listen more closely to the rumble.

The sound you hear is not thunder, but God calling you to rise and live your life with purpose and strength. Face the violent winds with courage.

The following is the last entry from Gray's journal, before her sight failed her. I can't imagine better words to leave you with.

But the basic reality of God is plain enough. Open your eyes and there it is! By taking a long and thoughtful look at what God has created, people have always been able to see what their eyes as such can't see: Eternal power, for instance, and the mystery of his divine being.

Romans 1:19, 20